WAKE UP, SIR!

A NOVEL

Jonathan Ames

SCRIBNER

New York   London   Toronto   Sydney

SCRIBNER
1230 Avenue of the Americas
New York, NY 10020

A portion of this work was previously published, in different form, in *Conjunctions*.

SCRIBNER and design are trademarks of Macmillan Library Reference USA, Inc.,
used under license by Simon & Schuster, the publisher of this work.

For information regarding special discounts for bulk purchases,
please contact Simon & Schuster Special Sales at 1-800-456-6798
or business@simonandschuster.com

DESIGNED BY ERICH HOBBING

Text set in Bembo

Manufactured in the United States of America

1   3   5   7   9   10   8   6   4   2

Library of Congress Cataloging-in-Publication Data
Ames, Jonathan.
Wake up, sir!: a novel/Jonathan Ames.
p. cm.
1.Young men—Fiction. 2. Alcoholics—Fiction.
3. Authors—Fiction. 4. Valets—Fiction.
I. Title.

PS3551.M42W34 2004
813'.54—dc22
2003070357

ISBN 0-7432-3004-3

For Blair Clark and Alan Jolis
(in memory)

Acknowledgments

The author would like to thank the following individuals and institutions: Priscilla Becker, Brant Rumble, Rosalie Siegel, *Conjunctions* magazine, the Guggenheim Foundation, the Medway Foundation, and the Corporation of Yaddo.

"Live and don't learn—that's my motto."
—ALAN BLAIR

PART I

Montclair, New Jersey

CHAPTER 1

Jeeves, my valet, sounds the alarm ★ A physical description of my uncle Irwin, the gun fanatic, and a rundown of his morning regimen ★ I rush through my toilet and yoga ★ A delayed ejaculation of fear

"Wake up, sir. Wake up," said Jeeves.

"What? What is it, Jeeves?" I said, floating out of the mists of Lethe. I had been dreaming of a gray cat, who, like some heavy in a film noir, was throttling in its fists a white mouse. "I was dreaming of a gray cat, Jeeves. Quite the bully."

"Very good, sir."

I started slipping back into that cat-and-mouse confrontation. I wanted to see the little white fellow escape. It had very sweet, pleading eyes. But Jeeves cleared his throat respectfully, and I sensed an unusual urgency to his hovering presence which demanded that the young master rally himself from the luscious pull of dreams. Poor mouse would have to go unsaved. No happy ending.

"What's going on, Jeeves?" I asked, casting a sleepy eye at his kind but inscrutable face.

"There are indications, sir, that your uncle Irwin is no longer asleep."

It was only under these alarming circumstances that Jeeves would interrupt my eight hours of needed unconsciousness. He knew that the happiness of my morning was dependent on having as little contact with said uncle as possible.

"Groans from the bedroom, Jeeves? He no longer dreams—probably of firearms—and is staring at the ceiling summoning the courage to blight another day?"

"His progression into the morning is further along than that, sir."

"You heard his feet hit the floor and he's sitting on the edge of the bed in a stupor?"

"He's on his stationary bicycle and he's davening, sir." Jeeves had picked up the Anglicization of the Yiddish from me, adding the *ing* to *daven* (to pray) as I did.

"Good God!" I said. "This is desperate, Jeeves. Calamitous!"

Coming fully awake and now nearly at the height of my sensory powers, I could make out the spinning of the bicycle's tires, as well as my uncle's off-key Hebraic singing—his bedroom was just fifteen feet away down the hall.

"Do you think there's time, Jeeves?"

"There is very little room for error, sir."

I am usually unflappable and rather hard-boiled, if I may say so, but this predicament first thing in the morning shook me to the core. For several months now, with rigorous discipline, I had just about managed never to see my uncle before noon.

"How has this happened?" I asked. I didn't want to fault Jeeves, but he had never before let my uncle get so far as the stationary bicycle without awakening me.

"Your uncle has risen quite early, sir. It is only eight-thirty. If you'll excuse me for saying so, but I was performing my own toilet during the first stages of his morning program."

"I see, Jeeves. Perfectly understandable." I couldn't expect utter vigilance from the man—after all, he was my valet, not a member of the Queen's Guard—*and* my uncle had thrown everything off by getting out of bed more than two hours ahead of schedule. This was an anomaly beyond the palest pale, and so our best defense—Jeeves's keen eavesdropping—had been wanting.

Well, I was in a bad way, but I like to think of myself as a man of action when shaken to the core, and so I threw back my blankets. Jeeves, anticipating my every move, handed me my bath towel, materializing it from his person, the way he is apt to materialize things from his person when they are needed, and so I dashed out of my lair, wearing only my boxer shorts, and shot myself into the bathroom, which is right next to my uncle's bedroom.

I had my own morning program to adhere to, but I was going to have to rush through it if I wanted to avoid my nemesis. Hurrying did not appeal to me—I would probably feel anxious the whole day—but an encounter with the ancient relative before noon would be worse. Then all my nerves would be completely unraveled and the day would be lost.

To avoid such an eventuality, Jeeves and I had memorized, in order to map out my every move, my uncle's morning schedule, which was as follows:

(1) Uncle Irwin's wife, my aunt Florence—my late mother's sister—would leave at dawn to go teach special education at the local high school, and she did this year-round, teaching summer school, as well. She was in her early sixties, but still working very hard—an angel in human form. My uncle would say good-bye to her each morning but immediately fall back to sleep. He was in his early seventies and a retired salesman of textile chemicals, though in the afternoons he peddled ultrasonic gun-cleaning equipment to police stations.

My uncle was a firearms expert and the house was equipped with a small arsenal. He was ready for another Kristallnacht or a siege by the FBI if there was a repeal of the Second Amendment. In case of a surprise attack, guns were hidden all over the place—behind shutters, in heating ducts—and he often wore a gun in the house, utilizing a special hip-holster. He called this *packing,* which has metaphorical resonance, I understand, in the homosexual community as well as in the NRA, which makes perfect sense since there is nothing more phallic than a gun; even phalluses seem less phallic, though, of course, the phallus did precede the firearm.

(2) Around ten-thirty each morning my uncle would awaken. He would groan several times and yawn lustily—his large stomach acted acoustically as a sort of bellows. He was a short, round man with a coal black mustache and a very white beard, and this unusual bifurcated arrangement of his facial hair gave him an uncanny resemblance, despite his Jewish origins, to a Catholic saint-in-waiting—a certain Padre Pio. This was discovered when a sweet and pious Italian woman nearly fainted at the local

Grand Union and pressed upon my Uncle Irwin a laminated card with an image of this Pio. My uncle then wrote to a Catholic organization and got his own such card, which he kept in his wallet as a form of identification, flashing it if he was in a playful mood at the synagogue or the shooting range or any of his other haunts. Pio was on the verge of sainthood due to his having stigmata—bleeding from the palms—and my uncle said that his carpal tunnel syndrome, brought on by years of clutching a steering wheel as a traveling salesman, was his stigmata.

(3) So after two to three minutes of these nerve-rattling, church-bellish yawns, whose purpose was to deliver oxygen to his organism, the blankets were thrown off. He would then turn on a small mustard-colored radio, which only picked up one station—a round-the-clock government weather report. The broadcaster's voice was dreary and unintelligible, and it enthralled my uncle for a good five to ten minutes each morning.

(4) Having then been apprised of the current meteorological conditions, he would go to the bathroom and pass water.

(5) After flushing, he'd come back to his room and begin to pray—on average about fifteen minutes.

(6) After prayer, he bathed—ten minutes.

(7) After bathing, around 11 A.M., he was down to the kitchen for his breakfast: microwaved oatmeal, banana in sour cream, hot water with lemon. He ate this hearty meal while reading *The New York Times* and listening to CBS news on the kitchen radio, which was played at maximum volume. The breakfast, due to the enormity of *The New York Times,* sometimes lasted as long as two hours, at which point he'd head out for the day to mix with the constabulary and speak of the benefits of keeping the barrel of one's gun free of dust and oil.

Well, that's the schedule—so if I played my cards right, I had bathed, breakfasted, and was safely sequestered back in my room before he even reached the kitchen table. Granted, the explosive radio-playing of CBS was unnerving and did not respect the boundary of my bedroom door, but at least there was no physical contact between myself and the relative. To feel properly aligned, mentally and physically, not to mention avoiding being shot or pistol-whipped, I needed solitude in the morning. You see, solitude is essential to producing art, and art in my case was literature: I was writing a roman à clef and needed to be left alone. Jeeves was about, but Jeeves was trained to be invisible. They teach you that at valet school.

Sometimes, though, if I was a little off my program, my uncle and I would pass each other on the three-step staircase that led from the kitchen to the bedrooms—it was a small, two-story, Montclair, New Jersey, house—and this was disquieting, but not the end of the world. He'd shoot me a withering glance full of disapproval, but the lighting was poor on that staircase, and so his mien undid me a little but not completely.

What was bad—avoided at all costs—was to be in the kitchen when he began to eat. Not only would he paralyze me with numerous withering glances, his eyes exuding all the compassion of iced oysters, but he generated in me an irrational reaction to the concussive sounds of his chewing. Without any doubt, the noises he made were obscene, but my response was uncalled for. I was his houseguest—well, practically a permanent resident for the last few months; he and the aunt had taken me in during a difficult time, acting like parents; I was only thirty, relatively young, but my mother and father had been deceased for many years—and so I should have been more tolerant of Uncle Irwin, but I found myself completely unraveled by the slurping cries of a sour-cream-soaked banana meeting its doom between his crushing molars and lashing tongue. Listening to him eat, my spine turned to jelly and I couldn't think straight for hours, which is why I had so precisely mapped out his schedule—the relative had to be avoided!

So, on the morning in question, the third Monday in the month of July, year 1995, I was in the bathroom, massaging my chin, and I decided I didn't have time to shave because of the crisis at hand, though it would be the fourth day I hadn't shaved—the old spirits had been a bit low, and when the spirits are low, I seem to lack the moral wherewithal to remove my whiskers—and a reddish beard was beginning to announce its presence. Meanwhile, my uncle was still singing and the bicycle wheels were whooshing.

But I wonder if I'm being clear about this bicycle business. I should explain that it was an eccentricity of my uncle's that he did his davening while on his stationary bicycle, which was actually a blue girl's bicycle that he had found at a garage sale and which had some kind of apparatus restraining its wheels so they didn't touch the carpeting of his bedroom floor. It was a speedless two-wheeler and provided very little resistance or exercise. He had been pedaling on it for years and was as stout as ever. But at least he made an effort. And he prayed. And though he wasn't an Orthodox Jew, he wore official davening gear: about his shoulders was his silky, white tallith with its blue stripes and fringes, and on his left arm and on his forehead were his tefillin—the leather boxes and straps favored by Jews for their morning prayers. The boxes, like a mezuzah, contain the Shema, God's directions to Moses, found in Deuteronomy. One of the lost directions, according to Jewish lore, is "Don't go out with a wet head!" Luckily, this important health command has been orally maintained for thousands of years.

So my uncle was bicycling and praying, and his tallith, had he been on a real bicycle facing the wind and the elements, would have been flapping behind him like a cape. I estimated that he was halfway through his prayers, and I quickly doused myself in the shower. Usually, I enjoyed lolling in the tub for a good fifteen minutes—a meditative Epsom-salts bath was the first station of *my* morning schedule—but this had to be forsaken.

With limbs still damp, I then sprinted to my room, towel wrapped around me, and just as I was closing my bedroom door, my uncle's door opened and in he went to the bathroom. A narrow escape.

Jeeves had laid out my clothes on the bed—soft khaki pants, green Brooks Brothers tie designed with floating fountain pens, and white shirt. My usual writing garments.

"Thank you, Jeeves," I said.

"You're welcome, sir."

"Nearly collided with the relative in the hallway, don't you know. Another thirty seconds in the shower, and all would have been different. Interesting the way fate works that way, isn't it, Jeeves?"

"Yes, sir."

I sensed a certain chilliness in the man, but pressed on with my theory. "All our lives we're saved from the hangman's noose by mere seconds, Jeeves."

"Yes, sir. If I may point out, sir, you have not shaved for four days." The source of his glacial attitude was revealed.

"I would have shaved today, Jeeves, but I'm economizing my every movement. We have at best ten to fifteen minutes in which to operate." I could see that Jeeves was still wounded. I tried to explain: "My uncle has thrown everything off by rudely changing his schedule. I'll shave tomorrow, I promise."

"Very good, sir."

I had soothed the fellow, and then I quickly pasted on my raiment, but I eschewed the tie.

"Your necktie, sir," Jeeves said.

"There's no time, Jeeves."

"There is always time for your necktie, sir."

"I can't risk it," I said.

"Your uncle is only just now drawing his bath, sir. I believe there is time enough."

"No, Jeeves," I said. "Also I've been meaning to tell you that I don't like doing my yoga while wearing my tie. Especially this time of year with the heat. From now on, I will put on the tie after breakfast."

"Yes, sir," said Jeeves. First the shaving and now the necktie. The man was cut to the quick, injured at his valet core. This was clearly a rough morning in our domestic life, poor old Jeeves, but he was going to have to show more sangfroid.

I flung open my door, raced down the stairs, flew through the kitchen, and ejected myself out the front door onto the small patio.

It was here that I performed my yogic exercises. My whole morning regimen (bath, yoga, no contact with uncle) was about achieving the right frame of mind—the correct mental pH, as it were—to toil at my novel. Usually, I did ten sun salutations. These really get the blood sloshing. You're continually going from standing upright to lying on your belly, then standing up again. What I would do was face east, prostrating myself to the sun, which penetrated through the tops of the summer trees, lighting up thousands of green, eye-shaped leaves. My uncle's house was nestled quite nicely in a bit of secluded woods—

very beautiful New Jersey, I've always said, a most unfair reputation. Of course, I'm biased, having grown up in the Garden State.

Due to the crisis that morning, I reduced the number of salutations to one. Then I lay on my back on the patio, which my aunt swept frequently, so there was no danger that my pants would be soiled. I closed my eyes and counted ten breaths. I always do this after sun salutations. I find that meditating on the back is more conducive to peaceful feelings than sitting in the lotus position.

I would like it, though, if I could sit in meditation like Douglas Fairbanks Jr., with my legs crossed at the knee, a thin mustache on my lip, and myself looking very dashing, but I don't think the soul, which operates like a chimney flue, has much draw when the legs are crossed like that.

Anyway, braced by my one sun salutation and my ten seconds or so of meditation, I went into the kitchen and Jeeves was there, beaming in at the precise moment that I made my entrance, which he's very good at. He's always appearing and disintegrating and reappearing just when the stage directions call for him.

"What's the status of the opposition, Jeeves?" I asked.

"Your uncle is dressing, sir. His attitude is that of one who has an appointment of some sort for which he is expected shortly."

"You mean to say that he's rushing off somewhere?"

"Yes, sir."

"No doubt some emergency meeting of the National Rifle Association or the Jewish Defense League."

"Perhaps, sir."

"I think I'll have to dine in my room, Jeeves. It's not pleasant, I know. But it's our only chance."

"I am in agreement, sir."

All I liked to have in the mornings in New Jersey was a cup of coffee, toast with butter, a glass of water, and the sports section of *The New York Times*—not to eat, naturally, but to read. I enjoy nothing more than to sit peacefully at a kitchen table, memorize the baseball statistics, and nibble my humble piece of toast. But this morning that would have to be sacrificed.

My aunt Florence, as she often did, had left a pot of coffee for me, and so I quickly filled my favorite blue Fiestaware mug and then tucked the sports section under my elbow—my uncle didn't read the sports and so he wouldn't notice its absence. Jeeves gathered a plate with some cold bread and butter. From the kitchen we charged up the three small stairs, myself in the lead, Jeeves picking up the rear of the formation. I was nearing the summit, on the second step, quite close to safety—my room just one more step and a yard away—but my uncle, unseen by me, was also thrusting toward the head of the stairs from stage right. And so it was only a mere half second later—into the hangman's noose after all!—that the unfortunate congress took place.

The physics was this: my head, in the lead of my body, was rising up the stairs, breaking the plane of the landing, just as my uncle was hanging a hard and hurried left down the stairs, with his belly, in the lead of his body, breaking the same plane. Two broken planes. A midair collision.

The nose of my plane went into his fuselage with not a little force. The wind was knocked from him, he breathed in caustically, and while his stomach collapsed a little, my neck, weak stem that it is, was forcefully and painfully shoved down into the shoulders. I also took right into my nostrils a dusting of baby powder which was emitted from his person, like a toad of the Amazon squirting poison when stepped on. The relative, you see, liked to generously coat himself with Johnson's powder after being in the tub, and I had grown to be mildly nauseated by its aroma. So taking that powder directly into the nostrils, right to the center of my olfactory glands, was quite the blow. Somehow, though, I righted myself on the second step, shakily holding the small banister, and miraculously, my coffee had not been spilled. Jeeves transported himself back into the kitchen.

"You idiot!" my uncle aspirated out of his Padre Pio beard. "You klutz!"

Then I, as often happens to me in moments of extreme stress, had a delayed spasm and ejaculation of fear. Whenever I'm scared, I register the scary thing for an instant rather calmly or sleepily: Oh, look, a rat has raced up my leg, I'll remark to myself—which actually happened to me one time in New York City, a trauma I've never quite recovered from—and after the rat reverses direction, having discerned that I am a person and not a drainage pipe, and runs

11

away, I suddenly realize what has transpired and scream at the top of my lungs.

So about two seconds *after* my uncle bellowed "You klutz!" when essentially the coast was clear, it was then that I responded:

"Noooo!" I yowled inanely, and threw my arms up to protect myself, much too late, and discharged from my person—behaving like my uncle's baby powder—was my cup of hot coffee, undoing the miracle of just moments before. The coffee spread itself like a searing, brown blanket on his yellow sport shirt, which, because of its thin material, did not prevent him from being scalded.

"Goddammit!" he cried in pain, pawing at his belly.

"I'm so sorry!" I said, mounting the last step, while my uncle recoiled.

"Am I burned?" he half demanded, half whimpered, as he pulled off his shirt. No one deserves to be showered with coffee. Not even frightening uncles.

I bent toward his belly to observe, and there was a thick, protective covering of hair on the stomach, much of it gray and a good deal of it white from the powder, and the skin beneath the hair and the powder seemed to be fine. A little pink, perhaps, but not the violent red of a serious burn.

"I think you're all right," I said, wanting to beg for forgiveness, but he retreated to the bathroom, his shirt in his fist like a rag, and I trailed behind like a fool. He regarded himself in the mirror and took a wet washcloth and held it to his stomach. He was rallying rather quickly. Hardy old thing. We regarded each other in the mirror. My thinning blond-red hair looked very frail, matching my mental state, and his mustache, like a mood ring from my 1970s youth, seemed to blacken further. And his eyes were as small as a lobster's, which is very small. Out of them shot death rays. Usually, as I indicated earlier, his preference was to have eyes that resembled chilled oysters, which was bad enough. So for him to switch over to lobster eyes was not a good sign—his repertoire of withering glances, taken from the worlds of mollusks and crustaceans, was expanding to keep up with his antipathy for me.

"I'm sorry I'm such an idiot," I whispered, and then I oozed down the hall to hide in my room.

CHAPTER 2

I attempt a little scribbling ★ The subject and hero of my novel are touched upon ★ Dating practices of wealthy senior citizens are explained in a sociological way ★ Jeeves, being quite literary, reassures me about the day's output of prose ★ I think back on how Jeeves came into my employ ★ Jeeves makes lunch ★ I make a decision

Careworn, you might have described me. Distressed and paralyzed would have also worked. I was lying on my bed. Too depressed to eat, I had gone without breakfast. Jeeves flickered like a beam of light to my left.

"Do you think a written apology, Jeeves, might do the trick?"

"I don't know if that is necessary, sir. It was an accident. Your uncle is not an unreasonable man. And from what you tell me of your inspection of his abdomen, no serious injury occurred."

"Perhaps you're right, Jeeves. But it is soupy. You know what they say about guests who overstay their welcome. Perhaps my tenure here has strained the blood ties. But I've been selfish, Jeeves. It's been good for the writing, this New Jersey air. Brings me back to my roots."

"Yes, sir."

"Maybe if I run the fingers along the keyboard now, my spirits will improve."

"You often feel better, sir, when you do a little work."

"Some iced coffee then, Jeeves. You know I can't write without it. Aggravating the nerves with caffeine always helps with the Muse."

"Yes, sir."

Jeeves trickled out to get the coffee. We knew the coast was clear. My uncle, after the debacle on the stairs, had gone about his usual

13

routine of assaulting a bowl of oatmeal, reading the newspaper, and listening to the radio. When the radio was shut off and we heard the front door slam, we knew that we serfs could run free and frolic and drink vodka and grab female serfs and sleep on the haystacks.

I sat at my desk and presently Jeeves arrived with my drink. I sipped the iced coffee and stared at the computer. I had only recently made the harrowing switch from the typewriter to the laptop, but there were decided benefits—one could play solitaire on the computer during momentary lapses in the creative process.

My first novel I hadn't even typed—I wrote it by hand and then gave it to a typist. But this was several years before. I had published rather young, only twenty-three, just a year out of college, but now at age thirty, while still a young man, I was practically washed-up. Hence my obsession with avoiding the uncle in the morning and being in the right frame of mind for writing. If I didn't produce a second novel, I would be a one-hit wonder. As it was hardly anyone read the book, *I Pity I,* but it *was* published by a major New York house, and so in my own little world I had something to live up to.

This new novel, which I had been working on for two years, was, as I mentioned, a roman à clef, except all the clefs weren't famous or celebrated in any way, except in my opinion. And I guess this is a bit strange since romans à clef are usually about well-known people, but it was a style that appealed to me—the protective covering of fiction over the caprice of real life. I hadn't yet changed people's names, except for my own, calling myself Louis instead of Alan. I've always been irrationally fond of the name Louis.

So the narrator of my novel was Louis (me), but the real hero of the story was my former Manhattan roommate, Charles, whom I planned to rename at some point Edward or Henry, thinking it was smart to stick with the names of British kings, especially since Charles was a real Anglophile and follower of the royal family. He was also an acerbic, failed playwright, but I thought he was brilliant. Unfortunately, no one else shared my opinion, only an obscure critic or two back in the fifties, and so he was a nearly penniless senior citizen, which is why he needed a roommate.

Charles did have some income from teaching composition at Queens College and from his monthly Social Security check, but it was barely enough to live on. I had the lofty ambition that though Charles's plays had failed to make him a great American writer, I would make him a great American *character.* So while living with him, I was writing about him, though he didn't know this—I worked on the book at the Ninety-sixth Street library or in the apartment when he wasn't home, and I kept my notebooks and the manuscript well hidden. I was always secretly jotting down things he said—his dialogue was wonderfully rich—but the ethics of the whole enterprise disturbed me: the act of stealing someone's life. And yet I didn't stop. I was driven by an imperious need—I had to produce a second novel!

After nearly two years of being roommates, we had a bad falling-out, and this led to my moving to New Jersey and taking up residence with the aunt and uncle. But I continued to view the book, which Charles was still unaware of, as an extended platonic love letter. You see, I greatly admired the man, despite the ending of our friendship, and my admiration was akin to love.

My title for the roman à clef was *The Walker,* since Charles was a walker for several wealthy Upper East Side ladies. This was a way for him to get some good free meals of the highest quality, which he very much enjoyed and couldn't have afforded otherwise.

As a walker, Charles didn't have to pay, because in the upper classes, as men and women get older, the roles, quite often, reverse: where once the man always paid, the woman now pays. These upper-class women in their seventies, eighties, or nineties have usually outlasted more than one husband, either through divorce or attrition (women live longer than men), and so they inherit and accumulate great wealth. The problem is they can't really attract new husbands or lovers or even more likely they don't want new lovers and husbands, but it *is* nice to have a man around, looks good socially—he opens doors, pulls out your chair, carries the luggage on trips—and so these wealthy women, these survivors, need male companionship. Thus, hovering around them, like blue-blazered seagulls, is always a roster of men who have no money, but do have a certain sophistication, which means they're quite often homosexual. "Walkers" is what they're called, seemingly because they walk alongside the woman, providing support. Sometimes they're referred to as an "extra man," as in you might need an extra man to complete the seating arrangements—boy, girl, boy, girl—at a dinner party.

It all works out rather well, because these men, these poor gay senior citizens, like their lady friends, can no longer attract lovers, but they're not alone—they find themselves, in their latter years, with women. The whole thing comes full circle: these men, these walkers, are engaging in sexless heterosexual dating, just as they must have fifty, sixty years ago when they were in the closet, which is where most homosexual men of that generation could be found.

So Charles was a walker and had the necessary costumes—one set of evening clothes and a variety of blazers, none of which were in good condition, but his ladies didn't notice as their cataracts were usually quite advanced.

I should mention that Charles wasn't clearly homosexual, despite my general depiction of a walker's attributes. Charles was very discreet on the subject of his sexuality, didn't think it was my or anyone else's business, and so none of my vampiric prying could get a disclosure, even after living together for two years. I was shamefully curious—as most people are—about what I shouldn't have been. But I guess we all like to know other people's secrets so that we can live with our own. Charles, in retrospect, was perhaps something quite rare, a heterosexual extra man, though in truth he seemed to be against all sex, which is a position not without merit.

Well, that gives you a general idea of the book I was working on—a portrait of a walker as an old man, and his worshipful sidekick, Louis (me). So there I was in New Jersey, sipping the iced coffee Jeeves had provided, and I picked up the novel where I had left off the day before. I slowly typed the following scene:

I was lying on the orange carpet and watching television. I was happily absorbing a Western. There was a big shoot-out going on and lots of horses were rearing up on their hind legs and kicking up dust, which made it hard for the gunslingers to see one another. The battle was rather long and protracted, and Charles came home in the midst of it, saw what I was watching, and didn't approve.

"Guns!" he said. "Americans are always shooting guns. They can't

outwit anyone, so they shoot them. . . . Put the news on. I can't stand Westerns. I want to see what's happening with the Saint Patrick's Day Parade. I wonder if this year it will finally be canceled."

I switched the channel with the remote control. Charles took off his winter coat and poured himself a glass of his cheap white wine. "Do you want some?" he asked.

"Yes, thank you," I said greedily, sitting up. He handed me a glass of the yellow-colored wine and sat on his couch. The sports segment of the news was being shown; it was eleven twenty-five.

"I don't think there will be anything about the parade," I said. "All the real news has already been broadcast. Now it's just sports and weather."

The sports report came to its end and then we gloomily watched the weather forecast—an ice storm was expected. Spring was a week away, but it was slow in coming. I turned off the TV.

"The homosexuals are trying to wreck the parade again," said Charles, sipping his wine. "Every year they protest and they take all the joy out of it for the Irish-Catholics. Gays have no tolerance for others' points of view. Why can't they accept that Catholics think homosexuality is a sin? They say, 'You can march in our gay pride parade.' But they wouldn't allow someone carrying a sign that says, 'Sodomy Is Wrong.' So why should an Irish-Catholic let someone carry a banner that says, 'We're Irish and Gay and Proud of It'? And there's nothing to be proud of. It's to be endured privately."

"Are you going to watch the parade if it happens?" I asked.

"No, I can't stand parades. Too many ugly people."

"What do you think of this, Jeeves?" I asked, and he evaporated and then reconstituted himself alongside me. Looking over my shoulder, he quickly read what I had produced.

"Do you think I have too much sitting down, passing of drinks, and taking off of coats?" I asked before he could comment. "Am I clogging things up? Seems like my characters are always walking across rooms and opening doors. Why can't they just appear places? And if I'm going to have all this movement, I should at least have a fistfight, don't you think, like in Dashiell Hammett?"

"Writing, I imagine, sir, is like seeing," said Jeeves. "You see the characters sitting and drinking and taking off their coats and so you have to describe it. And, furthermore, I don't think you have slowed down the narrative thrust with these necessary descriptions."

"But talking about the Saint Patrick's Day Parade is not very lively."

"I find it, sir, to be an amusing anecdote, and revealing of character."

"Thank you, Jeeves," I said gratefully. I felt rather fortunate. Not too many writers have valets who are of the literary sort. In fact, Jeeves and I were reading together, as a sort of two-person book club, Anthony Powell's epic, twelve-volume *A Dance to the Music of Time*. It's absolutely a stupendous work—almost nothing of moment occurs for hundreds of pages, thousands even, and yet one reads on completely mesmerized. It's like an imprint of life: nothing happens and yet everything happens.

Anyway, when I'd hired Jeeves just five months before, in February, I had no idea he was bookish. There was his very literary name, of course, but this didn't make me think he was an avid reader, it merely threw me for one hell of a loop. I mean, who ever heard of a valet actually named Jeeves? That's outrageous! That's like looking for a private detective in the Yellow Pages and stumbling across Philip Marlowe! What was the likelihood?

We all have cultural blank spots—I, for example, despite having grown up in the seventies, cannot distinguish the music of the Rolling Stones from that of the Who, though I am, through osmosis, aware of these rock bands—so some people might not know that P. G. Wodehouse, the premier British comedic writer of the twentieth century, wrote a celebrated series of novels about a young, wealthy idiot named Bertie Wooster and his wildly competent and brainy valet named Jeeves! I repeat: a valet named Jeeves!

So my hiring someone called Jeeves to be a valet is a stunning, improbable coincidence. And, you see, what makes this even more remarkable is that during the dark month of January, my first month with the aunt and uncle, I had fallen into a morbific depression and so had prescribed to myself the cure of reading lots of Wodehouse. I was using Norman Cousins as my role model because I had once heard on the radio that Cousins had healed himself of cancer by overdosing on comedic films—probably Chaplin, Keaton, the Marx Brothers, and Laurel and Hardy—and laughing himself into wellness.

I substituted an overdose of Wodehouse as a remedy—I'm more of a bibliophile than a cinephile—and it worked pretty well. By early February I had inched from black-lungish melancholy to drooping spirits. Then something really morale-boosting occurred: a check for $250,000 arrived with my name on it. Now, you don't see checks like that every day. For that matter, you don't see them every lifetime.

How this check had come into my possession was that two years before I had slipped on some ice in front of a Park Avenue building and broken both of my elbows—a disaster for a writer who needs his arms to type, but very good for a lawyer, a lawyer who likes to sue, and I found such a lawyer—Stuart Fishman. So two years later, rather quick for such things, I had been awarded $250,000—after Fishman took his well-earned $75,000—by the owner of the building because the doorman should have salted the area where I fell.

Well, there I was coming out of a depression thanks to that check *and* my reading cure, and I have to say I was sort of delirious from absorbing so many Wodehouse novels. He wrote ninety-six and I digested forty-three of them, including all fifteen of the books that feature Wooster and Jeeves. And this delirium produced an unexpected thought: Why don't *I* hire a valet? For years, I had lived frugally off the inheritance from my parents' early deaths, and that money had just about run out, but now I was a rich, young quarter-millionaire! *Why not have a valet?*

I mentioned the idea to Uncle Irwin since, after all, I was living in his house, and he remarked rather forcefully, "You're insane!"

So I dropped the matter, but then a few days later, in a rare act of willfulness, I called a domestic-help service, while Uncle Irwin was out selling gun-cleaning equipment and Aunt Florence was at the high school. The service promptly sent me Jeeves and I was immediately impressed by the man, but when he told me his name, I was taken aback and said to him distrustfully, "Did you change your name to Jeeves to bring in the business?"

"No, sir," he said. "Jeeves has long been my family name, since before my grandparents emigrated to this country from England."

"You're American?"

"Yes, sir."

"But you sound English to me."

"I have, sir, what you would call a Mid-Atlantic accent, which is sometimes mistaken for an English accent."

"Yes, you're right. I hear it now. But, anyway, it's awfully odd that you're named Jeeves, if you know what I mean. It's throwing me for a bit of a loop."

"I can appreciate, sir, your reaction. I imagine that you are making reference to the character Jeeves in the novels and stories of P. G. Wodehouse."

"Yes, that is what I'm making reference to!"

"Well, all I can tell you, sir, is that it has long been the theory in my family that the young P. G. Wodehouse must have encountered a Jeeves or a Jeaves with an *a,* in which case he changed the spelling for legal reasons, but, regardless, he thought it a good name for a valet and went on to use it with phenomenal success, but to the detriment of real Jeeveses everywhere."

"I see." I didn't say it, since I didn't think it was my place, but I wondered if Jeeves had gone into valeting out of desperation. A sort of "if you can't beat them, join them" approach, like being named Roosevelt and feeling compelled to run for president. "Have you considered changing your name to ease the burden?" I asked.

"No, sir. Regardless of the circumstances, one takes a certain pride in one's family name."

"Yes, of course," I said, and as Jeeves explained all this, it made me wonder if Frankenstein had once been a common German name, and then I recalled a fellow at Princeton, my alma mater, named Portnoy, who got a lot of razzing. So Jeeves wasn't alone with this kind of name problem, and his explanation about the whole thing was certainly sympathetic and calmed any thoughts I had that he might have been some kind of conman/valet. Thus, I was ready to hire him on the spot—he was everything I was looking for, there was about the man an aura of serenity and competence—but I thought I had better not appear too eager, so I pressed on with my interrogation.

"Well, thank you for clearing up this name issue. . . . So, do you have any allergies I should be made aware of?"

"No, sir."

"Do you belong to any political groups or apolitical groups?"

"No, sir."

"Clubs?"

"No, sir."

"Do you have any hobbies?"

"No, sir."

"No hobbies? Fishing? Leaf-pressing? Bodybuilding? Crossword puzzles?"

"No, sir. I like to read."

"Me, too! That's my only hobby, *and* a weakness for the sports pages."

"Very good, sir."

Well, that was it. I was sold. The man was perfect. So, feeling rather omnipotent with my quarter million dollars in the bank, I offered Jeeves the job and he accepted, and thus it came to be that the good old fellow entered my employ.

The aunt and uncle, fortunately, didn't say a word about it, cowed I guess by my having a servant, and, too, Jeeves was quite expert at staying out of their way. Also, because of my settlement, I started paying my aunt and uncle a generous rent, and this may have helped them to not be bothered by Jeeves's occupying the other spare bedroom.

So Jeeves was unquestionably a great addition to my life, and the fact that he could help me with my writing was a spectacular bonus. After producing that page about the Saint Patrick's Day Parade and receiving Jeeves's kindly stamp of approval, I said, "Well, I think I've written enough today, Jeeves, and I'm famished. Can you put something together in the way of nutrition? All I've had in my mouth today are my teeth."

"Yes, sir."

In no time at all, he fixed me up some sardines, tomatoes, and toast. It was a splendid feast, and afterward I was ready for my nap. Usually after lunch I need to sleep—my constitution and digestion are, in this way, rather Mediterranean in spirit.

I laid my head on the pillow, and though I was quite tired, I found myself worrying about the situation with the aunt and uncle. I really had overstayed my welcome. It was time for me to move on, and in that moment I made an imperial decision.

"Jeeves," I called out.

He poured into the room. "Yes, sir."

"Jeeves, how do you like the mountains?"

"I am not opposed to mountains, sir."

"Well, I was thinking that tomorrow, you and I should disappear for the rest of the summer. We'll take the car"—I owned a 1989, olive green Chevrolet Caprice Classic—"and motor up to the Poconos. We can rent a cabin and commune with the Hasidic wives of Manhattan diamond merchants, and I'll work on my novel in that mountain air, which I imagine will be invigorating."

"A very good plan, sir."

"After my siesta, start gathering the Blair necessaries. We'll attempt to break free of Montclair tomorrow. I think you'll enjoy the Poconos, Jeeves."

"Yes, sir."

I was sure my uncle Irwin would be glad to see me go, especially after I had burned him that A.M., but my aunt Florence, I thought, might be against my leaving—she was very fond of me. She'd never had any children of her own, and I think I had become something of a son figure and so I was concerned she might take it hard that I wanted to leave for the summer, if not for forever. But I saw the coffee debacle as a sign for me to move on, because a guest—even one thought of as a son—must know when to leave, even if the guest has nowhere to go.

CHAPTER 3

❧

*Dinner at the Kosher Nosh ★ Why a Jewish predilection for con-
stipation can be lifesaving ★ A Chinese family momentarily dis-
tracts ★ An unexpected contretemps ★ A sad good-bye*

A few hours after my nap, it was time again for calories and I was at
the Kosher Nosh restaurant with the old flesh and blood—Aunt Florence and Uncle Irwin. Jeeves was home, doing who knows what—
probably writing letters to fellow valets in servitude in far-off lands.
Meanwhile, I was meditatively chewing on a large, wartish, dark
green pickle. I had already broached the coffee matter during the car
ride to the restaurant, and my uncle, as Jeeves had predicted, was perfectly reasonable and forgiving; so now, with each bite of my pickle,
I was gathering up the courage to tackle the next difficult issue—to
let the old f. and b. know that their beloved nephew was going to take
wing the next morning.

It was part of our normal routine to go to the Kosher Nosh on
Monday nights. It was a delicatessen restaurant with about fifty
simple tables, all very close to one another, and the whole place was
bathed in bright fluorescent lights. On one side of the establishment
was the dining area, and on the other was a thirty-foot glass counter
filled with all sorts of meats and salads and knishes of various origins,
and behind the counter were usually about half a dozen yarmulked,
white-smocked countermen, who engaged in playful Yiddish banter and efficient meat-slicing and shouted with authority, "Next!"

The clientele of the Kosher Nosh were ancient Jews who had no
business eating pastrami sandwiches. They hardly looked like they
could walk, let alone digestively break down noxious smoked meats.

23

But there they were, happily absorbing substantial portions of kosher brisket, corned beef, pastrami, roast beef, chicken, hot dogs, tongue, liver, and steak.

I was as Jewish as any of the *alter kockers*—that's "old codgers" in gentile—present at the Kosher Nosh, but my surname Blair (originally Blaum but changed at Ellis Island), and my somewhat Waspish appearance often have me mistaken for a gentile. But my palate—I love pastrami and Cell-Ray soda—in contrast to my looks is a dead giveaway and decidedly Semitic, as is my digestion, which, like with most Jews, is constricted at best. If anyone should be vegetarian, it's the Jews. But we may have developed constipation in a Darwinian way. We've spent centuries hiding in cellars during pogroms, inquisitions, and holocausts, and so if you don't have to go outside to the bathroom, where you might get killed by a passing Cossack, inquisitioner, or storm trooper, then you live longer and pass on your genes, including the lifesaving constricted-bowel gene.

So every Monday at the Kosher Nosh, I got my weekly pastrami fix, and it was the one communal meal where my uncle's mastication didn't completely unman me. The other chewing noises coming from the tables around us were all so ghastly that his noises seemed to be lost in this gruesome chorus; in fact, in the world of the Kosher Nosh, the gurgles and spittles and frothings of his chomping were normal, and so their power over me was somehow nullified.

We placed our order with an exhausted, ready-for-the-grave waitress—for some reason, the Kosher Nosh only hired newly minted female senior citizens; it was a restaurant of the aged serving the even more aged. And it was while I was nervously starting in on a second pickle to pass the time and muster courage that an Asian family of four poked their heads into the dining area. This seemed very unusual. They just stood there, father, mother, a son, and a daughter—all of them clearly uncertain about storming this gathering of Israelites in Montclair. We weren't a fierce bunch of Jews, but if all the elders wielded their aluminum walking sticks at the same time, we could make a dangerous mob.

"Look," I said to my aunt and uncle, because of the novelty of the occurrence. "A Chinese family. Or maybe Korean. I don't think they're Japanese."

"They should come in," said my aunt Florence. "The food here is the best."

"I wonder what they're thinking, looking at all these Jews eating corned beef and ready for heart operations," I said.

"They're thinking," said my uncle, "'must be a good place—there's Jewish people here—that's always a good sign.'"

My uncle, despite a number of faults, often displayed a quick and amusing wit, which I admired. I smiled appreciatively at the cleverness of his remark and even let out a little laugh.

But my aunt, who at sixty-three looked no more than fifty with her honey-colored hair twirled in a challahlike, teenagelike braid, did not understand why I had giggled at my uncle's rejoinder. Her sense of humor, like her braid, was a bit naive, though in all other areas she was bright and sensitive. "What's so funny?" she asked.

My uncle was momentarily incapable of speech; he had grabbed and was destroying a pickle, nearly swallowing the thing whole—all tables came with an aluminum canister filled with the phallic green wands soaking in brine—and so it was left to me to explain to my aunt. "You know how when we go to a Chinese restaurant," I said, "or when any Jewish person goes to a Chinese restaurant, and if they haven't been there before and they see Chinese people eating there, they'll say, 'Look! There's Chinese people—that's a good sign.' Well, these Chinese people—if they're Chinese—have come to a Jewish restaurant and it's a good sign to them, according to Uncle Irwin, that there are Jews here."

"Oh yes," said my aunt, smiling sweetly, "I get it now."

"I think," I said, "it would be interesting someday if Chinese people ate Jewish food as much as Jewish people ate Chinese food. There should be Jewish fast-food places, like the Chinese have. Instead of wonton soup, chicken soup; instead of egg rolls, egg matzo; and a Jewish fortune cookie could be a piece of *rugelach* with a stock tip or something from a Jewish investment bank. You know, so people could make fortunes."

My uncle Irwin shot me one of those oysterish glances he specialized in. You know, where the eye is all cold and dead and runny. It wasn't as fearsome as the lobster look he had given me that morning, but it wasn't what you would call a tender glance. He didn't like it when I posited unusual hypothetical situations, like Jewish fast food and fortune cookies. To be honest, he thought I was a bit loony and something of a layabout. One time, he burst into my lair while I was working on my opus, though, actually at that moment, I was playing solitaire at the computer as a way to stimulate the Muse—she often likes it when I play solitaire for an hour or more. But when my uncle saw the cards on the computer screen, he shouted, "So this is what you do in here all the time! Talk to yourself and play solitaire!"

So before things went too far downhill at the Kosher Nosh and became overly frosty because of my Jewish fortune cookie idea, I thought I had better break the news about my leaving.

"I have something to announce," I said, flourishing my pickle like a green and swollen extra finger. "I'm going to take off for the Poconos for the rest of the summer. I've burdened you enough these last few months. But I'll be in frequent contact and will flood you with postcards of rural landscapes."

Uncle Irwin, to my surprise, continued to beam oysters at me. I wanted to tell him that oysters were *trayf* and had no place here at the Kosher Nosh. I had thought he would be glad to hear I was leaving.

In spiritual contrast, my aunt Florence's eyes were not at all oysterish—they looked sad and concerned. "Alan, I've been worried," she said. "I was going to suggest tonight, after we had our food, something very different from you going off to the Poconos." She paused, steeled herself, then continued, "I think maybe you should consider going back to rehab."

"We know you've been drinking again," growled my uncle. "We took you in when you had nowhere to go and the way you thank us is by hitting the bottle."

This was a contretemps I had not foreseen. I lowered my pickle to my plate, like dropping my sword. Then the Asian family took the empty table next to us. I smiled at them, wanting to welcome them to the promised land of brisket, but this smile was a cover-up while I tried to put together a defense. One came to me: I would drop my shield to go along with my pickle sword. No defense.

"Yes, I've been drinking," I said, taking the honest path, but then, swerving, I continued, "though not to excess. One medicinal glass of red wine each night as a sleeping potion. They say it's good for your blood. If the French didn't eat a lot of fat and smoke cigarettes in the delivery rooms of hospitals, they would live exceedingly long lives due to all the red wine they go through." I hadn't meant to produce such a disquisition of facts about the state of French health, but when nervous, I'm prone to obfuscation, not to mention lying.

"Alan," said my aunt, and she looked at me with love, "the Flatleys"—she was referring to the next-door neighbors—"asked us if we were putting wine bottles in their recycling bin. I said no, of course. And then they joked that somebody was going through two or three bottles a night and trying to pin it on them."

"That's why you closet yourself in your room all morning, isn't it?" said my uncle. "You're hungover! You're supposed to be writing your book."

"I do write my book. And I don't drink at night. It must be Jeeves!"

"Jeeves! You're insane!" exclaimed my uncle with anger. But he was quite right to be furious with me—I shouldn't have tried to smudge Jeeves's character as a way of oiling out of a tough spot.

My aunt ignored this Jeeves exchange. "I spoke to Dr. Montesonti," she said, and my mind reeled. The dreaded Montesonti— the nerve specialist at Cedars Grove rehab in Long Island where I'd had an unfortunate residence! He had told me that I was a maniac, in the classic sense of the word, which appealed to my ego a little, but he had wanted to destroy my relationship with my Muse by prescribing lithium. *"I will not go on lithium!"* I had protested. *"It's only a salt,"* he'd argued. *"I don't like salt,"* I had riposted, and luckily for me he couldn't force me to take that horrible seasoning. And then I miraculously escaped his clutches when my insurance ran out.

"Montesonti is a terrible doctor," I said to my aunt and uncle. "What kind of psychiatrist is grossly overweight and chews Nicorette gum?"

Aunt Florence didn't respond to my statement; she clearly had her speech prepared and pressed on with it:

"He recommended that either you come back to Cedars or we find you a place out here. But he also said that if you refused to go back to rehab, that we were to ask you to leave. That by letting you stay, we were enabling you. That we had to give you tough love. Your mother would want me to love you any way I can, and if the doctor feels that tough love is the best kind, then that's what we have to do. . . . Will you go back to rehab? You hardly went to AA, and you haven't stopped drinking on your own, as you promised. And that was our contract—a quiet place to do your writing if you don't drink. So either it's rehab or we can no longer have you in the house."

I could see that my aunt hated to say this, but she thought she was doing the right thing, and perhaps she was.

"You use up a lot of electricity, you know, with that computer, playing solitaire," said my uncle, "and you don't need to run the hot water the whole time you're shaving. Just turn the water back on when you rinse the blade." These were obviously economic grievances that he had been harboring for some time.

"Irwin, that doesn't help matters," said my aunt. Rarely did she speak harshly to him. My uncle, chastised, savaged another pickle, and it disappeared into his Padre Pio beard, never to be seen again. The Chinese family to our right were studying the Talmud-sized menus and consulting with one another in their native tongue. A shade, in the form of a waitress, arrived with our soups. We all had ordered mushroom barley, but now our unity in soup seemed quite sad. Our shared preference for barley soup had, over the months, given me an odd sense of family, despite whatever tensions existed between myself and the uncle, but the discovery of the wine bottles by the Flatleys had shattered this. My uncle started to eat; my aunt and I were too upset to begin.

"I understand your position entirely," I said to my aunt Florence, trying to gather myself with dignity; my uncle's head was bent to his bowl. "You've been wonderful and good to me and I'm very grateful. I promise you that my drinking is not out of control. . . . At least I don't think it is. So I don't want to go to rehab. It almost killed me the last time. . . . So I guess it's good timing, my decision to head for the Poconos."

I peered into my soup, ashamed. Barley and vegetables floated listlessly in the overcast broth. And yet, in that murk, I could make out my reflection—my eyes in that soupy mirror were two black coins. I didn't recognize myself.

"You're thirty years old," said my uncle. "You're a free agent.

Just don't put me in your book, if you ever write it. I want to write my own novel about being a salesman. Arthur Miller wrote the play, but I'll write the book."

"I won't write about you, I promise," I said.

My uncle, satisfied, ate his soup. My aunt took a sip of water, and then she said, "We love you, Alan. Please, please be careful."

"I will be," I said.

"He'll be all right," said my uncle to reassure her. "Eat your soup," he then barked, commanding both of us, not wanting us to waste food, and I did so numbly, without tasting it. I avoided my aunt's eyes for the rest of the meal. Naturally, I didn't have much appetite. My uncle had my sandwich wrapped up, told me to eat it for lunch tomorrow. Not an ungenerous man, he paid for dinner.

Later, at the door to my bedroom, my aunt hugged me good-night, and when she released me, she said, "I love you very much. . . . Irwin is fond of you, too. Loves you, you know, even if he seems gruff most of the time. He's liked having you here. If you stop drinking, you can always come back to us."

"Thank you," I said. "I love you." She didn't look like my mother, even though they were sisters, but telling her I loved her was almost like saying it to my mother, something I hadn't been able to do since I was twenty, except in my mind.

"We probably won't see each other in the morning unless you get up when I do," she said, "so let's say good-bye now."

She opened her arms for a second hug. We held each other. "Please don't hurt yourself with the drinking," she said, and let go of me.

"I won't," I said.

Then my aunt Florence walked down the short hall to their bedroom. My uncle was playing his weather channel. He played it at night, too, a habit from his days as a traveling salesman when he needed to know the weather just as much as a sailor.

I lay on my bed, once again careworn. How terrible to be alcoholic. You just want to quietly soothe and maybe poison yourself, but you end up poisoning those around you as well, like trying to commit suicide with a gas oven and unwittingly murdering your neighbors.

I started rubbing the bony center of my nose, which I always rub when things have gone badly. Then midway through this nose massage, I heard a slight aspiration—Jeeves, like humidity, had accumulated on my left. Jeeves, I think, is closely related to water. They say we're all 50 percent H_2O, but Jeeves is probably 90 percent. Jeeves and water seep in everywhere, no stopping them, like this underground lake that starts in Long Island, I'm told, and then pops up in Connecticut. So Jeeves spilled over from his lair, the bedroom next to mine, and was now standing alongside me, like mist on a mirror. "Yes, Jeeves," I said.

"Will you be needing anything, sir, before I retire?"

"A new brain, Jeeves."

"Really, sir?"

"I've made a mess of things. Aunt Florence found out about my tippling."

"Most troubling, sir."

"I've hurt her terribly. I should be lashed. If we weren't heading for the Poconos, she was about to give us the boot. She said she has to practice 'tough love' on me, Jeeves. And I don't blame her, but she's been overly influenced by those admirable twelve-step programs. But I need more than twelve steps. For what ails me, I require that whole staircase in Rome."

"Most vexing, sir."

"They say it all comes from low self-esteem. Maybe I can order chest-expanding equipment from Charles Atlas. That might help."

"Perhaps, sir."

"My aunt also said she doesn't want to enable me. All this language is strange, don't you think, Jeeves? *Enable. Tough love.* I think *enable* should be switched to *spoil rotten.* . . . And that's what you do to me, Jeeves. Spoil me rotten, just by listening. It's a great comfort."

"I endeavor to give satisfaction, sir."

We weren't about to throw ourselves on each other's neck, but it was a moment awash in tenderness and bonhomie.

"Good night, Jeeves," I said.

"Good night, sir," he said and I blinked and he was gone.

CHAPTER 4

A dream with a lovely element ★ My face has a problem, well, two problems ★ Stiff words with Jeeves ★ A cataloging of sport coats and a summary of my twenties as related, in a way, to sport coats ★ Stiff words with Uncle Irwin ★ A change of plans—the Hasidim aren't where I thought they were—but a pleasing alternative is presented

I woke fairly early, around eight-thirty, and all seemed quiet. No uncles were up and racing their stationary bicycles and creating havoc, and so I was confident that Jeeves and I would have a pleasant, midmorning start. I thought it would show character if we were on the road before noon.

"Morning, Jeeves," I said. He was at the bedside with my bath towel, having sniffed out that the young master was conscious. I smiled at Jeeves. Had no effect on him. Inscrutable as always. It's relaxing, though, to have an inscrutable person about—no fatiguing one's self with scrutinizing, if you know what I mean.

"Good morning, sir."

"Had another dream, Jeeves."

"The cat and mouse again, sir?"

"No, this dream was about a girl, though I would like to know what happened to that mouse. Anyway, this girl was leaning over me . . . her face right above mine. I think I was lying on my bed or maybe on the ground somewhere. Her eyes were blue. Very light blue. Kindly eyes, Jeeves. Her hair was blonde, but not very blonde. She said, 'I love you, Blair.' I couldn't believe it. Couldn't get any words out in response. Too shocked. Cowardly. Then she was gone and I was walking around an odd city with menacing buildings. Make anything of it?"

"Would appear to be a hopeful dream, sir."

"You think it's an omen for our trip? Maybe she's a god of some sort who will look after us."

"Perhaps, sir."

"I like how she called me Blair. Very intimate using my surname that way. Don't you think, Jeeves?"

"Yes, sir."

"But maybe she's not a god. Maybe I'm going to meet her in the Poconos. Maybe she's a blonde Hasid. We had both better keep an eye out for a girl like this—dark blonde hair, blue eyes. The nose was straight and fine, Jeeves, an elegant nose, and the lips were pink, not too full, but womanly. Quite vivid, my memory of her."

"Yes, sir."

"When she said she loved me, I felt that I loved her. A very strong feeling, Jeeves. I wish I could have said something. But I was scared. Then I was in that terrible city. Not New York, not anywhere recognizable."

"Perhaps you will dream of her again, sir."

"You know, I was in love once, Jeeves. My heart still hurts sometimes. It's like sciatica . . . I think, 'Why didn't she love me?' And then I get this pain. . . . But I wish I were in love again. I'd like to have a new someone. You know that song, 'Good Night My Someone'? It was in some musical I saw on TV. According to the song, that's what you say at night to the person you love when you haven't met them yet. They're just out there somewhere. Maybe this blonde is out there. . . . I'd like to tell someone I love them, Jeeves."

"A very human longing, sir."

"Hard facing life by myself, Jeeves."

"Yes, sir."

"You, of course, cushion the blow considerably."

"Thank you, sir."

"Sorry to start the day with such talk, Jeeves."

"Perfectly all right, sir."

"I'm not being very stoic," I said, and inwardly I chastised myself—get moving, Blair! So I stored the memory of the girl from

the dream in my mind, like a picture in a wallet. "My towel, Jeeves,"
I said, rallying bravely.

"Yes, sir."

Out of respect for my aunt, I had not drained the two bottles of
wine that were hidden under my bed, and a sober night's sleep
had me feeling rather hale for my mountain adventure, and maybe,
too, the lack of booze had sprung the girl from my subconscious.
Perhaps there was something to abstention. So I swung the Blair legs
out of that very good New Jersey bed, relieved Jeeves of my towel,
and set out to follow my usual regimen of bath, shave, yogic exercises, newspaper, and coffee. Even on a travel day, I wanted to stick
with my routine—you know, not wanting to jinx things.

But the ceremonies began poorly. My toilet was not a success.
Something had gone wrong with my face during my eight hours of
unconsciousness—the body is a mystery—and I didn't feel very
good now about traveling. It's hard to be courageous about setting
off for the unknown when your face isn't working, but I was going
to have to press on, regardless. It was either the road or rehab. So I
retreated to my room and quickly upholstered myself with the
day's costume that Jeeves had laid out: brown linen pants; light blue
shirt; my green paisley tie, which is especially good for travel since
paisley looks like things in motion, either butterfly wings or sper-
matozoa, depending on your worldview; check sport coat; black
socks; and wing tips, which are also good for travel—taking flight
and all that.

As I completed noosing my tie, Jeeves insinuated himself into the
room, and I hid my face from him. But Jeeves sees all. He cleared his
throat, like a bell tolled at the start of a round of boxing.

"Yes, Jeeves?" I said, acting like there was nothing wrong.

"If I may say so, sir, you have again forgotten to shave." There was
a quiet severity to his articulation.

"If you will notice, Jeeves, I have shaved most of my face." I
matched his quiet severity with confident severity.

"The upper lip, sir, has been neglected."

"What of it?" I felt myself weakening. My upper lip was under
attack and not very stiff.

"It is not appealing, sir."

33

"Show a little courage, Jeeves, some creativity," I said with false bravado. "I am aspiring to a Douglas Fairbanks Jr.-Errol Flynn look. Not to mention Clark Gable."

"I do not advise such a look, sir. It is not suitable for a young gentleman."

"Are you saying Douglas F., Errol F., and Clark G. were not gentlemen?"

"They were actors, sir."

Jeeves had me with that one. A crushing blow. It was all over. I had to concede. What was I thinking? Actors! So I came out with it. I couldn't filibuster the fellow.

"Listen, Jeeves," I said. "Morale is low. Very low. Rally round! I have a spot on my lip, that's why I didn't shave. The mustache is meant as camouflage. Hair on the upper lip is better than a pimple on the upper lip. Well, actually two pimples. Have you noticed that my spots are always symmetrical, Jeeves? Must be glandular—glands on the right and left of my body must get clogged at the same time. A kind of stereo effect. Remember last month, I had a pimple on the right cheek and one on the left cheek in parallel locations?"

"I am barely able to discern these upper-lip blemishes, sir, that you refer to. They are neglible and like most blemishes will not be noticed by anyone, whereas this unfortunate mustache is readily apparent and will be perceived by the most casual glance."

"But I can't tolerate pimples, Jeeves. How can I face the legions of barmaids and hoteliers and Hasidim that we are sure to meet in the Poconos with these things on my face?"

"They are hardly visible, sir."

"There's no reasoning with me, Jeeves. I know I distort the spots, but I can't help it, and we should both be grateful that I didn't make things worse and attack myself in the bathroom."

"Yes, sir."

I wasn't joking when I said that an attack on the self had been averted. You see, when it comes to blemishes, I'm like one of those people who feel the need to throw themselves into a body of water when they are on a boat, even though they know that such an act is irrational. So it's the same thing with me and pimples—I know I shouldn't squeeze them, but I can't help myself. I am the Hart Crane of acne.

You see, it's more of a mental, pathological condition than a skin condition. I actually have quite a good complexion, but on the odd occasion, three or four times a year, when I get a pimple—and they're often quite tiny—I look in the mirror and see the Elephant Man and begin to assault myself.

But Jeeves couldn't empathize. He probably hadn't had a pimple in years. His skin was above such things. I did think, though, that maybe I could win Jeeves over to my side by giving him the psychological angle.

"My condition is hereditary, Jeeves," I said. "I remember, as a boy, seeing my father in the bathroom intently staring at himself in the mirror, his fingers applied to some invading blemish. His face would be devastated for weeks as a result of his prodding—his pimples transformed into bruises. It made a deep impression on me, Jeeves. The sins of the fathers *are* visited on the sons. So it's in my blood to assail my own face, but I hope you acknowledge the fact that I fight this inheritance. Hence the mustache!"

"Yes, sir."

"So if you could put up with this nascent lip hair, now that you understand its roots are in a childhood trauma, I would be exceedingly grateful. If you notice, I have put on my tie for my yoga. I am holding on to the mustache, but I am bending on this other issue. This is known as give-and-take. I am not an unreasonable man, Jeeves."

"Very good, sir." He was coolly remote, but conciliatory. He knew he couldn't win every battle, and I *had* relented on the neckwear. So, trying not to be demoralized by my pimples, I did my yoga, then had some toast and coffee, while I memorized the box scores and batting averages, only to have to do it again the next morning. The worship of sports is merciless this way.

While I studied the *Times,* Jeeves took out to the car my two large suitcases and garment bag, which was swollen with my diverse sport coat collection. I don't have many possessions, and certainly no baubles, but I do pride myself on my sport coats. They are really my only jewels, though it's more like they're a knight's armor. I'm able to sally forth in style and engage the world when I have a sport coat on. Wallet, keys, pens, a little notebook, change, a paperback novel—everything I need to survive, except maybe water—all fit into the various pockets. For me a sport coat is not unlike Batman's utility belt, which I remember admiring as a small boy during my American childhood, years before my sense of myself as an American got somewhat clouded by reading too many British novels.

So here's a quick rundown of my sport coats, not in order of preference, but as they occur to me:

(1) 1950s rust-colored Brooks Brothers affair made of burlapish material, discovered at a Princeton yard sale. Always solicits kind remarks, despite some eccentricity in its hue. Lining was disintegrating for some time, and I felt like that character in the Gogol story who was embarrassed by the shabbiness of his coat, but a master Italian tailor on First Avenue in New York City resuscitated the garment.

(2) 1993 gray Harris Tweed, from Brooks Brothers. An emotionally sturdy jacket. I could climb mountains wearing this tweed. Fills me with confidence. Very good in the fall and winter. Couldn't get by without it, really.

(3) 1989 gray-striped seersucker, with a neck, from perspiration, permanently yellowed, like a cigarette smoker's teeth. But I am in favor of this jaundiced collar, gives the jacket character. Picked it up at the Princeton University store, but couldn't afford the matching pants, which I don't mind, a whole seersucker outfit is too attention-grabbing; I prefer a pair of khaki pants as a complement to my seersucker jacket.

(4) 1992 Brooks Brothers blue blazer. If one's sport coats were as important as one's inner organs, then the blue blazer would be the lungs—absolutely essential; you can survive without the seersucker, for example, the spleen of sport coats, but try getting by without a blazer! Though, as I indicated above, my gray Harris Tweed actually outranks my blazer.

(5) Sullivan's of Albany middling corduroy fellow, picked up at a church thrift shop on Eighty-sixth Street in Manhattan, year

unknown. Rarely worn, but hard to throw away. Just thinking about it, though, makes me feel bad for my neglect. I'm going to make a real effort to include it more regularly in the rotation.

(6) 1984 plaid green-and-blue summer coat, from Harry Ballard of Princeton. Needs frequent dry cleaning, seems to hold on to perspiration in a rather unforgiving way, but can be very charming. I have a love-hate relationship with this coat.

(7) 1986 blue linen summer coat, from Hazlett's of Princeton. Very handsome, a summer blazer essentially, and wrinkles in an attractive way that makes me feel like a character in a Chekhov play. Interesting that my sport coats provoke thoughts of Russian literature. Had never made the connection before this moment.

(8) 1990 spring-and-summer-weight check, from Harry Ballard. I often rely on this coat too much and don't appreciate it. It's so solid I take it for granted. Will try to work on that. It's my Harris Tweed for the warm seasons.

As you can see there's a preponderance from the Princeton region of sport coats, which is a very rich region for jackets, rivaling if not surpassing Cambridge and New Haven. It is where I first began amassing my collection, and that's because I was stationed there for a number of years, first as an undergraduate and then as a regular citizen. After graduation in 1986, I stayed on in the town of Princeton for another six years, during which time I wrote and published my first novel; fell in love and stayed in love, until I had my heart crushed; tried writing a second novel, but couldn't; and between the writing problems and the loss of the girl began to slowly lose my mind.

Then I moved to New York, to jump-start the writing process and forget the girl, and for two years, 1992–94, I lived with Charles and made progress on both fronts, writing and forgetting. But I have to admit I was hitting the bottle too hard, which eventually caused Charles to kick me out and me to end up in rehab, where I completely lost my mind, which is what I do, I've noticed, and that is to treat my mind like a set of house keys: lose it and then happily find it, only to lose it again. And one shouldn't treat one's mind this way, but these things happen. Anyway, this all explains why my sport coats are either from Princeton or New York—where you live is where you acquire your sport coats.

Well, after loading the automobile with my garment bag and my suitcases, Jeeves came back in and reported that he was going to give the Caprice a thorough inspection—oil, water, and tire pressure. "Very good, Jeeves," I said, and he siphoned himself back outside, and I cleaned up my breakfast dishes.

In the refrigerator, while putting away the milk, I noticed that my aunt had put together a bag lunch for me—my half-eaten sandwich from the Kosher Nosh, a pickle in foil, and an apple. She had attached a note, which gave my heart pause:

Dear Alan,
  I love you and Irwin loves you. Call if you need us.
  You're very dear to me. Please watch your drinking. But if you do want to stop drinking and go to meetings or to rehab, you can always come back to us.

                                        Love,
                                        Aunt Florence

I girded myself so as not to be weepy. It's always unnerving when people are loving. The slightest act of kindness—taking the time to put a lunch together, write a note!—directed at my person and I fall apart. Goes against one's core beliefs about one's self. Sets off a skirmish on the inside. I'll be the first to admit it: my whole unconscious—well, I'm somewhat conscious of it—outlook on life is built on the premise that I can't stand myself and should be shot. So if people love you, it makes it difficult to go about your business of being blissfully self-destructive and impulsive.

But I pulled myself together—didn't let my aunt's note unravel my plans for quitting Montclair—and made a final check of the bedroom, where I gathered my last and most essential belonging, my writing instrument—my laptop computer. As I left my room, my uncle's door opened wide and he emerged at the end of the short hall. Sunbeams, coming through a window in his room, bathed him in a radioactive orange light. He stepped toward me like a solar fireball. He was in flaming bathrobe and ignited Pio beard.

"Good morning, Uncle Irwin," I whispered before I was burnt alive: I was Icarus and he was the sun. I was trying to fly away in my wing tips.

"Are you growing a mustache?" he demanded, and he was right on top of me. The fire around him receded, though the hall behind him was still ablaze. I wasn't used to having such an acute, sober sense of sight in the morning. Thank God, I had been drinking all those months in New Jersey. I didn't know that this little hallway was so perfectly aligned with the sun, like Stonehenge, but in Montclair.

"Yes. I am growing a mustache," I said, not liking the tone of his question.

"I don't think it's working. It looks like you've been drinking orange juice."

He was referring to the reddish-orangish nature of my facial hair, and I didn't appreciate his remark. First Jeeves, and now Uncle Irwin. This fledgling mustache was under attack from all directions, but this only stiffened my resolve.

"I am trying to single-handedly bring back the Douglas Fairbanks Jr.-Errol Flynn-Clark Gable look," I said coolly. I didn't intend to mention, naturally, the blemish motivation, or the fact that actors aren't gentlemen. "When people see me at gas pumps on the state highways during my journey and in roadside restaurants, a ripple effect will occur. A grassroots movement. You may find yourself, in a few weeks' time, bowing to the pressure and thinning out your own considerable mustache."

"Listen," he said, "if you get pulled over by a state trooper, don't say anything. Just give them your license. It will upset your aunt if we have to come get you again out of some rehab or psychiatric hospital."

Usually, I don't register insults or sarcastic remarks directed at my person. I lack some type of translation device or hostility radar. I absorb the comments as if they are perfectly polite statements. And it's only later, well after the fact, that it dawns on me that I've been treated rudely, which is not unlike my delayed response to danger and horror.

Anyway, that morning I was in unusual form; perhaps it was sobriety—I had been quick to defend my lip hair against the orange-juice comment, and when my uncle followed that up with this psychiatric-hospital barb, I knew that another affront had been made. I then gave it back to the uncle as good as he had given it to me. We were at the very spot of the previous day's congress and I made reference to this.

"If I had a cup of coffee, I would be sorely tempted to douse you, Uncle," I said, brandishing my laptop as if it were a coffee mug. Some type of oedipal fury, repressed for months, was being unleashed between us. Though since he was my uncle, I guess it was more of a Hamlet fury.

"You did that on purpose yesterday, didn't you?" he growled. "I've always said that you're as nutty as a fruitcake."

"I'm not the one who thinks he's Padre Pio and has more guns than Al Capone! And I should think that the proper remark was 'as fruity as a fruitcake.'"

His eyes widened. Verbally, I had struck quite a blow. I turned my back to him and went down the three steps to the kitchen, Poconos-bound in a hurry. There was a good chance the back of my neck was in the sights of a .38.

"Wait a second," he said, following me into the kitchen and moving with considerable speed. "Slow down . . . I'm sorry! . . . I don't want you to leave on a bad note . . . I apologize! I'm upset, because your aunt is upset. We're both worried about you."

I turned and faced him. His mood-mustache looked warm and his apology was generous. I endeavored to soothe him.

"You and Aunt Florence shouldn't worry about me," I said. "I'm stronger than the two of you think. I promise you, I'm going to be all right. I swear."

"Well, where in the Poconos are you heading?" he asked.

"I'm just striking out into the whole territory. I'm relying on kismet. I want to find a cabin and get some writing done. My idea is to locate a summer Hasidic community."

I felt my uncle straining to give me one of his oysterish eye beams, but he held it in check. Also, he couldn't argue with my desire to be near fellow Jews, though it wasn't so much their Jewishness that I wanted proximity to, but, rather, their timelessness—fashion-wise the women are trapped in the 1940s and the men are in the nineteenth century, and both these time periods appeal to me. It's nice if you can combine regular traveling—like going to the Poconos—with time travel.

"You won't find Hasidim in the Poconos," said my uncle. "They're in the Catskills."

This was devastating intelligence to receive, right on the verge of takeoff. "Are you sure the Jews haven't branched out to the Poconos?" I asked the uncle, thinking that perhaps the Diaspora had spread to more than one mountain range.

"Don't be ridiculous. Pennsylvania and the Poconos are for the Irish and the Germans. The Jews are in New York State. You should go to Sharon Springs. That's in New York. You want Hasids, Sharon Springs is loaded with them."

"Really?" I was intrigued.

"You can take mineral baths there; that's why they like it—for the *shvitz* baths. I used to pass through Sharon Springs for business. There's a nice hotel there, the Adler. It has a kosher dining room. That's where you should stay."

This Sharon Springs and the Adler seemed perfect. Mineral baths—a cure—would give the adventure a sanitarium ring to it. Ever since I read *The Magic Mountain,* sanitariums (not rehabs!) have had a romantic draw for me, and, too, it was appealing, after all, to have a firm destination, to not rely entirely on kismet, which isn't always so reliable, this being one of the drawbacks of kismet. So I told my uncle that I would follow his advice and go where he suggested. "I can work on my novel and take a cure at the same time," I added. "Soaking in baths is very healthful."

To aid my withdrawal to Sharon Springs, he went to his office in the basement—a bunkerlike space alongside the boiler, which always struck me as dangerous, since it was in his office that he stored his considerable munitions—to procure me a map. We then studied the map together on the kitchen table, and huddling so close to his person, the secondhand fumes from his baby powder were overwhelming, but I survived, like a commando, by breathing through my mouth. He traced a route for me and estimated that I could be in Sharon Springs in four hours, if I didn't violate the speed limit. He was very keen on my keeping a distance between myself and the constabulary, but I didn't take offense. All had been forgiven.

"Thank you so much, Uncle Irwin. Sharon Springs sounds ideal!" I said, and with that we shook hands good-bye. "And thank you for *everything* you've done for me, for taking me in all these months, you've been very generous."

We then unclasped hands, the uncle actually smiled at me, and I gathered together my things, including the map, which was a gift from him.

He walked me to the door. He said, "I'll miss you until I see you again."

"Me, too," I said.

There was a twinkle in my uncle's eye and it occurred to me that something wasn't quite right in his parting comment, but I decided not to meditate on it. So I walked across the patio where I had done my sun salutations in the mornings and suddenly I felt a bit weak in the legs and my forehead went cold. I was scared. Scared to leave. But, thinking that my uncle might still be in the doorway watching me, I couldn't let myself fall apart. I soldiered forth to the driveway, and when I saw Jeeves sitting in the front seat of the Caprice, my fears left me entirely. It was hard to stay frightened when I remembered I wasn't alone.

CHAPTER 5

Motoring along and pulling free ★ A dangerous contract with my
fellow citizens ★ A discussion of death ★ A discussion of the "other
half"

We biffed along silently, both of us rather quiet and solemn at the
start of our journey. But don't think we were morose, just contemplative and preserving our strength after the effort expended in
breaking free of Montclair.

My Caprice was a spacious cruiser, well insulated from the
world—one motored along the highways as if sitting in a middle-
class living room equipped with an engine and tires.

It happened to be a perfect day for driving a living room. There
was a terrific clarity to the July midsummer light—no atmospheric
muddle, no moisture. The palette of the day was simple, primary:
the sun was white, the sky was blue, and the road, freshly paved, was
black. Trees alongside the highway, despite being perfumed with car
exhaust, were green and flourishing, showing off their chlorophyll
with pride.

We were on Route 287, heading north for the New York State
Thruway. Traffic was fairly thick and I tried to catch glimpses of my
peers as they zipped past me. Who were these citizens? Where were
they off to in such a hurry? Where was I off to? They all looked
tragically self-absorbed and self-important; they had stricken, tormented faces. But then I remembered that's how everyone looks.
That's how I look.

But I wondered if I should trust my fellow self-centered New
Jerseyans. Driving together at speeds in excess of sixty miles per
hour perhaps is a dangerous social contract. I did feel well armored

in my Caprice, but the fragility of my life even within such a sturdy vehicle was readily apparent, though why I cared about my life is something of a conundrum. Supposedly, according to my core beliefs, I should be shot—I know this because I'm always saying to myself, as a sort of mantra, "I should be shot"—but I also, if I look at the facts, have a strong instinct for self-preservation, because I really don't want to die, at least not in a painful car accident. Like most people, I'm a curious mixture of opposing forces: I think I should be punished—shot—but I loathe pain; I think often of suicide but have a fear of death. Well, if nothing else, all these opposing forces give me a certain balance.

Befitting my middle-of-the-road outlook on life, Jeeves and I were in the center lane, surrounded by antagonists. I had a speeding truck of prehistoric dimensions careening on my left, a slow-moving, narcoleptic senior citizen on my right, and in the rear there was a tailgating sociopath, who was evidently homicidal as well as impatient.

I said to Jeeves, "Do you ever think of dying?"

"Only when I'm in a car, sir, with someone I don't know, don't know their driving, that is."

"But you trust my driving, don't you, Jeeves?"

"You're a very good driver, sir."

"But with other people, as they careen along, you think, 'This could be it'?"

"Yes, sir, I've often thought this."

"Then you resign yourself?"

"Yes, sir."

"That's just what I do, Jeeves. But we're too polite, you and I. So many times in New York City, I didn't have the courage—and I was paying for the service!—to ask a cabdriver to slow down. But then I would rationalize my cowardly behavior by thinking that if he slows down, then I'll be altering our destiny and maybe some accident which we would have avoided will occur. Follow my thinking, Jeeves?"

"Yes, sir."

"But I do think we're well protected in this Caprice, Jeeves," I said, putting up a bold front. "Other than the trucks, I think we'd crush all the other cars, and also a lot of cars tend to flip over when things get rough, so I really do think we'll be all right."

"Very good, sir."

"But driving is tiring, so let's plan to take a coffee break in an hour or two and mix with the locals and see how the other half lives."

"Yes, sir. A coffee break, in an hour's time or more, will certainly be welcome."

"But about this other half, Jeeves," I said, contemplating my previous statement, "what half do you think we are?"

"I imagine, sir, that all halfs are simply the other half."

I let what Jeeves said swirl around in the Blair brain. It seemed like very good stuff. "You may have said something profound, Jeeves. Well done."

"Thank you, sir."

But then the Blair brain kept working, which it often does, and I found I wasn't yet ready to mail in Jeeves's aphorism to the patent office. I was going to have to knock the fellow down a peg. "Though, I do wonder," I said, "owing to our small numbers, if we qualify as a whole half. You see what I mean, Jeeves?"

"A point to consider, sir."

So we both considered this and our heady discourse was a pleasant distraction for me, especially while every other available nerve of mine was engaged in the serious business of negotiating the road and keeping us alive. Even if I sometimes purported to having mixed feelings about my own life, I certainly didn't want to hurt Jeeves.

PART II

Sharon Springs, New York

CHAPTER 6

Arrival in Sharon Springs ★ Has something catastrophic occurred?
★ An allusion to Stephen King, the American Dickens ★ Diffi-
culty purchasing a phone card ★ You have to let people kill them-
selves ★ Unexpected news ★ Solicitations of a sexual nature ★
Another change of plans

It took us seven hours—instead of the estimated four—to reach
Sharon Springs. You see, after our first coffee break, I made the
executive decision that we should pursue a route of scenic back roads.
This had the advantage of an aesthetic upgrade, as well as featuring
less peril in the form of other drivers.

We stopped at several country restaurants for coffees to go, but we
didn't do much anthropological mingling, as I had wistfully
intended, with the *"other half."* Once we got going, a sort of road
focus took over, and we were intent on achieving our destination,
even if we were now taking a more circuitous route.

When we made stops, we just ordered our coffees and made
use—as a direct corollary to the absorption of these coffees—of a
number of diverse WCs, which would seem to be an innocent and
necessary office of the body, but it turned out that my numerous
visitations to these washrooms contributed to an unfortunate disaster, the details of which I will convey later.

Upon arrival in Sharon Springs, I was both triumphant and
exhausted. But not so tired that I couldn't appreciate my lovely
surroundings—it was a hilly, rustic little town, nestled at the bottom
of some manly, hairy-chested mountains.

"It's beautiful here," I exclaimed to Jeeves.

"Quite, sir," said Jeeves.

"This is going to be our Magic Mountain, Jeeves . . . well, our Jewish Magic Mountain. It looks ideal for a cure."

"Very good, sir."

And just then, as we came into that pretty burg, in a display of remarkably good timing, we ran out of fuel. Both Jeeves and I had been grossly unaware of that important gauge, but lucky for us the Caprice had a tank of enormous battleship proportions, nearly twenty-four gallons, and so we had made it all the way to Sharon Springs before the thing gave out.

We were able to coast down a hill to a filling station, which seemed deserted—no other cars were at the pumps. In fact, the whole town seemed deserted. I sensed an unnatural quiet and stillness. Had a plague descended on Sharon Springs? Was I existing momentarily in some kind of bestselling horror novel? Hadn't I seen something once on TV, a movie adapted from a novel by Stephen King, America's Dickens, though I've never read him, which showed a abandoned, murdered town just like this? The gas station we rolled into was situated on a brief main street, which also featured a deli, a bar-restaurant, and a church, but there were no people about. No people, no moving cars, no Hasidim. It was ghostly, but attractive. Jeeves and I were the only people in the world still alive.

My fears of a plague were relieved, though, when I spotted a man with the gray, anguished face of a gargoyle. He was peering at me from the window of the small market, which was the financial center of the gas station. At some point in America's history gas stations metamorphosed into small grocery stores, specializing in foods—no doubt also made from petroleum—meant to destroy one's health.

We gassed up the Caprice and then I went inside the market to pay for the petrol. I approached the cashier-gargoyle, who grimaced as he sucked the life out of a cigarette, and I gave him the necessary American currency, but required some change. While he fiddled with the register, I held my breath to avoid his air pollution, and as I did this, I spied a rack of phone cards behind the man and decided to check in with the aunt and uncle, to let them know that the prodigal nephew was prodigaling well.

"How much for one of those twenty-dollar phone cards?" I

asked, exhaling. Then I breathed through my mouth, hoping to lessen the effect of the man's exhaust, just as I had done earlier in the day with the fumes from Uncle Irwin's baby powder. Unfortunately, I was protecting my nose but sacrificing my mouth—there's no winning!

"Twenty dollars," snapped the cashier, while crushing his cigarette in an ashtray. One has to be thankful for small gifts—I could use my nostrils again. He handed me my change for the gasoline.

"I mean how many minutes are on a twenty-minute card?" I said, correcting myself.

"The card is twenty dollars, not twenty minutes," he said with annoyance, and he eyed me curiously and angrily, appraising me as a subnormal, I feared, and then he started up a new cigarette. This was torture.

But I had to give it one more go. My mind was strained from hours on the road and perhaps I had killed some brain cells while holding my breath, but certainly I could manage this inquiry.

"How . . . many . . . minutes . . . are on a twenty-dollar card?" I asked, and by the end of my request my whole IQ seemed to be fully available.

"I don't know," said the Sharon Springian, and he swiveled on his stool and went to dislodge the card and brought down several of them to the floor.

"Fuck," he said quietly, and then with some exertion got off his perch, disappeared behind his counter, and resurfaced with the phone cards in one of his coarse-looking mitts. There was color now in his gray cheeks and he was out of breath. I hoped his lawyers were in contact with the tobacco companies. Just bending over had nearly killed him. "Four hundred minutes for twenty dollars," he said finally.

"That seems like a fair investment," I said, and was tempted to tell him that smoking was dangerous, and that doing so in such close proximity to gas pumps was even more immediately lethal than cancer. But I knew it wasn't my place to counsel him. There are so few people one can help in life. "May I then have a twenty-dollar card?" I said, keeping our relationship purely commercial.

Rigorous transaction completed, I repaired to a phone booth outside and connected myself to Montclair. My uncle Irwin answered.

"Hello, relative!" I said into the instrument.

"Are you broken down?"

"No, I'm in Sharon Springs! Just as you recommended."

"When did you get there?"

"Just now."

"Why'd it take so long? You got lost?"

"No. I took back roads to make the trip more scenic and self-improving. But thank you for your directions."

"I'm glad you weren't arrested."

"I'm a good driver!" I protested.

"Listen, you had a phone call. Somebody from a place called the Rose Colony. They want you to attend. They said they took you off a waiting list. What is it, another rehab? That will make your aunt happy."

"My God!" I shouted. "I can't believe the Rose Colony wants me! . . . And it's not a rehab. It's the most prestigious artist colony in the United States! It's a place for working on one's art."

"That's too bad it's not for drinking. You need to work on that more than your writing. I'm glad I didn't tell Florence and get her hopes up. . . . I'll give you the number. You're supposed to call before five, you have fifteen minutes."

He gave me the number and I went to write it on the first interior page of a weather-abused, dangling phone book, which was a common spot for jotting down numbers, as several other phone exchanges were scribbled there, accompanied by offers of homosexual copulation. Such things went on even in Sharon Springs! But I wasn't surprised. The human sex drive is relentless, especially the homosexual human sex drive. One finds it everywhere, it knows no dark corner—or, for that matter, dimly lit corner—where it cannot trespass. But it's not just homosexuality that is prevalent: old-fashioned heterosexuality is still the most popular form of sensuality between two people. Drive past any school yard—somebody is producing these children, though I understand that enrollments have been dropping. Homosexuality is perhaps then making headway in terms of overall subscription, while of course self-abuse remains the most popular form of sensuality overall, though not between two people, unless the two people are self-abusing in each other's company, which is often a happy compromise in both the homosexual and heterosexual communities.

Anyway, I thought it was clever of these randy Sharon Springians to put their solicitations inside the phone book. It gave the numbers more credibility than the personal advertisements I had read in all the WCs on the way up to Sharon Springs. It was as if the phone company itself were endorsing these come-hither notes. I have to confess, though, that those washroom jottings, despite the lack of any official sanction, had piqued my interest. As Jeeves and I drove along the country roads of New York State, I had thought about what I read in those toilets. For example: "Meet me at 5pm for a good sucking." Five P.M. when? All days of the week? Someone else had also wondered about this and written, "What day?" But there was no answer. And so this mystery plagued me.

In another toilet: "I'm straight but I like to suck cock. Meet here at midnight on Fridays." Had anyone shown up on a Friday? I would never know. Was the note left in this calendar year? These solicitations were incomplete narratives. I found it very frustrating.

And who are these people? I had wondered, and I had a knee-jerk desire to give these strangers, these bathroom lotharios, a call, when they were good enough to leave their home phone number, which they often did. But why did I want to call? Part of it was morbid curiosity, to see what kind of people would leave their home numbers in a toilet, but also, like most human beings, I am not without some homosexual fantasies—in my case, usually with a prison cell as a backdrop after I have been convicted of a crime I didn't commit, which makes it a rather complicated fantasy.

So there I was on the phone with Uncle Irwin and once again confronted with depraved notes. Rather striking was the competitive nature of some of the advertisements of these Sharon Springs inverts. One man, named Angelo, wrote, "Call me anytimes. I love to suck kock for hours. I am the best in the area."

And a man named Tim wrote, "Who knows better than a man how to suk dik? Don't call Angelo, call me." These men were competing in a small marketplace, so it was smart, I imagine, to boast, and they clearly weren't ashamed of their sexuality or their spelling, though I wondered if they were purposely misspelling. Was this some sort of gay code? More mysteries! More frustration.

Distracted by all this, I didn't get the number the first time Uncle Irwin gave it to me. "Can you run that past me again, please?" I asked.

He grunted with annoyance, but came out with it, and this time I jotted down the Rose Colony's number, and I happened to put it right next to an exceedingly compelling note: "I love to have my pussy kissed, call Debbie, 222-4480." Now this was unusual—extraordinary even. There were about a half dozen notes on this phone book page, but this was the only one from a woman, and in all the WCs I had visited that day, there had not been a single epistle from a female.

I have to say I found the use of the word *kiss* to be unexpectedly seductive and charming, almost Victorian. I was quite tempted to maybe steal the page and consult it later. Who was this Debbie? But the notion of calling a stranger was ludicrous, and there were more important things to consider—the Rose Colony! So I told my uncle Irwin to give my aunt Florence my love and we hastily rang off so that I could call the colony before five.

Six months before, in mid-January, I had applied to the Rose, which is located in Saratoga Springs, New York. I had read an article about the place in *Poets & Writers* magazine at the Montclair library, where I had gone one afternoon to take refuge from Uncle Irwin. Then a day or two later there was a mention of the colony in *The New York Times*.

Well, you know how it is: something starts appearing in front of you repeatedly, and you take it as a sign—so after spotting these two articles about the colony, I sent in an application and in March they sent me back a letter informing me that I had been placed on the waiting list. I had been more pleased than disappointed. It was enough of a victory just to have been wait-listed. I had sent, as my writing sample, the first chapter of my novel, *I Pity I*. But now I was in! Off the waiting list! A real triumph!

Wanting to share my good news before calling the colony, I beckoned to Jeeves to come over from the car. He conveyed himself across the asphalt.

"Yes, sir?"

"Jeeves, remember I was put on the waiting list at the Rose Colony?"

"Yes, sir."

"Well, I just called Uncle Irwin and the Rose Colony had called the house, looking for me, and they want me! I'm to call them this moment. This could mean a change in our plans, Jeeves, but a good change, I think."

"Yes, sir."

"Aren't you happy for me, Jeeves?"

"Yes, sir."

I think the fellow may have been a bit road-weary himself. The old vocab wasn't too diverse at the moment; he could have come up with something more enthusiastic than his standard "Yes, sir," but I thought of my own road-weary verbal struggles in purchasing the phone card, so I forgave Jeeves for not spicing up his side of the master-valet discourse.

I turned to the phone and performed the necessary manipulations.

"This is the Rose Colony," answered a woman's voice.

"Hello," I began, not very creatively, but the openings of phone conversations have their conventional limits. "I'm Alan Blair and I was informed that I've been removed from the waiting list?" I added an interrogative at the end of my speech to not seem too presumptuous and to display the proper humility.

"Oh yes . . . There's been a cancellation, and if you can come, if you're free, we'd love to have you. I'm Doris, the director's assistant."

"Very nice to meet you . . . on the phone that is," I said, clutching the instrument as if it were the woman's hand. "Well, my calendar is remarkably clear and I'd be happy to come to the Rose Colony. I'm about to take a cure in Sharon Springs, but will gladly flee Sharon Springs for Saratoga Springs. In effect, spring from these springs to your springs. When can I report for duty?"

I immediately worried that I was overdoing it linguistically in an attempt to please and amuse and be obsequious, but Doris appreciated my efforts. "You're funny," she said, and chuckled sweetly. "You can come up in two days, on Thursday—a room and a studio will be ready—and we can offer you a residency of six weeks, all the way to the end of August."

Six weeks. This was incredible. Even better than communing with Hasidim would be the chance to commune with fellow artists. Then it occurred to me that I had better tell her about Jeeves. There probably weren't too many artists who had their own valet, but I figured the place, being a nineteenth-century mansion, as reported in *Poets & Writers,* would have servants' quarters where Jeeves could bunk. "I should tell you," I said, "that I'll be bringing my man, Jeeves."

"Your man, Jeeves. Not your man, Godfrey?" she said, again laughing pleasantly. "That's funny. We need a Jeeves around here. I'm a big Wodehouse fan!"

I didn't let on to Jeeves, who was floating off to my left like one of those squiggly things on the surface of the eye, what the Rose Colony woman had said. Wanted to spare his feelings, if I could. This Wodehouse business was upsetting to him, though he'd never brought it up after our first interview, but I could tell that it rankled. After all, he wanted to be his own man, his own Jeeves, which was perfectly understandable. "Well," she said merrily, continuing, "you'll have two rooms, a studio and a bedroom, and in the studio there's a cot, so you can put your Jeeves there. But I want to borrow him!"

"Yes, well, I'm glad that's all fine with you," I said into the phone, with some severity, having no intention of sharing Jeeves, he wasn't chattel. I kept the steel in my voice and said, "So he'll take his meals with the staff in the kitchen, if that's all right . . . And I come up in two days, correct?"

"I haven't read Wodehouse in years, I have to read him again," she said, giggling, and still pursuing that annoying theme, poor Jeeves, but then she rallied her forces of concentration and said, "Yes, come up in two days." And before we rang off, she provided me with directions, which I memorized, they were so simple. Saratoga Springs was only ninety minutes away from Sharon Springs! New York State was clearly loaded with springs—I could probably swim to the Rose Colony through subterranean channels if I set my mind to it.

CHAPTER 7

❦

Driving to the Hotel Adler ★ I lecture Jeeves on the nature of tormented Jewish sexuality ★ The Hotel Adler is on a sloping hill and looks about to topple over ★ I use my charm on the ancient innkeeper ★ Dreary thoughts about my parents

The next step, naturally, was to secure a room at the Adler. I went back into the market and solicited the advice of the cashier as to how to find the hotel, and he generously directed me, pointing out the window: "It's about two miles down that street over there, on the right." But then he added, "I don't think the place is open."

I chose to ignore this remark. I didn't want it to spoil my Rose Colony news, and I didn't tell Jeeves what the cashier had said when I joined him in the Caprice. No reason to alarm everyone on board. And the cashier was probably wrong. Addled, most likely. His mind shrunk from pulling too hard on cigarettes, which force the temples to squeeze the brain.

I can be single-minded, you see. I had come all this way, seven hours of driving, and to think that I might not stay at the Adler would be debilitating. I lacked the inner resources to get back on the road and find a motel. So if I believed the Adler was open, it would be open. I'm an advocate of positive thinking, even if it's irrational positive thinking.

We drove down a hilly, tree-lined street. I was proceeding at about ten miles per hour, not wanting to somehow miss the hotel. We passed beautiful old houses with lovely porches, but still there were no people, until at last I spotted a single male Hasid—age indeterminate since after a certain point all male Hasidim seem to be about sixty—standing on a porch, looking to the sky. He was fiddling with the fringes poking out of the bottom of his shirt and he was probably making a *brucha*.

"There's a Hasid, Jeeves!"

"Yes, sir. His garb would certainly indicate this."

It occurred to me, as we drove past him, that the Hasid may have been having an impure thought instead of making a blessing. The Hasidim, in my experience, are quite sexually tormented, though probably not more than any other type of people, if I really think about it, and certainly not any more than the average Jew, who is almost universally sexually tormented.

"Jeeves, why do you think that we Jews are almost universally sexually tormented?"

"I had not considered that Jews were afflicted in this way, sir."

"Oh yes, Jeeves. We Jews are completely out of control when it comes to sex. I think, as I do about many things, that it may be Darwinism."

"Really, sir?"

"Oh yes. Wild Jewish sexuality must be an inherited trait, an evolutionary adjustment to shortened life spans due to pogroms, genocide, bad colons, and general dislike. We may not live long, but we're so libidinous we manage to procreate before we're killed. But this sexuality, Jeeves, which saves us, also gets us in trouble, causing more shortened life spans. We Jews are always making headlines for having affairs or doing something perverted, and non-Jews don't like this. Either they find it distasteful or they're annoyed that they're not getting any action. So it's some kind of mad, insane cycle that only we Jews could find ourselves in: we fornicate a lot to keep our race alive, but all this fornicating causes more resentment and hatred, which results in more inquisitions, pogroms, and genocides, not to mention quotas at Harvard."

"I should point out, sir, that gentiles also have many sexual problems."

"That's true, Jeeves. It seems that everyone has a problem with sex. Certainly the Muslims do, though the harem was a pretty good invention. The Asians have a nice attitude about it, except for foot-binding, which looks very painful, but that's mostly gone out of style. I do think everyone would be a lot happier if we all laid eggs on our own and could just have friendships and didn't need to mount and penetrate one another."

Before Jeeves could respond to my egg idea, we passed several Hasidim, men and women, sitting in rocking chairs on the porch of another old wooden house. They looked wonderfully out of place here in the wilds of upstate New York. In the wilds of America. Everything beyond the reach of New York City—about seventy-five miles—feels to me like *America,* an exotic country I have rarely, in my life, visited. New Jersey, according to my personal sense of geography, is also not America.

"Hasidic homesteaders," I said, regarding them on their rocking chairs. "Probably getting ready for an orgy. You know, Jeeves, despite my understanding of the Jewish libido—my own libido!—I have in the past been guilty of prejudice directed at the Hasidim when it comes to *their* sexual problems. It's just that it's so easy, with their top hats and beards, to spot them in peep shows and strip clubs. It's hard for them to sin anonymously like the rest of us—and so I've tended to form an unfair and imbalanced impression of the Hasidim."

"Their costumes *are* distinctive, sir."

"But who am I to judge, Jeeves? If I wasn't in such establishments in the first place, I wouldn't be able to come up with these unsound opinions. I can't characterize a whole clan because of a few wayward fellows."

"The Hotel Adler, sir. I advise turning."

"Yes, Jeeves. Thank you for spotting it."

There it was—the magnificent Hotel Adler. It was on the right-hand side of the road at the top of a steep, rising lawn, at a grade of almost sixty degrees. I floored the Caprice up the driveway.

The Adler was glorious: white-painted, wooden, and three-tiered, like a cake, with red wainscoting playing the role of icing. There were large green doors and an enormous front patio. It was the kind of hotel you don't see anymore. I don't know when you did see such hotels, but you certainly don't see them now.

It showed its age, though. The roof was sagging, the paint was chipping, the grounds were hoary, and the whole building seemed to be tilting forward, as if it were ready to topple over from exhaustion. It had been beautiful for too long. There was the unmistakable aura of lost grandeur to the place, but lost grandeur, I find, is always more grand than regular grandeur, if you know what I mean.

I pulled into the gravel parking lot and made the acute observation that there were no other cars, which, naturally, was not a good sign, but—like the cashier's warning—I chose to ignore this. Jeeves stayed in the Caprice and I mounted the long concrete staircase, which led to the patio and front doors.

With utter confidence, I pulled on one green door and then the other, and both were locked. My positive thinking, at this point, was nearly dried up. Still, I didn't quit. I saw a doorbell, rang it, and pretending that I wasn't on the verge of a crisis, I casually peered at myself in the glass of the window beside the front doors. I adjusted my tie, smoothed my thin but elegant hair, and stroked my fledgling orange mustache, and then I became an old woman with a kerchief on her head. It was a bit disarming to transform like that, to turn so rapidly, like Tiresias, into an aged representative of the opposite sex. I wondered if it was the d.t.'s—I hadn't taken a drink all day.

Then the doors opened and my kerchiefed old-woman self addressed me. "What do you want?"

Her accent was Yiddish and her figure was Russian, and I realized that an optical misunderstanding had occurred. This lady, heeding my ringing of the bell, had simply approached the window on her way to the door, just as I was looking at my reflection. It's always good when these phenomena can be explained by science and reason.

"I very much want a room," I said. "Are you open?"

"No. We had a fire. We open again one week. You come back then." Her face was round and fleshy, the skin yellow-brown from age. She was about five foot two and wore a faded blue housedress. Her slippers were ancient, flesh-colored, and may not have been removed in years. She was anywhere from sixty-five to ninety-five. Her eyes were older than that. They had seen Moses come down the hill and trip with the tablets, which is when the word *klutz* was invented. Her bosom was substantial. I felt a pang of desire for the young woman she had been in the nineteenth century.

"I can't come back in one week," I said, pleading. "I need a room now. I've been traveling for hours. To send me back out there might kill me. I would really like a room. Money is not a problem."

I removed my wallet from my sport coat pocket to emphasize this salient point.

"We had a fire," she said.

"But do you have any rooms that weren't burned? Please?"

"Yes. We have rooms. But closed one more week. Come back one week."

"*Nu,*" I said, hoping to charm her with my Yiddish, "can't you make an exception?" I smiled at her and held my wallet as if it were quite heavy, thinking this might be a winning combination—a smile from a nice Jewish boy who knew a word or two of Yiddish and who had a thick billfold.

The *nu* melted her. She let me into the Adler and to the front desk. "My son out shopping. I take care of you."

I gathered from this communication that her son was the owner or the manager. Behind the front desk was an open door which led to an apartment, her lair; perhaps she shared it with her son. She was charging me $40 a night, which was more than equitable. I paid for two nights, and then she started rummaging through a box of keys, making a good deal of clanging sounds. The keys were thick and old.

"Do you want me to fill out a registration form?"

She didn't answer me. I took this to mean no. I tried another question. "Does the room have two beds?" I asked. "My valet is with me." I didn't want to push things and ask for two rooms. Jeeves and I would have to rough it and be unconscious together in close proximity. But we could handle it; our relationship was unusually warm, I felt, and, too, it never hurts to save money.

"Two beds," she said. She was still making loud music with the keys. I waited patiently and looked about me. The lobby had a few sagging couches and chairs. The ceiling was very high and there was a large center staircase which led to the upper floors. The lost grandeur, except for the high ceilings, was less apparent on the inside—the interior was merely shabby.

From the fire, the place smelled of smoke, but I also detected that distinct bouquet one associates with the homes of old Jews. What is the source of this odor? I happen to like it. It smells like family and love to me—like the homes of my grandparents and my other old relatives, all of them gone now, though. But what are the ingredients of this smell? Mothballs? Matzo balls? Chicken broth? Chopped liver? Jewish anxiety? Yahrzeit lamps? Is it the smell of the past? Does the present have a new scent?

The Russian woman located the appropriate key. "Two oh four," she said. She was a woman of few words. Conserving her energy, I imagined. She handed me the key.

"Where was the fire?" I asked, since there were no signs of it in the lobby, except for the burnt odor.

"Third floor," she said.

"What caused it? Someone misbehaving and smoking in bed?"

"*Vas?*" I think she was a little hard of hearing, and though her English was clear, I didn't sense a profound grasp of the language.

"Someone was smoking in bed and set the third floor on fire?"

"Shabbas candles."

"Smoking Shabbas candles in bed!"

The woman didn't laugh. I pressed on. "Thank you very much for bending the rules."

"In morning you want bath?"

"A bath?"

"*Shvitz* bath."

"Oh yes. Here in the hotel?"

"Yes, in the basement."

"You'll run a bath for me even though you're closed?"

"You don't want a bath?"

"Yes . . . Yes, I do. What time in the morning?"

"Morning."

I liked the Old World feeling of that. Morning. No precise schedules. No anxiety of keeping a set appointment. "That's fine," I said. "I'll take my bath in the morning. Thank you so much for everything."

"Two oh four," she repeated, and pointed to the wide staircase. Then, done with me, she shuffled back toward her apartment.

"Zei gazint," I said to her retreating form, hoping to charm her with more Yiddish, but she didn't take notice.

Jeeves and I climbed the staircase. He carried our two bags. There was a mezuzah on the door to our room—they were on the doors to all the rooms. I found this to be comforting: it was nice to be somewhere so Jewish. When one is a minority, it's always pleasant, if not surprising, to be in an environment where one's practices are the rule rather than the exception.

I unlocked the door, but before crossing the threshold, I kissed my fingers in a sloppy, smacking way, and then put my wet fingers to the mezuzah, which is how my father used to do it. To mimic the dead is a good way to remember the dead. It's like when I do my yoga, I think of my mother and her earnest attempts at it when she was first sick. She was trying to save her life and someone had recommended yoga. My father died when I was seventeen of a heart attack, and my mother, perhaps poisoned by grief, died three years later of cancer.

So when I do these things—kiss mezuzahs, my morning sun salutations—it's my way of honoring my parents and also getting them back for these brief moments, though it's only like catching a glimpse of them out of the corner of my eye.

If I try to see more of them in my mind, a fuller picture, it's quite painful. It hits me that I can't ever again have just one day with them, and the pain of this thought actually becomes physical. It's like a knife is being drawn across the inside of my belly, though I don't feel the sting of the blade, just the sensation of being sawed in half. I collapse inward, a weird mixing of the physical and the emotional. I get sucked down by this terrible grief and then I start hating myself, because I can't really recall their faces. I was too horribly selfish. It's that wretched human problem of spending a lifetime with someone and never looking at them. So if I want to see them, I have to resort to the envelope of photographs I've held on to, but the pictures feel too thin in my hands, too pathetic, and anyway I don't want to see them in the past, I want to see them *now*. I want them to be alive. I'd like the chance to know them this time. But if I can't have that, more than going to any beautiful place in the world, I'd love to see my father and mother one more time, just for a day or an hour, and then maybe after that I could die or if need be continue to live.

Jeeves put our bags down. I sat on the bed that was closer to the door. I told Jeeves that I needed to take a nap.

"Very good, sir."

"I'm so tired, Jeeves. All that driving. *And* the good news about the Rose Colony. Good news can be tiring, you know."

"It's been a strenuous day, sir."

"A very strenuous day, Jeeves. Do you think I should just sleep through to morning?"

"I don't recommend it, sir. It's not even six o'clock. If you went to bed now, I fear that you would wake at two A.M. and be very unhappy. I would suggest, sir, a one-hour nap now, and then a simple meal at the restaurant we saw in town. The one across from the gas station. Its sign indicated that it is called the Hen's Roost. I can wake you in one hour."

"You think that's the best plan, Jeeves?"

"Yes, sir."

I smiled to indicate my grateful compliance. It was soothing to have Jeeves do the thinking. It's not easy taking care of one's self, determining nap lengths and all that, but with two people it's a manageable job. So Jeeves looked after me, but that didn't mean I couldn't look after Jeeves, to make sure he wasn't suffering in silence. I inquired, "Are these close quarters all right with you, Jeeves? It's a bland little room, I know. But the beds seem to be of quality. I hope you find this setup adequate."

"The accommodations are fine, sir. You should lie down now and I'll wake you in an hour."

"Why don't we just set the alarm and you take the night off, Jeeves. We can just leave the room unlocked. Come and go as you please. See what Sharon Springs has to offer. Take the car, if you like. You worked very hard with that map today. Very good folding and unfolding."

"Thank you, sir," he said, and he accepted my offer of a free evening. Then he opened a window—the room was a little stuffy—and set my little travel clock for me before leaving to explore Sharon Springs.

"Stay out of trouble, Jeeves," I said.

"Yes, sir." He closed the door.

I undressed and lay on top of the bed, too lazy to pull back the thin blanket. I thought momentarily of the two bottles of wine undrunk from the night before and hidden in my bag, but I pushed those wine bottles out of my mind. "No drinking!" I said to myself. I wanted to show Aunt Florence and Uncle Irwin, even if they weren't around to witness it, that I could stay sober if I wanted.

Then my prenap thoughts went from wine to love, a logical progression since the quadrant of the brain that craves alcohol is probably deeply aligned with the quadrant that craves love, and so I thought of that blonde girl I had dreamt about. I was hoping I would see her again. It was like when I would spot someone in a café in New York and we'd have eye contact but I'd lack the nerve to say anything and then the girl would leave, and so I'd vow to return to that café at the exact same time for days on end until I saw her again, but it was always an empty vow. I never would do such a thing. I feared the humiliating folly of it—either the girl would never return or if she did, she'd reject me since I had misread her the first time. But now my own subconscious was like a café, one I could easily return to, in fact could not avoid, and so maybe that girl would come to me again in my dreams, and this time if she said, "I love you," I'd say it back and we'd see what would happen.

Well, these thoughts, like a light, began to dim, and then I fell asleep and the day's struggle was temporarily—but only temporarily, I'm afraid—over.

CHAPTER 8

*The ruined bathhouse ★ Peer pressure ★ The mostly sad history of
Sharon Springs ★ I come up with how Sharon Springs will be
saved, as well as an idea for a screenplay ★ I eat my dinner and
read some Dashiell Hammett ★ I join the fray and hold forth on
the nature of professional wrestling, while momentarily contemplating the Homosexual Question and the Jewish Question ★ A
rash phone call ★ Two intuitive, internal voices, one forceful, one a
milquetoast, wrest for control of me*

Napped, showered, and refreshed, I took it upon myself to walk up
the long hill, roughly two miles, to the Hen's Roost. Jeeves hadn't
taken the Caprice—who knows what he was up to—but I had done
enough driving for the day. Also, some exercise, walking, would be
good for me. I hadn't dreamt of the girl during my nap, but I was in
good spirits. After months in Montclair, I was on an adventure!

About half a mile from the hotel, on the opposite side of the road,
I came upon the ruins of an old wooden bathhouse, which I hadn't
noticed on our way to the Adler. The outer shell of the long, narrow
building was intact, but its roof was only beams. Drawn to ruins, I
snuck inside. Who doesn't enjoy ruins? It's like getting to read a person's diary, albeit that of a dead person.

But what had happened to Sharon Springs? It was getting an
A+ in the Lost Grandeur department, but I should mention that the
beauty of Lost Grandeur is a sad beauty, mournful, the beauty of a
graveyard, and the cause of the Sharon Springs' sadness was a mystery to me.

Inside, the bathhouse was gutted—the floor had dissolved. I
walked on dirt strewn with sections of pipe. The place reeked of sul-

fur. There were still rows of old rusted tubs, like rows of coffins. It was spooky imagining that people had once bathed in these tubs, healing themselves. The division of rooms was still visible: there were door frames and walls, and on one wall there were hooks for towels, and built into another wall were cubbyholes with faded metal name tags. This bathhouse had once been a destination, a place you went often enough, over the course of years, over the course of a life, to have a name tag in metal. On one door frame was the ubiquitous mezuzah.

I walked out what was once a back door and immediately there was a steep, forested hill, almost right up against the building. Some large rocks were at the bottom of the tree line, and running between them was a steady current of water, making the narrow strip of land in the back a muddy stream.

I crossed the stream and cupped my hands to the pouring water coming through the rocks and took a drink. It was salty and sulfurous, like rotten eggs, and I loved it. Made me feel good. I swallowed as many mouthfuls as I could. This was the spring that had fed the baths. It was a happy moment in nature for me, but then I destroyed it by wondering if deer urine could seep through the earth and pollute the spring with microbes. Hadn't I read something alarming in the Science section of *The New York Times* about deer urine?

Well, it had been a nice moment while it lasted; one can't ask for more. I did think it unlikely that deer microbes could travel through rock, but still my Thoreauish enchantment with nature had passed.

I returned to the road, and on some of the porches of the old white houses there were more Hasidim now, men and women sitting in straight-backed chairs or rocking chairs, and in the driveways a few children rode bicycles. It was summer twilight, always the most beautiful time of day—so beautiful that man can't seem to mar it, and the world, sensing this, seems remarkably and momentarily untroubled.

The children looked happy on their bicycles; they had sweet smiles, and I liked the boys' odd wispy curls dangling in front of their ears. It made me feel good to see the children being gleeful, especially in contrast to their somewhat unhealthy pallor and formal clothing.

At the top of the hill, across from the gas station, I penetrated the Hen's Roost—first there was a bar and then off to the right a dining room. An old fellow in a baseball hat was at the bar sipping a glass of gold-yellow beer; he was the only customer. I half expected to see Jeeves on a barstool, but he had found his diversion elsewhere. Perhaps he was in the beautiful Sharon Springs forest, performing a Spartan rite; that's the kind of thing Jeeves might do, I thought. The short, heavyset bartender, who had a distended belly which looked very difficult to carry around, addressed me: "Drink or eat, my friend?"

The "my friend" was quite welcoming. "Eat," I said, though the beer the old fellow at the bar was drinking looked awfully tempting. But I felt strongly that I had better stay on the water wagon. If I drank and something did go wrong, I couldn't expect Aunt Florence and Uncle Irwin to bail me out.

"One minute," said the bartender, and he went into the kitchen. He reemerged with a plump woman, who was wearing a white apron and black pants. Her reddish hair was in a frizzy perm. "My wife will take care of you, and if she doesn't, just let me know," he said, grinning, conveying to me facetiously, man-to-man, that he kept his woman in line.

She smiled agreeably at his banter and sat me in the dining room at an old oaken booth, the table of which was deeply marked with the carvings of initials. All the booths were oak and scarred this way and so were the tables in the middle of the room. It occurred to me that germs and bacteria could readily collect in these scars—hard to keep such a table clean. My mind, I noted, was listing toward germy neurosis after imbibing that deer urine in the woods.

The bartender's wife said, "You want something to drink, sweetheart?"

It was easy to see that the Hen's Roost was a congenial establishment, despite its health hazards. I surmised that she and her husband were in the habit of only serving friends, thus they were comfortable with bandying about terms of endearment like *friend* and *sweetheart*. It was nice to be welcomed. Very human. It didn't seem like too many gentleman travelers—strangers like myself—must cross the threshold of this charming, rustic inn.

"I will be prudent and have only a club soda," I said steadfastly.

She smiled at me from beneath her curly crown of red hair, but at the precise moment that I concluded my brave announcement, I glanced to the bar—I was in the booth closest to the drinking area—and saw the old fellow in the ball cap take a last and satisfying swig of beer. His mug looked absolutely romantic as he put it down. He motioned for a refill. I want to do that, I thought, and succumbing to peer pressure, I quickly said, "Actually, I'd like a beer."

"We have Miller on tap. That all right?"

"Yes," I whispered, mortified at my alcoholic weakness, and she walked away.

I was ashamed that I hadn't been able to stay on the wagon for even forty-eight hours. I looked at my fellow tippler at the bar. A milk-white ribbon of hair stuck out of the back of his hat, and what was visible of his neck, above his collar, was a crisscrossed slice of red meat. Awfully far north for rednecks, I thought, and I blamed him for my going back on the booze. He lifted his refilled mug and drank. I looked away. *Why did you do this to me?* I said to him in my mind.

The waitress came, bearing, like a chalice, my glass of beer. "Here you go, sweetheart. Enjoy."

"Thank you," I said, very much the weakling. She smiled and departed.

The beer was before me now. I can simply not pick it up, I thought. I won't drink it, and when she returns, I'll ask her to take it away, explain to her that I've changed my mind.

As soon as I completed that trickle of consciousness, my hand shot out, the mug was lifted, and the beer was in my mouth. It had been a feeble resistance—a little tree standing up against a hurricane. With the beer in my mouth, there was a feeling of transgression, of doing something purposefully unnatural, and I was thrilled by this transgression—the cold excitement that comes from doing some- thing wrong. Then I took a second long sip, nearly finishing the beer, and feelings of transgression left me. There was no more awareness of possibly doing myself harm, whether I found it thrilling or not. You see, that Tennessee Williams click arrived almost immediately. The click that says: Everything is going to be all right. I guess it's a lie, but it's a very believable lie.

I raised my glass a third time, finished the beer, and privately toasted the old man at the bar. I wasn't upset with him anymore. I was—probably because of a weakened liver—already, after just one beer, in a mildly intoxicated state, and the ancient farmer was now my boon companion.

I motioned to the waitress, miming a refill. She arrived quickly. I was glad. I was impatient now that I had started. "Sweetheart, you finished that one in no time," she said, but without judgment. I smiled at her. All was well. I drank up. And I deserved to drink: I was going to the Rose Colony! Cause for celebration!

Presently, I studied the bill of fare, and though I had the highest trust in the good intentions of the Hen's Roost—after all I had been called "friend" once and "sweetheart" three times and the beer was delicious—I decided to avoid anything that could be dangerous, such as the odd Cajun dishes they were offering and any of the fish entrées, especially since we were a good distance from the Atlantic, not to mention the Pacific.

I figured that chicken would be the house specialty—Hen's Roost and all that—and when the waitress came to take my order, I inquired, "Is your chicken free-range?"

"We broil it on the range."

"I mean, is your chicken organic?"

"Oh no. Organic chicken is much too expensive. But our chickens are very good. Everybody loves them."

It's very hard not to commit cancer suicide in America; we should all just be eating dark green lettuce and living in bunkers with air filters. So I resigned myself and ordered the broiled chicken breast, mashed potatoes, and house salad. Also, a pitcher of beer to wash down the cancer. Unfortunately, I'm one of those idiots who knows everything about health and is in a constant state of alarm, and yet I continue to do everything I shouldn't do.

My pitcher of Miller arrived, and feeling gregarious, I engaged my sweet waitress in conversation.

"I don't mean to be rude," I began, "but what has happened here in Sharon Springs? It's very beautiful, but the town seems to be empty and I came across this old bathhouse which is in ruins."

Well, my inquiry was honey to a bee. Or is it honey to a bear? I'm not very good with proverbs and folk sayings, so what I'm trying to communicate is that my waitress was very eager to provide an answer, practically an oral history, the town legend as it were, to my question. There was still no one else in the dining room, and she really launched into her tale and I drank my beer and listened.

What I gathered is that in the middle part of the nineteenth century, Sharon Springs was maybe second only to Vichy when it came to attracting European royalty and American royalty (millionaires) who were in need of a cure. Dukes, princesses, and earls from the Continent, and Vanderbilts, Rockefellers, and Astors from New York, all came to bathe in and drink the waters of Sharon. But then the railroad was expanding at the end of the century, and a line was built from New York to Albany, and suddenly everybody was going to Saratoga Springs, which was just north of Albany.

(Saratoga! I didn't tell my waitress that I, too, would be going to Saratoga; it seemed to be a fresh wound for her, though the original abandonment had occurred one hundred years before.)

Thus, by the beginning of the twentieth century, Sharon Springs was just about forgotten, its popularity usurped by its rival Saratoga Springs, and then when the Depression came around, it was nearly destroyed. But when World War II ended, the town and its people were brought back to life and flourished for the next forty years.

"Germany paid for the Jews to come here after the Holocaust to get healthy," she explained. "They gave them thousands of dollars as a way to say sorry. Also, I think they had to give them the money, part of an agreement they signed. So all these Jews, thousands and thousands of them, *the survivors*"—this phrase seemed to have special import for her; it must have been said over and over during her childhood—"and their new children would come from New York City. Manhattan mostly. But a lot from Brooklyn and the Bronx, too. They'd bring their own cooks, it had to be kosher, you know. But we also had jobs. Lots of jobs. We made very good money. It was wonderful when the Jews were here. We all loved them. They got better here. That made everybody feel good, put the war behind us. But they couldn't live forever, and their grandchildren and great-grandchildren don't want to come here. They're too Americanized. They want to go to the Jersey shore or Disney

World, places like that. So it's all over. I don't know if Sharon Springs will make it this time. We miss the Jews."

"I noticed there were several Hasidic families in town," I said, trying to console her, though I didn't mention that she was serving a Jew that very instant. I didn't think *that* would console her. Rather, it would have made us both uncomfortable. I could tell from her speech—the way she had said *kosher* with just the slightest trace of derision, despite her love for *the Jews*—that she assumed I was a fellow gentile, which was understandable: I was wearing my blue linen blazer, brown linen pants, thinning blond-red hair, and Douglas Fairbanks Jr.-Errol Flynn mustache.

"Yes, there's some Hasidic people," she said, "but that's all that's left. A couple hundred. We used to have ten thousand Jews here in the summer and many would come all year-round. They loved the water. Not for swimming of course."

Her husband called to her from the bar and I nursed my beer. It was a fascinating town history, very interesting to think that this had once been a place that royalty came to and then later Holocaust survivors—princes and earls followed by devastated Jews. It made the rusted tubs at the bathhouse even more funereal.

But who would be next? Who would follow the royalty and the Jews? I wondered if the homosexual community was on to Sharon Springs. A few homosexuals were in the area, as evidenced by those notes in the phone book I had read earlier, but that wasn't the kind of homosexual I had in mind. I was thinking of wealthy urban homosexuals in search of weekend homes and how those fellows are always good at sniffing out beauty, knowing the value of a place before anyone else. The West Village, Provincetown, Fire Island, San Francisco, New Hope, and all of ancient Greece came to mind.

It then occurred to me that what these places shared in common was access to water, even New Hope, Pennsylvania, which was on the Delaware and not far from Princeton, and I thought how homosexuals, like all advanced forms of civilization, are drawn to water, and then I thought—*Sharon Springs has water! And not only water, but ruined bathhouses ripe for restoration! Bathhouses!*

This was great news! I wanted to call the waitress over and tell her that everything was going to be all right, that the homosexuals were coming, but it did cross my mind that she might take this pronouncement in the wrong way.

This was frustrating. I felt like someone who commits a good deed but can't tell anyone. I knew in my gut that everything was going to be all right with Sharon Springs, but I couldn't share with her this good news, even though she was clearly so brokenhearted over the fall of her town. I could only take solace in knowing that someday Sharon Springs would be revived, that it would have a third act!

Act I: Royals.

Act II: Jews.

Act III: Gays.

Still, I needed to tell someone that I had figured out what would save Sharon Springs. I was proud of my line of thinking, and so I decided—under the influence of the beer I was drinking, which had made me rather drunk; I was halfway through my pitcher—to have an imaginary conversation with Jeeves, since I knew he would be a good listener if he were actually there with me.

"Jeeves," I said to the imaginary Jeeves, "know what's going to save Sharon Springs?"

"No, sir."

"Gay men!"

"Really, sir?"

"Oh yes, Jeeves. Gay pioneers. They'll revive the local economy. I can feel it."

"Very good, sir."

This was working perfectly. It was almost like talking to the real Jeeves. I drank some more beer and continued the conversation.

"We should open a bed-and-breakfast, Jeeves," I said. "The homosexuals will need a place to stay while they look for old farmhouses."

"Could be very profitable, sir."

"My thinking exactly. You know, Jeeves, this whole thing brings to mind a movie I loved as a boy, *The Russians Are Coming!* But in this case, it's the homosexuals that are coming."

"I'm not familiar with this film, sir."

"I remember watching it on TV with my father—probably in the early seventies. It's a Cold War comedy about this Russian submarine that breaks down off of Nantucket. Naturally, a Russian sailor falls for a young girl on the island, lending a Romeo and Juliet twist to the whole thing. At least that's my memory of the plot."

"Very good, sir."

"Starred Alan Arkin. My father always liked Alan Arkin. He liked most Jewish actors."

"Yes, sir."

"The scene I remember most vividly is of a young boy—and I was a young boy when I saw the movie, so I must have identified with him—running down a street shouting, 'The Russians are coming! The Russians are coming!' . . . You know, Jeeves, a funny title for a porno movie would be *The Homosexuals Are Coming!* Or a farce. Better yet a pornographic farce. Comedy and nudity have rarely been paired, at least not in an interesting way. You know, Jeeves, instead of opening a bed-and-breakfast, we should make such a movie. *The Homosexuals Are Coming!* could be a humorous *Caligula*. . . . After I finish my novel, I'll write the screenplay. As homage to *The Russians Are Coming!* we could set it in Nantucket. A musical theater group could set sail from Provincetown, wash ashore in Nantucket, and a young boy could go racing down the street shouting, 'The homosexuals are coming!'"

"Potentially very amusing, sir."

"And the island would be upset, just like when the Russians came. Also, there'd have to be a Romeo and Juliet romance. . . . The son of the mayor of Nantucket could fall for one of the troupe members, probably in a dune. And another troupe member could fall for a girl and convert to heterosexuality. Naturally, I'd like to work in some female nudes. As director and screenwriter that should be my prerogative. Also, I'd give Alan Arkin a cameo, as a nod of love toward my father and the earlier film."

"I think that would be very good, sir."

Just then my food arrived and a fresh pitcher of beer, and I thought it was high time to stop my imaginary conversation. You know you're very drunk when you talk to yourself at great length, and I thought I had better slow down my intoxication by nursing at my breast of chicken.

To go along with my food, I took out of my sport coat pocket the book I had chosen to read with my dinner, a collection of Dashiell Hammett short stories, featuring his forever nameless private dick, the Continental Op. I love Hammett. He's the master of facial descriptions and fight scenes, and he's also very good at depicting neckwear. No one has written more poetically about ties than Hammett.

After a third pitcher of beer, which I had in lieu of dessert, I couldn't focus too well on Hammett and his hero, and I was a good candidate for some oral surgery. I paid my bill and left a 30 percent tip, compensating in my own small way for my fellow Jews' abandonment of Sharon Springs.

Despite already being loaded, I wanted to keep drinking at the bar, which now had several patrons. There were a number of other senior-citizen farmers, colleagues of the fellow with the vivid neck, as well as a few middle-aged American males of a certain genus—bald, heavy fellows wearing eyeglasses purchased from *Gun and Rifle*. They were reliable, decent men, capable of all sorts of masculine endeavors: fixing things, shooting deer, getting up early in the morning for work and drinking bad coffee. Besides the bartender's wife only one female was at the bar—a tired-looking fifty-year-old blonde who was on the arm of one of the middle-aged gents.

I joined the fray at the bar, where I was welcomed with great camaraderie. When I'm drunk, people seem to like me and I think it's because I like them. I like them when I'm sober, but I'm too shy to let them know. So there was lots of pleasant banter between me and these Sharon Springians.

"Why are you wearing a tie?" asked one fellow.

"I use it to wipe my mouth," I said, and drew my tie up and gave my mouth a good wipe and everybody was enchanted. It was a very friendly group of men. We mostly talked about baseball, a subject on which I'm an expert, owing to my daily memorization of the sports pages, and there was a game on the TV for us to comment on.

Well, I bought them drinks, they bought me drinks, and I was happy to be out in the world again after months of seclusion and solitary tippling in my room in Montclair.

Toward the end of the festivities, only a few of us were left at the bar and everyone was getting rather silent and contemplative. I directed my attention to the television from which a wrestling match was now being broadcast. I hadn't seen wrestling in years, not since I was a boy, but I was aware that its popularity as a form of entertainment was growing rapidly. I tried to study what was going on to decipher its appeal, but the attraction of this staged grappling, however, was lost on me. I thought maybe it was an acquired taste.

"Do you like wrestling?" I asked the gentleman next to me, whose impressive gut was the twin of the bartender's gut.

"It's stupid to me," he said, "but my sons love it. Me, I enjoy a real fight, like in hockey or football."

I studied the wrestling some more. Two fellows with shaved bodies, wearing bikini underwear, were assuming various homo-erotic positions. Has no one pointed out the Greekness of this? I wondered. And then I thought, Why am I so fixated on homosexuality today? First, I'm intrigued by provocations in bathrooms, then I conceive of a gay-oriented film, and now I'm seeing homosexual subtext in wrestling! Why must I always be raising the Homosexual Question? Clearly, I have not answered it yet. That and the Jewish Question.

Well, I made a drunken mental note to channel my desire for answers to the H. and J. Questions into my novel when I got to work at the Rose Colony. I would address my confusion through my writing, my art.

I continued to watch the wrestling and I wondered, still ruminating on the H. Question, if seeing men embrace each other in a combative ring was somehow, for the American psyche, a safe expression of this form of sensuality. One of the wrestlers had pectoral muscles the size of serving trays, and at the climax of the choreographed battle he suffocated his opponent between his formidable breasts. This was the other fellow's scripted undoing, because shortly thereafter, he was on his belly, his leg was pulled back, he was ready for a good sodomizing, and the match was over.

"I think wrestling is like pornography," I said to the man with the distended belly whose sons liked wrestling, though I didn't mention to him the Greek angle. "It must be a formula. Porno and wrestling. In both cases, you have people with absurd bodies pretending to do something. In one they pretend to fight and in the other they pretend to be attracted to each other. There must be catharsis for both audiences in the exaggeration of it all. You know what I mean, sir?"

The gentleman didn't respond, though, to my thesis on wrestling and pornography, and then the bartender screamed out, "Last call," and eager to get one more beer in my system, I didn't pursue any more discussion on the meaning of simulated grappling.

It was 2 A.M. when I got off my barstool, and all the alcohol I had been storing in my proverbial wooden leg shot to my head. It's always a revelation to sit and drink for hours and then stand up and find out that you're twice as intoxicated as you realized. That's why it's good to drink in bed, as I had done in Montclair. No sudden shocks.

I thanked the bartender for an excellent evening, then staggered out of the Hen's Roost. The other patrons got into their trucks and station wagons and disappeared into the darkness. I had arrived at twilight and now black ink was spilled across the sky.

I walked across the street to the gas station, which was still open. I thought I had better buy a bottle of water, hoping to fight off somewhat the next day's inevitable hangover, and as I approached the entrance to the filling station's commissary, I spotted the telephone I had used earlier in the day. I suddenly wished I had somebody to call. You know how it is when you're drunk—you're vulnerable to sentimentality and want nothing more than to talk to somebody on the phone and say, "I love you."

Unfortunately, I had no such person to call, certainly not Aunt Florence under the circumstances, but then in a moment of alcoholic genius, I remembered the phone book with all its solicitations.

Next to where I had scribbled the Rose Colony's number—and I thought that I should probably cross it out before someone mistakenly called the Colony looking for an illicit encounter—I saw the message that had appealed to me earlier, though I find this all very embarrassing. It was the one from Debbie, where she stated what she liked to have done, but it's silly of me to beat around the bush, to pussyfoot around, to stall any further, so in case you don't remember, I'll reproduce the message: "I love to have my pussy kissed, call Debbie, 222-4480." Again, it was the use of the word *kissed* which I found so beguiling.

Removing my phone card, I gave her a ring, which was very selfish of me, considering the hour, but when one is drunk, one is notoriously prone to selfish behavior. But even drunk, what was I thinking? Well, I was terribly lonely, and, too, I had always wanted to try one of these numbers that people leave in toilets and in this case a phone book. But I needed my IQ to be reduced, to have the top of my brain sheared off by beer, before I was able to pursue this curiosity, which had been reinflamed by all the numbers I had seen scrawled in the restrooms between Montclair and Sharon Springs.

"Hello," answered a woman with a sleepy voice after about the sixth ring.

"Is this Debbie?" I asked, and I was aware that my speech was slurred.

"What?"

"I'm calling for Debbie," I said, trying to speak more coherently.

"Who is this?" Her voice now wasn't at all sleepy.

"I'm sorry to call so late . . . I read your message here at the gas station . . . My name is Alan. Would you like to come here? I'll buy you a wine cooler. Whatever you like. The bar is closed or I'd buy you a drink there. We can sit somewhere and talk. I'd love to talk to you . . . ?"

I phrased it as a question to make myself less intrusive, if that was at all possible.

"You got my number from the gas station?" She sounded angry.

"No, the phone book," I said, and my intuition told me I should hang up right now, but some overriding drunk intuition told me not to. The overriding one said, *You're talking to a woman. Don't give up now. You never know what might happen.*

"Where are you?" Debbie asked.

"I'm at the gas station."

"And you want to buy me a wine cooler?" Her voice seemed to soften.

"Anything you like. Or if you know of a bar that's open—the Hen's Roost just closed—I can get you a drink."

"All right. Stay there at the gas station. You're at the one across from the Hen's Roost?"

"Yes."

"Stand outside. I'll be right there." She hung up.

The overriding intuition, who may have been as drunk as me, said, *"See. You're going to meet a woman!"* The other intuition, who had somehow stayed sober, said, *"Start running to the Adler now. This is too good to be true, so it can't be true. Get the hell out of here."*

Naturally, I didn't listen to this sober, milquetoast voice of reason, and I went in the store to buy some chewing gum. I didn't want Debbie to be too put off by the alcohol on my breath. Remarkably, the same fellow who had been working there earlier was still holding down the fort these many hours later. "You want another phone card?" he said.

"Oh no, I have many minutes left. Thank you for asking. Just want some chewing gum."

He was probably on his eighth pack of cigarettes, the smoke in there was as thick as the bar's, which I hadn't minded while drinking. Under the influence, I don't notice cigarette smoke, except to be upset when I smell it on my sport coats the next day.

I was tempted to share with the cashier my good news, but I thought this could be indiscreet: he might know Debbie, it was a small town.

I went back outside to wait for her by the phone booth, and I tripped on some curbing and fell to the pavement. I righted myself and seemed to be in one piece, just my hands were a bit raw.

"Pull yourself together, you have a woman coming to see you," said the forceful intuitive voice, and to help pull myself together I chewed a piece of gum, and either from the taste of the gum or the booze or nerves or a combination of all three, I nearly vomited, but managed not to, though I spit out the gum. I was really falling apart moments before my date. My hands were scraped and my throat was scorched from the stomach bile which had risen like a flame and then sunk back down.

"Don't blow this, Alan!" admonished the voice. The other voice, the sane one, was pouting, silent, beaten into submission.

I leaned against the building, closed my eyes, pulled myself together, and waited for Debbie. It was a long shot, but maybe she really would be nice to me. I couldn't be the only lonely person in the world.

CHAPTER 9

I meet Debbie ★ I search for the right words ★ I meet a Hill ★ I do things I didn't know I was capable of ★ An arduous journey

I may have blacked out for a few minutes, because it felt as if I had lost some time, like I was waking from a dream. Then a large, elevated pickup truck pulled in, its high beams trained on me. For a moment, because of the blackout, I didn't know where I was. But then I remembered: I was in Sharon Springs, at the gas station, waiting for Debbie.

The lights were blinding—they were at eye level because of the truck's unusual suspension and its impressive, swollen tires. Somebody came down from the passenger side of the truck; the figure seemed to be that of a woman. Then the figure, now clearly a woman, was in front of the lights, and she stopped there, didn't come closer. I took a step away from the wall, but maintained a respectful, wobbly distance. It had to be Debbie.

"Did you call me?" she asked, and I wouldn't characterize her tone as welcoming, but she had to be sure I wasn't just some idiot standing outside the market of the gas station. She had to be sure I was the idiot who had called her.

"Yes," I said. "I'm Alan."

She was a robust female specimen, not a classic beauty like the girl in my dream, but I was thrilled that she had come out in the middle of the night to meet me, to give me a chance. Her hair was dyed a limp blonde—the roots were dark. Her chest, in a halter top, was formidable and appealing, and her somewhat chubby face was extra-puffy, I could see, from being woken in the middle of the night. She looked to be in her late thirties. It would be nice to hold her. It had

81

been a while since I'd held a woman, and so I was more than happy at the idea of snuggling up against this tough-looking gal.

"Where'd you get my number?"

"From the phone book . . . I've been drinking . . . I know it's crazy, and I'm sorry it's so late, but—"

"You looked up my number in the book?"

"No, the note you left . . ."

What could I say? She was wary of me. I searched for the right romantic words, but before I could come up with something seductive and charming about the unusual circumstances of our rendezvous, she tapped the hood of the truck and the driver's-side door swung open nastily.

It hadn't occurred to me when she came from the passenger side that she was perhaps not alone, that someone else had to be driving, but there's only so much one can consider in these highly charged situations which involve calling women who leave notes in phone books, especially when one's blood-alcohol content drops the old IQ to a figure lower than one's body temperature.

Hence, a large, mean ball of a man stepped out of the truck and gave me a rather nasty stare, which he seemed to have been rehearsing for some time, perhaps the last forty years of his life. He could have matched iced-oyster glances with Uncle Irwin. He was in a blue T-shirt and jeans, his head was a large globe with bristles, and his belly was distended, which seemed to be the vogue in Sharon Springs. He was a few inches short of six feet, but he made up the difference in his width. He looked like a small hill.

This hill soaked in the Blair dimensions—I'm about six feet, 160 pounds, most of it in my leather wing tips, I'm afraid—and then he advanced toward me with a single, historically unfriendly salutation: "Motherfucker!"

Seeing a hill move stunned me. It was not unlike that time a rat crawled up my leg. I froze. Then this human landmass was right in front of me. He said, "Why'd you call her?"

"I'm sorry—" I began, but then he coldcocked me, which is to say he struck me without warning, though I think it would have been highly unusual for him to have verbally alerted me.

The nature of his coldcock was that his fist, the size of a small toaster, smashed me right on the nose. There was a high-pitched crack—the sound of a pencil violently snapping comes to mind—and the pain was cruel, disgusting, like I had been hit with a hammer.

I didn't fall, but there was some kind of eclipse, even though it was already night, because all light in the world was extinguished. I saw only the blackest blackness, and in this sightless world I reached up to my nose, feeling for it like someone reading braille. My nose, I discovered, had moved over to the right side of my face, finding that it was no longer wanted in the middle. I heard someone scream, "Oh, God!"

That someone, I realized, was me. But that's all right. Agnostics are allowed to pray under these circumstances; it's one of the benefits of our position.

Then some of the lights came back on just in time for me to see the Hill's fist enter my blue linen sport coat in the area of my stomach. This brought the bile and puke, which I had swallowed earlier, back up to my mouth, and I fell to the ground, but heroically I didn't vomit.

I couldn't breathe very well, though, and I couldn't see much. It felt like I was looking through the tube of a drinking straw. I saw one of my hands on the sidewalk. That was all my field of vision could take in. *My poor hand,* I thought.

I was vaguely aware of being scared and sad that this was happening to me. But there was a curious detachment. I could sense the Hill just standing there. He seemed to be resting. Perhaps I had been punished sufficiently. I deserved what was happening. I had made a terribly selfish mistake with that phone call, so my beating was justified, but maybe enough was enough. Blood was now pouring out of my nose onto the ground as I knelt there, hunched over, trying to breathe.

I wasn't really drunk anymore. I was something else. Not drunk. Not sober. Beaten. Noises were far away, muted. I made out the Hill saying, "Fucking call my girlfriend," and Debbie saying, "Fuck that pervert up." And through the drinking straw that was my field of vision I saw a work boot speeding toward me, right for the eye that was looking through the straw, and I rolled and caught the boot on the shoulder. That hardly hurt at all compared with the crumpling of my nose and the devastation of my stomach, and I was so emboldened by this lesser pain and avoiding a kick to the eye that I tried to crawl away.

The blow to my shoulder woke me up a little and my vision was now functioning almost normally. As I crawled away, humiliated, I looked back and saw the bottom portion of the Hill advancing with menace. I observed what appeared to be a knee, and I don't know where I got such a smart idea, but just as the Hill was on top of me, I kicked out my leg with great force—months of yoga did have their benefit—such that the flat sole of my leather wing tip met the Hill's knee and it was a brief skirmish but my shoe won.

The knee went backward, which is not how knees are designed to operate, as I'm sure you know, and it was rather grotesque to see a knee buckle like that, even a malevolent knee connected to a dangerous human Hill.

I couldn't believe it. I had directed my leg as if it were something I had practiced, like a serve in tennis, and the Hill shrieked and then all of him collapsed and he was on the asphalt with me, looking pained and vulnerable and human. Even cruel Hills have an attachment to the proper function of their knee joints, and I was horrified to have so injured someone and tried to convey with my eyes—I don't think I was capable of speech—my regret. But I did think that maybe it was a fair exchange, almost biblical—a knee for a nose.

I then rose up, thinking it was all over, but the Hill got to his good knee and went to punch me in the groin, but it glanced off my sturdy hip bone. I was stupidly shocked. Hadn't he seen my apologies in my eyes?

Then he quickly took another swing and punched my left knee, tried to do to me what I had done to him, but mine didn't buckle, thank God, he caught me on the side of the knee. And before I knew it, I intuitively sent my right foot, my thick leather shoe, back into action, into an opening, which happened to be his mouth. The Hill let out another cry and his lips were painted with blood. It's amazing how quickly the mouth produces blood, but I shouldn't have been surprised, since when I floss my teeth there's so much blood that I think of running to the Red Cross and making a donation.

When my shoe was out of his mouth, the Hill and I, in a moment of closeness—fighting is quite intimate, actually—locked eyes again. We were both in disbelief that I was getting the better of him, and our eyes communicated this. Then he spit out two crimson-colored teeth.

But it still wasn't over. The Hill was a worthy opponent. He tried to stand up, made it about halfway, and took a wild swing at me and missed. I then swung my right fist—the size of a good paperback dictionary, no toaster, but not insubstantial—into the side of his head, into an ear, which felt soft and fleshy, though the skull underneath was hard. A terrible pain went through my hand and wrist, and I think a terrible pain went through his ear and head, because he crumpled to the sidewalk, holding his ear with one hand and covering his face with the other, like a child who doesn't want to be hit any more.

Then I was convulsed with incredible terror—the old, procrastinated reaction to something traumatic—and I started to shriek and run, I had to get out of there, but a fierce monster in a halter top—Debbie!—flashed claws at me, but I was able to brush her out of the way with a sweep of my arm, like a running back, and I saw her stumble but she wasn't injured—it's one thing to dismantle Hills, another to strike a woman—and then the cashier stepped out, holding a baseball bat. "What the hell's going on?" he asked, but I ran by him, screaming like someone deranged, and fueled by adrenaline which hadn't been tapped in years, I was off on a crazed sprint for the Adler, with blood still coming out of the thing that had once been my nose.

Fearful that the Hill was going to pursue me as soon as he got up, I raced down the dark street, then jogged, and then with my adrenaline petering out, I hid, exhausted and frightened, under some bushes by a house, near where I had seen the Hasidic children riding bicycles. I lay on the ground, disbelieving of what had happened to me. I gingerly put dirt on my nose, thinking madly that the soil could heal me.

I lay there a few minutes, but scared to be discovered, I forced myself to get up, walked some more on the dark road, some stars and a wedge of moon lighting the way, and I made it to the ruined bathhouse and hid in there. I thought of spending the night, maybe in one of the tubs; there was just enough moonlight to make out their shape, but being in there was too frightening. I couldn't take it.

So I got out of the bathhouse and started walking and jogging; it was endless, two miles seemed like a hundred, and I kept expecting the Hill to come after me, perhaps with a gang of friends to finish me off. Or maybe the Hill couldn't get up and Debbie had called the police and a cruiser was going to find me and arrest me for assault, not to mention battery, not to mention inappropriate phone calls.

But no police or vengeful gangs pursued me. I safely reached the Adler, and with my last bit of strength, I dashed up the concrete steps. The front door was open. Thank God, the old lady had left it open for m; how could I have rung the bell and let her see my face?

I tiptoed through the dark lobby and then went quickly up the staircase to my room, through the door, past the mezuzah.

"Jeeves! Jeeves!" I cried.

CHAPTER 10

Jeeves to the rescue ★ Things look bad for my jacket and worse for me ★ A few hours' sleep, some would call it passing out ★ A discussion of my flaws ★ A last look and then a departure

"Yes, sir?"

"Jeeves! I've been mortally wounded!"

"It appears, sir, that you've had some type of accident."

"Accident? A piece of bone from my nose may have entered my brain! I was in a fight to the death with a member of the Hells Angels and I'm wanted by the police. Oh, Jeeves, what are we going to do? I really screwed up this time."

"May I suggest, sir, that you lie down and I will take care of your injuries."

"Am I disfigured, Jeeves?"

But before he could answer, I went to the bathroom to look in the mirror. With a washcloth, I carefully dabbed off some of the dirt I had smeared my face with.

Well, I'd always had a bony nose, with a prominent bump at the top, very similar to George Washington's nose, should you happen to have a quarter in your pocket and want to take a look, and now that bump, as I had determined earlier, was way over on the right.

This made sense since the fellow I'd tangled with had struck me with his right-hand toaster, which had sent my nose, like an English sentence, from the left to the right. The nostrils, stubbornly, were still in the middle. The skin over the bump was cut open. The blood had dried, but the wound was lumpy with granules of earth. The whole nose was frightfully and eerily swollen, and the nostrils were filled with thick, stopped blood, and there was dried blood all over my chin.

"I've wrecked myself, Jeeves . . . I'm mutilated." I tried to touch my nose, but the feel of it repelled me.

I held back tears.

"Please lie down, sir."

Jeeves was showing a great deal of sangfroid at the sight of my dried *sang,* and his calmness had a hypnotic effect on me. Like a tiny boy, I held out my arms to him and he began to remove my clothes—the lapels of my favorite blue linen sport coat were bloody, but maybe the jacket wasn't ruined. One always hears that blood can't be washed out, but it often is. This business then about permanent bloodstains on clothing must be a rumor to keep people from attacking one another, though it's not a very effective rumor since a good deal of attacking still goes on.

Anyway, I lay on the bed and Jeeves gently bathed my face. Then he applied a damp washcloth to my nose, in lieu of ice.

Undone by it all, I passed out.

Around six-thirty in the morning there was a harsh banging on the door. I was shot into consciousness. But not just consciousness. Full coherent panic. My God, it's the police, I thought.

Jeeves was by my side, holding a wet compress. "Jeeves, it must be the sheriff," I whispered. "Should we climb out the window?"

"There's no fire escape, sir."

The banging continued, then speech. "In there—you want *shvitz* bath?" It was the old lady.

"Yes . . . of course . . . very good . . . thank you. . . . I'll come down in twenty minutes. That all right?"

"We heat the water. Come in thirty minutes," said the old lady through the door.

"All right," I said. There was silence. She had left.

"I'm only stalling her, Jeeves. We have to flee at once. I'm sure to be traced here to the Adler. I told everyone at the bar I was staying here and the cashier at the gas station knows—I asked him for directions."

I went to the bathroom to start getting ready and regarded myself in the mirror. I looked worse than I had a few hours before. The swelling had really set in. I looked like I was wearing the mask of a boxer. A boxer who wasn't very good. The space between my eyes, at the top of my nose, which was normally an indentation—in fact, most people have an indentation there unless you are a horse or a member of the horse family, like a zebra or a burro—was puffy, bloated.

I've overheard discussion of a certain arrangement of features known as a unibrow; well, I had a *uniface.* I was all snout, and to the left and right of this grotesque snout were already two black eyes. And beneath the snout was my Fairbanks Jr. mustache. But no pimples! The blows I received had done something to my pimples. Knocked them into submission! How innocent—how vain! how foolish!—I had been just one day before when my greatest concern was two spots on my upper lip.

Seeing my face took something out of me and I wasn't quite ready to flee. Fleeing, most will agree, requires a good deal of energy. So instead, I sat on the edge of the bed to inspect the rest of my person. There was a black mark on my stomach—some kind of horrible blood bruise—and two blue-red bruises on my hip and shoulder respectively. Also, my right wrist and hand were tender from the punch I had thrown, and both palms were scraped from when I had fought the curbing before fighting the Hill. I experienced pity for my body, like it was something separate from me, something that should be valued, but had instead been vandalized.

I was about to cry and leaned forward to hold my face in my hands, but blood rushed into my nose, such that I thought my head might explode. I lay back, to drain the blood elsewhere. I was also hungover. Hungover and bludgeoned! I couldn't cry, after all. It hurt too much.

Jeeves cleared his throat.

"What is it, Jeeves?" I whimpered.

"If I may inquire, sir, you were hysterical last night and I didn't want to further upset you with an interrogation, but I am curious to know how you came to blows with a Hells Angel and why you are wanted by the police."

"There's no point in explaining things, Jeeves. I should just be shot."

"Perhaps, sir, if you tell me what happened, I can provide some counsel."

"I'm too wiped out."

"I only require the headlines, sir. A brief summary."

"All right," I said.

It wasn't fair to keep the fellow in the dark, so I related the tragedy to Jeeves, confessing all. He absorbed my tale like some kind of magus and then he spoke with great sobriety and sanity. First of all, the message in the phone book, Jeeves hypothesized, was some kind of prank perpetrated on the femme fatale in question, not authored by Debbie herself, and so I was in the wrong for having made the phone call. But it was his feeling that we weren't in great danger of the law, that such a fellow as I had fought with was unlikely to seek out the police, and if he did, there was the old fall-back of self-defense. The woman, though, might have cause for action, but the whole thing was so absurd that the local constabulary would probably be baffled as to what to do.

He did think we should leave for Saratoga Springs this morning, since as a keen observer of my psyche, he knew that I would feel too anxious to remain in town. We could get a hotel room in Saratoga and then report to the Rose Colony the next day, as expected. I could explain my injuries by telling them that I had been in a minor car accident.

Time would take care of the body was his overall opinion, and I was not to touch any more alcohol. Jeeves was rather stern on this point—"I really do think, sir, that you show every sign of being alcoholic, floridly evident in last night's episode, and so the only recourse, I can see, is abstention"—whereas in the past he had simply looked the other way while the young master gargled the crushed grape.

I humbly accepted his prescription of temperance, but wondered if there wasn't more I could do. "Do you think I should write a letter of apology to the woman and to the man?" I asked Jeeves. "Perhaps from her phone number there's a way to get her address."

"Your intention is good, sir, but I think a letter would not have the desired effect. Anything having to do with you would most likely cause more pain, and a letter, I'm afraid, would be misunderstood by the parties in question. I do understand your willingness to make amends, but it's probably best to see your injuries as your form of apology. Your burden, as it were."

"Yes, Jeeves," I said. What a mess I had made, but I had to pull myself together.

We gathered our few things and slipped out of the Adler. The old lady must have been in the basement tending to my bath. I felt bad leaving her without explanation, but I had paid for two nights and so my conscience was more or less clear.

We got into the Caprice and I started the engine. Through blackened eyes, I took a last look at the tall, leaning Adler. Mist was coming off the morning grass and so the foundation of the hotel was lost in a cloud hovering close to earth, and it was all rather lovely and eerie, but this wasn't the time to meditate on beauty, and so I put the car in reverse and then aimed it for Saratoga Springs and the Rose Colony.

PART III

Saratoga Springs, New York

CHAPTER 11

Jeeves and I sequester ourselves at the Spa City Motel ★ Empathy experienced for criminals ★ I ice my nose and read a little Anthony Powell ★ A black depression ★ Thoughts of suicide ★ Jeeves helps me to rally

It was the beginning of the racing season in Saratoga, but we managed to find a room. Right on Broadway, we checked into a 1950s sort of hostelry: a bright blue paint job, a splashy sign, a bar in the lobby, a pool the shape of a kidney and the size of a kidney—in short, the kind of place where you have a healthy fear of getting lice from the blankets. The Spa City Motel was its nom de guerre.

"What happened to you?" asked the desk clerk, who was a misshapen little fellow.

"Car accident," I said, and the terseness of my tone indicated that no further conversation would be necessary.

It was a day infested with July sunshine, but when we got into the room, on the second floor, I pulled the curtains. Was feeling rather criminal, you know, still expecting the long arm of the Sharon Springs law to tap me on the shoulder and arrest me for breaking a fellow human being's kneecap and for making a harassing, ill-advised phone call to an innocent female.

Thus, I peered out the slit of the curtain, glancing at the parking lot below, and I felt a surge of empathy for criminals all across America, many of whom at the precise moment were also no doubt peering nervously out of curtain slits, waiting for other long arms of the law to reach them, which well those long arms should, since I am all for criminals being arrested. You see, I was only empathizing with how nervous criminal behavior makes you feel; in no way was I approving of behaving criminally.

"Oh, Jeeves," I said, clutching the curtain, "life is so difficult."

"Yes, sir."

In the parking lot below, I saw a squirrel run from a trash bin to a tree, which it nimbly and efficiently climbed. What an athletic and perfect little creature, I thought. Then I imagined that squirrel running up my leg, noting, as I did, that there's not much difference between a squirrel and a rat, just some fluffy hair on a tail. Then the squirrel leaped majestically from a tree branch to a phone line. I admired him. He knew exactly what to do at all times. You wouldn't see him drinking to excess at the Hen's Roost.

"Animals don't seem to get into trouble," I said to Jeeves. "They're much more sane than human beings."

"Why don't you lie down, sir," said Jeeves, clearly not wanting to engage in a discussion on the flaws of man and the perfection of animals. "I will make an ice pack for your nose."

This seemed a wise course of action, and I let go of the curtain and lay down on the nearer of the two beds. Jeeves left the room and made quick use of the Spa City Motel ice machine, returning with a bucket of the necessary ingredients for a cold compress.

So there I was, icing my nose, which also soothed my hangover. I would have liked to sleep, but it was impossible while icing myself, so with my free hand I held open my Anthony Powell novel, forgoing Hammett, thinking that Powell would mix better with my ice pack since his prose is wonderfully chilled, but after just a few minutes I had to stop reading as I felt myself overcome by the blackest of depressions. I took stock of my life:

I was an alcoholic who had been beaten to a pulp.

I had no home.

I had lost, over the years, almost all my friends.

My parents had both been dead for more than a decade, and what family I did have, an aunt and uncle, I had alienated.

The closest I had come lately to a girlfriend was literally in my dreams—the blonde girl who'd said, "I love you, Blair."

I had published one novel, but that had been seven years before.

I was thirty years old and a complete failure—I only had money because of a lawsuit.

Was there anything positive about me? I could only come up with one thing: I had been accepted to a prestigious artist colony, but how was I going to show up there the next day with my face so damaged?

I was feeling as low as they come. Or as low as I come, anyway. So hungover and broken-nosed, I covetously eyed the plastic bag which lined the small garbage can next to the night table.

A writer I admire, Jerzy Kosinski, used a plastic bag to kill himself, and ever since he pulled that stunt, when I am beyond consolation, I think of putting a plastic bag over my head, which is symbolic of a lower rung of depression and self-pity than when I merely think, "I should be shot."

I ran through the fantasy: I pictured the bag over my head, a strange sleep following, and then no more having to put up with myself. But also, I thought, no more suspense, no more wondering if there might yet be a happy ending, or at least a pleasant middle. And then, too, the greatest deterrent came to mind: the pain I would cause the few people—well, maybe one person, Aunt Florence—who loved me.

There was also Jeeves. I didn't want to presume that he loved me, but if I did kill myself I was sure that it would upset him considerably. Also, if I went the Kosinski route, it certainly wouldn't look good on his résumé. I imagined that the suicide of an employer would be a real blemish for a valet, and I didn't want to do that to Jeeves. So rather than mar his record by killing myself, I sought his counsel.

"Jeeves," I said, "I'm running on fumes. Despairing, if you follow me. So I'll put it right to you: Do you think there's anything worthwhile about me?"

It was a rather bold-faced cry for help and flattery, but I was desperate. His back was to me and he didn't say a word. I waited. I waited some more.

"Jeeves!" I said.

"Yes, sir."

"Did you hear my question?"

"Yes, sir."

"Well, I'd like a response. Terrible to leave a fellow hanging. I'm not exactly feeling like Norman Vincent Peale. A combination of Norman Bates and Vincent Price is more my mood at the moment."

Again Jeeves was silent. I may have baffled him with my references to the cinema. He's aware of some things, major movie stars like Clark Gable and Douglas Fairbanks Jr. and Errol Flynn, but the fellow's absorption of modern culture is minimal at best. But I didn't have time to illuminate him on movie arcana and explain myself.

"Jeeves!" I said. "Please tell me something that's halfway redeeming about myself!"

"I'm sorry for the delay, sir. There are so many things about you that are worthwhile that it is difficult to choose a single quality."

"Really?"

"Yes, sir."

"Enough with the yes, sirs, let a compliment rip. I don't want to tell you what I've been thinking about that plastic bag in the garbage can."

"Well, sir, I find you to be a kind person. Tolerant of others."

"You really think so, Jeeves?"

"Quite, sir."

"So I look the other way when others have faults?"

"Yes, sir."

"Sort of a noble characteristic, you'd say?"

"Yes, sir."

This pleased me and then I cast the inner eye over some of my recent relationships to see if Jeeves's assessment was correct. I quickly struck upon a possible glaring exception.

"Was I tolerant and kind to my uncle Irwin, Jeeves?"

"I would say so, sir. You knew that your society disturbed your uncle and so you did your best to avoid him, which I think, sir, shows a great deal of kindness and respect."

I thought Jeeves was missing an essential point: as much as my uncle did not yearn for my society, so I did not yearn for his society. We were equally nonyearning. But, looking at it from Jeeves's perspective, I could see that I hadn't been unkind to the uncle, so I was free to put Jeeves's compliment on the credit side of my ledger.

"Thank you, Jeeves. I appreciate you being kind to *me,* and I won't press you for any more compliments, unless you feel like letting one casually slip."

"Your mustache, much to my surprise, sir, is coming along rather nicely."

"Oh, thank you, Jeeves!"

"You're welcome, sir."

"Your words are like aspirin, Jeeves. Very soothing. I've taken two and will call the doctor in the morning."

"Very good, sir."

"Think I'll try to sleep now, Jeeves," I said. "Gather my strength for reporting tomorrow to the Rose Colony. Those artists are bound to be a terrifying lot, and having a broken face won't make things any easier. Yesterday, it was hard to imagine facing the world with two pimples."

"Some rest is a good idea, sir."

"Well, thank you for this ice, Jeeves." I handed him the compress. "We'll let the nose thaw while I nap, and then refreeze it when I wake up."

"Yes, sir."

It was around 10 A.M., but I slept until late in the afternoon, despite the fact that the Spa City Motel blankets felt dirty and reeked of cigarette smoke. But I was so tired, the soiled bedding was of no consequence.

When I woke up, we ordered some Chinese food to the room, watched television, and then did a little reading, and all the while I kept icing my nose. Jeeves might have liked to explore Saratoga, but I wasn't up for it, and he generously stayed by my side. After we finished reading, we discussed Powell and *A Dance to the Music of Time,* having lapsed somewhat in our book club discussions, and we both agreed that the character Widmerpool was one of the most repellent creatures ever found in literature.

"It wasn't directly intentional," I said, "but during this war period Widmerpool more or less brings about the deaths of Stringham and Templer. His orders as their military superior destroyed them, and it must be because they snubbed him at public school. . . . Public school in England really does a lot of damage to people. But

I think all the sadism in those schools makes them good poets. The British are much better at poetry than Americans. Anyway, I can't stand Widmerpool."

"I imagine, sir, that justice will be served."

"You're saying that Widmerpool will get it in the end?"

"That is my feeling, sir."

"A good reason to keep reading."

"Yes, sir."

And so our discussion went. Then I got back into bed around nine o'clock. I pulled the covers to my chin and said, "Jeeves, I'm worried what those artists will think about my face."

"I wouldn't be concerned, sir."

"But it's hard not to worry about what people think since they do think. There's no getting around it."

"Very true, sir."

"Well, regardless, I had better rest."

"I would agree, sir."

So I slept through until morning, nearly ten hours, and I needed it. My episode in Sharon Springs had taken a good deal out of me: I had burned the candle at both ends, as well as the middle.

CHAPTER 12

Another movie reference escapes Jeeves ★ We drive past the comely Saratoga racetrack ★ The two front teeth of the Rose Colony ★ A first glimpse of the Mansion and thoughts of castles and seductions ★ Two asylum inmates—I mean artists—are briefly encountered ★ Some foreboding, but not much ★ Setting goals with Jeeves

By 9 A.M. we were in the Caprice. It was another sunny day, good for skin cancer and playing tennis. I had on dark sunglasses and was wearing a floppy cotton hat, purchased at the Princeton Woolworth's years ago. It was the kind of hat that pensioners wear in Florida and other warm climates. I was trying to obscure my injuries and felt like the Invisible Man, absent the bandages.

"Jeeves, I feel like the Invisible Man," I said as I started the car.

"People often feel that way, sir," said Jeeves.

"I'm not speaking psychologically! I'm referring to the Invisible Man from the movies."

"Very good, sir."

If I *had* been speaking psychologically, I might have commented to Jeeves that my mood was rather good. The despair of the previous day, like my hangover, had just about lifted. I was even mildly hopeful, though still a bit anxious. Reporting to the Rose Colony was like the first day of school. Would I measure up? Fit in? Would my face frighten them? Maybe my nice clothes would distract them from my injuries, should I have to remove my glasses and hat. I was wearing khaki pants, my check sport coat, light blue shirt, and yellow-green tie with clock faces—a good first-day-at-school outfit, applicable as well to artist colonies.

The Rose was located on the edge of town, about a quarter mile

101

past the famous Saratoga racetrack, which we got a good look at as we drove past, and it was lovely. The track came with an ancient—by American standards—wooden grandstand, and there was, of course, the requisite mile-plus dirt oval, which had an expanse of emerald-colored grass in the middle for "turf" races and the steeplechase.

The track and the colony were on Union Avenue, and separating the two was a stretch of dense forest, and in the middle of these woods was the rather secretive entrance to the Rose, privacy being of the utmost importance for artists, since you don't want the tax-paying public to know about the creative process—how much napping and procrastinating are involved—because otherwise what little funding there is would be cut immediately.

If one didn't pay rigorous attention or have an excellent navigator like Jeeves, it would be very easy to miss the shadowy, mouthlike opening to the place. There was the smallest of faded signs, wooden with old painted script, *The Rose Colony, Private Property,* and behind the sign, at the top of the colony's drive, there were two ivy-covered stone columns, like two ancient front teeth, which must have supported an elaborate gate in the nineteenth century when the colony was the estate and home of a steel baron.

"On your right, sir," said Jeeves, "is, I believe, the entrance."

I had to make a rapid pull on the Caprice's steering wheel, but executed the maneuver without driving into the ditch on the side of the road, though I skidded to an awkward stop, breaking just in time before hitting one of the stone teeth. I backed the car up and then entered the driveway in the fashion most often associated with entering driveways.

"Sorry, Jeeves," I said. "Hope you weren't too jostled."

"Perfectly all right, sir," said Jeeves.

"Well, that's something of an auspicious start, but that's why they have the phrase *auspicious start,* because one often starts that way," I said, trying to cover up my embarrassment for the sloppy turn.

"Very good, sir."

We proceeded down a long, shadowy sylvan drive—on both sides was a continuation of the thick forest, with moody, sun-blocking trees. We passed a small, dark green pond, and then the driveway began a steep, winding ascent, trees still obscuring one's vision to the left and right, until suddenly we were at the top of a plateau, and revealed to the enchanted eye was a rolling, hilly lawn, about the size of a football field, and at the top of the lawn was the Mansion—an American castle. Built from blocks of silver-flecked stones imported from Italy, it was four stories in height and was loaded with picture windows, ivy, eaves, a copper roof, numerous wooden shutters, elaborate weather vanes, a porte cochere, and—if one looked closely—depraved gargoyles.

I stopped the car. I was thinking cinematically. Whenever you see a movie about the British upper class, which is almost always set on an enormous estate, first there's the aerial shot of the country "home" or "seat." It gives one a full sense of the place's majesty.

Then you zoom in for a close-up, usually of a servant going in some pantry door, carrying a recently shot bird or a bottle retrieved from some secondary wine cellar.

Then there's another close-up of some lord of the manor standing in a window looking repressed, bloated, scheming, and troubled. This is often followed by an interior shot of a woman sitting in front of a mirror, brushing her lustrous, gorgeous hair—blonde or brunette—while wearing just a slip. She's usually filmed from behind, but we see her face in the mirror, which gives us the rare treat of seeing, simultaneously, the front and back of a beautiful woman. And you get the whole story in those images—wealth, loneliness, and sex. The Rose, I thought, would definitely be served by such a sequence of movie takes.

"It's glorious, Jeeves," I said. "Like Brideshead."

"Very elegant, sir," said Jeeves. "A handsome structure."

At the other end of the lawn from the Mansion was a fountain with marble nymphs. A jet of water kept the nymphs cool in the July morning sun. It struck me that this fountain, with its spray and small pool of water, would be an advantageous spot for romantic assignations if one could lure poetesses there late at night.

I took my foot off the brake and drove farther into the grounds. The road curved, leading us behind and then past the Mansion. When Doris, the director's assistant, had given me directions, she had told me to go to a white wooden building marked simply as

OFFICE to check in. Thus, we continued on the asphalt drive, beneath a colonnade of trees, and up ahead were two people, artists, presumably, walking together.

"My future colleagues," I said to Jeeves.

As they came into sharper focus, I made out that these two creative souls were a man and a woman. We pulled alongside them and I stopped the car. I smiled kindly through my rolled-down window, acknowledging my fellow artists, my bruises hidden by my disguise, and my smile was met by a specimen out of Brueghel—the woman, in her fifties, had a long, jellyish nose, gray teeth, and copper, wiry hair that had a life of its own and not a very pleasant life at that. Her companion was a stoop-shouldered fellow whose arms were slack along his sides in an unnatural fashion, as if he were heavily sedated, and his thick eyeglasses were slanted spasmodically. One of the lenses was in front of his eyebrow—didn't he notice?

They both lowered their heads to peer into my car and looked at me quizzically. I said, "I'm checking in today."

But this didn't seem to register. I tried a different tack. "Can you tell me where the office is?"

The man pointed and said in a listless voice, "Just up ahead." He did add a weird, feeble smile and I smiled back and said, "Thank you," and the woman smiled at me. It was an orgy of smiles with us three, but it was all very strange: the female's eyes had a look of terror in them and the man appeared to be on the verge of collapse. So, thinking it wise to end this encounter, I pushed down on the gas pedal. A shudder of foreboding coursed through me. What kind of place was this? They looked more like inmates at an asylum than two of the country's finest artists. Had I escaped being banished to a rehab by my aunt Florence only to attend some kind of creative loony bin?

We presently pulled alongside the office. It appeared to be a once-grand stables, now renovated to act as the bureaucratic center of the colony. Behind us loomed the Mansion.

"Those two were the walking wounded, Jeeves," I said. "I hope they were the exception and not the rule here at the Rose Colony. . . . Not to be unkind, since you said I'm a tolerant person, but they were unquestionably disturbed."

"Artists are often temperamental, sir."

"*Disturbed* going too far, Jeeves? . . . Well, to be fair then, those two were probably poets. Poets are the most afflicted in all the arts. Their hearts are like furnaces and their bodies disintegrate from the internal pressure and heat, though male poets are pretty much wrecks from the start, otherwise they wouldn't go in for it."

"Perhaps you should check in, sir."

"I need to gather myself a moment, Jeeves. Feeling a little nervous."

"I understand, sir."

There were a few parked cars, but no people. The place was quiet and tranquil. The immediate grounds were a mixture of lawns and trees, and in the distance were some renovated barns, perhaps artists' studios. I tried to calm my nerves by having a pleasant thought about that fountain of nymphs, and then I asked Jeeves, "Do you think there might be attractive young female poets here?"

"It is certainly a possibility, sir."

"Young poets haven't burned up yet. It's only if they keep at it that they start to fall apart."

"Very good, sir."

"Maybe the girl from my dream is here, Jeeves. Wouldn't that be remarkable?"

"Yes, sir. Quite remarkable."

"Know what's interesting, Jeeves?"

"No, sir."

"My dream girl is actually a dream girl. See what I mean?"

"Yes, sir."

"Isn't that interesting?"

"Quite, sir."

"Well, I hope my dream girl dream girl is here."

"Yes, sir."

"I have three goals, Jeeves, for my time here at the Rose Colony."

"Indeed, sir?"

"One, to fall in love—maybe with my dream girl or just a regular girl. Two, stay off the booze, and, three, finish my novel."

"Those are three admirable goals, sir."

"I'd like to throw in finding God. But I always think these things come in threes and that you're not allowed to ask for four."

"That is the norm, sir."

"A way around it perhaps is that finding God is a sort of constant goal and so doesn't have to be listed. You know what I mean, Jeeves? It's sort of a permanent Roman numeral I, and the others are just regular numbers: 1, 2, 3. That Roman numeral does give it a Catholic air, though. But that's all right. Essentially I'm a pantheist-agnostic. I worship many deities with equal amounts of confusion. . . . So, God, if you're listening, finding you is my number-one goal, and if you want to help me with the other three goals, I won't object. . . . I hope you don't mind me praying in front of you, Jeeves."

"Not at all, sir."

"Well, I guess I should go into that office, but I'm still scared, Jeeves."

"No need to be afraid, sir."

"But my face, Jeeves, and, too, this is a famous artist colony, even if the poets are mad-looking, and I'm a struggling writer at best."

"They accepted you, sir, so they value your talent. And you can simply tell them you've had an accident, which is not untrue."

"All right, I'll plunge in there, Jeeves. I don't want to but I have to. It seems like we're always doing things in life we don't want to do."

"One often has that impression, sir."

"I'm sorry I'm whining, Jeeves. In I go!"

"Very good, sir."

CHAPTER 13

*I am welcomed by three kindly women ★ For a moment, my sanity
is in question and what causes this—my fractured nose or acute
withdrawal from alcohol? ★ A remembrance of the psychic effects
of plastic surgery on a high school colleague's nose ★ A return to
sanity, and some discourse about Brown University and the origins
of its name ★ An unmasking and the telling of untruths ★ I meet the
novelist Charles Murrin and we proceed to the Mansion ★ I'm
shown my glorious rooms ★ An invitation to drink ★ I repeat certain untruths, but I'm used to it now, telling untruths, that is*

The office was comprised of three women sitting behind desks,
arranged in a sort of pyramid—two desks at the base and one at the
point. It was some kind of hierarchical arrangement. They all looked
up at me.

"Is Doris here?" I asked. "I'm Alan Blair—"

"Welcome to the Rose!" said the woman at the point of the pyramid, presumably the leader. She was a solid, gray-haired lady with
flushed cheeks and a sweet smile. "I'm Doris! And look at you!
Nobody has shown up here in a jacket and tie in years."

She then introduced me to the other two ladies, Barbara and Sue,
and they murmured welcomes. Barbara was rather old, late sixties
with white hair, and Sue was rather young, early twenties with red
hair. She was pretty, maybe a college intern.

All three women radiated sweetness, though there was a bit of a
rough, take-charge quality to Doris—she came over to me, shook
my hand vigorously, then commandeered me to a chair alongside
her desk.

"Dr. Hibben is out of town for a few days," she said. "Normally he'd say hello and give you a warm welcome, but you'll meet him when he returns."

"Dr. Hibben?"

"Dr. Hibben, our director," she said and smiled, and I didn't like the sound of this—a doctor!

"What type of doctor is he?" I asked, and for a moment I doubted my sanity. Had I perhaps ended up in an asylum after all, deceiving myself into thinking it was an artist colony? And if this was true, then it was some kind of double insanity: insane enough to think an asylum is an artist colony, but also insane enough to be accepted to an asylum!

Doris didn't answer my question about Dr. Hibben; she was preoccupied, searching for something in her desk drawer. My mind raced. It had to be an asylum. The director was a doctor, and the grounds were too calm and idyllic, perfect for a nerve farm. And those two I had seen staggering up the drive weren't poets but patients, just as I had feared. Of course, they might have been poets who had become patients, since the history of mentally ill poets is famously long. Regardless, they were patients now!

But how had this happened? How did I come to be in an asylum? I had applied to this place during the dark month of January, when I was in the throes of that terrible depression, before my thinking had cleared up, before Jeeves and my quarter-million-dollar settlement had both come into my life. So had my application to what I thought was an artist colony actually been a call for help to a private, elite nuthouse? A call for help I didn't even know I had made due to mental fogginess and muddle? And now a bed was free and so they had taken me off the waiting list?

"Sorry," Doris said, handing me a form that had been the object of her search. "I couldn't lay my hands on this. What did you want to know? What kind of doctor is Dr. Hibben?"

"Yes," I whispered, and looked at the paper she had handed me—a medical history form! I *had* committed myself!

"Dr. Hibben has a Ph.D. in art history," Doris said good-naturedly. "He was at Brown for years, but now we have him."

"Yes, of course," I said, and I felt my sanity return instantaneously; it had only been a case of temporary insanity, which is very useful for committing murder, but not so practical in other situations. But thank God I wasn't at an asylum! Someone with a Ph.D. in art history could only be running an artist colony, not a nuthouse. But why had I been suspicious even for a moment? What was wrong with my thinking?

Well, I had to go easy on myself, I realized, and not be upset if my judgment of things was off. I was booze-free for only twenty-four hours—I could be having delirium without the tremens. Also, my nose had been rearranged, and this could definitely affect one's perception of reality, at least according to some nineteenth-century psychiatrists who believed that the structure of the nose determined the psyche, to which there is some merit, I think, otherwise why would so many people go in for nose jobs? Their psyches become a mess from having overly large noses; then the noses get shortened and their psyches feel better, at least cosmetically.

I saw this psychic rearrangement happen to a girl I knew in high school. She was a blonde with a good figure, but she had an enormous, catastrophic nose. She was ostracized and had no friends. Then one summer her parents sprang for plastic surgery. When we all returned to school, no one knew what to make of her. Then a football player asked her out. Suddenly she had friends. She became "cool." She was considered beautiful, pretty, but I could see that in her eyes there was still the look of the ugly girl she had once been, a hint of fear that it would all be taken away from her. By the end of the year that look in her eyes was almost extinguished, but a trace was left. Still, her psyche must have felt a lot better. With a short nose to go with her other attributes, she was destined to be courted often and eventually married and impregnated, which was the goal of most of the girls from my middle-class New Jersey high school. But then her children would have big noses. No escaping one's self. Her husband would wonder where his children's noses had come from. Perhaps the marriage would dissolve. He might suspect infidelity. She wouldn't be able to tell him the truth—*I'm ugly.*

Well, life is never easy, that's for sure. But *my* life was now a little easier. I was at an artist colony and not an asylum. This was a positive.

"So Dr. Hibben was at Brown," I said. "I've always wondered why it was called that. Never looked it up. I'm lazy that way. Must be for someone named Brown, can't be for the color, right? Be interesting, though, if schools were named after colors, like Red University, but of course white and black would have to be avoided. Red might not work either. Too closely associated with Marx. I went to Princeton. Our colors were orange and black."

Doris gave me a look and I thought I had better shut up. What was I doing running my mouth with my personality all rearranged nasally and a brain reeling from no alcohol?

So I shut my trap and began to fill out the medical form, and as I endeavored to indicate that I had no allergies and was taking no medications, Doris said, "Are you all right? Have you been in an accident?" I could feel her looking at me more closely, noticing that something was amiss with a person who wore his sunglasses and hat while inside. Also, the edges of my bruises were somewhat apparent. My Invisible Man costume was only good for a quick pass, not a penetrating gaze.

"Yes, I have been in an accident," I said. "Nothing serious."

"What happened to you?"

I wasn't really prepared for such a vigorous cross-examination. I didn't like having to lie; I'm much better with omission. But I rallied.

"A fender bender," I said. "I was struck from behind"—in my mind's eye I saw the Hill's fist coming at me—"and my face went into the steering wheel, breaking my nose, if you can believe it."

"This is terrible! When was this?" asked Doris. Old Barbara and young Sue were silent, listening attentively to our conversation.

"Two days ago, after we spoke," I said.

"Are you in a lot of pain?"

"Just a little throbbing. It's really okay."

"What did the doctor say?"

"I didn't go to a doctor, but I'm fine. The nose is swollen and pushed a little to the right, but it's nothing drastic. I could stand to be more on the right. I tend to be too liberal in my policies, though I'm not against prayer in schools, which I think would help with test scores."

"Let me see what you look like," Doris said, with a touch of drill sergeant and a touch of one's mother, but with more drill sergeant than mother. I could see that she thought I was a nutty artist who didn't know how to take care of himself, and that she felt her job was to look after such artists.

"It's not too bad," I said. "But I feel embarrassed. That's why I'm wearing this hat and glasses."

"You don't have to be embarrassed in front of me, I used to be a nurse. So take those glasses off and the hat. We may have to send you to the hospital."

I didn't like the sound of this at all. It's been my experience that if you go to a hospital, they like to hold on to you. That's how I ended up in rehab in Long Island. You go for a simple emergency-room visit to Beth Israel for alcohol poisoning, and next thing you know you're on a detox unit for ten days, and then Long Island for a whole month, where you meet nightmarish physicians like Dr. Montesonti.

Thus, in that moment, I felt I should never have come to the Rose Colony. I should have stayed in Sharon Springs. . . . No, I should have stayed in Montclair. . . . No, I should have stayed in New York. . . . What was I thinking? I had nowhere else to go. This was terrible, I had burnt all my bridges.

I said nothing and made no motion to remove my disguise. I was paralyzed. I had just been breathing easy that this wasn't an asylum, but there was already talk of carting me off to a hospital.

"Let me see what you look like, dear," Doris said. "Don't worry, I can handle it." This time there was a little bit more mother and less drill sergeant to her tone of voice, which appealed to me. I respond well to mothers. Some people don't like mother figures, but I'm all for them. I took off my hat and glasses. The use of *dear* had done the trick.

"Oh, my God," she said. "Are you going to sue the people who hit you?"

The scab on the bridge of the nose, which the sunglasses had obscured, was gruesome but healing. I had two black eyes, though why they're called black is silly—the blood that had drained and formed pools beneath my eyes was a rather gorgeous mixture of blue, green, and even yellow; and I still had a snout, but it had gone from being the snout of a horse to the snout of a dog.

I said, "I know it doesn't look good, but I'm actually mending rather quickly. I probably won't sue. . . . There was no damage to the car. I was simply thrown forward. It was sort of my fault—I wasn't wearing my seat belt."

That was an incredible bit of quick thinking. If I hadn't said anything, she might at some point have noticed that my car was unscathed and she'd realize something was fishy. But I didn't feel good. I was in the prevaricator's spiral: lies give birth to more lies. That's why I prefer omission. Keeps things simple. Of course, there was the truth, but I didn't think it would make a good impression to say that I had been in a drunken brawl.

"How's your breathing?" asked Doris.

"Perfectly fine."

"Your septum is probably all right. I can't force you to go to the hospital, but I do think you should get looked at. We can take you to the emergency room."

"I honestly don't think that will be necessary. But if I don't continue to improve over the next few days, I'll take you up on that."

Doris seemed resigned. She wasn't going to fight me on this. I could read her thoughts: *Have to let these foolish artists do what they're going to do.* I began to relax a little. I had lied, but survived.

"You're being very brave," said Doris.

"You poor thing," said the grandmotherly Barbara, and young Sue, the attractive coed, made some sort of cooing, nonverbal noise.

I said to all of them, "Well, a man's nose is meant to be broken at least once in his life."

This was a rather good pronouncement, which I hadn't considered before, and I liked its vague sexual implication, especially as young Sue appeared to lower her gaze in a sweet and feminine way.

I then finished the medical form and was handed a sheet labeled "Emergency Contact Information." For this I put down Uncle Irwin, though in an emergency he was quite likely to recommend that my life support be shut off, so it gave me a certain morbid pleasure to scrawl his name.

Doris filed my papers, and then using a walkie-talkie, she contacted one of my fellow artists, whose role on the campus was to act as a greeter that first day. I put on my hat and sunglasses, and within two minutes of Doris's transmission, this very tiny fellow with a shock of silver hair and unusually light blue eyes came to the office to gather me and lead me to my rooms. He was in his sixties, a novelist I hadn't heard of by the name of Charles Murrin, and was rather gnomish in an appealing way. We shook hands and then I said to Doris, "Thank you so much for having me, I'm thrilled to be here," and then I said to Barbara and Sue, "Nice to meet both of you," and with these pleasantries taken care of, Murrin and I quit the office.

Jeeves stayed in the car, and I let him know with my eyes to wait there. I thought it would make an odd first impression for Murrin to meet my valet, might provoke jealousy. Most writers can't afford valets. Murrin and I headed for the Mansion.

"Where are your bags?" Murrin asked. "Were they dropped off at the Mansion? You took a taxi from the station?"

"They're in my car. I drove. I'll collect them later."

"I can help you, if you like," he offered, which was very kind of him, though my garment bag of sport coats would have outweighed him.

"Oh, that's all right, I'll get them later," I said. "I'm eager to see my rooms."

As we walked, Murrin briefed me on our feeding schedule:

Breakfast was from eight to nine in the dining room; lunch was a solitary affair—a lunch pail and a thermos of coffee would be left for me in the mudroom each day (this was done for all the artists); and dinner was served from six-thirty to eight.

"What will you be working on?" Murrin then asked as we strolled beneath a ceiling of tree branches. My feet stepped in and out of striations of sunlight and shade. Then I looked up and the Mansion loomed in front of us like a gigantic, otherworldly spaceship made out of granite.

"A novel," I said, answering Murrin's question. "And what are you working on?"

"Also a novel."

"I offer my condolences."

Murrin smiled. "Nice to meet a fellow sufferer," he said.

"I'd rather be a fellow traveler. But is a fellow traveler a communist or a Mason? I always get confused. Be nice, though, if being a novelist was like being a Mason. Be fun to have a special ring."

"Oh yes," said Murrin, and he gazed at me sweetly. Bringing up a fondness for rings had perhaps sent the wrong message. This Murrin, perfectly charming, was evidently homosexual. The Homosexual Question had arisen yet again!

I quickly surmised that Murrin's tiny stature—he was only about five feet two—had early on shaped his sexuality, had made the competition for women too difficult, and so he had entered an arena where he could be loved, which was more than understandable. We all must find the right arena. Of course, there could be other reasons for why he preferred men, but I had often noted that tiny men were homosexual, though I had also noted that dwarfs were usually quite swaggeringly heterosexual. Well, it's very hard to figure these things out, to make definitive statements about human sexuality.

We entered the Mansion through a side entrance, into the mudroom, which, despite its name, was a handsome, country-house living room with floral-patterned couches and large, old chairs and several tables loaded with literary journals and art magazines.

"After dinner," Murrin said, "people sit here and read the paper, play Scrabble or chess or hearts. We don't have TV at the Rose, but sometimes people go to the mall for a movie."

"I see." I had the immediate impression of having stepped into a simpler time and place where adults gathered on a summer night to play cards.

In the adjoining room there were two long tables, one for the colonists' mail and one loaded with old-fashioned metal lunch pails and thermoses. Murrin located my lunch pail and a thermos, both of which already had my name on little tags, and this pleased me immensely. The thoughtfulness! I happily took my two items, and then Murrin led me to a winding back staircase. We went up one flight to the hall where I'd be staying, which was a narrow, dark passage. There was a palpable hush to the Mansion—a quality of quiet akin to sound.

"This is the old servants' wing," said Murrin, "but you'll be the only one on here, which is nice and private." We walked down the hall; there were closed doors to the right and left. "These other rooms are used for storage, and this is your own bathroom." He pointed out the appropriate facility, which had an ancient tub with clawed feet. "You're lucky; you're one of the few people with a bathroom all to yourself."

I did indeed feel lucky. Sharing a commode with strangers is always a nerve-racking disaster. Such a thing is better left to college students and soldiers and convicts, people who are young and strong and can withstand the rigors of communal living.

At the far end of the hall were the two rooms, side by side, that were mine: a bedroom and a writing studio.

"These aren't the most elegant accommodations," said Murrin as we stood in what would be my writing studio. "Young male writers are often put here on their first visit. In the main part of the Mansion some of the rooms are enormous, but I've always liked these two little rooms. Very Spartan. Good for young men."

"Where do you stay?" I asked.

"I'm on the fourth floor, just a tiny bedroom. But my writing studio is a cabin in the woods. A few of us have cabins."

In my writing room there was a large oak desk, an empty bookshelf, and a cot where Jeeves could bunk. The floors were old dark wood; there were timber beams in the ceiling. My desk faced a window with a view of the sloping lawn that led to the fountain of nymphs, and in the far distance I could make out mountains. I put my lunch pail and thermos on the desk. I was going to work well in such a room.

We went into my bedroom. It had an old antique single bed, a little letter-writing desk, and an antique armoire for my clothes. It all felt like such an honor—all this so that I could write. I was very grateful.

Murrin pointed out a map of the colony on the letter-writing desk and we studied it together. It clearly illustrated what I could find on the six-hundred-acre grounds—barns converted to artist and composer studios, three other houses where artists also had rooms, a pool, a tennis court, a famous rose garden (hence the name of the colony), and a forest with trails and several ponds.

"This is like heaven," I said.

"Yes, it's wonderful," said Murrin. "I've been coming here for thirty years . . . have made many friends. . . . If you like, most of us get together for drinks on the back terrace before dinner. Around six. Be a good chance for you to meet people."

"Thank you for the invitation," I said, and I felt a shiver of concern at the mention of drinks. *Drinks before dinner*. I had to be strong. "I hope it's all right that I only take temperance beverages." This was an unnecessary admission, but I wanted to be vigilant about not drinking.

Murrin laughed at my use of the word *temperance,* but then he peered at me, trying to see if I was serious or not since I didn't smile or join him in laughter, but my sunglasses hid my eyes, so he wasn't sure. "Of course you don't have to drink, if you don't like," he said, playing it safe. "But do come so you can meet everyone. We're filled to capacity, about forty of us. A fun group."

Then Murrin looked at me more intensely; like Doris, he had seen through my Invisible Man facade. He said, "Has something happened to you? You seem to have two black eyes."

"I've had an accident," I said. "A car accident. That's why I'm wearing this disguise of hat and glasses. My face is a bit gruesome. I was rear-ended and broke my nose on the steering wheel, which caused the black eyes."

This repetition of my earlier lie was quite easy. I've observed that a lie repeated begins to feel like the truth. When it spawns new lies, that's a problem, but just repeated by itself, the lie comes rather naturally.

"Are you in pain?" asked Murrin.

"Only mentally."

"Me, too," said Murrin, smiling. He was a good-natured fellow and I felt he was someone you could trust—he was old and gentle and funny.

"Can I ask your opinion about something?" I said.

"Yes, of course," said Murrin generously.

"Well, do you think it would be all right if I wore my hat and sunglasses to dinner? Or would it seem strange? The alternative is my bruised face."

"Why don't you come in your disguise," he said. "It will give you an air of mystery."

"That's what I'll do then," I said, and was relieved that Murrin had seemingly no desire to inspect my injuries.

"Well, I'll let you settle in," said Murrin. "But I always like to suggest to people to just relax their first day. Get a feel for the place, and then start working tomorrow. Go for a nice walk and a swim in the pool."

"I'm a bit anxious to get working."

"Well, whatever you want to do. That's the main thing at the Rose Colony. You do what you want. . . . So maybe I'll see you for temperance beverages at six," Murrin said, teasing me a little.

"Sometimes, I'm intemperate," I responded, my alcoholism suddenly asserting itself, wanting to leave open a door for a drink to splash in. Murrin grinned knowingly—or was it unknowingly? People rarely take another person's drinking problem seriously, and why should they?

"Whatever you want to do," said Murrin, "that's the only rule." Then he left me in my room. My own beautiful room in the Mansion of the Rose Colony.

CHAPTER 14

I arrange my desk, in preparation for literary flight ★ I cull my notes for material, coming across odd things about the brevity of life and the cause of hair loss ★ One note leads to a discussion of out-of-body experiences with Jeeves, whom I mark as a likely candidate for having had such an experience ★ I type up a scene about New York's clubs, which leads Jeeves and I to discuss, in order, the Racial Question, the Jewish Question, Fitzgerald, the Great American Novel, and my own plans for myself as a novelist

I didn't take Murrin's advice. As soon as Jeeves unpacked my things, I sat down at that desk to get to work.

I had my computer open, and my pens, pads, and thermos of coffee were at the ready. My *Concise Oxford Dictionary,* 1960 edition, replete with my preferred British spellings, was there for moral and spiritual support, though I'm too much of a coward to use the spellings in my own work.

Anyway, there I was, like a pilot in his cockpit. My desk was my instrument panel, and being on the second story of the Mansion added to this flying motif.

I took in the lovely view out my window—green lawn, marble nymphs, old trees, blue sky, and far-off mountains. A bird, unseen in the tree closest to my window, made a cry, once, and then a second time to make sure it had got it right the first time. Another bird responded in a slightly different key. A mother calling to a child to come home for lunch? The child answering? All was well with the world. The birds were singing! The sky was a kindly blue! I was at a writing desk!

I poured myself a cup of coffee from my thermos. I drank the

119

coffee. It was weak, thin, nothing more than warm brown water, but that was of no consequence. Coffee for me is a placebo: it just has to be there, regardless of taste. I can't write without it.

The first thing I did was take out my notes, which I kept in a large shoe box. To try to have some order, I had placed the notes in about fifty letter-size envelopes, and so the box was overflowing. My notes—kept on various mad scraps of paper—were my observations and thoughts on things, but mostly they were witty, off-hand remarks or long speeches that my old roommate Charles had made.

On the outside of the envelopes were neatly printed messages to myself as to what I might find inside, for example:

Charles on New York Society
The Time We Snuck into the Opera
Charles on Women
Charles on the Royal Family
Our Troubles with Cockroaches, Fleas, and Pigeons
My Thoughts on Charles
My Thoughts on Sex

I felt a little sad looking at the envelopes. I missed Charles. But he didn't want anything to do with me. My drinking had made living with me as a roommate intolerable, and it was while I was in rehab that he had kicked me out—he had no faith that I would reform.

And now that I was trying to reform—off the booze for twenty-four hours—it didn't really make a difference. I was writing a novel about him, which I was hoping to publish someday, and I knew he would never forgive me for this, no matter how loving my portrayal of him might be. He'd find it humiliating that I would reveal to the world how penniless he was and how dependent he had become on the women whom he escorted. But I felt mercilessly compelled to write the book—he was too great a character to pass up. Also, I was selfish—it was me or him. My money from the settlement wouldn't last forever. I had to write a second novel to survive *and* to prove to myself that the first book was not a fluke, that I was, indeed, a writer. And every writer needs a subject and Charles was mine.

So I had to harden myself and be ruthless. I brushed aside, as always, my misgivings and my guilt, and pressed on with the book in order to make proper use of this glorious writing room the Rose Colony had given me. Also, once I began working, my bad feelings always went away as I experienced an odd joy in reliving and reshaping my time with Charles, and, too, in my mind, which mollified my guilt, I was making him a hero, even if he would never see it that way.

I put my hand in the shoe box and randomly chose an envelope and interestingly enough came up with one that I had labeled: "My Random Thoughts That Perhaps Can Be Given to the Narrator."

I removed a torn scrap of paper, like a fortune cookie's note, and it said, in my handwriting, though I didn't remember writing it:

I keep repeating to myself: Life is short. Life is short. Life is short. Will I shorten it further if I keep repeating that? Have the character based on me think this.

That wasn't very helpful, so I took out another slip of paper. This one also featured a litany:

I wish I wasn't going bald. I wish I wasn't going bald. I wish I wasn't going bald. Well, that didn't work. Those three wishes make me think of the Wizard of Oz. Doesn't Dorothy have to say something three times?

I should sing "If I only had hair," but to the melody of "If I only had a brain." I could also sing that song, though. I have no hair and no brain.

I am probably losing my hair because of sex-with-self. Loss of minerals. When I look at other bald men, I know this is true for them as well. Baldness is the Mark of Cain for self-abuse. What's more stunning is that all the men with hair are somehow refraining, and many of them look quite depraved. Well, you never know what goes on in someone else's life. Some people may look depraved but are quite nice. So the narrator could assume that Charles doesn't touch himself since he has all his hair.

I wasn't sure when I wrote that note, either. It was odd receiving these messages from an earlier self. I did consider, though, with some happiness, that I was making progress on one front—of late I had been feeling good about my hair. My thinning had reached some sort of elegant stasis, or so I told myself.

I removed one more note:

I'd like to have an outer-body experience. Maybe the character based on me could have one. Since I probably can't have one in real life, my character could.

"Jeeves," I called out.

Jeeves transfused himself from the bedroom to the writing room. "Yes, sir?"

"Have you ever had an outer-body experience?"

"Do you mean, sir, an out-of-body experience?"

"Yes, you're right, Jeeves. . . . I must have confused *out-of-body* with *outer-borough.* Anyway, have you ever had one?"

"One what, sir?"

"What do you think? An out-of-body experience! Lifted out of your body and gone somewhere else. You strike me as the type who might be good at this sort of thing. So you could tell me what it's like to leave your body and I'll write about it. I'd like to put such a phenomenon in my book."

"I'm sorry, sir, but I've not had an out-of-body experience."

"Really? I'm surprised. Would you like to have one, Jeeves? I'd get one for you if I could."

"No, sir, I don't want one."

"Well, I'd like one, Jeeves. You would think with my yoga I could get one, but ten sun salutations probably isn't enough. . . . It would be a relief to get out of my body every now and then. I often feel I'm jumping around in a costume that doesn't fit right."

"I'm sorry to hear that, sir."

"No need to fret, Jeeves. At the moment, my body seems to fit pretty well, though my nose is throbbing. It'd be nice if my nose could have an out-of-body experience, leave me with a suitable, temporary replacement nose, and come back when it's healed. Sort of a positive spin on that Gogol story. You follow me, Jeeves?"

"At some distance, sir."

"Well, that's all, Jeeves. I'm very excited to get to work, even with a throbbing nose."

"Very good, sir."

I drank some more coffee and returned to my shoe box and went to the "Charles on New York Society" envelope. I took out a large scrap, upon which I had jotted down an excellent exchange between Charles and myself on New York's clubs. This dialogue, I felt, could comprise the next day's scene after the Saint Patrick's Day Parade discussion. So I typed up the following:

"I wish I was a member of the Yale Club," I said to Charles. We were having an early-evening glass of wine. This was in lieu of cocktails since we didn't have any hard liquor. He was sitting on the blue couch, which was also his bed. I sat on the white couch, crossing my legs at the knees, trying to affect a Douglas Fairbanks Jr. pose. "So many of Fitzgerald's stories take place at the Yale Club," I continued. "Be romantic to have a club to go to for a drink and meet friends."

"I'm sure the Yale Club is destroyed," said Charles. "They probably have women members. The best clubs don't take in women. The best clubs are still fascist holdouts. Randall Chatfield, an old fruit, resigned from the Players Club because they took in women. He wanted them to take in boys. The Explorers Club is good, but you have to be an explorer."

"It's probably silly of me, though, to fantasize about clubs as these romantic places," I said. "I don't really want to be a member now, but a member in the 1920s, when Fitzgerald was around. The problem with that is, if I went back in time to the twenties I couldn't be a member since I'm Jewish."

"Well, if you can go back in time, then you can also change your religion. I would think that time travel gives you great powers."

"But I wouldn't want to change my religion."

"Then stop whining," said Charles, admonishing me. "And stop romanticizing about clubs. They didn't take in Jews. You have to accept this. It's the way things were. In the twenties, the best hotels used to have signs: NO JEWS, NEGROES, OR DOGS. And this upset many people; they liked to travel with their dogs. The rich still like their dogs. Prefer them to children. Less expensive."

"If they're rich, why does it matter?"

"Don't be stupid. The wealthier you are the cheaper you are, and nobody is more barbaric to their children than the rich."

"Well, I guess I don't want to go back to the twenties. Too racist. It's racist now, but not quite as bad."

"I hate that word. I told my students that I thought Scandinavian women were the most beautiful and so they called me a racist, and I explained to them it's preference, not racism. I also told them I have great admiration for blacks. They're one of America's first families."

That took about an hour to produce, fixing the dialogue, getting it just right. When I had it at a somewhat acceptable level, I called for Jeeves.

He insinuated himself back across the hall. "Yes, sir?"

I read him the day's efforts. "Very good, sir," he said when I had finished.

"You think so, Jeeves?"

"Yes, sir."

"I do seem to be fixated on Douglas Fairbanks Jr. *Gunga Din* must have mesmerized me at some point. But maybe it's a passing phase. Though I am enjoying having his mustache. Well, I can always remove him during the next draft. I don't think too many people will know what posing like Douglas Fairbanks Jr. means. I'm not sure I do."

"Very good, sir."

"You did pick up, Jeeves, that I'm trying to subtly address the Racial Question and the Jewish Question? And some hint of the Homosexual Question, with the mention of Chatfield."

"Yes, sir. You touch on these matters in a most subtle way."

"There are so many Questions, Jeeves. Have you noticed?"

"Yes, sir."

"There are also a lot of Problems. The Monogamy Problem, the Mind/Body Problem, the Designated Hitter Problem in baseball . . . Naturally, I'm most curious, in a self-centered way, about the Jewish Q. For the Nazis it was what to do with us, but for me the J.Q. is: 'Why are we hated?'"

"An exceedingly difficult question, sir."

"We Jews would like, of course, to figure out how not to be hated, either changing ourselves or changing the haters, but maybe we just have to accept that we're hated, like they advocate in AA— that you have to accept you're alcoholic. So we Jews just have to accept that we're hated and move on. . . . I wonder if there's a twelve-step group for Jews to help us work on this, though I guess that's what the synagogue is for, which makes sense since most AA meetings are held in churches. So Jewish AA, which, I guess, is just Judaism, is held in synagogues and instead of twelve steps you have Ten Commandments."

"Perhaps, sir."

"Well, in my book, Jeeves, I'll simply pose these Questions. I won't come up with any Answers. But that's all right because you don't have to be conclusive in novels about the human condition. When you write the Declaration of Independence or the Constitution or directions for brain surgery, then you have to be firm, but with novels it's enough just to ask the Questions. People don't expect too much from literature. They just want to know they're not alone with being confused."

"An astute observation, sir."

"Know what's upsetting to me, Jeeves? Writing that bit about the Yale Club and Fitzgerald made me think how most writers I admire hated Jews. Including Fitzgerald. They shouldn't publish people's letters. Inevitably you spot the anti-Semitic remark from one of your heroes and it breaks your heart. . . . Oh, well. Even if Fitzgerald was anti-Semitic, I still say *The Great Gatsby* is the Great American Novel. People keep talking about the Great American Novel as if it hasn't been written yet, but it has. By Fitzgerald. It has everything American: money, sex, cars, liquor, forging a new false self, prose like cocktail music, New York City. What do you think, Jeeves?"

"You make a convincing argument, sir."

"Thank you, Jeeves. . . . I do think, though, that even if Fitzgerald wrote the Great American Novel, he *was* wrong on one thing: there being no second acts in American lives. I think he said that because he died so young. He missed his own second act—his elevation from being out of print at his death to being in the canon. . . . Well, maybe he did prove his point, since his second act came in death, not life, but I think people live so long nowadays because of vitamins that they do have second acts."

"Quite possibly, sir. Life has been extended."

"You know, Jeeves, *I'm* not trying to write the Great American Novel. My ambitions aren't that far-reaching. But maybe my book will be the Great New Jersey Novel, since it's about me leaving New Jersey for New York, but always knowing in my heart that I would return to New Jersey someday, as I did when I moved in with Aunt Florence and Uncle Irwin in Montclair. Maybe that will be the end of *The Walker*—moving to Montclair and having Uncle Irwin shoot me. It will be like the end of *The Great Gatsby,* but instead of a pool, since they don't have one, he could shoot me in the tub because I'm wasting hot water. . . . I'd like to be killed at the end of my novel. . . . Do you think that's too morbid, Jeeves?"

"All tragedies end in death, sir."

"I do intend for it to be a comedy, but maybe the ending could be tragic."

"Very good, sir."

"Well, I'm not going to write the Great American Novel. That's for sure. I don't have to write the best book about the whole country; one state is good enough for me. Of course my first novel was also about New Jersey *and* losing my parents. Maybe I'm working on a New Jersey cycle, like Wagner and the *Ring* cycle."

"Sounds promising, sir."

"You're very patient, Jeeves. I'm sorry if I bore you with talk of my literary plans."

"Not at all, sir. I enjoy listening to you."

"Thank you, Jeeves . . . and thank you for listening to my passage."

"It was my pleasure, sir."

"Well, I had better get back to it."

"I will leave you then, sir."

"Wait, Jeeves, did you hear something? A voice? But like God—faraway and deep?"

"Yes, sir."

"This is incredible. . . . Could we both be having the same auditory hallucination?"

"No, sir. I believe what we are hearing is the loudspeaker from the racetrack. We passed the course on the way here and the races must be commencing."

"You're right, Jeeves. Thank you for clearing that up. Well, it's not too distracting, that voice; I can pretend it's my Muse. . . . Maybe in a few days, if I work well, we can go over to the track and give them some of our money."

"Very good, sir," said Jeeves, and then he breezed out of the room to let the young master resume his labors.

And so I passed my first day at the Rose Colony—happily culling through my box of notes, like picking at a roasted chicken for some skin or dark meat; typing up scenes; sipping my thin brown coffee; listening to the far-off voice of the track announcer; eating the lunch in my pail; ignoring the throb of healing in my nose; and occasionally staring at the beautiful and unexplored green estate just beyond my window.

CHAPTER 15

I take a bath, but feel terribly anxious at the thought of facing my Rose Colony colleagues ★ I put on my armor, laid out by Jeeves, but don't feel very brave ★ Jeeves comes up with a scientific system for improving self-esteem, bucking up my morale considerably ★ I sally forth

I took a short nap at five, and then it was into the tub by five-thirty to get ready for the gathering on the back terrace. I love baths, but felt nervous as I lolled there. The hot water was expanding my nose, which seemed dangerous, but more important I was quite agitated as I replayed in my mind my exchange with Murrin: "See you for temperance beverages at six!" "Sometimes, I'm intemperate . . ."

Why had I said this? Now he was going to thrust a drink into my hands, I just knew it. I should have stuck to my guns as a committed teetotaler, but I had weakened. Why was I always weakening in life and never strengthening? It must be gravity. We're always pulled down, never up. But I had to be strong. I had to figure out a way to not drink.

I had attended several AA meetings in the rehab and a few when I moved to Montclair, but I had stopped going for one simple reason: I wasn't ready to quit, I loved drinking too much. Perhaps that's two reasons. Anyway, I wanted to stop now. My nose had been reduced to splinters because of booze, and everything that had gone wrong in my life could be traced back to alcohol. And if I got drunk at the Rose Colony, I would surely screw something up. So I tried to remember some of the things I had heard in the meetings, despite my best efforts not to hear anything, and a few AA notions, as I understood them, did come to mind:

(1) That life got better without booze—this was encouraging to consider and seemed like it must be true, especially if booze was always leading to blackouts and broken noses and other such mishaps.

(2) That I had a physical allergy to the stuff, which made it impossible for me to control my intake—this definitely appeared to be the case. I almost never had one or two drinks, except if there wasn't more available, which was always profoundly frustrating.

(3) That if I didn't pick up the first drink, I wouldn't get drunk—this one I sloshed around in the brain for a while; it seemed of vital importance. All right, Blair, I said to myself, just don't take one drink and you won't get in trouble here at the Rose Colony.

But this was high math. Some kind of physics of behavior. If you don't take the first drink, you won't get drunk. But how do you not pick up that first drink?

I couldn't remember them covering that in the meetings. I scrambled for the answer. Surely they had gone over this. It was essential. But I couldn't bring anything to mind. I hadn't been paying proper attention! I had missed the most crucial lesson: *I didn't know how NOT to pick up the first drink!* This was a nightmare! It was like that terrible dream where you have to take an exam but have forgotten to attend class all semester, which is made worse by the fact that you're not even in college anymore, and so in some sort of mad dream-logic you think the degree you've had all these years is fraudulent, confirming a core belief about yourself—your inherent charlatan nature.

I put my face in my wet hands. My fingers were shriveled, like a child's. I *was* a child! A pitiful little thing. I was infantilized by my own stupidity. I had no idea how not to drink. I wished someone would help me. I felt wildly distraught.

But then this feeling of distress lifted because suddenly solutions began to present themselves: All I had to do was skip the first drink and get right to the second drink. Or just call the first drink "the second drink." Simply rename it. I was a writer: I was allowed to play with language. After all, they said in AA, "Don't pick up the first drink." They didn't say anything about the second drink. Or I could just pick up two at once and guzzle them at the same time. This way I wouldn't be going contrary to their advice.

Then I was distraught again. See what I was up against? Sick thinking! I had started out trying to firm up my resolve to *not* get drunk and then came up with a plan *to get* drunk. Madness! But there was a root cause for this crazy thinking: How could I face these people at the Rose without taking a drink? I'd be a complete failure:

(1) I would be boring.
(2) I wouldn't be able to talk.
(3) I wouldn't fit in.
(4) They'd see that I was dumb and ugly.

But if I had a drink, I'd be charming, not at all boring, and I'd be attractive, or so my warped brain told me. But my warped brain did have ammunition: I *was* ugly. I had a swollen nose and two black eyes. And there were going to be women! Maybe my dream girl.

Well, I was up against it, that's for sure. Things were looking very dark. My mind was cleaved: I wanted to drink, but I knew I shouldn't. It was agonizing to be so conflicted.

I emerged from the tub and trudged to my room with my towel wrapped around me. Jeeves had laid out my clothes on the bed: check sport coat, light green Brooks Brothers shirt, blue tie with hummingbirds, khaki pants.

"Excellent ensemble, Jeeves," I said, trying to show a brave front.

"Thank you, sir."

I glued on my costume. It somewhat buoyed my spirits. The hummingbird neckwear may have been laced with an antidepressant. Also, a good tie, by cutting off the flow of blood to the brain, can often enhance one's mood.

I perfected my noose, got the knot just right, and was ready to sally forth courageously. But then I couldn't. Not enough blood had been cut off by the tie. The mind still operated. I sat on the bed.

"Don't want to go, Jeeves," I said.

"Why, sir?"

"Not feeling very good about myself."

"This is unfortunate, sir."

"Makes me want to drink. I don't think I can face these people without alcohol."

"I think it is very important, sir, that you not drink. We concluded as much after the incident in Sharon Springs."

"I know, but it's not easy, Jeeves. I feel savagely insecure."

"I'm sorry to hear this, sir."

"You see, Jeeves, I don't know how to behave in a group setting. One-on-one, I can do quite nicely, but add a few people and have it resemble anything like a party and I fall apart. I don't know what role to play, though I'd like it to be one of those roles with an arrowhead over the ô. A rôle. That appeals to me. Feels leading man in an erotic, European way. . . . But I don't know how to get assigned such a part. . . . So I'm afraid I'll drink. But at least when I drink, I can speak to people. . . . Oh, Jeeves, we're in the soup again. I know it!"

"You don't have to drink, sir. It is absolutely unnecessary."

"But they won't like me!"

"If I may suggest, sir, why not try cultivating a more imperious attitude. Try thinking of yourself as vastly superior to all those whom you will meet tonight."

"Do you think this is wise, Jeeves? Superior types are not very pleasant."

"I'm hoping, if you may allow me, sir, to bring you to something of a middle ground. By thinking yourself superior you will compensate for the low feelings you have and will perhaps find yourself properly relating to others as an equal, of no more or less worth."

"A kind of pulley system, Jeeves? Yank up the self-loathing with self-importance to a fighting weight of general humility?"

"Precisely, sir."

"You're something of a wonder. You know that, don't you, Jeeves?"

"I am merely trying to assist you, sir."

"Well, if no one's told you lately: you're a wonder. I would like to give you an out-of-body experience for your birthday, whenever that is. But I know you don't want one. So I'll have to come up with something else. . . . An electric shoe buffer? . . . Anyway, you've helped me immensely. This pulley idea is brilliant! I'm going to march down there and face these people. I'll think I'm greater, secretly know I'm lesser, and come across as a nice chap. And the result will be: no drinking, a decent meal, conversation with artists, and then as soon as dinner is over, I'll come up here, read Anthony Powell or maybe Hammett or Raymond Chandler, I have one of his books with me, and go to bed early. Then back to the novel tomorrow. That's what's really important: the novel! I have to live for the novel. All else is immaterial."

"Very good, sir."

"Well, I'm off then." I got up from the bed. "Oh, thank you, Jeeves," I said, as he handed me my sunglasses and floppy Woolworth's hat. "These *are* necessary. That Murrin fellow said it would make me mysterious. Maybe that's good."

"One more thing, sir."

"Yes, Jeeves?"

"Your mustache, sir, is improving each day."

"Thank you, Jeeves! Very kind of you to say so. That information is certainly helpful for my new imperious attitude. I guess my mustache is like the Eiffel Tower: at first met with resistance and then appreciated."

"I would agree, sir."

"Well, thanks as always, Jeeves, for boosting my morale."

"You're welcome, sir."

"I'm going to sally forth now. . . . Do you think Sally Forth would be a good stage name for an actress?"

"Quite winning, sir."

"I agree. If I ever meet an actress with a terrible name, I'll suggest Sally Forth. Or any woman with a terrible name. Doesn't have to be an actress."

"Very good, sir."

CHAPTER 16

Murrin collects me and makes a favorable comment ★ We go to the main hall and I am impressed by its museum-quality elegance ★ I meet a poetic pair and witness a muscular kiss ★ I am introduced to everyone, including three senior citizens and a writer whose work I admire and who happens to look like a pirate on the high seas ★ A young girl beckons and I follow

I sallied forth all the way to the bottom of the staircase, had a case of jitters, and was going to sally right back to Jeeves's bosom and suggest we skip out and get dinner in town, but at the bottom of the stairs I was met by the diminutive Murrin.

"Was just coming to fetch you, in case you were feeling shy," he said, and his light blue eyes were rather electric until one got used to the glare. "The first night here is always the hardest, like most things in life."

I wasn't sure if he was speaking epigrammatically or flirtatiously. Regardless, I tacked forward—with my own adverb—diplomatically. "Very kind of you to be concerned," I said, though inwardly I was cursing him for having sought me out. I couldn't go through with this first night of drinks and dinner. Jeeves's pulley system was already too hard to operate: I've never been mechanically inclined.

"I just want to assure you that you don't have to feel nervous," said Murrin. "Everyone is always so scared their first night. But no one's going to bite. And you're looking fine with that hat and sunglasses, and I didn't say it before, but I like your mustache. I haven't seen a thin one like that for some time."

This compliment, so soon after Jeeves's compliment, worked on me like a shot of B_{12}—my spine, which had been ready to dis-

135

solve, seemed to firm up. I stopped my inward cursing of Murrin. He was a generous person. A kind remark from a fellow human being is one of the greatest gifts you can receive. I need to hand out more of them myself. The price is certainly reasonable.

"Yes," I said. "My mustache seems to be getting positive reviews from most critics. Have you seen *Gunga Din*? I modeled this lip hair after Fairbanks Jr."

"Really? I'm sure I saw *Gunga Din* as a boy, but I can't picture Douglas Fairbanks Jr., or Senior for that matter. . . . Well, let's go meet everyone."

Murrin then led me down a paneled service hallway, which twisted and turned a few times, the kind of thing that is expected of service hallways in mansions, until we emerged into a grand chamber, the main hall, which was the size of two basketball courts end to end, to put things in a layman's sporting terms.

There were beautiful old carpets; a very high ceiling with lacquered timber beams; a broad, red-carpeted staircase that made most other staircases I had met look woefully malnourished by comparison; gigantic pastoral oil paintings; lush antique couches and chairs; a tinkling marble fountain, which was next to the original oaken front door; antique vases with fresh-cut roses and irises; and all of it, except the flowers of course, preserved from the end of the nineteenth century for late-twentieth-century artists to mingle in. It was like a museum diorama, but for once in life you got to step over a red rope and live in the past.

Off this main hall, Murrin pointed out, was a chapel with old wooden pews, now used for concerts, and there was also a drinks room, where people could gather for cards or Scrabble if they didn't want to meet in the mudroom. The dining hall was across from the chapel, but I couldn't see it just yet as its enormous sliding wooden door wouldn't open until six-thirty, at which time a dinner gong would be sounded. Up the main staircase, Murrin told me, was a library, a number of lounges, and a dozen or so bedrooms, with another dozen bedrooms on the third and fourth floors.

Quite striking, at the far end of the main hall, was a splendiferous wooden chair, built like a throne. It even had a little roof with elaborate carvings—very unusual to see a chair with its own roof.

Beside the chair was an enormous picture window—about the size of half a tennis court—that looked on to the back terrace.

But what was most notable about this throne was that perched on its red-velvet cushions were two dark-haired men of equal size, one on the lap of the other, and their mouths were conjoined in a rather passionate kiss.

Despite my frequent querying of the Homosexual Question, I had never before that moment actually seen two men kissing quite like that. I may have observed a quick peck between males on a West Village street corner, but French-kissing by two lovers of the Greek arts was something completely new. The twin aspect of this embrace was what struck me. It was not like seeing a man kiss a woman: the large encompassing the small, the coarse fusing with the delicate. Rather, this was like arm wrestling between two equally matched opponents. Furthering this metaphor, they looked, to me, like human biceps sucking on each other, and perhaps this was my feeling because they were wearing tight T-shirts and their muscular arms were squeezing the life out of one another.

"That's Luc and Chris," said Murrin with some disdain. "They've just met. Going a bit wild. Some people are upset about it."

Then the two people I had seen earlier in the day came down the red staircase holding hands. It was the man with the cockeyed glasses and slack shoulders, and the woman with the copper hair and tormented face.

Murrin made the introductions: "This is Alan Blair, a young novelist, and this is June and Israel Greenberg, both poets." My initial assessment earlier in the day was correct: they *were* poets! A married poetic couple!

Up close they seemed much less deranged than when I had passed them in the Caprice, though the physical and psychic hardship of the artistic life was in marked evidence. But they had each other, which, I imagine, was a great comfort. Even if life had gotten the best of them, they weren't alone, and they were certainly very sweet to me in their remarks of welcome and the friendly smiles they directed at my person. So I shouldn't have judged them on the wreckage of their bodies—their souls, one immediately perceived, were gentle and kind, probably because they had been so beaten. A prolonged crushing in life often results in a humble nature, though it can just as often cause bitterness and defeated rage.

The four of us headed outside, passing the throne where Chris and Luc continued to hold each other, though none of us looked directly at them, granting them privacy, even if they didn't want it.

Outside, there was quite a festive gathering, and the air was warm, but sweet, and the end-of-the-day light infused things with a murmur of color, a summer rouge. Almost all the colonists, nearly forty people, were present. The back terrace was long and wide, like an Olympic swimming pool—it's difficult, I find, to give a sense of size without referring to the measured world of athletics—and was made of gray flagstone. There were green plastic chairs and several green plastic tables populated with bottles of wine and stacks of clear plastic cups. There were also flagstone benches around the edges of the terrace, and people languished in various sitting positions or stood and chatted. Everyone had a clear plastic cup in hand, filled with yellow liquid—jaundiced white wine!

Murrin took me around, introducing me to people, and I was nervously proceeding as best I could and was too busy surviving to feel superior. Murrin wanted me to meet everyone, so we didn't linger for small talk, just a smile, an exchange of names and mediums—novelist, sculptor, composer, poet, painter, nonfiction writer—and that was it, though after we would part from each visual artist, Murrin would give me a quick sketch of their work. It appeared that the painters and sculptors all had a signature style, a gimmick, as it were—the sculptor who built children's models without directions, the painter who made portraits of portraits, the sculptor who made sculptures out of paint, the painter who created paint-by-number canvases and allowed his patrons to daub on the color, and so on.

I noted that not a single other male was in jacket or tie, or even just a jacket for that matter, but I wasn't terribly surprised, since most men don't have sport coats of the right weight for a warm summer evening. But despite everyone being casually dressed, the setting and atmosphere were undeniably glamorous: the diminishing sunlight, the Mansion looming behind us. Most everyone was recently showered—hair wet, eyes shining, skin blushing. And the light was flattering for all of us, even the sweet Greenbergs glowed. Everyone was excited and aroused. They were all happy to be out of their lives for a little while, to playact, to live the way the wealthy had lived one hundred years before—drinks before dinner on the terrace of a mansion.

And even though I wasn't using Jeeves's pulley system, I was doing all right. On the handshake front, I was actually excelling—not once were my fingers squeezed in a way that I found embarrassing, which is usually a worry of mine when I shake hands.

Furthermore, no one seemed to be bothered by my costume of hat and sunglasses. In fact, there was one tall, melancholy fellow, a middle-aged writer, who was wearing an eye patch. His getup was certainly stranger than my own, which made things, I felt, easier for me. He was dressed in a rather unassuming manner—jeans, a white oxford shirt—but one rarely comes across eye patches these days, so I must have looked, in my hat and glasses, relatively sane and normal by comparison. And it was after Murrin had led me away from this pirate-writer that I realized why his name—Reginald Mangrove—was familiar. I had read and enjoyed one of his books, *Hell Is Other People,* and I almost never read contemporary literature, lagging behind, as I am, with all the old masters. So I looked forward to speaking further with R. Mangrove.

As I met everyone, I was surprised to observe that I was one of the younger people present. Most of the artists and writers ranged from their forties to their sixties—Murrin, for example, was in his sixties— and there were two intriguing senior-senior citizens who appeared to be in their late seventies or early eighties. One was an ancient woman who had high cheekbones and a beautiful head of white hair. She wore a long, flowing blue dress and had enough makeup on to paint a small yacht, but I could see that she had been a great beauty once. Her lipstick was bloodred and she leaned on a cane. She was a painter, though according to Murrin she was legally blind, which is a term I've never fully understood. Are such people arrested if they leave the house without their glasses? The other elder was a silver-haired, graceful fellow with an exceptionally long and gorgeous nose—he was a Pulitzer prizewinning poet.

There was a smallish contingent—about ten—of younger people, in my age range of late twenties to early thirties, and we were equally divided between the two existing genders, but there was only one young poetess, when I had been expecting a whole squadron. The other young women, it turned out, were all visual artists.

The lone poetess, though, was rather comely—a waifish ballerina type with strawberry blonde hair, and she was talking with a pretty, young photographess when Murrin made our introductions.

Side by side, these two young women—neither of them, I should add, was my dream girl—looked like workers at a health-food store, dressed as they were in some latter-day hippie apparel. The poetess was in a thin peasant's frock and the lenswoman wore a tie-dyed shirt, and one of them was definitely giving off the distinctive aroma of patchouli.

Murrin introduced me to a few more people, and after I had met almost all my fellow colonists—all that remained were a handful who had not come for drinks—Murrin said, "You're not drinking, right?"

"Yes, not drinking," I said with strength and resolve.

"I'm afraid there's no club soda tonight," he said, "but I'll see if I can pick some up for tomorrow night. And maybe cranberry juice. Would that be good?"

"That's very nice of you, but don't trouble yourself."

"Well, I'll see what I can do. . . . And now *I'm* going to indulge. I hope you don't mind."

"No, of course not," I said, and I was glad that Murrin, after all my worries in the tub, wasn't being pushy at all on this matter of tippling.

He left me then to procure for himself a bottle and plastic cup from one of the green tables. I could see he wanted me to fend for myself, like letting an animal out in the wild and hoping it will survive.

So my first act of fending was to walk over to the edge of the terrace, engage no one, and ensure that I would engage no one by turning my back to the crowd.

Everyone was chatting away behind me, and to show them that I was a self-contained, thoughtful person, I pretended to take in the lush green lawn and the marble nymphs in the distance.

I pretended so well that I actually did begin to take in the lush green lawn and the marble nymphs in the distance. I found it all rather pastoral and soothing and was startled when there was a tap on my shoulder. I turned, expecting it to be Murrin having come already to rescue me.

But it was the young female photographer. Diane was her name. She had dark hair and pretty features—large, heavy-lashed brown eyes, a perfect straight nose, a sprinkling of freckles, and full, seductive lips. Her chin was a little strong and her teeth were crowded, but these imperfections were attractive. To go with her tie-dyed shirt, she wore a short, faded pink skirt. She had a small, high bosom and lovely tan legs that ended in rubber sandals. My nose determined that she was not the one doused in patchouli.

"Do you want a glass of wine?" she asked. She held a bottle and a plastic cup.

"Oh no, thank you," I said.

This seemed to stump her momentarily. She rallied. "So how are you doing? Are you freaking out to be here?"

I recognized her argot to be that of my generation. I paused, then said, "Enough about me. How are you?"

A friend had once used this remark on me when I inquired how he was doing, and I had always wanted to try it, but the humor of it failed to impress Diane. I didn't know if she was humorless or if I was humorless. My remark only seemed to indicate to her that I was in dire need of alcohol.

"Are you sure you don't want a drink?" she repeated. "I know it's weird the first night." She smiled at me. She was beautiful. "Are you sure you don't want one?"

She was too beautiful. I felt stabbed by loneliness. I was incapable of talking to this girl. A joke I had saved for years had failed terribly. She held the bottle and the cup. I said to myself: I'll tell her I can't drink, that I'm on medication.

"I'm taking antibiotics," I said, and feeling embarrassed for sounding like a milquetoast, I looked down at her rubber sandals and her dirty, stubbed toes, which struck me as fiercely erotic. She was a sexy female animal! I wanted to kiss those feral toes! Kiss her everywhere. "You know, I will have a glass of wine," I said suddenly. "I was only joking about the antibiotics."

I felt the sick spike of adrenaline that accompanies such willfulness. But wine, I knew, was the way to get to those toes—if I loosened up, I could have a shot at her. So yet again, like in Sharon Springs, the fascistic alcoholic impulse had taken over and spoken on my behalf. Why are fascists always such forceful speakers? Mussolini and Hitler, for example, could really hold an audience. If only liberals were that good at oratory. JFK and Martin Luther King and Lenny Bruce all were, but we know what happened to those three. I guess it's dangerous for liberals to speak well. That's probably what inhibits them.

"You *should* drink," said Diane. "You should celebrate being here." She poured and then handed me the cup. "I left mine on the table."

She started walking over to one of the tables, through the happy crowd of colonists and their floating cups of wine. She intended for me to follow her. I held my own plastic cup of yellow nitroglycerin. Some of my resolve came back. I'll just hold it, I thought. I'll fit in by holding it, but won't drink. I followed Diane. Her calves were brown from the sun and beautifully shaped. I raised the cup to my lips.

CHAPTER 17

*Cervantes and Pavlov are proved correct ★ I exhibit **Under the Volcano**-ish behavior ★ A general impression of the dining room ★ I sit with a painter, Sigrid Beaubien, the novelist Mangrove, a fiction writer named Alan Tinkle, and a poetess called Lenora ★ Conversation begins with novels but then focuses primarily on a bat problem in the Mansion ★ That old question of Asylum vs. Artist Colony briefly returns ★ I reenact a battle ★ A force of nature, in the shape of a woman, who is in possession of a remarkable nose, makes an entrance*

The dinner bell gonged just as I finished gargling that first glass of wine, at which point there was a general stampede into the Mansion. I thought of something I had read once in *Don Quixote* about artists and food, how they can't control themselves when presented with free nutrition. Well, that was the case at the Rose Colony—everything was free, including the food, and so when that bell gonged, the artists raced into the dining room, and I would have behaved similarly but my needs in that moment were elsewhere.

So while they stormed in, I smartly availed myself of another glass of wine, which I gulped down in solitude on the now abandoned terrace. I did consider that perhaps I should stick to just two glasses of wine for the evening, but this thought was like a balloon that has been let go by a child at a park. I proceeded to drink a third glass!

This drinking maneuver, while properly anesthetizing me, did affect me adversely when it came to the seating arrangements inside. There was a long table that ran down the middle of the room, which sat about twenty people, and then there were three satellite tables that had room for eight each. I ended up at one end of the large table, while Diane and the poetess, who was named Lindy, were at one of the smaller tables. I had commenced on this latest drinking campaign with the idea of gaining intimacy with Diane—we had exchanged but a few comments over my first glass of wine: she was doing a series of photographs of herself disguised as various animals, which seemed to correlate with what I had observed of her pawlike feet—but now she was, temporarily, beyond my reach. By drinking those extra glasses of wine on the terrace, I had missed an opportunity to sit with her, but the alcohol was a pleasing mistress in its own right. Its first kisses—that initial rush of intoxication—were, as always, delightful, though inevitably the wine was sure to turn on me.

But regardless of what alcoholic doom might await me, I was presently in a good mood—only three drinks under my belt—and the dining room was splendid. An unlit chandelier dangled in the center like an enormous diamond earring, and sunlight came through the lead-paned windows, suffusing the room with a solar-hued beauty. The walls were wood-paneled, and there were glass cases displaying antique plates that looked like works of art.

The main table, where I was sitting after getting a plate of food from the buffet line, was incredibly heavy and old, and the chairs surrounding the table were high-backed antiques, with little hungry-looking gargoyles carved into the frames.

I found myself directly across from Mangrove, the eye-patched novelist, and on my right was a short, little fiction writer, about my age, a fellow named Alan Tinkle. He had profuse curly hair and a rather manly jaw. We shared the same *prénom,* but he had been dealt an unfair blow in the surname department.

That first night we had salmon steaks, mashed potatoes, steamed spinach, and salad, and all of it quite good. There were more bottles of white wine spaced out down the middle of the long table, like traffic cones; conveniently there was a bottle right in front of me.

On my left was a female painter by the name of Sigrid Beaubien; she was in her late forties and quite pretty, in a fading-beauty way, with elegant, expressive hands, smooth bare shoulders exposed in a sleeveless tunic, a long pale-white face, and jet-black hair, pulled tight to her skull. She readily engaged me in conversation.

"I always like to meet the new arrivals, so I welcome you," she

144

said as she picked at her salmon, removing bones. "Every few days there's someone new, but also someone leaves. It's sad. Someone is born and someone dies."

"Dying is a severe way to look at it, don't you think?" said Mangrove from across the table.

"It feels like dying to me," she said. "I hate it when I leave here every summer. I can't believe that it will go on without me. . . . Alan here is our newborn." She smiled at me in an eerie fashion and she spoke in a whisper, and people who speak in whispers are almost always insane. They want to draw you near so they can kill you. I drank my fourth glass of wine.

"What are you working on?" asked Mangrove, trying to save me from Beaubien. There was tension between those two. An old affair, I sensed, hung between them like a fishing line caught in a tree. I could see where they had once been attracted to each other: she was crazed in some sort of dramatic, whispery way, and he, dramatically, had only one eye. But my keen intuition said that they weren't a couple now.

"A novel," I said, answering Mangrove, and feeling loquacious because of the wine, I kept going: "I don't want to embarrass you, but I read *Hell Is Other People* and liked it very much. I'm a big fan of noir. Your character who kills people by not paying attention to them was brilliant."

"Thank you," he said, and he looked simultaneously delighted and uncomfortable to be praised publicly. His pale pink lips lifted momentarily into a smile, but his expressive nostrils twitched oddly, and then his features resumed a more normal, severe countenance. He had close-cropped black hair that was of the same color as his eye patch—there was no hint of gray, though he looked to be in his late forties. His one eye was brown.

"What are you working on now?" I asked.

"A memoir," he said. "But I'm calling it a *mem-noir*, since I'm telling my life story as a murder."

"You're so depressing, Reginald," said Beaubien. "Why don't you lighten up?"

"You're the one who said that leaving here is like dying," said Mangrove.

145

This spat between Mangrove and Beaubien was further indication of their previous alliance. But before Beaubien could reply, Mangrove was engaged by the woman next to him on the subject of bats. This woman, a somewhat rotund fifty-something poetess named Lenora, had just sat down with a second helping of spinach and didn't realize she was interrupting a fight. So Mangrove talked to Lenora, and Beaubien busied herself with some salmon, and I craned my neck to look at Diane, who was absolutely not craning her neck looking for me, which was mildly disappointing. She was busy eating and talking with Lindy. When one goes in for neck craning to spot new objects of affection, you hope to find their eyes searching for you as well, but the fact that Diane was not looking for me was not an indication, I rationally conjectured, that I had no chance to win her affection.

I turned back to my salmon and caught something of this bat parlance between Mangrove and Lenora. It seemed that the Mansion was rife with bats at night and Mangrove was the resident expert at catching them, employing a net and gloves, and this was no small feat on his part since the bats were possibly infected with rabies.

"It's ghastly," said Beaubien to me. "One was flying around my room two nights ago. I couldn't sleep at all, even after Reginald caught it."

"I like bats," said Tinkle. "They're misunderstood creatures."

"Is it true that if a person gets rabies, they shriek when they see water?" asked Beaubien.

"Rabies's scientific name is hydrophobia, which people associate as a fear of water, but I think it's called hydrophobia because of the foaming that occurs," said Mangrove. "But I'm not sure that humans foam at the mouth when they have rabies. They just die rather quickly. Bats *can* kill you if they bite you."

"See, you *are* morbid! I won't be able to sleep the rest of the summer," said Beaubien. "It's bad enough there's a ghost in this Mansion."

"There's no ghost," said Mangrove.

"I had a mouse infestation in my house," said Lenora, who wasn't all there, I felt. She had a permanent fixed smile and struck me as one of those conversational declaimers: people who make remarks that are in the general vicinity of the discussion but are not in direct response to any previous comments.

"I can't stand bats. They look like rats with wings," said Beaubien. "Flying rats."

"I once had a rat crawl up my leg in New York," I said, indulging somewhat in conversational declaiming myself, but when it comes to that rat story, I can hardly control my impulse to shock and regale and relive.

"My God," said Beaubien.

"It was racing across a sidewalk and panicked, mistook me for a lamppost or something, and went right up to my knee before it realized I was human. Luckily it didn't bite me, though my kneecap may have been difficult to sink teeth into. I don't know if I'll ever recover."

Mangrove raised an eyebrow over his eye patch as I recounted my rat story, and I very much wanted to ask him how he had lost his eye, but etiquette forbade such an inquiry.

"I'd like to be a bat," said Tinkle, not commenting on my rat speech. "Then I could sneak into people's rooms."

"I'm very happy with my room this year," said Lenora.

Beaubien chose to let out a cackle at this, thinking it funny, and I sipped from my fifth glass of wine and shuddered internally for a moment as I had the recurring thought that maybe I *was* in an asylum, after all, but I was so nuts that I kept thinking I was at an artist colony. The people around me were definitely unbalanced. Beaubien's cackle was straight out of *The Snake Pit,* there was something zany about Tinkle, Mangrove only had one eye, and Lenora's face was etched in a kind of merry grimace.

I craned my neck again and peered at Diane. She still wasn't seeking me out, but at least she wasn't mad, as far as I could tell. She was just beautiful and had dirty feet. And there was Murrin holding forth at the far end of my table with the Pulitzer prizewinning poet, and those two didn't seem to be suffering from lunacy. So the shudder passed. I *was* at an artist colony, not a loony bin. But I was going to have to talk this over with Jeeves. It was along the lines of another Problem or Question. It was the old Appearance vs. Reality Dilemma that used to show up on my Shakespeare exams at Princeton.

I tucked into the mashed potatoes to lay some sandbags down against the wine. Lenora was back to praising Mangrove for his abilities to protect everyone from the bats, and there was an overall din of conversation and scraping of forks in the air, and then Mangrove addressed me.

"Have you been in some sort of fight?"

"Yes," said Beaubien. "Your sunglasses and hat are hiding something!" There was an excited quality to her whisper; she was hungry for distraction and intrigue.

I took a healthy dose of my sixth glass of wine, then said, "It's rather embarrassing, but, yes, I was in a bar brawl."

This was a case of *in vino quasi-veritas.* I had told Murrin and Doris that a car accident was the source of my injuries, but now, drunkenly, I had spoken a half-truth, but wasn't so drunk as to tell a whole truth, to say that I had been in a fight across the street from a bar, which isn't exactly a bar brawl.

"What happened?" inquired Mangrove with a novelist's curiosity. He was definitely pro-me since I had praised *Hell Is Other People,* so his asking wasn't invasive so much as a genuine expression of interest and even concern. And this led me to think that at some appropriate juncture I could find out what had happened to him, but at the moment the focus was on me, so I said:

"Well, two nights ago, I was in a town called Sharon Springs at a bar called the Hen's Roost—"

"What a funny name," said Beaubien.

"And I was drinking and watching a baseball game, and this fellow took an alcoholic dislike to me, perhaps because I was a stranger and it was a bar of locals. Anyway, I went to the men's room and when I returned, he had taken my stool. I made the mistake of saying, 'I was sitting there,' and he shoved me. I then made the mistake of thinking that if someone shoves you, you should shove them back, and so I did, imagining that would be the end of it. I knocked him off the stool, but he certainly wasn't injured. His next action was to punch me in the face, which I had not been expecting at all, and he broke my nose immediately."

"This is worse than hearing about that rat," said Beaubien. "I can't stand it."

"Were you knocked out?" asked Mangrove.

"I didn't lose consciousness, though the punch sent me to my knees, but then I rose up and threw a roundhouse right."

I stood up then to demonstrate this. I was taking to my story like a real raconteur—I was rather intoxicated, which was making me extroverted—and I threw a vicious right hand through the air, re-creating the moment when I had struck the Hill with my decisive blow.

"And I caught him in the ear, clearly injuring him, at which point everyone converged on us and the whole thing was broken up."

A general hush had fallen over the room, as everyone sensed that something unusual was taking place, my fellow artists catching out of the corners of their eyes my hatted-and-sunglassed figure standing and pantomiming a Joe Louis right hand. I was momentarily the center of attention. Then I sat back down. Conversations around the room started back up.

"I've never been in a fight," said Mangrove.

"Let's see what you look like," said Beaubien.

"Can you get that bottle of wine?" I asked Lenora. I had finished off the bottle in front of me, and she was closest to the next bottle up the table.

I poured a glass.

"You're putting it away," said Tinkle.

"Painkiller," I said, "for my face."

"I approve," said Tinkle, smiling at me. He was a curious fellow: as tiny as Murrin, but with a jaw like Zeus.

"Will you show us?" said Mangrove.

"Please," said Beaubien.

"That's why I'm drinking," I said. "Building up my courage."

I filled the glasses of Tinkle, Mangrove, Lenora, and Beaubien— my four new friends. Even if they were crazy, I was now feeling warm toward them all; it was partly the alcohol and partly the seat-ing arrangement—that we had all been thrust together at one end of the table—but I really did like them. We clinked glasses without making a toast. Then I removed my sunglasses and Woolworth's hat. Again there was a hush in the room. The clinking had alerted the others to more strange behavior from our quarter. The other artists

149

strained to look at me, caught a glimpse of my swollen, misshapen nose and black eyes, and then their chatter recommenced.

"You look sexy to me," said Beaubien. "Very manly." And though she was a whisperer and whisperers always put my guard up, I did feel aroused by her remarks. Most men are suckers for praise. Also, she was not without her charms—pretty face, slender shoulders, an elegant neck.

"Did he hit you in the eyes?" asked Mangrove, obviously an area of interest to him.

"No," I said, "the black eyes are the runoff of blood from the nose."

"You certainly took a beating," said Mangrove.

"I've considered plastic surgery, just the wrinkles around my eyes," said Lenora, "but what if they make a mistake?"

"You're not going in for plastic surgery, are you?" Beaubien asked me. "A broken nose on a man is a sign of virility."

"No, I don't think I'll have surgery," I said, and then at that very moment a woman came into the room and there was a rush of air. Her presence was so forceful that conversations, for the third time, became muted as we all noted her late arrival. This woman headed for the food.

"Ava," said Beaubien with feline jealousy.

I took in the dimensions of this creature, and I have to say that all thoughts of Diane and my brief attraction to Beaubien were dismissed, displaced, and disregarded. I had never seen a more stunning female. She wore a simple white cotton dress that could barely contain six feet of Amazonian legs, glorious breasts, and a nose. A nose! The most incredible nose I had ever seen in my life. Enormous, bumpy, hooked, with flaring nostrils the size of shot glasses. The nose looked like some sort of mad knot on a tree, but it was in the middle of her face, which was an Italian face, an oval Roman face. Her hair was a thick brown pelt of curls, and as she swung her arms, I could see sexy hair coming out of her armpits, alongside her full Sophia Loren breasts.

But it was the nose. The nose is what did it. There's a French phrase that covers the experience of immediately falling in love with someone; it's called a *coup de foudre,* which I've always translated, perhaps incorrectly, as a piercing of the heart. Well, what I experienced when I saw Ava was just that, but with an added element—it was a *coup de foudre par le nez.* Her nose had pierced my heart. I was in love. Head over heels in love.

She filled her plate with food and walked across the room to the table behind us. I turned to look at her. She paused by her chair before sitting down and faced me directly. Rays of sunlight, coming through the windows, went right through her thin white dress. The tops of her legs were illuminated, and I don't know if I was hallucinating, but I thought I could just make out the hint of her mound, of dangling private beautiful hairs, as defined by sunlight, which would mean she was pantyless. Real or hallucinated, it was the most beautiful thing I have ever seen—this forbidden glimpse of the silhouette of her mons. I was temporarily in possession of X-ray vision. Then she sat down. In shock, I finished my eighth glass of wine.

CHAPTER 18

In the drinks room with Beaubien ★ Somewhere along the way a switch from wine to port has been made ★ I'm given something of a life story, while craving more port ★ My mustache gets another five-star review ★ I come very close to taking decisive action ★ Tinkle makes an entrance

I hadn't drunk that much, only about two bottles of wine altogether, but shortly after the vision of that nose, I lost nearly an hour and a half. This was not an unfamiliar experience during my drinking career, but my liver must really have been getting pulpy for me to go on autopilot after such a small amount.

I came out of this blackout to find myself alone with Beaubien in the drinks room, sipping a glass of port. It was half past eight and dark outside. The room was shadowy, two lamps in the corner were lit; the walls were painted a dark somber red, good for whiskey-sipping by nineteenth-century millionaires. There were various chairs and sofas keeping one another company. I scraped around in my mind for what had transpired over the last ninety minutes. Nothing floated to the surface. I must have finished my meal, had coffee and dessert, and then at some point found myself alone with Beaubien. She seemed to be in the middle of a monologue, a life story perhaps:

". . . because of what happened, I ran away from home many times. Then in my twenties, I lived on a commune in the woods of Oregon. We were all vegetarians and everyone had many lovers . . ."

I nodded politely at this, it sounded rather *As You Like It,* but I was trying to get a grip on things and couldn't give her my full attention. I checked my sport coat for vomit. None. That was good. My hat was on the floor, but this didn't seem to indicate that anything too

153

strange had occurred. My sunglasses were in my front sport coat pocket. I did feel rather sober, oddly enough, the blackout serving like some kind of alcoholic nap, but I cringed inwardly, thinking of how I was going to have to confess to Jeeves that I had fallen off the wagon with almost no resistance and had already blacked out. I hadn't even tried to conduct a masquerade of social drinking. Oh, God, I was doomed. Alcohol was going to kill me. To put such thoughts away, to recapture intoxication, I finished my glass of port, but I needed more.

Beaubien and I were on an olive-colored divan, and her bare, attractive legs were pulled up beneath her. She was wearing an elegant gray skirt and a sleeveless, peach-colored tunic. Her naked shoulders continued to be naked. I noted that she was sitting rather close to me. I desperately wanted to get my hands on some more port, but I didn't see the bottle. She was still in the middle of her whispery monologue, which seemed rather difficult to interrupt:

". . . I had my first show in Paris, which was a great success, but I was hysterical in my thirties and so I went for analysis. I slept with *many* younger men. That was flattering. Now I'm in my forties and not hysterical and would like to marry. Reginald and I used to date, but we're too alike. . . . Many women my age are having children. They say the forties are the new thirties. . . . One time I saw my analyst's notes when he had to leave the room. He had written only one thing and underlined it several times: 'borderline personality disorder.' I looked it up at the library and completely disagreed with him and stopped going. But I miss it sometimes. The things that happened to you in your childhood don't go away. You know what I mean?"

"I think so," I said. "Is there any more port?"

She pointed behind me to a sideboard with a number of bottles.

"Would you like some more?" I asked.

"Yes," she said.

Piloting myself over to the sideboard, my basic motor function seemed to be good. Legs were steady and my hand grasped the port in a commanding, purposeful manner. In my mind, I thanked my limbs for behaving so nicely. I came back with the bottle and refilled our glasses.

"Thank you, Alan," she said.

I took a swig and felt some of my earlier blissful retardation return. "You were speaking of your childhood," I said.

"My father was a terrible man. I was an unusually beautiful girl."

She put her hand on my sleeve. This was the strangest seduction I had ever experienced, especially since I was more or less coming to at some penultimate moment. Though my senses were a bit dulled, I felt that she was cryptically referring to incest and sexual abuse— "things that happened in your childhood," "terrible man," "unusually beautiful girl"—while simultaneously making a play for me. She wanted me to both pity her and desire her. I wished I could return to my blackout. She should never have quit analysis. My mind reeled. Why were so many people sexually abused? I, for one, have never found children appealing in a sensual way. Well, one time at the ocean I did find a young girl's buttocks to be extraordinarily beautiful, the way they looked in her bathing suit; she may have been only nine years old, but this was purely an aesthetic reaction, though it was a powerful one, such that I still remember it. Regardless, I am certainly not a pedophile, and if I had a young daughter, I wouldn't go into her room, as I imagined Beaubien's father must have, and commit atrocities. Poor Beaubien!

"Your mustache is so attractive," Beaubien whispered, and squeezed my arm. "I love it. I love men with mustaches."

She really did have a borderline personality disorder, though I wasn't sure of this condition's exact pathology. But I hypothesized it must have something to do with faulty borders, which was manifest in this loony confession/seduction. She was telling me too much about herself, making herself too vulnerable: she had no borders. But her hand on my arm was arousing. A woman's touch, even the touch of a woman who is nuts, can be very powerful. And the desire to console her—sexually and emotionally—activated my own lunatic sense of chivalry. Somebody had to save this mad beauty. Why not me?

But I sensed a classic dilemma forming: Do you take the woman you can have or do you try to go for the woman you really want? I wanted Ava and that nose, and short of Ava, there was still Diana and her dirty feet.

But I could have Sigrid Beaubien. Wouldn't have to risk rejection. Her hand was not lifting from my sleeve. She had praised my mustache. Her eyes were humid; they beseeched me. The pupils were so dilated there was just a rim of brown. She was insane. Possibly on drugs. She had very nice legs. She was a whisperer. Her shoulders beckoned to be grabbed in my manly fists. I imagined that she was quite good in bed in a hysterical, thrashing sort of way, though I also imagined her taking a letter opener or a scissors and gouging out one of my eyes as I lay in bed with her. I don't know why this particular image came to me, but then I wondered if maybe she had gouged Mangrove's eye.

So despite every possible warning signal—whispering, inappropriate confession, admission of psychiatric diagnosis, bragging about numerous lovers—that hand on my sleeve was a siren's call, which I was going to answer. I've always chosen the wrong romantic partners, and now was no time to change. Life is circular and repetitive; both Nietzsche and Shakespeare have confirmed this.

"I'm glad you like my *mustache,*" I said in a hushed, seductive tone, indicating with my emphasis that we were talking about more than mustaches here, and I knew that I could lean forward and kiss her. I was about to put my hand in her dark hair, to push it away from her face as an opening move. This would be my first caress, followed by the leaning in with my port-flavored mouth, but Tinkle came into the room just as I had sent out the orders to my nerve endings to begin action. With his intrusion, though, all military-sexual advancement came to a sudden halt. I did lurch a little on that divan, rocking forward as if with a myoclonic jerk, the spasm that occurs right before sleep, and Beaubien's lips, which she had just noticeably parted, were now re-formed into a tight-lipped smile.

"Am I interrupting?" asked Tinkle.

"No," said Beaubien, though she was unmistakably irritated.

"I wanted to offer Alan a welcome to the Rose Colony cigar," Tinkle said, "if he likes to smoke." Then addressing me directly: "That is, if you'd like a cigar."

"Yes, a cigar would be very nice," I said.

"We have to smoke outside. No smoking in the Mansion," he said. "But if you two are talking, I can find you later."

"Yes, we're talking," said Beaubien rather coolly.

"Could we continue later?" I asked. "I've had quite a lot to drink and going for a walk and smoke would be good for me."

This was a lie, of course. A cigar might make me very ill, but I had immediately perceived Tinkle's arrival as a sign from the gods that to kiss Beaubien on my first night at the Rose was to court disaster. Putting aside the issue of the women you want versus the women you can have, in this case Ava versus Beaubien, I knew that Beaubien was just too much for me. She was older and sexy and beautiful, but before my lips had even touched hers, I knew it would all go horrifically wrong, which, naturally, had been part of the attraction. To put my hand in a flame. So Tinkle had saved me. I stood up before Beaubien could actually grant me permission to leave, which forced her to do so.

"All right," she said. "Go smoke your cigar. But I want to keep talking to you. I'll be in here or the mudroom. Find me."

I could see there was already hurt in her eyes, that she was injured, but if I went further, it would only get worse. I was drunk, but I had some wits about me. I wasn't going to come find her later, but she'd forget about me soon enough. And I had behaved, more or less, like a gentleman, so I was in the clear. I bent down to pick up my hat and left the drinks room with Tinkle.

CHAPTER 19

*Drinking and smoking with Tinkle ★ I provide counsel, playing
the rôle of Ernest Hemingway ★ Tinkle tries to kill me*

I was in Tinkle's room on the third floor of the Mansion, smoking
one of his cigars and drinking his whiskey. After we left Beaubien, I
had casually mentioned the need for more alcohol, so we had come
up to his room to smoke instead of going for a walk, since it was in
his room that he could properly introduce me to his bottle of Wild
Turkey, which is not the most expensive whiskey, but in the right
light it can look very attractive, and Tinkle's room had the right light.

At first I had refused the cigar, but then after a sip of Tinkle's Wild
Turkey, I had put one in my mouth and was reminded of Hans Cas-
torp's affection for cigars in *The Magic Mountain,* which, as I may have
mentioned, is one of my favorite books of all time. When Hans
finally kissed Claudia Chauchat around page 600, the book literally
flew from my hands in ejaculatory pleasure. For six hundred pages
Mann had teased us with an attraction between those two! He had
been sadistically patient. Well, it was worth it. Only one other time
has a book flown from my hands, and that was when Sancho Panza
vomited in Don Quixote's mouth after Don Quixote had vomited
in Sancho's mouth. I highly recommend reading *Don Quixote* just for
that passage.

Anyway, Tinkle's lead-paned windows were open and we had a
fan blowing our cigar exhaust out into the night, since smoking
wasn't allowed in the Mansion, due to the fire hazard it posed to
such an old building. The dark summer sky was visible to me. I felt
rather at peace. I was holding my liquor, and guilty thoughts about

159

falling off the wagon had been banished. The cigar was making me feel good, not nauseous. All was well.

Like my own accommodations, Tinkle's chamber was somewhat monastic: a bed, a desk with a typewriter (Tinkle, I surmised, was an old-fashioned writer), and an easy chair, which I was at the moment inhabiting. It had a stick shift on the side for a footstool. I popped the stool, extended my legs, and admired my wing tips. I put my hat on the floor. Tinkle sat at his desk.

"Thank you for saving me from Beaubien," I said.

"Why saving? You looked to be in a good position. I feel bad for interrupting. I'd go for her in a heartbeat."

I had misspoken—had nearly besmirched Beaubien's character. To rally out of that, I compensated with an admission. "Well, you see, I have my eye on Ava. Her nose is extraordinary."

"You have a thing for her nose?"

"I think I do."

"I also have sexual problems," said Tinkle.

"I'm not sure my thing for Ava's nose qualifies as a sexual problem. It's a very beautiful nose."

"I'm sorry," said Tinkle.

"That's all right," I said.

"But I really do have sexual problems," said Tinkle.

"I understand," I said.

"Can I talk to you about something personal?"

I was enjoying the man's tobacco and whiskey, the least I could do was to provide some counsel, though I wondered if everyone at the Rose was so forthcoming. First Beaubien and now Tinkle. But it made sense: I was new on campus and they were probably desperate for a friend. I popped the footstool down, to show that I was serious and sympathetic. "Tell all," I said to Tinkle.

He leaned forward. His posture was confessional. "I'm like a broken water pistol," he said. "I fire sideways."

"Have you seen a urologist?" I asked, and I didn't say it, but I wondered if Tinkle's name had subconsciously caused him to suffer in this area. Growing up, I knew a girl with the surname Hiney, and this probably shaped her destiny. She was relatively normal-looking but she was reviled. I remember her singing a solo in the fourth-grade choir and someone screamed out derisively, "Hiney!" Everyone in the auditorium laughed and the poor girl's will was broken. Up until that point she had been singing beautifully. I had even thought for a moment, with some kind of nine-year-old's intuition, that her lovely singing voice might erase the years of ridicule. But some bully must have sensed the same thing—*Hiney!*—and robbed her of her triumph. I wonder what's become of her. Her family moved after the fifth grade. Maybe they went to a foreign country where the name Hiney wasn't a detriment. That's the best one can hope. A name can determine a great deal. Look at Jeeves, poor fellow. Very hard for people to take him seriously.

"My problem isn't physical," said Tinkle. "It's not something a urologist could help me with."

"Well, if you're shooting sideways, that sounds physical to me. . . . I'll have some more whiskey."

In my mind, this was like when Fitzgerald had consulted Hemingway on the size of his—Fitzgerald's—genitals, at least that's what Hemingway reported in *A Moveable Feast.* So I played Papa to Tinkle's Scott. He poured me some more whiskey.

"Now explain to me how shooting sideways is not a urological, physical issue?" I asked, and I wondered if I should bring up, after all, the Hiney story, point him in the direction of uncovering the possible name-related psychosomatic root to his problem, but it also occurred to me that perhaps his organ had somehow become bent. Maybe a bicycle accident? Or perhaps a rapidly descending toilet seat had gotten the best of him. I had heard of such things happening and had narrowly avoided that guillotinish fate myself a few times. Every now and then people idiotically put rugs or some kind of quilt-work on the back of toilet seats, and such coverings cause the lids to be unpredictable and spastic. Only lightning-quick reflexes have saved me during these crises. Perhaps Tinkle didn't have such good reflexes.

"I guess it's more that I misfire without provocation," said Tinkle. "Things set me off. I have orgasms when I don't want to."

"So you're not shooting sideways?"

"No."

"Why did you say sideways, then?"

161

"Maybe because it happens in my pants and I'm constrained."

"So sideways does come into it, but not because of structural damage. . . .What sets you off, then? A woman's perfume? That often arouses me. Or a hint of a woman's body odor?"

"No. Body odor could do it, but I usually don't get that close to a woman."

"You don't always have to be so close. I once went into a stationery store and the girl behind the cash register had exposed armpits and was fumigating the place. But I loved the smell. Responded priapically. I nearly misfired, myself. I lingered in there for a long time, pretending to be interested in a fountain pen that was also a cigarette lighter. She was ordinary-looking but her smell was incredible. She may have known this and didn't bathe to compensate for her plain features. I did return there at least twice, wanting to just breathe in her fragrance, arouse myself, and rush home. Except she was never there again. Frustrating when things like that happen. Very difficult sometimes to figure out a stranger's schedule."

"Like I said, a smell can trigger me. But it doesn't have to be as obvious as that. See that thermos lid?" asked Tinkle. There was indeed the lid of a thermos on the floor. It was upside down and could be used as a drinking cup.

"That sets you off?"

"It could."

"What about it? The shape? That fact that it's a receptacle?"

"No. The shape doesn't matter. I sexualize everything. A shoelace. A lamp."

I eyed the thermos lid, submitting it to a test of attractiveness, to see if I had the same condition as Tinkle, but I found it simply to be a lid, though I was intrigued by this notion of finding all things erotic. I don't know if it was the booze, but I sort of wished that I could find thermos lids sexy. I looked at it again. The oval nature was appealing, but that's as far as it went. I looked at his desk lamp. Nothing. I resumed my counseling session with Tinkle.

"You're not having an orgasm right now, are you?" I asked without judgment, like a scientist.

"No, whiskey dulls it. That's why I drink a lot."

"How many orgasms a day do you manufacture?"

"Along with heavy drinking, I do preventive masturbation four or five times a day so that I can go out in public."

This all sounded oddly familiar. Then I reassured myself: I might have shared some of his symptoms, but that can be said for most psychiatric illnesses.

"Why do you think this has happened to you?" I asked. "Maybe you should see Oliver Sacks. It could be neurological. Like the man who thought his wife was a cocktail waitress."

"I don't get any sex. That's my problem. I'm thirty-one; I haven't had sex in nine years."

What could I say to comfort him? Nine years was a terribly long time. One hardly goes nine years without doing most things, except maybe trips to the Far East. So nine years without something as meaningful to a person's sense of well-being as sex was a dire stretch. Poor Tinkle! I had recently gone about seven months—the duration of my posting in New Jersey—but that was nothing compared with what Tinkle had endured.

"What about going to a prostitute?" I asked.

"No. I'd fall in love."

"You're a romantic. That's admirable. But you had better give it up. Going to a prostitute is better than walking around having orgasms because of thermos lids and lamps and shoelaces."

"It would be too depressing that the only way I can have sex is to pay for it."

"Listen, if everyone thought that way, a whole industry would collapse. It's not depressing! Well, maybe for a few minutes afterward, but it's worth it. Especially in your situation."

"I can't. I'd feel bad for the woman."

Tinkle was stubborn on this issue. What the hell could I do for him? I wished I could get Jeeves to help me figure this one out, though I didn't think the pulley system would work on such a severe case.

"Do you go on dates?" I asked.

"Sometimes, but I never get a second date, or if they go out with me at all, it's only out of pity. And now I'm liable to come if they even stand next to me or if I see them handling a fork. So I haven't gone on a date in a year. I'm dangerous."

"You're a good-looking guy," I said. "I don't understand."

Tinkle just stared at me, imploring me with his eyes not to force him to bring up the issue of his height. He was fairly attractive—he had nice curly hair, the jaw of a longshoreman, and the stocky body of a wrestler. But, like Murrin, he *was* terribly short, though it hadn't made him homosexual, as far as I could tell; everything he said pointed to a desire for intercourse with females. Nevertheless, I did think of suggesting homosexuality to Tinkle, as a sort of temporary solution, but this struck me as an injurious proposal. Also, just because he was short didn't mean he couldn't get a woman, though it no doubt made things more difficult. After all, it's nearly impossible for a person of normal height to get a woman. But something had to be done for Tinkle. I decided to hammer away at him on the prostitute angle. He needed to know that he could function like a man and not a leaky water pistol. This would be the first step of his recovery.

"I really think going to a brothel would be the best thing for you," I said. "Would demystify the whole act and recalibrate you so that you only find women appealing and not objects. And it will give you some confidence. If money is an issue, I'll happily advance you five hundred dollars. I received a settlement a few months ago and my wallet is bursting at the seams. Let's get a good one. This is a horse town. The racing season has started. There's bound to be beautiful women who will take care of you, get you working properly again. I stayed in a shabby place last night, but I saw some fancy hotels on the main drag. We'll go to one of those places, sit at the bar, drink, and discreetly ask the bartender how to proceed."

I saw myself and Tinkle, my little companion, at an elegant bar, two beautiful women approaching. Perhaps I, too, would indulge. In the past, when I'd first moved to New York, I'd had a few experiences in that realm, mostly disastrous, but initially it's always pleasant, a sort of a revelation to cut right to the chase with a woman. Still, Tinkle was right: you felt bad for the prostitute, no matter how jaded she might be, and afterward you were terribly depressed. But maybe this time in Saratoga it would be better. That's always the lure, though, *this time it will be better, different,* which seems to be the hook with most vices. Gambling, sex, alcohol, drugs, Chinese food—you always give these things a second chance or a hundredth chance, but something healthy, like kayaking, if you don't go for it the first time, you never try again.

"I can't go to a prostitute," said Tinkle. "I know I'll fall in love. I'm pathetic. Also, I have another problem which I should tell you about. . . . But the coming *is* getting worse. I have wet dreams every night, no matter how much I drink or masturbate. Last night I dreamt that I saw two dogs humping and that made me come. I'm afraid to go to sleep tonight. What if I dream of lobster claws?"

"More whiskey," I said. My ability to empathize was getting the best of me; I couldn't take much more of Tinkle's misery. I felt a black depression inching around the edges of what had previously been a good mood. Lobster claws! The man's psyche was booby-trapped. He poured me two more inches of Wild Turkey. "Were you one of the dogs, or just watching?" I asked.

"Just watching. And when the dog finished, I finished."

"What's your other problem?" I whispered. I inwardly shielded myself for another blow; I don't know how Freud and Jung did this for a living.

"I have hyperhidrosis," Tinkle said.

"What's hyperhidrosis?" I asked.

"I sweat too much."

"Were you actually diagnosed by a doctor?"

"Yes."

"How do you get hyperhidrosis?"

"Genetics. And stress. Stress sets up the genetics."

"All right, you sweat a lot. Extra showering and deodorant, that's all. Maybe a pill. They give incontinent people pills to dry them up. Maybe you could take one of those."

"Nothing works. But it's just not sweating from the armpits. My hands are incredibly moist. It's disgusting. If I touch a woman, she'll think I'm a sponge."

"What about nine years ago? Who did you sleep with then?"

"An older woman. A lesbian."

"If she was with you, then she was bisexual, not a lesbian."

"She was more lesbian than bisexual. She had never been with a man. I was a six-month experiment. Now she's back to being a lesbian."

"Well, she reverted to form after a pleasant six months with you. More important, what did she think of your hands?"

"She didn't mind."

Tinkle looked completely defeated as he recalled his love affair. I wondered if it had been the extent of his sexual experience. "Is she the only woman you've ever been with?"

"Yes. The only woman I've been with was a lesbian."

"Listen, there are a lot of fellows who would die to be able to say that. . . . You have to focus on the positive: she didn't mind your hands. This hyperhidrosis can't be that bad. Let me shake your hand."

He shook his head no.

"Come on. Please. I have to see if you're exaggerating."

He went to wipe his hand on his pants. "No," I said, stopping him. "I want the full effect."

We shook hands. His hand *was* very slick and chilled. It did feel like a sponge. I said nothing. I didn't know how the guy could take it. I couldn't take it. I felt myself mentally crumbling. I finished my whiskey. Tinkle poured me some more.

"I have to use pens that aren't water-soluble," he said. "I try to avoid shaking hands or at least give my pants a quick wipe. . . . One time I was on a date, it was winter, and I was in this woman's car. She kept asking me why my side of the windshield was fogging up. I said the defrost must be broken. This is what I live with."

"The hyperhidrosis fogged up a window?"

"Yes."

"You're like a superhero," I said, trying to summon a smidgeon of enthusiasm for his affliction. "You cause windows to fog, ink to run. You're a force of nature. That's a positive way to look at it."

"I do think positively about it. It's a curse and a gift. . . . God knew I would always be alone so he made me self-lubricating."

Tinkle gave a maudlin smile, then said, "There's one more thing."

I slumped deep into the chair. I nodded my assent, like a slave stoically taking another lash from his Roman master.

"I saw a spot the other day on the *head*," said Tinkle, laying into me, not holding back. Cruel Tinkle! I wasn't cut out for this kind of treatment. "I think I have penile cancer. When something gets overused, the cells begin to fragment. That might be what's happening."

"You need to see a doctor," I lisped. My voice was barely audible. Tinkle had defeated me. I was psychically destroyed. I was no Hemingway. This latest announcement pushed me over the edge.

"They'll probably have to cut off my penis," Tinkle said, reveling in his martyrdom and further destroying me mentally. "My life will be over before I've even had a life."

"Don't speak this way; it's not healthy," I croaked.

"Don't worry, I have a plan," said Tinkle. "I'm going to turn into a bat. I'm going to burn a cork and put blackface on, like Al Jolson. I'm going to sneak into women's rooms here in the Mansion and they'll never see me."

"Please tell me you're joking," I pleaded. Tinkle was either insane or madly drunk or both.

"No, I'm going to become a bat. It will be a performance piece. Everyone is scared of the bats here."

"You're not going to molest anyone, are you?"

"No, I'll just stand in the shadows unseen. They don't see me now. It'll be the same thing."

"Listen, this is crazy. Forget this bat business and penile cancer business. I'm sure you're fine. I'm always seeing things on my penis that aren't there. Everyone does. It comes with having a penis. . . . Please . . . you don't have cancer and you don't have to impersonate a bat. You have to think about your work, your writing." I waved my hand in the direction of his typewriter. "Live for that. I've had a number of setbacks myself lately—look at my face—but as long as I keep working on my novel, everything will be all right. So forget about sex and crazy performance pieces. What is it you're working on?"

"It's like Mangrove's book, but a little different."

"What is it? Tell me," I begged. The fellow's life had to have some purpose.

"A novel in the form of a suicide note."

The pain came to an end right about then.

I blacked out.

CHAPTER 20

A talk with Jeeves about detaching with love, as opposed to detached retinas ★ I give a speech on the possible interpersonal application of the lifeguard motto

"Oh, Jeeves," I said. I was in bed. It was morning. My brain was a blister and my mouth was an old leather wallet without any money.

"Yes, sir?"

"Oh, Jeeves . . ."

"Yes, sir?"

"Stop it, Jeeves. Please. I'm sick. I'm not fit for a duet."

"Yes, sir."

"Please, Jeeves. No more yes, sirs."

"Very good, sir."

I closed my eyes. I thought I might vomit. I steadied myself with a yoga breath.

"Some water, Jeeves."

Jeeves vanished. Went to the bathroom and returned with a glass of water. I propped myself on an elbow and got down all of that nourishing cocktail of two parts hydrogen, one part oxygen. Sunshine lit the edges of my thin, white curtains and gave the room a yellow, early-morning glow. I looked at my travel clock: only seven-thirty. I unpropped myself and lay down flat.

"Well, Jeeves, disaster has struck again."

"I can imagine, sir."

"I fell off the wagon."

"I know, sir."

"Do you hate me, Jeeves?"

"Of course not, sir."

"But you should. I went back on the booze. It wasn't even forty-eight hours."

"Your behavior, sir, is undeniably alcoholic."

"Then you should hate me, Jeeves."

"No, sir, I am detached."

"Like a retina? You won't look at me?"

"Not exactly, sir. I once overheard your aunt Florence speaking to your uncle Irwin about the philosophy behind the Al-Anon meetings she attended. She told him that she was detaching from you with love."

"What do you think that means, Jeeves?"

"That she loved you, sir, but there was little she could do for you. She was acknowledging that she felt helpless to aid you, but that your self-destructive behavior did not preclude her from loving you—at a safe remove."

"So she didn't hate me for being alcoholic?"

"Correct, sir."

"And you don't hate me?"

"Yes, sir."

"Yes, you do hate me, or, yes, you don't hate me?"

"I don't hate you, sir."

"Sorry to make you spell things out, Jeeves. I've sawed my IQ in half with all the liquor I consumed."

"I understand, sir."

I felt dismal. Nauseous. Brain pinched by dehydration. Morally defeated. Nose throbbing.

Jeeves stood patiently by my side. Sunlight continued to illuminate the borders of the curtains, like a flame curling the edges of a piece of paper. I did some more yoga breaths, trying to heal myself.

But then suddenly a terrible ice pick of fear shot through my consciousness. I couldn't recall how I had got back to the room or what had happened after that insane Tinkle had driven me to the point of collapse. Might I have gotten into some kind of mischief? It had happened before during my blackouts. In college, I had, according to my friends, smashed my head into the glass of a beautiful antique wall clock in one of the more elegant Princeton eating clubs and said, "Time has no effect on me!" Sober I would never have damaged an old clock or made such a vainglorious pronouncement.

And one time in New York, I had been in a bar in the East Sixties, watching a boxing match around 10 P.M., and that was the last thing I remembered until I came to a little after 4 A.M. when I was found beneath a parked car on Eldridge Street on the Lower East Side. It was November and quite frigid and I had lost my overcoat. All that was protecting me from the elements was my wonderful and faithful Brooks Brothers gray tweed. But what behavior: losing a coat, lying beneath a car!

The Eldridge Street bartender whose bar I had been patronizing—so I was later informed—had closed up for the night and was leaving with his Icelandic girlfriend when he spotted my feet comically and tragically sticking out from beneath the car's license plate, like a drunk witch.

He roused me, got me out from beneath the car—no easy task— and told me I could have died from exposure. Then I vomited, narrowly avoiding this kindly man, and he and his girlfriend took me to their home, where I continued to vomit for at least two hours, holding on to their toilet with what little strength and life force I had. The bartender went to sleep and his sweet blonde girlfriend attended to me. I kept apologizing, and I remember her saying, as she sponged my face with a wet towel, "You don't have to say you're sorry. I'm from Iceland. We do this all the time."

A few months later, I read in the Science section of *The New York Times* that Iceland, a beautifully named country, has a high incidence of alcohol abuse. So the gods were looking after me, sending an Icelander to care for me when I needed one most.

I'll never know how I got from the East Sixties to Eldridge Street, quite a distance Manhattan-wise, or what I did for nearly six hours. That part of my life is forever lost, as are many other nights. And I never saw that kind bartender or his wonderful girlfriend again.

"What time did I get in, Jeeves?" I asked with trepidation.

"A little before ten, sir. Rather early."

This was very encouraging. From what I could recall, I had gone to Tinkle's room around eight forty-five. I was with him for at least half an hour, maybe forty minutes. That didn't leave a huge blank spot of time in which I might have perpetrated something embarrassing. I would have to ask Tinkle what had happened. I didn't relish the idea of seeing him again so soon after what he had done to me, though I didn't think he was a bad fellow, just hopelessly unfavored by nature and life.

"A little before ten; that's very good news," I said to Jeeves. "I think I lost consciousness around nine-thirty. So there's hope that I didn't do anything too crazy. . . . Do you see any fresh wounds or bruises?"

"No, sir."

"Oh, Jeeves, I'm sorry you have to know me. I'm a hopeless dipsomaniac. Did I say anything embarrassing to you?"

"No, sir. You simply wanted to go to bed. You did manage to tell me that a Mr. Tinkle had been most unkind to you, but you didn't specify in what way he was unkind."

"It's not so much that he was unkind, Jeeves. But the poor fellow is in worse shape than me, if you can believe it. I may have a broken nose and a drinking problem, but this Tinkle is really up against it. I don't think your pulley system would work for him. Maybe lifts in his shoes might be effective, but from what I've read, those things don't really work. . . . This Tinkle confided in me, Jeeves. Told me all his problems. It was like radiation. He melted my interior defenses. Psychically I needed one of those flak jackets they give you at the dentist."

"I see, sir."

"Some more water, Jeeves?"

"Yes, sir."

I downed another fortifying glass of H_2O, then got out of bed. I was fairly steady. I looked out the window; it promised to be a beautiful day. Maybe everything would be all right . . . well, as soon as I learned from Tinkle about my missing half hour. I sat back down on the bed and consulted my nose with my fingers. Still pulpy and throbbing, but the swelling seemed better. I meditated on what had gone wrong with Tinkle and tried to explain it to Jeeves:

"You see, Jeeves, with Tinkle, I probably should have detached with love, if I had known the concept. But instead of detaching, I attached and was sucked down."

"Most unfortunate, sir."

"I should have known better. During my training as a lifeguard, when I was a teenager, they warned you about this. The lifeguard's motto is 'Reach. Throw. Row. Go.' The first thing you do is try to reach the victim with a pole or one of those hooks. If that doesn't work, you throw them one of those circular things. One's impulse is to get it around their head, like a horseshoe, but you're not supposed to do that. It's to land in front of them. But if the circle thing doesn't work, then you take a boat and clobber them with an oar and then drag them on board. And if you don't have a boat, then you *go*. The absolute last thing you want to do with someone drowning is actually get in the water with them. The death instinct has taken over and they will try to kill you, bring you down in their panic. Most of my lifeguard training was like martial arts, how to subdue someone so you can save them. So remember, Jeeves: 'Reach. Throw. Row. Go.' I think this theorem can be applied to human relationships outside the swimming pool."

"Very interesting, sir."

"It's exactly like this detaching with love business. I wonder if Al-Anon got its principles from the lifeguard guild. But with Tinkle I didn't remember my training. I jumped right in and the fellow shoved me down. Oh, Jeeves, I can't even begin to tell you his struggles. And earlier in the evening I had been accosted by an attractive madwoman, a Sigrid Beaubien. . . . And there's an exceedingly beautiful woman named Ava, with the most unusual nose. . . . Overall, it was a strange first night. Do you think this is really an asylum and we're under the delusion that it's an artist colony? I keep thinking this might be the case, and I've been meaning to ask you your opinion on this."

"I am quite sure, sir, that we are at a center for the arts."

"What makes you so sure, Jeeves?"

"I just am, sir."

"All right, Jeeves, I believe you. The lack of medical personnel, or at least visible personnel, certainly would support your argument."

"Yes, sir."

"I wouldn't mind some medical assistance with this hangover, though it's not too bad at all. The initial reports were gloomy, but I'm rallying."

"I suggest, sir, a bath, and then if you can stomach some food, you should go to breakfast and have some eggs. The proteins and minerals in eggs, as you know, are very good after a night of drinking."

"Yes, some eggs would be very good."

Jeeves conjured up my bath towel. "Thank you, Jeeves."

"You're welcome, sir."

"And, Jeeves, I'm going back on the wagon, I promise," I said, but as I spoke I could hear the flimsiness of my own words, of my resolve, and Jeeves could, I was sure, hear it as well.

"Very good, sir."

"You're detached, aren't you, Jeeves?"

"Yes, sir."

"I don't blame you. That's the best position to take. I wish I could detach from myself. But it doesn't seem that one can apply the lifeguard principles or the Al-Anon principles to one's self. The only recourse then if I'm drowning is that I must swim."

"A logical conclusion, sir."

"Well, I'll go practice in the tub."

"Very good, sir."

"I'll do the dead man's float."

"Yes, sir."

"That was an attempt at black humor, Jeeves."

"I understand, sir."

CHAPTER 21

Yet another division of the Western world is arrived at ★ A misstep with Tinkle, but then a good discussion follows ★ I join a table and hear two bits of gossip ★ I am falsely accused, or am I?

About half the colonists were present for breakfast, while the rest must have been breakfast abstainers, which I noted with some interest. In one's quest to continually divide the world, I think one can safely say that the world is divided between those who pursue breakfast and those who don't.

As soon as I entered the half-full dining room, I spotted Tinkle advancing in the direction of the coffeepot. Everyone else was arranged at the constellation of tables, having already plundered the steaming trays of eggs, potatoes, bacon, and oatmeal. Large serving bowls of fresh fruit, granola, and yogurt were also vying for attention.

I headed right for Tinkle. Had to clear up this business of my missing half hour. Walking across the room, I was self-conscious, aware of my fellow colonists casually glancing at me—I was still the new recruit, an object of curiosity—but I was far less nervous than the night before when I had had to meet them all for drinks. I was sans hat and sunglasses, thinking at this point it would be stranger to continue my masquerade, since most everyone had seen my face or at least caught a glimpse of it at dinner.

"Morning, Tinkle," I said a little bashfully, catching up to him at the coffee station.

"I prefer Alan," he said, flinching a little around the eyes. It was hard for him to assert himself, I could see, but on the issue of being called Tinkle, it must have been something he was prepared to do, regardless of how difficult it might be. I felt stupid for being insensitive. "I hope that's all right with you," he continued, "unless it's too weird to use your own name."

"No, not at all . . . I apologize."

"No problem," he said, and smiled and poured himself a cup of coffee. He had forgiven me, which was good: I had to pump him for information.

"So how are you feeling?" I asked, starting slowly, while attending to the administration of my own cup of coffee.

"A little hungover," he said, "but not bad."

Lenora came over to the coffeepot and we all said, "Good morning," and then she added, "I used to only drink ginseng tea."

We absorbed this news flash, and then Tinkle put milk and four spoonfuls of sugar into his coffee, which was a little unnerving. I take my coffee black with no sugar. Tinkle then headed for a small bread table and I adroitly followed him and watched him put two slices of whole wheat into a toaster which was manifesting a very loud ticking sound, a cross between a metronome and a nuclear device. We waited for his toast.

"Thank you very much for the cigar and your whiskey last night," I interjected while we contemplated the toaster. "Though something *is* troubling me a little. I seem to have blacked out at some point . . . Did anything untoward happen?"

"You really blacked out?"

"Yes. I do that sometimes. Weak liver. So did I do anything I should regret?"

"I don't think so. I was talking your ear off, and then you did look like you were kind of out of it, and you said you had better get to bed, but you wanted one more drink. So we had one more. Maybe that's when you blacked out."

"That may have been the decisive moment."

"Your eyes were pretty strange. You said you were reading Anthony Powell for your book club, and then you kind of lectured me on Powell as the British Proust but better than Proust. Do you remember any of that?"

"No. I don't remember discussing Powell. I apologize if that was terribly boring."

"No, it was interesting, you're passionate about him. But I'm sorry if I made you drink too much and I'm sorry I rambled on and dumped all my problems on you . . . I was also really drunk."

Tinkle looked at me. He was a little ashamed, but also brave and forthright, prepared to accept the fact that he had let me know his most troubling secrets.

"Please, don't worry about last night," I said, and then I did morbidly wonder if he had dreamed of lobster claws grasping him, but I thought it better not to ask. "I enjoyed talking to you. I hope I helped a little. . . ."

"Yes, you were very nice," said Tinkle. He was quite a different person this morning than the night before: more normal and reserved. But this was entirely understandable. We all have multiple selves, especially those of us who drink heavily. I find that I'm a different person with every human being I meet. I try to match my personality to theirs like a pair of socks to a pair of pants.

"So I must have gone right from your room to my room?" I asked, and that toaster was ticking loudly—counting off the seconds of our ever-diminishing lives and the warming of Tinkle's bread.

"Yes, I walked you to your room. You weren't sure if you could find it. The Mansion *is* like a maze."

"Oh, thank you for helping me."

I felt confident now that nothing embarrassing had occurred while I was blacked out, and then Tinkle's toast announced itself, leaping rather high and startling me. But Tinkle, unfazed, gathered the two squares of bread and put them on a plate with some butter.

"All right if I sit with you?" I asked. I suddenly really needed Tinkle: to go sit at one of the tables with the others, all by myself, was beyond me, though none of the young females, including Ava, was present, which would have made things even more daunting.

"Of course," he said, smiling, indicating that even if the night before had been embarrassing for both of us, we had drunk together and this meant something, possibly friendship.

So I followed him to one of the smaller tables where Charles Murrin was holding court with five of the colony's more senior members, including the poetic Greenbergs, who were happily gorging themselves on granola and yogurt. I imagined they were very concerned with their bowels—who isn't?—and from that thought I pictured them individually on the commode, and I shuddered as certain images flashed across my mental screen. My mind often goes in such directions, a disgusting tendency, and I think it does this to torture me.

I don't know if it's common, but I am self-diagnosing myself as having a Mind/Mind Problem. Most people, including some very famous philosophers, have a Mind/Body Problem, and I have that as well, but I have this additional Mind/Mind Problem, where the mind tortures the mind. It's very annoying. The gods, clearly, are testing me. Well, I'm trying not to fail.

Despite the scatological nightmare I was temporarily screening inside my head, I took my seat and said hello to Murrin and the other tribal elders. Everyone acknowledged me and smiled, and they also warmly greeted Tinkle—we were junior officers but welcomed into the fold. I took a few sips of my coffee, then got back up to get a plate of eggs and toast.

Everything tasted especially delicious, which is often the case after a night on the tiles, and as I rapidly metabolized my carbohydrates and proteins, I listened to the table's conversation and soaked up my eggs with a lot of gossip. It appeared that the night had produced two scandals. The first scandal involved Sigrid Beaubien, who, as related by Murrin, had come into breakfast earlier and had been rather hysterical, claiming that a crime had been committed. The whole thing was rather mysterious, but I will try to summarize the basic facts of the case, as I heard them:

For some reason Beaubien left her slippers every night outside her door—she may have had the Japanese and Scandinavian fetish which smartly prohibits footwear in one's living chambers, though why she prohibited slippers is a bit severe and rather inexplicable—and when she went to retrieve them this morning, some odd thief had removed the slippers and left behind two pieces of paper upon which the slippers had been traced; the tracings had been cut from larger sheets of paper with a scissors to better capture the exact shape of the stolen slippers, like the etchings of dead bodies at a crime scene.

This was all fairly interesting and amusing, though I felt a shiver of intuitive concern, having nearly seduced or, rather, been seduced by Beaubien on the night the crime had been perpetrated.

"She's very upset," said Murrin to the table at large. "I think she's going to tell Dr. Hibben. I really wish she wouldn't. It's just a silly prank."

"Must be a visual artist," said the elderly Pulitzer prizewinning poet with the dashing nose, whose name was Kenneth—the poet that is, not his nose. As far as I know, his nose had no name, but it was certainly elegant, a kind of Dorian Gray nose, much younger than the rest of his face, and almost a twin in shape and expression to Peter O'Toole's nose in *Lawrence of Arabia,* which may be the greatest male nose in the history of cinema.

"Leaving behind replicas of the slippers is not the kind of thing a writer would think to do," Kenneth continued. "A note perhaps, but not a paper cutout."

"I think a writer could handle a pair of scissors," said June Greenberg, her copper hair glinting with morning sunlight.

"It could be a composer. They're very prank-oriented," said a rugged, acne-scarred midfifties sculptor named Don, who worked only with steel and was noticeably missing half a thumb.

The next bit of gossip concerned the two lovers Chris and Luc, the pair I had seen last evening kissing on that thronelike chair. Here again, I summarize:

In their all-consuming passion for each other, Chris and Luc had more or less started living together, putting two single mattresses on the floor of Chris's room. This had been quite upsetting for the cleaning staff, who were mostly older Saratoga matrons not used to men shacking up together—supposedly condoms had to be removed from the garbage can. And then this morning the cleaning staff had really been pushed over the edge when a sheet was discovered in the Dumpster behind the office. That would have been bad enough—throwing away a sheet, thus wasting the money and resources of a nonprofit organization—but this one had an enormous burn hole. Well, all sheets are marked with the room they come from, and this piece of incriminating evidence was from Chris's room. So two of the cleaning ladies had come to Murrin's chamber early this morning to let him know that they would be reporting the burnt sheet.

Murrin had gotten this scoop, I assessed, because if the colony was anything like a prison, then Murrin, as a "greeter," was the most respected prisoner, and the staff—the equivalent of prison guards— wanted to give him a heads-up on possible trouble. Fire was the main concern of the administration of the Rose Colony—the place was an antique tinderbox—and so there were certain to be repercussions in our quiet artistic lives. As I sat there, I was able to make this prison analogy from my extensive reading of prison novels, a genre that is one of my favorites because of its metaphorical portrayal of our universal existential crisis—we all feel trapped and we'd all like to escape.

"After the cleaning ladies told me about the sheet, I went to Chris's room," said Murrin, concluding his tale, "and I woke those two very bad boys up. I asked them about the sheet. They had thrown it over a lamp for mood lighting while they were screwing last night! They were so caught up in the act, they didn't realize it was on fire. They could have burnt down the whole Mansion!"

"That's romantic of them, but dangerous," said Sophie, a sixty-something painter, whose canvases were only painted one color— black. She was famous for having produced hundreds of all-black paintings, forcing a reappraisal of the color, though perhaps the same conclusion was arrived at: very dark. She was silver-haired and had the attractive figure of a much younger woman. Her shirt was open, revealing an appealing cleavage that spoke to me oedipally. "Why didn't a smoke alarm go off?" she asked. "We all could have been killed."

"I wonder if the hole in the sheet was actually for some kind of erotic ritual?" asked Kenneth with some irony. He smiled mischievously. It pleased him to think of Chris and Luc fornicating. He was an old homosexual with a beautiful nose.

"I've heard a rumor," I said, wanting to join the discussion, "which I've never been able to substantiate, that the Hasidim, for religious reasons, employ holes in sheets."

"That's the oldest, stupidest rumor there is," said Israel Greenberg, whose glasses were still as cockeyed as the day before. "That's right up there with drinking blood on Passover!"

He seemed to think that I was slurring Jews, but he didn't know

I was a Jew myself, and regardless my remark had not been offensive, at least I didn't think so. But my gentile attire may have thrown Israel off—I was wearing my seersucker jacket and hummingbird tie. There was a moment of uncomfortable silence, in which I didn't know what to say.

Tinkle, the good fellow, tried to rescue me and jumped in with "A fire would have killed all the bats. Some people would be happy if that happened."

No one knew what to make of this declaration, and Tinkle looked at me with sad eyes. Had he spoken in code? Did he want a fire to kill him? Hadn't he told me he wanted to impersonate a bat and that his book was a prolonged suicide note? But then I had a pleasant thought: I'll drag him to a brothel tonight, that'll fix things! This thought was then followed by the idea that I would have to be drunk to do this, and my brain didn't register a protest. My fascistic alcoholic thinking was already gearing up and I wasn't even finished with my hangover!

Then I said to Israel Greenberg, trying to smooth things over, "I didn't mean to say anything rude about the Hasidim. I admire them greatly and recently almost joined their clan."

"Really?" said June Greenberg, and Israel Greenberg looked at me skeptically through the one lens of his glasses that was actually in front of an eyeball.

I was caught in an exaggeration. I hadn't meant to magnify my connection to the Hasidim, but I was trying to compensate for having appeared anti-Semitic.

"Well, I sort of almost joined," I said, backsliding. "I went to Sharon Springs, a vibrant Hasidic enclave, and was going to take a cure there and study them and walk among them, more like a journalist than anything else, but then I was called to come here."

The Greenbergs seemed somewhat mollified, and Murrin found all this beside the point and brought the conversation back to a more relevant group discussion: "So Dr. Hibben is going to have to do something about Chris and Luc. It's going to be very uncomfortable. He may have to kick them out, or at the very least give them a warning. That's why I don't want Sigrid going to him about her slippers. He'll really think we're all coming unglued."

Beaubien took this as a cue, without knowing it, to come into the dining room and head right for our table.

"Here she comes," whispered Kenneth to Murrin, as a warning to not speak further about her.

As she approached, I saw that in her hand were two pieces of paper—the tracings of her slippers!

She came right over to me, waved the two sole-shaped cutouts, and made a startling accusation, "You did this, didn't you!"

She delivered her line with great drama. It was a real *"J'accuse!"* My tablemates, Israel and June G., Kenneth, Don, Sophie, Tinkle, and Charles, and everyone else in the dining room looked at me.

First an accusation of anti-Semitism and now thievery!

Beaubien was a woman scorned. Just because I hadn't come back to finish that kiss I was Suspect No. 1 for this slipper crime. I didn't know what to say.

"You stole my slippers!" she charged, or rather recharged, since I had not responded to her first detonation.

"No," I managed to get out. "I swear I would never touch your slippers."

She seemed to take this the wrong way. "Don't insult me," she said.

"Sigrid, sit down," urged Murrin. "Alan wouldn't take your slippers."

"Why wouldn't he?" demanded Beaubien.

"He just got here," said Murrin, and this didn't seem to clear my good name with anyone, Beaubien or my tablemates, who had just witnessed me being caught in a white lie about my association with the Hasidim. If I was capable of lies, then I was perhaps capable of slipper theft. Clearly, no jury would have found Murrin's reason to be a compelling argument. If anything, my novice status, my unknown character, *and* my battered face all worked against me.

"I swear I didn't take your slippers," I said with sincere desperation, though there was a glimmer of doubt in my mind. Tinkle said he had walked me to my room during my blackout, but maybe he hadn't walked me all the way or maybe I had turned around . . . but I didn't know where Beaubien was staying and I didn't have access to scissors. But still . . .

"Sigrid, please, sit down," said Murrin. "Someone is just playing a silly prank on you. And Alan here is a sweet young fellow. He wouldn't do anything to your slippers." But Beaubien, despite Murrin's entreaty, remained standing; she was livid.

"I'd be flattered if someone took my slippers," said June Greenberg, trying to console her.

"It's not flattering. And I went to Dr. Hibben and showed him these," Beaubien said, indicating the paper cutouts. "He said he'll make sure my slippers are returned. I don't need this kind of thing when I'm trying to paint!"

"Of course not," said Sophie, kindly showing allegiance to a fellow painter, while at the same time trying to calm Beaubien down.

"Everything will be all right," said Murrin.

"I know he did it," said Beaubien, pointing at me, and my blood sugar behaved diabetically—a terrible feebleness and fear washed over me and I thought I might faint. And then Beaubien walked out of the room.

CHAPTER 22

The high rate of diabetes in our country goes up by one ★ An alibi is provided ★ The high rate of diabetes goes down by one ★ My neck turns to rubber and then firms up ★ Too much testosterone can cause hair loss ★ Mangrove competes in the Tour de France ★ A tie is touched ★ Serotonin and testosterone can equal euphoria, if mixed properly

"She goes crazy every summer," said Murrin. "Don't let it upset you."

"Usually over a man," said June Greenberg. "And you're this year's *objet.*"

"She's a little hysterical," said Sophie. "The bats really get to her and she's always talking about there being a ghost in the Mansion."

My blood sugar was really going nuts: I was in deep diabetic peril. Any moment now I might need an amputation. Beaubien's accusation had slaughtered me. I felt as frail as a butterfly. I'm not cut out for confrontations. I can barely handle mild opposition.

"But who took the slippers?" asked Kenneth.

"Reginald Mangrove?" offered Sophie. "That's who Sigrid was crazy for a few years ago."

"No. Reginald is too self-absorbed to pull such a stunt," said Murrin. "It would never occur to him."

"*Did* you do it?" Donald, the half-thumbless sculptor, asked me.

"No, I didn't do it, I swear," I said. "I don't even know what room she's staying in."

"He was drinking with me last night," said Tinkle, "and I had to walk him back to his room. He didn't know how to find it. If he had taken her slippers, I would have seen it."

185

Thank God for Tinkle. He wasn't the most reliable witness—his comment about the bats dying in a firestorm had weakened his credibility—but he spoke with authority and clarity when it came to my whereabouts. He secretly knew his alibi for me wasn't fool-proof—my blackout and my near kiss with Beaubien had to be causing him to question my innocence—but he had, nevertheless, come to my defense. He was a good person! His statement seemed to remove any doubts my tablemates may have had about me, which was a great relief. Other possible suspects were then discussed, and my diabetes went into remission.

I was still shaky, but I managed to gum some scrambled eggs and choke on some coffee. This had been a horrible start to my day. It was worse than any morning encounter with Uncle Irwin. In fact, I would have liked to sic Uncle Irwin on Beaubien. He would be an equal match for her, and oddly enough as I sat there numbly trying to chew eggs, I felt something akin to fondness for that bearded Pio imper-sonator. I imagined him brandishing a pistol and shouting at Beaubien, "My nephew-by-marriage would never steal your slippers."

I finished my breakfast and then excused myself from the table. I was pretty worn-out. In my mind Uncle Irwin was my defender, someone who could be angry on my behalf, a surrogate anger-figure, but my real response to the Beaubien situation was to skip anger and go right to depression. I wanted to crawl back into bed and start the day over. Tomorrow.

"See you later," said Tinkle as I stood up.

"Yes, see you later," I said, and with my eyes I thanked him for coming to my aid.

I started to limp off, but Murrin took hold of my sleeve. "Don't worry about Sigrid," he said. "Whoever took the slippers will probably put them back by her door today and this whole thing will blow over. You just go do your writing and forget about this slipper business."

"Okay," I said.

I left the dining room and staggered in the direction of the mud-room to get my lunch pail. I was going to hide in my chambers all day. I didn't want to see any of these insane people for some time. I'd sleep all day and then skip dinner and treat Jeeves to a nice meal in town.

In the mudroom, my blood sugar was given another jolt.

Ava was there.

She was searching among the forty or so lunch pails for her own. To get mine would bring me into close proximity to her. I didn't feel capable of that. I was already completely weakened by Beaubien's attack. If I got too close to Ava, I thought my head might start to dangle from my neck, like someone with no muscle control. So either I had to retreat and go up the back staircase to my room, which would look foolish, or I could walk right past her and exit the Mansion and pretend to be going for a morning stroll. I chose this latter maneuver and headed for the door. Lunch pail in hand, Ava turned from the table and faced me and said, "We haven't met. You must be new."

"Yes," I said, and sure enough my head felt supported by a thin rubber pencil eraser. I wonder if other people lose their ability to support their head when their nervous system is overwrought and their sugar goes haywire.

Her nose, at close range, was spectacular; it was too much for me. In the nose department, she made Shylock look like a Barbie Doll. And her full breasts, barely contained in a bright yellow halter top, were a close second to her nose for piercing my heart.

She was also wearing flimsy running shorts—in other cultures they might have been used as a bandage for a small wound. She had been out jogging—the sexy hairs in her armpit, which I caught glimpses of, were damp. *I* was damp. I had all the strength of a puddle.

She also had green eyes. You really can't beat green eyes. Blue eyes, brown eyes, speckled, gray—all those shades you can more or less deal with. Give somebody green eyes and they can rule the world.

"I'm Ava Innocenzo," she said. I was taller than her by at least three inches, but it seemed as if she were towering over me. Tall women have that effect on me. Maybe women's heights, like their shoe sizes, are on a different scale. Ava was five feet nine, but in men's height she was six feet four.

"I'm Alan Blair," I said.

She offered me her hand; we shook. She had a powerful grip, which I met with equal force. This pleased me. Muscle control wasn't completely lacking, after all. And contact with her seemed to infuse me with life. My neck stopped behaving like an eraser.

"We have one Alan already," she said. "Alan Tinkle."

"Yes, I've met Alan Tinkle."

I was capable of a firm handshake and my neck was functioning, but my tongue, in the form of interesting discourse, was lagging way behind. It's those precise moments in life when I'd like to be charming that I am at my most dull. I could have said something inventive about there being multiple Alans, or taken advantage of Tinkle's last name and told her I was Alan Tinkle-Toes and that I was from England and that many people there have hyphenated surnames.

"What do you do?" she asked.

"Writer." It was all I could manage. But to hell with charming dialogue. I was feeling very strong. This woman was doing something to my blood chemistry. I wanted to lunge at her, hold that nose in my fist, like some kind of handle, and nurse at her breasts. My desires were a mixture of the violent and the infantile. In other words I was feeling quite manly.

"I can't write. I can't spell for shit," she said.

"I'm sorry." I visualized spinning her around and taking hold of her hips and mounting her from behind. My earlier diabetic imbalance had been replaced by an overrelease of testosterone, which they say causes balding. Some people's hair turns gray in an instant; well, my hair was going to completely eject from my head due to the flood of male hormone in my system. Either that or I was going to misfire like Tinkle.

"But I don't care about spelling," she said. "I send in grant applications with every word misspelled, but nobody says anything. They don't expect artists to spell."

I was on the verge of catastrophic hair loss and a public emission, but I redirected these internal forces in the form of a verbal storm, especially in comparison with my previous output in our conversation. I apparently had regained my tongue, and then some:

"Well, many writers are also terrible spellers. Fitzgerald, supposedly, was an atrocious speller. . . . Might be interesting to have a spelling bee for famous writers, expose their weakness. . . . PEN should do it as a way to raise money or something for writers in prisons, though most writers like prisons for the material and might not want to be released; Jean Genet did his best work behind bars. Of course he liked prison life for other reasons as well. . . . I wouldn't mind a prison stay, though the shivs make it unappealing. . . . Wait a second, I wonder why it's called a spelling bee. Do you know?"

"I don't know. That *is* weird. Why spelling *bee*? Why not just spelling *contest*?"

As she spoke, I held my eyes away from her breasts, but her breasts were so full that I didn't need to see them to see them, if you know what I mean. I was picking them up on sonar. And of course her incredible nose was right in front of me—convention allowed me to look at that—and I wanted to smother it in kisses, while grabbing a fistful of her thick hair.

"Spelling *contest* is more direct," I said. "Though spelling *bee* sounds more fun, but it makes no sense. . . . You don't say 'hot dog–eating bee,' for example. . . . I might do well in a spelling bee, though I have a preference for British spellings, but not the conviction to use them."

"Were you in a fight?" she asked, obviously losing interest in the spelling topic. She was studying my nose and eyes. A nose to match her nose, at least in its unusual character.

"Yes, I was in a fight," I said proudly. I could see a glimmer of respect and interest in her eyes. I sensed that my savage face, with its caveman attributes, appealed to her, and I rapidly diagnosed that she would be drawn to brutal fellows. It would take a caveman, after all, to subdue her, since she was so physically imposing. And I felt myself rising to the challenge. I was nearly as tall as her now. I was growing! I had gone from an internal height of five-four or so to nearly five-nine. If only I could reach my natural length of six feet, then maybe I could have her.

I know this doesn't quite make sense with her being six-four in men's height, but that's a theory whose kinks I haven't completely worked out. I think what happens is that I shrink and women grow. Even short women appear tall to me. If a woman is five-three, in my eyes she comes in at about five-eight. . . . Well, it's all a jumble. Essentially, a massive distortion somehow takes place, that's all we need to know.

189

"Who did you fight?" she asked.

"It was a bar fight with a stranger. He got me pretty good, but I also got him."

I threw a punch to show off for her in a masculine way. Unfortunately, eye-patched Reginald Mangrove came into the room at that very moment and saw me throw the punch. He looked at me with some curiosity, catching me, as it were, boasting in the very same manner I had boasted at dinner. How embarrassing.

But then there was the hint of a smile on his face, and I knew that he had generously assessed what was going on. He realized I was being a peacocky male for the purposes of trying to conquer a female, and as a man of the world with only one eye, he didn't judge me for this.

"Morning, Alan," he said, and he was wearing the outfit of a competitor in the Tour de France. He sported a tiny white cap, a yellow T-shirt, and black stretch pants, which came to the knee and looked obscene. Very few people can wear those kind of pants and not look depraved. Mangrove, I'm afraid, fell onto the depraved side of the ledger, though he seemed to be unaware of this. Most middle-aged sport hobbyists seem to be deluded in this way when it comes to their costuming.

"Good morning," I said.

He said hello to Ava, she said hello to him, and then Mangrove clicked across the floor. His shoes were the kind that plug into the pedals of fancy racing bicycles.

"Have a good ride," Ava said.

"Thank you," he said, and left the Mansion.

"He does thirty miles every day before he starts writing. . . . Well, I better get *my* day started," Ava said.

"Okay," I said, and smiled weakly and stared at the articulation of her nostrils. Her nostrils led to her full lips. She had the nose of Durante and the mouth of Bardot. I felt defeated and hopeless—she didn't want to talk to me anymore, and since I couldn't attack her, I felt like killing myself.

When women really stun you, you want to die. It's an inversion of the lustful violence one feels. The desire has become pain, which is its natural course, according to the Buddhists. Desire = Pain. I learned this on the back of a ginger tea box. Most of what I know of Buddhism—and my yoga moves—comes from tea boxes.

So I had to remove the desire to remove the pain. In the case of Ava, I had two options for achieving this: the Tinkle method of self-release or the conqueror-caveman method. At the moment, the Tinkle option looked the most viable, which is why I felt hopeless. Around the six thousandth time in life, the prospect of self-release as a pain reliever begins to feel a bit grim.

"You don't look like the kind of guy that gets in a bar fight, but I like your tie," Ava said, not ending our conversation, after all. She fingered my Brooks Brothers neckwear. "I love these little birds."

Jeeves had repeated the hummingbirds, pushing them back into the tie rotation sooner than usual, and I was incredibly grateful to him—Ava was touching me. Well, touching my tie, that is. But my tie was like a part of me, more so than with most people. Then she let go of it. She had appraised the small portraitures of the birds as a visual artist, but still she had touched it, touched me, and I had a growth spurt. I was at my full height and was now taller than Ava!

"It's my favorite tie," I said.

"Do you wear a tie every day?"

"I try to."

"Why?"

"I like to. Gives me a false sense of purpose."

"Well, I'm glad to meet somebody interesting around here. . . . See you at dinner tonight." This was another abrupt conclusion to our conversation, but it didn't wound me this time. I felt good about our whole meeting. She had noticed me, touched me, and praised me. What more could I ask for on a first encounter?

"Okay," I said, "see you tonight."

She smiled and then left the mudroom for the main hall. I was free to watch her backside. My testosterone valve was completely open, and I felt the serotonin valve open, as well. My bloodstream was rich with ingredients and I was happy, euphoric, and jocund. And since I was in such a good mood, I'll add ecstatic to the menu.

I collected my lunch pail and flew up the stairs to my room. My

Beaubien-inspired drooping spirits had reversed completely. There was much to tell Jeeves. Last night's feeling upon seeing Ava was confirmed. I was in love!

Of course, I knew it might only be physical infatuation. But you know how it is. One thinks it's love, and sometimes, once or twice in a lifetime, it is.

CHAPTER 23

A meditation on love, probably all wrong ★ I give Jeeves my head-
lines—the gossip page and the crime blotter ★ A plot to catch the
slipper thief, but has a perversion also been mistakenly stolen?

Jeeves was just finishing the corners on the young master's bed. His
back was to me and so absorbed was he in the perfection of his task
that he didn't hear me come into the room, which was unlike
Jeeves—my catching him unawares; it was always the reverse.

So I was oozing love for the world, and there was Jeeves making
my bed—selflessly being kind to me, thinking of me, wanting to
please me. Well, I almost felt like crying.

You see, every now and then I glimpse a person in my life for just
an eyelash of time, and the dearness of this other human being—in
this instance, Jeeves—strikes me as a revelation, and my love for
them becomes so obvious and clear, not obscured by judgments or
fears or distractions—the rush of life—and it's a very beautiful feeling, and I'd like to tell the person, but I'm not sure I can express it,
maybe it would frighten them, or maybe it will frighten me to say it,
maybe it will sound hollow and false, and right next to this feeling of
my love for them, like something across a breach, is the fragility of
it all, the mortality of it all, the hopelessness of it all, and I sense the
coming loss before it has even happened, and then usually the mind
clouds over and I'm back to pressing on to the next event.

It's all very confusing. One of my problems is that I mix up love
and pity. I can't really distinguish the two, but maybe they do go hand
in hand, because as soon as you love someone, you don't want
them to feel pain. But you know they will. You see the tenuous illu-
sions they surround themselves with to keep going, how easily they

could be hurt and crushed, and so you pity them, in the same way that deep down you pity yourself for the very same reasons.

Regardless of how gloomy it all is, I should tell people I love them, but I don't do it nearly enough. When I was living in Princeton, I had a friend who was dying from a brain tumor and he knew he only had about six months to live, and on the phone one day he said to me, in lieu of good-bye, "I love you." It wasn't going to be our last phone call and I wasn't his closest friend by any means, but I could hear in his voice that he was going to say this now to everyone; there was no need anymore to hold back. I thought I should adopt the same policy with the people in my life, but I wasn't able to, though to my friend I could say it whenever we spoke over the next few months until he died.

Anyway, I was looking at Jeeves and feeling a good deal of affection for him. My adoration hadn't turned dark in my mind yet—it hadn't turned to pity—and he must have sensed something because he suddenly snapped out of his gurulike bed-making trance and turned and said, "Yes, sir?"

I think it would have made Jeeves uncomfortable if I had suddenly blurted out, "I love you." But in his case maybe things don't have to be explained or said out loud. So even though my sentimental engine was running on all eight cylinders and my foot was on the pedal, I kept things off our relationship and went right to a heralding of the day's current events.

"Brace yourself, Jeeves."

"All right, sir."

"Are you properly braced?"

"I believe so, sir."

I sat on the newly made bed and motioned to Jeeves to take the chair at the letter-writing desk. Thus situated, I was prepared to give him a full account of all that had happened.

"I have headlines, Jeeves."

"Very good, sir."

I paused for effect, and then let him have it: "I'm in love! You can print it in bold. Splash it across the front page."

"Excellent news, sir. Delightful."

"I feel wonderful, Jeeves. Full of life and beans . . . Is that the correct saying?"

"I don't know, sir."

"What about spelling bees, Jeeves. Why are they called that?"

"I apologize, sir. I don't know the answer to that question, either."

"That's all right, Jeeves. These mysteries don't really plague me, they just momentarily annoy."

"Understandable, sir. . . . If I may ask, sir, with whom have you fallen in love?"

"Ava! I mentioned her earlier. The one with the extraordinary profile."

"Are you sure you're in love, sir?"

"You mean, I might just be smitten?"

"Perhaps, sir."

"I've considered that, Jeeves, and it's highly likely. But it's fun to feel in love. And the most promising development is that she seems to like me. I don't think it's going to be one of those one-sided affairs."

"Very good, sir."

"She appreciated my tie, for which I have you to thank. I'm glad you went with the hummingbirds again this morning. She grabbed hold of it. A woman doesn't do that sort of thing if she's not drawn to you. She was admiring the artwork, but on some level she must have wanted to touch me or wasn't so repulsed as to *not* want to touch me. When a woman is not repulsed, that's half the battle."

"I am pleased that the hummingbird tie was a satisfactory selection, sir."

"More than satisfactory! The tie won her over. . . . You know, Jeeves, I'll tell you one thing—she's not my dream girl dream girl. Kind of a photo negative of her. Which is interesting, now that I've put it that way. Maybe the subconscious is some kind of negative or reverse telepathic imprint of the future. You see what I mean, Jeeves?"

"I believe I understand, sir, to a certain degree the concept you wish to express."

"I don't fully get the concept myself, Jeeves, but I sort of get it. A lot of my concepts, I've noticed, are like that, which is a bit frustrating. They're not fully thought out. I don't seem to have the intellect to take things all the way. I hit a mental wall."

"You do quite well, sir."

"You think so, Jeeves?"

"Yes, sir."

"Thank you, Jeeves. . . . Anyway, what do you think of the name Ava? Besides its obvious attribute as a palindrome. Good for a femme fatale?"

"Ava is a lovely name, sir."

"She is lovely, so she matches her name, though she *is* a bit rough around the edges. She said she couldn't 'spell for shit.' But I like her earthiness."

"Very good, sir."

I lay back on the bed and Jeeves sat dutifully at the letter-writing desk with admirable posture. I closed my eyes and on the inner Ziegfeld I saw myself taking Ava in my arms, my hands in her thick hair . . . but then a dark shadow passed in front of this image, as if the mental celluloid had been burned. I sat back up.

"There is another headline, Jeeves."

"Yes, sir?"

"From the crime blotter, I'm afraid. I was accused by this Sigrid Beaubien character of stealing her slippers. She made quite a scene at breakfast. Denounced me in front of everyone. Tried to organize a lynching. My sugar went completely berserk. I almost went blind from diabetes."

"Most vexing, sir. She claims that you took her slippers?"

"Yes. . . . The others seemed to be on my side; they have her characterized as a hysteric who sees ghosts. But I'm not entirely cleared. I'm sure everyone suspects me a little after her accusation. . . . And my blackout does give me some pause. I didn't come back here last night with a pair of women's slippers, Jeeves, did I?"

"No, sir."

"And if anyone would know, you would."

"Yes, sir."

"And we're not in possession of any scissors or cutting shears?"

"No, sir. Why do you ask?"

196

I further explained to Jeeves the nature of the crime—the tracing of the slippers and the manufacture of cutouts and how Beaubien left the slippers outside her door each night. He took it all in stride, but did say, "Very strange, sir."

"Yes, it is strange. Strange that she leaves slippers outside her door and strange that they were taken. I don't blame her for being upset, but she overreacted. She was ready to kill me. It's very uncomfortable to be hated, Jeeves, especially in an environment like this—no escaping her, really. I mean it's worse than living with Uncle Irwin. I wasn't his favorite person, but he didn't exactly loathe me. I just kind of bothered him. But this woman, I feel, hates me. I want to be able to concentrate on my writing and my love infatuation with Ava and not worry about Beaubien and her damn stolen slippers. . . . You know, if we caught the thief, that would clear my name with her and everyone else."

"That would firmly establish your innocence, sir."

"Any idea how we could achieve this, Jeeves?"

"Well, we might leave your shoes outside the door tonight, sir, and try to apprehend anyone who might make off with them."

"Excellent thinking, Jeeves!"

"Thank you, sir."

"But don't you think we should leave my slippers outside the door? This person might only go in for slippers and not shoes."

"A relevant distinction, sir."

"Could just be a prankster or an actual slipper fetishist. We have to cover all the bases. So to be on the safe side, we'll bait him with slippers, assuming it's a male. It could be a female, but most sociopaths are male. Females take out their troubles on themselves, for the most part."

"Yes, sir."

I contemplated our catching this possible slipper fetishist, and I distractedly ran my finger along my mustache. It was rather sensual to stroke myself this way, and this led me back to the inner Ziegfeld and the movie I had started to run: Ava in my arms.

But how two people kiss is always a great mystery. It doesn't make sense to me when I think about it. One tilts the head and then somehow these two mouths come together. Nevertheless, I tried to visualize our kiss—the physics of it—but I was botching the whole thing, my choreography was all off. Mouth issue aside, I imagined that our considerable noses would be crushed against the other's face, and then I really fumbled the camera—the mind shoots the picture and screens it at the same time—and I saw her nose go in my mouth. But this aroused me. I indulged myself with this bit of scenery chewing, and then, chastising myself, I turned off the inner projector and camera. I was suddenly feeling more than a trace of concern about this nose business and sought to express my anxiety to Jeeves.

"There is an element to my love affair that disturbs me, Jeeves."

"Indeed, sir?"

"It's somewhat embarrassing . . ." Jeeves looked at me calmly; his was a face you could trust. I shot out my confession: "I think I'm overattracted to Ava's nose, Jeeves. I've never had that before. Never been drawn to a nose quite so powerfully. I can't explain it."

"Does sound unusual, sir."

"If I understood Freud or had actually read Freud, I'd say it was some kind of transference, having recently had my own nose altered."

"Perhaps, sir."

"But that doesn't fully satisfy me. . . . It may be that her nose is in the shape of a female body. The nostrils are like haunches."

"Really, sir?"

"Sorry, Jeeves, I don't mean to be vulgar. I'm trying to understand its power over me. Maybe it's like getting two women in one."

"That is certainly a possible psychological explanation, sir. But have you considered that it is merely an attractive nose and you find it appealing?"

"It goes beyond that, Jeeves. . . . You know, I once read about a nose fetishist in Krafft-Ebing's *Psychopathia Sexualis*. I don't remember the details, but I remember being fascinated. . . . I wonder if by reading that years ago, I've caused myself to have the same condition. I've heard of novelists and screenwriters who read some book as a young boy, forget about it over time, and then years later produce a book or screenplay which is a twin to the original, not realizing they've stolen the whole basic plot and theme."

"I've also heard of this phenomenon, sir."

"Maybe I've done that with the case history of this nose fetish—except I've stolen a perversion, a mental problem. . . . I'm such an idiot! It would be much more lucrative to steal a book. I can't do anything right! . . . I used to read Krafft-Ebing as a boy to arouse myself. Probably wasn't healthy to be reading cases of sexual psychosis for that purpose and now I'm paying the price. I was a twentieth-century Jewish boy in New Jersey reading about nineteenth-century German sexual deviants; I might as well have been reading *Mein Kampf.*"

"I understand, sir."

"I can't believe this has happened to me, Jeeves. This is worse than what Oscar Wilde went through. His was a love that dare not speak its name. My love doesn't even have a name that it can't speak. . . . Nose-love? Nose-sex? That's ridiculous. . . . I won't even think of the implication of the word *nasal*. . . . I wish I had *Psychopathia* with me now . . . lost it some time ago. I'd like to read that case history again and get to the bottom of this."

"Could be very instructive, sir."

I tried valiantly to remember the specifics of the nose-fetish case, but couldn't bring it to mind. All I could vaguely recollect was an assault on a tram, but that was it. Then I had an excellent idea.

"Jeeves, let's go to the library," I said, "and find the Krafft-Ebing. If I'm going to fall in love with this woman and her nose, I need to understand everything that is motivating me. I just hope the library has the book and that some teenager hasn't stolen it for the same reasons that I once used it. . . . If they don't have it, Skidmore College is hiding around here somewhere."

"Very good, sir."

"Maybe I can incorporate it into my novel somehow. Make one of my characters have a nose fetish."

"Very good, sir."

And with that, we made our way to the Caprice and drove into town in search of the library and Dr. Richard von Krafft-Ebing's masterwork of human eros, *Psychopathia Sexualis.*

CHAPTER 24

An extract from Krafft-Ebing's Psychopathia Sexualis ★
A discussion with Jeeves about fetishes and AA ★ I do some reading, and Jeeves disappears into the stacks ★ A contemplation of my
ignorance, but then I give myself a pat on the back ★ Jeeves and I
discuss an idea for a new novel

Case 88. (Binet, op. cit.) X., aged thirty-four, teacher in a gymnasium. In childhood he suffered from convulsions. At the age of ten he began to masturbate, with lustful feelings, which were connected with very strange ideas. He was particularly partial to women's eyes; but since he wished to imagine some form of coitus, and was absolutely innocent in sexual matters, to avoid too great a separation from the eyes, he evolved the idea of making the nostrils the seat of the female sexual organs. Then his vivid sexual desires revolved around this idea. He sketched drawings representing correct Greek profiles of female heads, but the nostrils were so large that insertion of the penis would have been possible.

One day, in a bus, he saw a girl in whom he thought he recognized his ideal. He followed her to her home and immediately proposed to her. Shown the door, he returned again and again until arrested. X. never had sexual intercourse.

Nose fetishism is but seldomly met with. The following rare bit of poetry comes to me from England:

> "Oh! sweet and pretty little nose, so charming unto me;
> Oh, were I but the sweetest rose, I'd give my scent to thee.
> Oh, make it full with honey sweet, that I may suck it all;
> T'would be for me the greatest treat, a real festival.
> How sweet and nutritious your darling nose does seem;
> It would be more delicious, than strawberries and cream."

Hand-fetishists are very numerous. The following case is not really pathological. It is given here as a transition one:

Case 89. B., of neuropathic family, very sensual, mentally intact . . .

I showed this remarkable passage to Jeeves. We were alone at a desk in the very nice Saratoga Public Library. "What do you think of it?" I asked him.

"A sympathetic portrait, sir, of a troubled person."

"And using that poem! Brilliant, don't you think?"

"Yes, sir."

"And isn't the prose delightful?"

"Very well written, sir."

"Granted it's in translation, but still . . . God, I love this stuff. No wonder I imprinted this perversion on my psyche and now suffer from it. . . . But I don't have it as bad as this fellow. I mean I'm attracted to the entirety of Ava's body. And as soon as I get to know her person, I'll be attracted to that as well. At least I hope so. So I'm not as bad off as X., right, Jeeves?"

"No, sir, I don't believe you are as afflicted as the person discussed in this history."

"I think what I have is the kind of fetish you can live with. You know, where it doesn't dominate your whole life and sexuality and you have to go to support groups and conventions and even vote for certain politicians. Cross-dressers, S-and-M people, and the men-who-love-boys are all the sexual equivalent of the NRA. . . . Foot fetishists aren't as well organized, I don't think. Then again, they can just go to a beach and have their fill. But with those other three, there are all sorts of meetings, newsletters, legal fees, expensive gadgets, dues . . . It's a big hassle, I imagine, to have a serious fetish. I mean, look at Uncle Irwin. The NRA has completely brainwashed him. I just have a mild case of nose fetishism. I don't have to change my whole life."

"I would agree, sir."

"So I feel better about this nose thing now, but I do need to change some of my life, Jeeves. I'm not really hungover, thank God, but I have to arrest this drinking. It's really getting out of hand. First a broken nose and then a blackout. And I blacked out the night my nose was attacked, now that I think of it. That's just not normal. I have to accept this and quit the booze. No more empty promises about getting on the wagon. I'm not a frontiersman. I'm an alcoholic!"

"I am in firm agreement, sir."

"I should call AA or something. Maybe go to a meeting here in Saratoga. There's something crucial I missed when I went to a few meetings at Montesonti's gulag and then in Montclair. This business about how not to pick up the first drink. Do you know anything about it, Jeeves? Could save me from calling AA."

"I'm afraid, sir, I don't. I do think a telephone call to AA would be helpful. I believe its methods are efficacious for abstention from spirits."

"All right, I'll call them later. Probably listed in the phone book. Smart of them to name it AA. I wonder if AA comes before all those companies with three *A*'s. Do you think that was their reasoning, Jeeves? Good placement in the phone book?"

"It seems unlikely, sir, but it is a possibility."

"Or do two *A*'s come after three *A*'s?"

"I will have to consult a phone book, sir."

"Don't bother. I'll do it later. . . . You know, if you have a drunk-driving accident, what's good is, you can look up Triple A and AA and kill two birds at once. . . . They should call AA, Double A. More catchy. . . . Then again it might conjure up notions of ordering a double, which probably isn't very helpful."

"Yes, sir."

It was not quite 10 A.M. and I spent the next delightful two hours reading *Psychopathia,* though I made sure to keep its cover flat on the table, which was a little difficult since it was a paperback and the book was rather thick, but I didn't want some Saratoga senior citizen or an impressionable child to glance at the cover and read what was written above the title: "The only newly and completely translated edition of the classic work on sexual aberration." It would give people the wrong idea about what I was doing in the library on a Friday morning. As it was, my bruised face was sure to arouse some suspicion, though my jacket and tie probably acted as a nullifying agent to a certain degree, making me appear to be the trustworthy character that I am, or, at least, aspire to be.

While I read, Jeeves lost himself in the stacks; he was probably boning up on plant life and fauna in the Saratoga region, something improving like that. Meanwhile, I was having a Proustian experience with the Krafft-Ebing. Reading the case histories again, I was transported back to my childhood home and the nights I had spent as an adolescent with a flashlight under the covers soaking up the beautiful narratives of *Psychopathia Sexualis*. The strange yearnings and acts of Krafft-Ebing's patients had thrilled me as a teenager, but I had also loved how Krafft-Ebing magnificently explained with great compaction and efficiency the lives of his subjects.

I can see now there was a certain parallel to my reading of the case histories and what had preceded that—my boyhood adoration of baseball cards. From the back of a card, from the player's statistics, you could tell if he was great, lousy, or mediocre; if he'd had potential but had fallen short and would forever be disappointed; if he was a late bloomer who could live with himself when his playing days were over; if he'd had one freakish year and never produced again; or if his numbers were piling up in a way that was admirable, perhaps Hall of Fame–ish.

The trajectory of the player's life and his career was all laid out, year by year, just as Krafft-Ebing had tried to show what had happened to the people in his book over the course of their lives, over the course of time. In both instances, I was drawn to the notion of human lives as understandable narratives, and from a young age, I was trying, like most people, to make sense of my own story, my own life, and must have subconsciously wished to see it explained on the back of a baseball card—my childhood dream—or in some case history—my potential adult reality.

I do wish I had read Freud as much as I've read Krafft-Ebing. Interestingly enough, Krafft-Ebing was Freud's superior in Vienna, against whom Freud rebelled. Krafft-Ebing was just compiling the facts of perversion, kind of like a stamp collector; he didn't really probe why people were disturbed, except to theorize once in a while that maybe a poorly shaped skull or a weak liver may have set someone off. That kind of thing. So Freud looked down upon and ultimately surpassed Krafft-Ebing.

Thus, I should know Freud inside and out. Every writer should. Instead, I only have watered-down knowledge of his theories from what I pick up in the culture, which is the intellectual equivalent of playing that telephone game. The same thing with Jung and Darwin.

Especially Darwin. I haven't read a single word of the man's work—whereas with Freud I own a paperback edition of *Interpretation of Dreams* and I tried once to read the first paragraph—and yet I use Darwinian interpretations to inform much of my worldview. No wonder I'm always screwing up. I back up everything with rumor and insinuation and overheard gibberish! My knowledge of a major religion, Buddhism, comes from tea boxes. I have to say, though, I have a better grasp of Buddhism, because of those tea boxes, than I do of Freud, Jung, or Darwin. I wish they'd condense those gentlemen's theories on tea boxes.

Having just said what I've just said, I realize, with great embarrassment, that I may not have been reading about Buddhism all these years. I can't believe my folly. I think it might be Hinduism. You don't hear much about Hinduism, so I assumed, as I drank all that tea, that it was Buddhism. But there's often a picture of a yogi on the tea box, and they don't have yogis in China. Yogis are from India, and I think the religion in India is Hinduism. And I'm pretty sure Buddhism was made in China, like so many other things, though the Buddha doesn't look Chinese. Confucius looks Chinese. But whatever happened to him? When did he go out of vogue over there? And what about the Koreans? What do they practice? Very little seems to be known about them, which may explain why we attacked them in the 1950s—fear of the unknown.

Well, I have to say I just demonstrated that I'm more of an idiot than I had previously realized. I'm the worse kind of idiot. I think I know things, but I don't know anything. I'm so colossally stupid, I may have a negative IQ. At Princeton, a friend of mine got drunk and in the middle of the night knocked over an enormous volume of the *OED* and in the morning discovered that he had killed his little kitten. That's how I should be sentenced to death: I should have the *OED* or the *Encyclopedia Britannica* dropped on my head.

Anyway, I had better go easy on myself. At least I make an effort to think about things. Have to give myself some credit.

★   ★   ★

Jeeves returned to the library table around noon—I had more or less finished gorging myself on *Psychopathia*—and I had an idea for a new novel, which I wanted to share with him.

"Know what's interesting about Krafft-Ebing's book, Jeeves?"

"No, sir."

"It ends with Case 238. I love the fact that they're numbered. Wouldn't a great title for a book be *Case 239*? I would write it as if 239 was the long-lost missing case history, sort of like the Dead Sea Scrolls, and this 239 would somehow solve the human dilemma of why everyone is so sex-crazed. You know, we make fun of rabbits, but there are a lot more people than rabbits."

"Very true, sir."

"I'll make it a grand philosophical book, masquerading as a case history. Kind of like what George Bernard Shaw or Thomas Mann would do—unrealistic characters who represent things, philosophical positions. In this case it would also be sexual positions. The book would be a sort of combination of *The Kama Sutra* and *The Magic Mountain*. I can also see it adapted as a musical, the way *Pygmalion* became *My Fair Lady*. The patient would be Everyman. He'd go by the initial *E*. I would try to write it in Krafft-Ebing's style . . . or it could be quasi-autobiographical. I could write my own case history, how my aberrant sexual behavior was my excessive reading as a teenager of Krafft-Ebing, which led me to having a nose fetish later in life. Something like that. Which makes it all very circular—how reading a book on perversion is a perversion, which also causes a secondary perversion. It's good when things in literature are circular. Gives the impression of profundity."

"I see, sir."

"I would write it as a letter to Krafft-Ebing. Some of the case histories are simply letters he received from people telling him of their abnormal behavior and begging for his help. And my letter would be extra forlorn since he's dead, and I'd be writing a letter knowing there'd be no response, no help."

"Excellent, sir."

"After I finish *The Walker*, I'll bang out *The Homosexuals Are Coming* screenplay, and then I'll tackle *Case 239*. It's good to think about future projects. Gives one hope."

"I would agree, sir."

"There is the possibility, though, that there may not be a whole novel in the concept. Or a musical. There may just be a title. Often-times that happens. If that's the case, all is not lost. I could have the narrator of *The Walker* think of himself as Case 239, a sort of interior, self-lacerating joke. . . . Of course, the narrator is based on me during the years when I was living with Charles and I've only just now come up with this 239 business, but I can take liberties since it's fiction. . . . And this Krafft-Ebing thing will be good, since in *The Walker* I'm making myself out to be a loony, unreliable narrator, which is the best kind of narrator to have, Jeeves. Allows you to get away with things, like not fact-checking. But he's not entirely unreliable. He's punctual and writes thank-you notes."

"Admirable traits, sir."

"Let's head back to the Rose, Jeeves. I've done enough research for today. I think I'll go for a swim in the pool. The cold water will be good for my nose. Then I'll spend the afternoon laboring with great industry. My reward will be seeing Ava at dinner."

"A healthy plan, sir."

"I think so, Jeeves."

On our way out of the library, I made a stop in the restroom and encountered this bit of graffiti over the urinal: *FREE THE BOUND PERIODICALS!* I was struck by the brilliance of this remark, and when I came out of the bathroom, I reported to Jeeves what I had read.

"Very interesting, sir," said Jeeves.

"Saratoga has hidden depths," I said as we left the library and walked to the Caprice. "There are subversive elements present here. Graffiti like that is better than any real estate brochure. We might consider settling down here after our tenure at the colony is finished."

"A promising notion, sir."

"Any town that promotes that kind of thinking is the place for us."

"Very good, sir."

CHAPTER 25

A religious discussion ★ A poisoned letter ★ A cowardly impulse; a brave response ★ A brave impulse; a cowardly response ★ Man, woman, animal, fruit, or vegetable? ★ A rigorous interrogation

The gods don't like to let my nerves untangle for too long. Why this is, I don't know. They gave me some peaceful moments in the library, but it had been nearly four hours since Beaubien had me craving insulin, so I was more than due for another disaster, which this time came in the form of a note. I had parked the Caprice, Jeeves was off on a nature walk in the woods, and I was sailing through the mudroom, all set to charge to my room and don my bathing trunks for a dip in the pool, when my eye was drawn to the mail table, where a plain envelope bearing my name was waiting to be picked up.

The old brain immediately squirted some serotonin into my system at the sight of the envelope, as it bore a resemblance to a letter, and letters, like dogs, always make me feel instantaneously happy. Unfortunately, I have very little contact with dogs and receive almost no letters. I should probably start a correspondence with a dog pound and combine the two pleasures.

Anyway, I took hold of the envelope and carried it with me up to my rooms, delaying the pleasure of finding out who had written me. It was some kind of internal colony correspondence—there was no return address and no address beneath my name. So I was free to fantasize that maybe Ava had written me a note, confessing her profound attraction and love for me and inviting me to her room to ravish her . . . that she'd be waiting naked on her bed, a rose in one of her nostrils. This was unlikely, but until I opened the envelope, one could

209

hope for the best, and so I stalled my great curiosity until I was at my desk.

Happily seated, imagining myself rushing to Ava's boudoir, I pried open the envelope as carefully as I would a can of sardines; I don't think I've mentioned this but I've been prone to paper cuts all my life. Put me near something sharp and it's as if my skin begs to be assaulted. I can't even begin to tell you of the scars on my hands from actual sardine cans and kipper cans, which is why it's great to have Jeeves about—no more slitting my wrists on those things. I did have to give up tennis at a young age since opening a new can of balls was such a hazard, but maybe now with Jeeves around I can take the sport up again.

Anyway, unfortunately, it was not a note from Ava to come ravish, though things began pleasantly enough—the epistle was typed on Rose Colony letterhead, which featured, embossed at the top, a large red rose twined around a miniature line drawing of the Mansion. But after this bit of stationery artwork, things took a decided turn for the horrible and the tragic. It was a lightning bolt from the gods. Curse them! Believe me, I understand well when good old Hamlet says that thing about "the thousand natural shocks that flesh is heir to." At the Rose Colony alone, I was well on my way to filling out my quota. Mental patients in the fifties didn't have as rough a time as I was having at a so-called peaceful artist colony.

Herewith, I reproduce the lightning bolt in question, sans rose and line drawing, I'm afraid:

THE ROSE COLONY

Alan,

Please come to my office as soon as you can; I'd like to discuss Sigrid Beaubien's slippers.

Dr. Roderick Hibben

As you can well imagine, I reeled at the sight of those words. My desk, with me seated at it, was suddenly in a tornado; we spun around the corners of the ceiling and I got a good look at the molding. Then we slammed back into place in front of the window.

My thoughts then went immediately to the two bottles of wine that had been in my bag when I left New Jersey. What had Jeeves done with them? I went to my bedroom and looked in both suitcases, but the bottles weren't there. And they weren't in any of the dresser drawers. Jeeves must have stashed them somewhere or shared them with the kitchen staff. This is one problem with having valets—they do all the packing and unpacking. He may have saved my hands from sardine tins and kipper tins, but now I didn't have access to my booze when I needed it. To hell with AA. To hell with the pioneer life of climbing on the wagon. I needed alcohol if I was going to face Dr. Hibben.

Then the other rational alternative, besides drinking, presented itself—fleeing. I'd start packing, and when Jeeves came back from playing Daniel Boone in the woods, we'd leave the colony, pronto.

I glanced out my window to see if Jeeves was visible and coming toward the Mansion, and thus our departure could be hastened, but I didn't see him. I did see Ava, though. She was striding in the direction of the barns, one of which was probably her studio. She was in the cotton dress she had been wearing the night before. From my second-story perch, she looked as beautiful as ever. Well, as beautiful as the other two times I had seen her.

Suddenly, I wasn't ready to flee. Seeing Ava, I was emboldened. I wasn't ready to throw in the towel or even a washcloth. I couldn't leave the Rose and give up my chance at Ava. So I'd go face this Hibben and declare my innocence. I'd even tell him my plan—well, Jeeves's plan—to snare the slipper thief.

With great courage, I sallied forth out of my room. I was a classic lover—not to be confused with a lover of classics, though I do love the few classics I've read—on a mission. I was Romeo, Cyrano, Tristan, and Case 88, all rolled into one. Nothing was going to come between me and Ava and her nose.

In the office, the three ladies were at their desks. They lifted their heads in unison at my courageous entrance; I stood in the threshold.

"Alan," Doris said, using my name as a form of greeting. Then she asked, "How are you feeling? How's your nose?"

"The nose is coming along," I said, and then I added with steel in my voice, "I have a note from Dr. Hibben; he wants to see me."

"Okay," she said, "let's see if he's busy."

She came out from behind her desk. I knew full well that she was aware of the Beaubien situation—she had probably produced the note that was in my pocket, since Hibben's name had been typed and not signed—but she discreetly didn't say anything. And I could see in the faces of the other two women, old Barbara and young Sue, that they, too, were cognizant of the missing slippers and the charges against me. The Rose Colony, as I mentioned, was like a prison—everyone knew everyone's business, almost before it happened, and now I had an appointment with the warden. Martial law was probably in place. If Hibben thought I was guilty of stealing those slippers, he'd probably kick me out, and I'd lose my shot at Ava. I had to prove to him I was innocent. I was doing it for love!

Doris led me down the short hallway that was to the left of her desk. This poorly illumined passageway culminated in a door half composed of frosted glass. She knocked and then opened the door a crack and said, "Alan Blair is here."

I didn't hear any response, but Doris opened the door wide. Clearly, a signal from the master had been given.

"Go in, Alan," Doris said, and so I walked bravely into Dr. Hibben's office, an image of Ava's profile pinned to my heart to give me courage, like Don Quixote fighting his battles for his lady, La Dulcinea.

Doris closed the door behind me.

Well, I wasn't prepared for what I then saw. I don't know if any sane person would have been. All my courage drained to my ankles and with it went my blood sugar. My bone marrow turned to butter. I took flight again and went for a spin around the ceiling, cleaning cobwebs, and then returned to my station in front of the door.

I wasn't looking at a man. Standing behind a large antique desk was some kind of hybrid of man, woman, animal, fruit, and vegetable. If only I had found those two bottles of wine!

I'll start with the dimensions. Dr. Hibben was a seven-footer, if you can imagine a pear that big. He had unusually wide hips and unusually narrow shoulders.

At the top of the pear was an enormous head, in the shape of a rugby ball, and this rugby-ball head was disastrously covered with orange-brown freckles, like an overripe banana. Had the man never heard of *skin cancer*?

There were tufts of orangish hair on the sides of the head, and near the top of all this, high on the rugby ball, were two kindly blue dots—his eyes, I presumed. His nose was hard to make out, lost as it was in a galaxy of freckles. A small pink hole, like the anus of a starfish, opened, and from far away I heard a deep voice say, "Alan. It's very nice to meet you."

He came around his desk and moved toward me, an arm the length of a python extended in my direction. I was in danger of a seizure; not only was he an incredible, frightening specimen, but he had draped his prodigious organism in seersucker! Not just a jacket, like I was wearing, but also pants. I don't own seersucker pants, relying, as I do, on khaki trousers to go with my jacket. And so looking at that much seersucker on Dr. Hibben—yards and miles of it—was like staring at one of those disco balls, which cause epileptic fits in people with weak minds, and my mind definitely qualified as weak due to alcohol abuse and reading without glasses in poor light. But the alcohol abuse turned out to be a positive. Instead of a seizure, the sight of him had me excreting reserve ethanol that my liver must have been holding on to in case of an emergency. So this shot of stashed-away booze calmed me down and I went from experiencing sheer terror to feeling simply afraid.

With two long strides, he was upon me and I was offered a freckled hand that I could have sat in. I put out what looked like a toy hand by comparison and watched it disappear, ingested all the way to the wrist, and I wondered if I'd ever see it again. He squeezed my swallowed hand in greeting, and some orange juice I had drunk in the fourth grade may have been extracted, and then Dr. Hibben's fingers, which were the size of aerosol cans, unfurled, and I took my hand back and was overjoyed to see it, and he said, "We're so glad to have you at the Rose Colony."

"Thank you," I managed to whisper, and I tried to look up at his head, but I hadn't done yoga for a few days and my neck wasn't that flexible.

He then repaired to the other side of his desk and indicated that I should take the chair in front of the desk. The room was cool, an air conditioner hummed in a window, and on the walls were paintings, which were obviously the works of former and present colonists—mostly mad abstractionist efforts, including one entirely black painting that must have been perpetrated by Sophie, whom I had breakfasted with. Also on the walls were old black-and-white photos of the colony from earlier in the century. As with most pictures from long ago, there are far fewer trees visible than are present today. At some point in time in America, trees have made something of a comeback, while of course suffering great losses elsewhere. But why no one comments about all the trees we have running around is something of a mystery to me. Seems like it's at least one delusional positive we could hold on to, while everything else goes up in flames.

"So how are you making out so far?" asked Dr. Hibben. "Settling in okay?"

"Very well, thank you," I said, feeling apprehensive, waiting for him to stop with the sweet talk and broach the slipper issue. I avoided his watchful gaze and stared mournfully into the vibrating field of his seersucker. I think it was reflecting off my own seersucker. Rarely—except maybe in Newport, Rhode Island—are two people dressed in seersucker found in the same room at the same time; it happens with the frequency of a solar eclipse and is probably as dangerous to the human eye.

"I understand you had a car accident before coming here."

"Yes . . . I wasn't wearing my seat belt, hit my nose on the steering wheel."

I wondered if word had spread from the inmates that I had been bragging about a bar fight. Well, it would be better to be caught in a lie to them than to Doris. If he confronted me on the two differing tales—car accident and bar fight—I'd tell him I was trying to save face, literally and figuratively, with my peers, while telling the truth to Doris. Though of course, I had actually lied to Doris and told something closer to the truth to the colonists. Well, it was all a mess.

"You don't need to go to a doctor?"

"No, I think I'm healing nicely, thank you."

I risked taking a look at his face, which sent a fresh jolt to my nerves, and I gripped the arms of my chair. Somebody had to ban this man from being allowed in the sun; he needed to be hooded, like a hawk, at all times. I directed my stare back into his seersucker, and the lines oscillated and I almost expected them to congeal into a television broadcast.

"I'm glad to hear that you're all right," said Dr. Hibben, and he paused, uncapped and recapped a pen, and then he pulled the rope on the guillotine and down came the slippers. "There's something I want to talk to you about . . . Sigrid Beaubien came to me this morning rather upset."

"Yes, I understand that something strange has happened."

"She says that her slippers have been taken. And . . . this is very embarrassing . . . you know, but she says you took them, and so I have to ask you, did you take her slippers? I'm sure you didn't, you know, but I have to ask. Each artist's stay here has to be protected so that they can work."

"I didn't take her slippers. I swear. She brought all this up at breakfast and I had a sugar attack. I don't know why she thinks I would do such a thing."

I looked him in the face, found the two blue marbles that were his eyes, and sought to convince him of my innocence. I was growing somewhat used to his appearance, like a nurse working on a burn unit.

"A sugar attack?" he asked.

"When I'm upset, it's like I've eaten a carton of ice cream; I become feeble. . . . This one time in New York, I was walking along and a rat mistook me for a garbage can and raced up my leg and made it to my knee before it realized I was human. I guess if I was an infant, he might have tried to eat me. But he simply reversed direction and went and told all his friends, I imagine. Well, after he left, I screamed and then my sugar disappeared, and I had to buy a bottle of lemonade to bring myself back around."

I regretted shooting out that rat story—I can't seem to help myself with that tale; I'm like a war veteran blurting out "Take cover!" at the most inappropriate moments. But Dr. Hibben didn't seem to hold it against me.

"I'm sorry to hear about this rat, sounds terrible," he said with empathy. And then he asked, "So you didn't take the slippers?"

"No, I swear, I didn't even know that Sigrid owned slippers. . . . But since I've learned of this crime, I was thinking of leaving my own slippers outside my door and maybe attaching a string or something to my wrist, so if I fall asleep, I can still apprehend this slipper thief. . . . I'm on a hallway, though, that doesn't see a lot of action, but still it's a plan."

"That's very nice of you . . . but I don't think someone is going around stealing slippers. I spoke to Charles Murrin and he thinks it's just a silly prank, and I'm in agreement, but I did want, you know, to talk to you, and now I can reassure Sigrid that it's not anything to worry about."

"I'm sorry she got so upset."

"Everyone responds differently to stress," he said.

"Yes, stress is very stressful," I opined rather moronically, and then continued in a more interesting vein, "I have noticed—in old novels anyway—that people used to say they were *distressed*, but nowadays they're so upset that they've shortened it to *stressed*. . . . I do think we should take a page from the navy's book and develop signals for distress, rather than yelling at one another. I think a flare is more effective than bad behavior."

I was alluding to my disapproval of Beaubien's attack that morning, but Dr. Hibben didn't respond. He just looked at me. He couldn't defend her actions, and so we had just about run out of dialogue on the Beaubien matter, and no cue cards offstage were presenting themselves. The good news was that it looked as if everything was going to be all right. Other than his appearance, it had been a rather easy grilling. We were free to pursue other topics, if we liked, and so I really wanted to ask him if he had sought counsel with a dermatologist, but I didn't want to overstep my bounds. I decided, therefore, to practice giving compliments, the way Jeeves and Murrin had complimented my mustache. So I said, "I like your seersucker suit. Between the two of us I don't think there's been this much seersucker in one place since the British colonized India."

"That's very funny," said Dr. Hibben. "And I admire your jacket, as well. . . . You don't have pants?"

"At the time, when I bought the jacket, I couldn't afford the pants," I said, which was true, but I also think a whole seersucker suit is just too much, too pajamas-like, too bright. Of course, on Dr. Hibben it was beyond too much; I wouldn't have been surprised to learn that Doris, Barbara, and Sue were coming down with glaucoma and were going to file a class-action suit against his suit.

"I see," said Dr. Hibben. "Well, khaki pants work very well with seersucker. And I like your tie. Are those hummingbirds?"

"Yes. This tie is beloved by all. . . .By the way, do you know the derivation of the word *seersucker*? After all the years of having this jacket, it just dawned on me that it's a very odd word. What do you think? *Seersucker*—a visionary who is easily deceived?"

"I don't know," said Dr. Hibben, "but I can look it up."

He consulted his dictionary and read aloud, "'Noun. Indian blue and white-striped linen. From Persian, *shir-o-shakar*.' Which, according to the dictionary, means "'milk and sugar.'"

"That's very interesting," I said. "I knew that seersucker came from India, but I didn't know about this Persian connection. . . . I wonder if in Iran they ask for seersucker in their coffee?"

Dr. Hibben chose that moment to open his little pink mouth rather wide, revealing an impressive set of bunched-together, yellow teeth, which he may have stolen from the George Washington museum, and he laughed quite loudly, with several heroic snorts. When someone Dr. Hibben's size laughs, it's like a gigantic bellows is pushing up a great reserve of repressed air, since the volume of their chest cavity is so much larger than the average person's.

Well, it was quite apparent that we were really hitting it off over this issue of seersucker, and I had to give all the credit to Jeeves. He had outdone himself that day with his selections. Both Ava and Dr. Hibben had fallen under my sway due to my wardrobe. My whole destiny might have been different if I were wearing my blazer and my floating-fountain-pen tie. With Dr. Hibben, I felt I had gone from death-row to favorite-son status.

When the snorting subsided, he smiled and said, "Well, it's very nice to meet you, Alan, and I'm sorry, you know, that I had to ask you about those slippers, but what we do here is very fragile in a way—the making of art—and so we have to coddle one another."

"I'm all for coddling."

With that, Dr. Hibben stood up and my stomach did tumble; I had grown accustomed to half his body, and seeing the whole thing again was a bit daunting. But I got to my feet, and out came his hand and so I sacrificed mine for another juicing.

"You might not know this," said Dr. Hibben as he let go of my desiccated hand, "but on Fridays my wife and I have everyone over for drinks after dinner. We're in the house on the dirt road beyond the pool. You'll see everyone walking in that direction. I hope you can come by."

"I will . . . thank you," I said, and left his office, trying to shake some blood back into my fingers. Dr. Hibben would be a good guy to have around if you needed someone who could remove lug nuts without a wrench. I said good-bye to Doris, Barbara, and Sue and walked back to the Mansion and contemplated what lay ahead of me:

Drinks before dinner.

Drinks during dinner.

Drinks after dinner.

It wasn't what you call an ideal program for someone struggling to stay sober.

CHAPTER 26

Preoccupations of artists ★ A ribbon of pavement ★ An emerald glade with a blue pool ★ An inspiring talk with Kenneth about homosexuality

Jeeves wasn't in our rooms when I returned. Either he was taking his lunch in the kitchen or he was still out communing with nature. I wondered if maybe he was trying to achieve an out-of-body experience to show off for me later. In any event, regaling him with the tale of my interview with Dr. Hibben would have to wait.

Wanting to proceed with my earlier plan, I put on my bathing trunks, wrapped a towel around my neck, grabbed my current volume of *A Dance to the Music of Time,* and headed out, once more, from the Mansion. In the distance, I could hear the announcer from the track, and I made a mental note that Jeeves and I should go over there someday soon and lose some money.

As I walked to the pool, the colony seemed deserted: everyone must have been off in their studios working or taking naps or hating themselves, the usual preoccupations of artists.

I had a good idea what Tinkle was up to, and I was sure he wasn't the only one engaged in this manner, it being another preoccupation of creative people and a by-product of the solitary work environment. This is not to say that noncreative people don't go in for that, but they usually work with other people in offices, and self-release in public is not tolerated, though of course it does happen.

I crossed paths with no one, and walking along the ribbon of pavement that wound through the colony, amid lawns, patches of forest, and outer buildings, I made my way to the pool, which was in its own private glade, enclosed by a thick protective wall of pine trees.

The sun was bright but not punishing—a kindly wind helped to make for a nice air temperature. And the pool, with its water looking so blue, was incredibly gorgeous, surrounded, as it was, by the emerald color of the grass and trees.

Beach chairs were scattered about the concrete lip of the pool, and there was a little house for changing. The great poet Kenneth, he of the beautiful nose, completing a sort of nose triangle with myself and Ava, was sitting poolside. He was the only person there, and as I approached, he motioned that I should come sit next to him.

"Hello," he said with a smile. It was a handsome smile that must have served him well over the course of his long life. There was something undeniably glamorous about him. Some people have it. It's called charm. They seem to give off a kind of magnetic field. But it doesn't so much attract as repel, but we're attracted to the things that repel us, so in the end it does attract. Seeing him lounging there, I recalled a bit of gossip I had gleaned from the *New York Review of Books* in a piece about the biography of Leonard Bernstein, and I made a connection with Kenneth's name that hadn't occurred to me before—he was the poet rumored to have been Bernstein's secret gay lover. "You've discovered," he said, "the best thing about this place—the pool."

"It's beautiful," I said shyly, sitting down on the beach chair beside him.

"Any news on the sandal scandal?"

"No. But I think it was slippers that were stolen."

"I prefer *sandals* since it rhymes with *scandal*." This made sense since Kenneth was a poet.

"Yes, *sandal scandal* does have a better ring to it," I said, glancing at him, and I saw that his old body was hairless, white, and that his muscles sagged beneath the skin, but I could see the outline of a physique that had once been attractive, even ideal, in a Greek sense. It was strange to me, though, that his old legs were hairless. Had seven decades of wearing pants worn away his leg hair or could he possibly shave his legs? Is that what Bernstein liked? Kenneth's smooth legs? My own body, in contrast, looked practically simian. I have reddish brown curls on my chest, and my legs look like the makings of an angora sweater.

I held in my lap, above my angora legs, the thick Powell tome, the third of the four volumes (each volume, which Powell titles movements, contains three novels; the third movement covers the years of the Second World War). Kenneth, glancing at the book, said, "I didn't think anybody read Powell anymore, though hardly anyone read Powell when they were reading Powell."

"There are still a few mad devotees around," I said.

"A few of the books are good, but on the whole the thing is a deadly bore, and he was a nasty man."

"But I love it."

"I won't hold that against you," Kenneth said. I could see that he was one of those people who have great convictions about things, what's good and what's not good. This is often a component of charm, though not always. And usually around such people I find it hard to speak, fearing that they will continually correct me and put me in my place about the aesthetic makeup of the world. But that day I felt as if I could almost hold my own with Kenneth. The air was too nice and the sun felt too good for me to be intellectually destroyed by him. Also, I had survived my encounter with Dr. Hibben: I was a world-beater!

"Well, I really do love *A Dance to the Music of Time,*" I said, not ceding my position. "I think it has changed my life. Makes me notice how everything repeats: my feelings, people, events. Powell often refers to Nietzsche's theory of eternal recurrence. I haven't read Nietzsche, but I think I get what he's saying—"

"Are you homosexual?" asked Kenneth, cutting off what could have been my dissertation defense.

This really was the Homosexual Question of all Homosexual Questions, not that there's necessarily more than one Homosexual Question, but you know what I mean. I hesitated a moment, not knowing if I should answer, but to not answer seemed worse, so I said, "No, I'm not homosexual."

I felt this was a true response, but there was also something untrue about it, and I wondered if Kenneth would perceive this and say that I was lying. After all, could I be an utter card-carrying heterosexual if, over the years, I'd had a recurring—speaking of Nietzsche—fantasy about life in prison? It all came from reading

Papillon during my adolescence, right around the time that Krafft-Ebing was putting its mark on me. The author, Henri Charrière (nickname: Papillon), describes a love affair between two prisoners on the island where he was held, and how one man had taken the rôle of the wife, and something about this had aroused me mentally and erotically and been plaguing me, periodically, ever since. Here I was, as an adolescent and in adulthood, completely attracted to females, but somewhere lurking in my psyche was a desire to be imprisoned and forced to play a feminine rôle.

"I hope you don't mind me asking," said Kenneth. "Whenever I meet a young man, I like to get that out of the way. Usually, I can tell one way or the other, but with some people, like you, it's less clear. You're all beaten up and bruised, but besides that your signal is strange. I didn't think you were gay, though it's hard to read that mustache of yours and you dress eccentrically. . . . I, of course, am completely homosexual. I don't like the word *gay,* but I use it when I have to."

"I don't mean to give a fuzzy signal," I said. "I was hoping with my mustache to convey a Douglas Fairbanks Jr.-Errol Flynn look. Also, William Powell, now that I think of it."

"William Powell wasn't a bad actor, he could be quite comedic, but Fairbanks Jr., like most actors, had no talent. But he had a face. That's all you need for movies. A good face . . . So you're a little bit off, like everyone else here, but I believe you when you say you're not homosexual."

"I'm not saying I'm one hundred percent heterosexual. . . . Doesn't Jung contend that we're all essentially bisexual?" I think I was hoping to win Kenneth's approval—one always wants the approval of charming people—by acknowledging some possibility of homosexuality for myself, but my remark didn't quite have the desired effect.

"Everyone is always saying Jung, Jung, Jung, and this bisexual bullshit. I haven't had a single sexual thought about a woman in my life. I'm the least bisexual person there is. I've always been entirely homosexual, even before puberty. . . . I was defiled when I was twelve by a man in his thirties. We were in a park. In Chicago, where I grew up. He took me in some bushes, and I loved it. I still love it. Psychologically, anyway. I can't do it physically. Hurts too much. But I'm still looking for that man who raped me. Seventy-eight and still looking. Don't think I'll find him."

I was silent. There was something very sad and human about what he had said. For a moment, I wondered idiotically if that man in the park was still alive, and somehow he and Kenneth could be reunited.

"I went back to that park for years," he continued, "but I never saw him again. He was dark. Have always liked men with dark hair ever since. But I did meet other men in that park. . . . And I always wanted the same thing: to be defiled . . . that's when I was happiest. Went on for decades, but in my fifties, I quit sex. No point to it anymore. I had piles. It's very painful. I didn't have sex for twenty years, but then last year I was in England lecturing and I met a young man about your age. He came back with me to the States; he didn't have a job. I gave him blow jobs for eight months. That was it. But I enjoyed it. A substitute for what I really like. We did try it once, but I couldn't do it."

As Kenneth spoke, I had something of an intellectual breakthrough, a glimpse of understanding about my own sexuality, and it all hinged on the word *defiled*. I wanted to get back to my room and write it down before it slipped away from me, but it would have been rude to leave Kenneth at that moment, though I didn't know how to keep the conversation going.

I was pretty sure before this talk with Kenneth that everyone at the Rose Colony was sex-crazed, but this confirmed it. I mean they were as sex-crazed as the regular human population, as sex-crazed as I am, but something about the place compelled people to confess to me about their erotic lives almost immediately upon being alone with my person. First there was Beaubien with her insinuations of incest, then Tinkle with his water-pistol problem, and now Kenneth.

"I've silenced you," he said.

"I just feel bad that you've never found that man again," I said, and I thought of how Kenneth must have been a very pretty boy when he was in that park, all of him as fine and as beautiful as his nose.

"Don't feel too bad," he said. "I don't think anybody finds that man."

Rather than say anything, I stood up and put my foot in the water, testing it. Testing the water, that is, not my foot. Though maybe it was my foot I was testing—whether it could tolerate the water's temperature. Oh, God, I don't know what's more difficult, life or the English language.

"Cold?" asked Kenneth.

"A little cool, but sort of nice," I said. "I think I'll go for a swim. Be good for my nose."

Kenneth nodded sympathetically, and through the trees the track announcer mutedly called for the start of another race. I got into the pool and did ten laps, racing only against myself. It was good to exercise and the aqua therapy was healing for my nose; I could almost sense the swelling going down. When I came out, Kenneth watched me towel off. I felt like Tadzio to his Aschenbach.

"You have a nice slender physique," said Kenneth. "Muscular but thin."

"Thank you," I said. "I do a little yoga." I didn't mention that heavy drinking seemed to have had a dissipating effect on me, but in a positive way, stripping off any fat. Some people get heavy on booze and some people disappear.

"You have bruises on your body," he said. The marks on my shoulder and stomach were fading but still visible.

"I had a fall." I picked up my book. It seemed okay to leave now. "I'm going to try to get some work done," I said, still mentally holding on to my breakthrough. "It's been nice talking to you."

"Nice talking to *you*," said Kenneth, smiling at me seductively. I knew from his smile that all his life he'd had power over people and could induce them to try to destroy him. Maybe it was the way he had kept his ego in check. And it hadn't completely sailed over my head that Kenneth had perhaps mentioned giving blow jobs to a young man my age as a veiled sort of offer. But it was an offer that didn't appeal. So his smile didn't seduce, it only made me feel like I couldn't save him. You see, I didn't want to defile him; it would have killed him to hear me say so, but there wasn't much left to destroy.

CHAPTER 27

I spell out for Jeeves my breakthrough with the Homosexual Question ★ Thanatos and Eros are touched upon ★ More whining on my part about not having read Freud and Jung ★ A contemplation of the loneliness of being a Siamese twin ★ Even if I'm a little bit defeated, I show a plucky spirit and press on with my work

Jeeves had returned from his nature romp, and I changed out of my wet bathing suit and glued back on my seersucker jacket and khaki pants.

Feeling lively and gregarious after my swim, I invited Jeeves to come sit with me in the writing room. I thought that if I orally ventilated my mental breakthrough, this would facilitate my turning it into prose, with the hope of finding a place to slip it into the novel.

I was arranged at my desk, and Jeeves was on his cot. We had a fan blowing on us, which was quite delightful. I had picked up my lunch pail and thermos in the mudroom on my way into the Mansion, and so I sipped some coffee, to further excite my intellect.

"Jeeves, you're not going to believe what I've been through in the last two hours," I said.

"Indeed, sir?"

I quickly told Jeeves of my interview with the frightening yet civilized Hibben. But this already seemed like back-page news, compared with my discussion with Kenneth. I then outlined that discourse for Jeeves. I told him how Kenneth had desired all his life to be defiled.

"A frank admission, sir."

"Well, when he told me that, I had a breakthrough with the Homosexual Question."

225

"A happy occasion, sir."

"But before I spell it out for you, let me ask—how were the woods?"

"Lovely, sir."

"You weren't working on an out-of-body experience, were you?"

"No, sir."

I was a little disappointed but I didn't let on. "So you had a good time, then?"

"Yes, sir."

"I'm glad. I want you to be happy, Jeeves. . . . We'll have to go to the track one day, and if I ever get a moment's rest, I'll go for a spin on the forest trails myself. But this Rose Colony really keeps a person busy."

"It *is* a stimulating environment, sir."

"Especially since everyone is on sexual red alert. I don't know if anyone here is actually having sex, but they certainly have it on the brain. . . . Wait a second, those two fellows are having sex, I forgot about that; here I am intellectualizing the whole Homosexual Question and those two are quite literally burning up the sheets. . . . Well, to each his own. They do it, I think about it. . . . So the thing with the H. Question is that I've never really known what the Question is. I'm not sure there even is one, but I once heard someone say the 'Homosexual Question,' so I assumed there must be one. It could be like the Jewish Question: Why are homosexuals hated? But I don't think they're as hated as Jews, though they're certainly up there. I wonder if Jewish homosexuals had to wear a pink triangle to go with their gold star in Germany? Or was one decoration enough? . . . Maybe they wore a pink star? . . . Anyway, what I've realized, Jeeves, is that the Homosexual Question is primarily, for me anyway, a personal question: Why do *I* have homosexual thoughts? And what do they mean? . . . Is it all right if I talk about this?"

"Perfectly all right, sir."

"Thank you, Jeeves . . . you're very kind. . . . I've been learning so much about myself today, it's incredible. First the nose-fetish business and now this homosexual breakthrough. One can go years without any insights and then in one day several mysteries are cleared up. . . . I'll try to make this coherent, Jeeves. . . . You see, ever since I read this book *Papillon* when I was about fifteen, I've had this occasional fantasy of being in prison and forced to play a feminine homosexual rôle. . . . It embarrasses me to tell you this . . . but I'm going to be brave. . . . So I'd have this fantasy usually when I was feeling low and self-hating, and as I often feel this way, this homosexual fantasy would recur with some frequency. But the thing is, it's not easy or desirable to get one's self thrown in prison, so the whole thing was quite impractical. And not being able to act it out, it sort of plagued me. I couldn't demystify it, couldn't find out whether or not it was really for me. So for years, it's had me somewhat wondering if I was homosexual. I knew it was unlikely, since I don't find men attractive and that seems to be a key component to male homosexuality, but nonetheless, I did have my doubts. And I'd really rather not have doubts, especially now that I'm on the verge of a romance with Ava. . . . So when Kenneth said he wanted to be defiled, I realized that's what I've wanted, at least in those low moments. Follow me, Jeeves?"

"At some remove, sir."

"Well, we're almost there . . . I'm trying to make sense. . . . Anyway, as you know, I haven't really read Freud, but I read a novel where some characters were talking about Freud's theories, one of which is that there are two draws on the human spirit: Thanatos and Eros. Death and sex. Destruction and creation. Kind of like the north and south poles for explorers. . . . We see it in children early on: the-building-of-the-sand-castle-and-then-kicking-it-down motif. . . . Well, when I'm low, I'm drawn to *both*! Sex *and* death. So I combine the two! I'm thinking of calling it *Thanateros*. Death through sex. Death of my *self*. By taking on the female rôle—in prison!—it's been a way for my psyche to punish myself *and* kill myself. To be *defiled*! To kill my *self* as I know myself, or is it 'my self' again?"

I spelled out for Jeeves the two versions—"myself" and "my self"—that were confusing to me.

"In this instance, sir, it would seem that both word combinations could apply."

"Thank you, Jeeves. . . . Now the thing is, I most loathe myself when I feel weak and helpless and inadequate. And for better or worse, I must think of the female as the weaker of the two sexes, and so when I'm feeling weak and low, I fantasize about playing the female rôle. This is denigrating to me, but I want to be denigrated because I don't like myself. . . . So the breakthrough is this: I now realize that this prison fantasy has actually been a positive and not something to be ashamed of. You see, my mind had sought out a scenario where I would be loved even if I was a weak, helpless thing. Because in *Papillon* the man loves his wife. They were happy on the island, even though it was a prison. That's what was so moving. . . . Eros also means love, which is important to consider. . . . So I want to die but I also want to live, and my fantasy has been a way for me to do both. Thanateros. To live through being loved, but to be loved by having my self killed, defiled, erased. But a new self is created, a female self. . . . Is any of this understandable, Jeeves?"

"A good deal of it, sir, though not all of it."

"You're right, Jeeves, I haven't fully worked it out. . . . I think my main point is that my homosexual thoughts are almost entirely psychological and metaphorical, which explains why I haven't, at age thirty, ever really needed to physicalize them. . . . And they're not bad, these thoughts, since at the root of them is a desire to be loved. You see, my mind is always working on that angle, even when I hate myself."

"Very good, sir."

"I should read Freud, though, to make sure I'm not botching everything. And I probably should read Jung. I read a novel that was all about Jungian analysis. Mostly it discussed the male's search for his anima, which sounds too much like *enema*. But the anima is the female self or something, which is probably what I'm looking for in Ava, but I'm supposed to find it in myself. And women are supposed to be looking for their animuses, I think. But nobody finds these things. We spend years searching for them by screwing around and a lot of babies get made by mistake, which probably keeps Darwin happy, and then we lose our looks and can't screw around anymore and we haven't figured anything out. . . . Oh, it's just a great big mess, actually."

"I would agree that it is a mess, sir."

"But it keeps me busy."

"Undoubtedly, sir."

"Keeps everyone busy. . . . But we're all so lonely due to our mass confusion. It's very frustrating."

"Indeed, sir."

"I wish it weren't so, but there's no way around it. I think even those two-headed Chinese fellows felt alone. One of them was alcoholic, which I can appreciate, and the other was what they called in rehab a *codependent.* So even Siamese twins have it rough. Don't you think?"

"It's not something I had considered, sir."

"Probably a good thing. Your brain doesn't seem to get cluttered up with things, the way mine does. I envy that, Jeeves."

"You have an excellent mind, sir."

"Thank you, Jeeves. . . . But I guess my breakthrough wasn't such a breakthrough, after all. But it was nearly a breakthrough, which is pretty good. For some people it doesn't even occur to them to have breakthroughs."

"Yes, sir."

"Well, I'm going to put this partial breakthrough into my novel. I'll inhale the rest of this thermos of coffee and type until I'm arthritic."

"Very good, sir."

CHAPTER 28

The Steps * I try my hand at scriptwriting * A wedding celebration * We're all chastised * An interesting story about teacups and
urine * Alone with Tinkle and Mangrove * Another tale of a
decimated heart * Beaubien is on fire * Mangrove, the hero * Talk
of transubstantiation

The Steps of Alcoholism that I was following went like this:

(1) Have honest intentions to stay sober.
(2) Do nothing to stay sober.
(3) Drink.

I didn't call AA as I said I would in the library, and when I was
offered a glass of white wine on the back terrace, I immediately
caved in.

Here's what the screenplay version would look like:

```
BACK TERRACE MANSION. DRINKS BEFORE DINNER —
FRIDAY NIGHT.

              FELLOW ROSE COLONIST
        Would you like a glass of wine?

              ALAN BLAIR
        No . . . . Yes!

Alan drinks.

Similar lighting and costuming as the night
before. Similar quantities of white wine
```

231

available. Same cast, with camera spending
time on more significant cast members, such as
Mangrove, Tinkle, Murrin, and Kenneth. Notably
absent: Ava and Beaubien. Diane, the feral
photographer, is observed by Alan and her
beauty is admired, but his heart belongs to
Ava.

As Alan continues to rapidly sip several
plastic cups of wine, becoming drunk, his
eyes happily scan the wine-drinking crowd—his
fellow artists. It's as if he's always been
here. He's joined by Mangrove and Tinkle.

I had only been at the Rose Colony for two days, but there was already a familiarity with everyone that was quite striking. Have a few meals and social gatherings with people and you feel like you know them.

Along with behaving alcoholically, what was happening to me at the Rose Colony is the exact phenomenon that takes place during a wedding celebration which spreads itself over a few days—you become very close to certain people and you can't stand certain other people, but in either case you *know* them, you're intimate in some way that is lacking in your everyday life.

So my two favorite Rose Colony members were Mangrove and Tinkle. We three men naturally sought one another out on the back terrace and then ate dinner together at one of the smaller satellite tables, where we were joined by Sophie and Don, my two breakfast-mates, and the ancient painter, named Janet, who appeared to be locating her food perfectly well, further mystifying me as to the nature of legal blindness. Meanwhile, Tinkle sat next to me and I looked upon him as the younger, smaller brother I never had, even though he was a year older than myself.

The Rose Colony, as I just tried to explain with my wedding celebration analogy, was a hothouse for emotions. Things grew quicker here than in the real world. It might have taken me years to feel close to Tinkle if we had met in the real world, but at the Rose Colony, by our third meal together, he was already a boon companion.

Beaubien, who had skipped the pre-dinner-drinks binge, was at the large table, and every now and then I felt a psychic stinging on my neck. She was obviously directing mental ice picks in my direction. Ava never came to dinner, which pained me, but I drank plenty of wine and was hopeful that I would see her later.

We had Cornish game hens, mashed sweet potatoes, and salad, and the dining room was abuzz with the usual sounds of eating, as well as conversation about a notice that Dr. Hibben had placed on the mail table before dinner. Herewith, I reproduce:

Dear Colonists,

Our physical plant is old and our greatest DANGER is fire. We need everyone to be very careful and responsible. Also, if anyone took Sigrid Beaubien's slippers, please return them to me. This is a community whose purpose is the accomplishment of serious work. We must not forget that. Let's try to get back into the spirit of things with a pleasant evening of drinks at my house after dinner. Come by around 8:30.

Dr. Hibben

From what I gathered, this was unprecedented. No one could ever recall a director of the Rose Colony having to take such an action. Occasionally individual colonists had to be warned or even excommunicated, but never had the colony at large been chastised. And so a herdlike fear was palpable—that if we didn't shape up, we would all be punished, even if we were innocent of the crimes that had so far been committed: sheet-burning and slipper-stealing.

As a way to counteract this group anxiety, or perhaps to enflame it, a history of bad colonist behavior, essentially Rose Colony lore, was the primary subject of our dinner-table discussion. Mangrove recounted a particularly florid tale, though his speaking voice was notably serious and flat, without affect. It was the voice of a major depressive.

"There was this English writer a few years ago, this was during the winter, who was nuts," he said solemnly. His eye patch was shiny and his good eye beamed out equal portions of intelligence and despair.

"He was sneaking into people's bedrooms and leaving teacups of his urine under their beds."

"I heard about that," said Sophie, who was wearing a black T-shirt, her favorite color. "What could he have been thinking?"

"What an idiot," said Don, the acne-scarred sculptor, who was interesting to look at—the crevices in his face were compelling and his half-thumb was also good visually. "If I found him in my room, I would have beat the shit out of him. What's his name?"

"Philip Goldberg," said Mangrove.

Of course, a Jew, I thought to myself. We're always so disturbed.

"The whole thing is disgusting," said Sophie. "How could such a person be allowed in here?"

"They've been letting kooks into this place for years," said Janet.

"He did publish a novel that was well received in England," said Mangrove.

"How'd they pin it on him?" asked Tinkle.

"I'm not sure," said Mangrove. "I arrived a few weeks after he had been asked to leave. But what I think happened is that one person found a teacup, told somebody, and then everyone began looking under their beds and discovered they also had teacups."

"But how'd they know he was the one?" asked Don.

"Again, I'm not sure," said Mangrove. "But they just knew it was him. He was strange. And then I think he did confess to Hibben when confronted."

"I wonder what he's doing right now," I said.

"Why?" asked Sophie.

"Whenever I hear about interesting people, even if they're interesting in disturbing ways, I wonder what they're doing at that precise moment. Though this fellow is probably asleep, if he's in England, which isn't very fascinating to think about, but at least the world at large is safe from him wreaking havoc."

"Seems like the teacups were sort of an English thing," said Tinkle rather astutely.

"A sick thing," said Don.

"I think you're right about the teacups," I said, addressing Tinkle. "Maybe that was his clue, a real English clue, so that he would be caught, like a serial killer who wants to be discovered."

Then the conversation moved on to other desperate characters who had lost their minds at the colony, and the list was rather extensive. But I wasn't upset by this, inured as I was at this point to the colony's resemblance to an asylum.

After dinner, Mangrove, Tinkle, and I made for Tinkle's chambers to have a conference with his whiskey bottle. We had about an hour before regathering with everyone chez Hibben for more white wine, though supposedly he sometimes provided gin. I was hoping that Ava would make an appearance there. I was still wearing my hummingbird tie and seersucker jacket, thinking it best to stick with the costume that she had responded favorably to earlier in the day. I could have given over to gloomy disappointment at not seeing her at dinner, but I was happily—and drunkenly—floating along with my two friends.

Mangrove, being the eldest and a natural leader, took the easy chair in Tinkle's room, the one with the stick shift that I had inhabited the night before. I assumed Tinkle's desk chair and Tinkle sat on his bed. We each had a healthy glass of whiskey, which we sipped like gentlemen, and Tinkle passed around cigars. He put on his fan, and we blew our smoke out the window.

We were silently enjoying one another's masculine company and I eyeballed our tall, melancholy leader, Mangrove. He looked quite dignified with his long legs and eye patch. He was closer to fifty than forty, but his bicycle riding kept him in good shape.

So there I was staring at his eye patch and then suddenly I said to him, unable to take it anymore, "How did you lose your eye?" I hadn't intended to blurt this out, but there it was.

"I haven't lost an eye," said Mangrove calmly.

I was too shocked to say anything, but not Tinkle. "What's with the patch, then?" he asked. Tinkle was his drunken, assertive self, as opposed to his more reserved, sober self, which I had encountered that morning.

"I'm trying a radical depression cure," said Mangrove. "I'm seeing a holistic psychiatrist in New York. He's attempting to shift the use of my brain over to the left side. I have become almost entirely right-brained, which is the creative side, and by overrelying on that side, I opened myself up for a severe depression when I had an emotional

235

trauma. The doctor said that I was the most depressed person he had ever met who was still alive."

"But the patch is on your left eye," I said.

"The right side of the brain controls the left side of the body," said Mangrove.

"I forgot that about the brain," I said. "It's like sailing. I hate when the left is right and right is left. You'd think, though, that it was the left side that would control creativity, but that must be my liberal bias. I have to say, though, this is all rather confusing."

"Is it working?" Tinkle asked Mangrove, and I wondered as he said that if an eye patch would help Tinkle with his misfiring. I was curious, though, as to which side of the brain controls the penis. I figured that since it's in the middle, probably both sides of the brain control it, which makes sense, because if one side of the brain breaks down, you still want your penis to work. So Tinkle would probably have to wear patches over both his eyes.

"I'm not sure if it's working," said Mangrove. "I've only been doing it a few weeks."

"So you're trying to slosh some activity over to one side, to the left side . . . with the hope of getting some balance, like a seesaw?" I asked.

"Yes," said Mangrove. "There are parts of my brain that haven't seen serotonin in years." He spoke with such seriousness that everything he said had the weight of grave truth, and it was fascinating to contemplate a brain that had areas starved of serotonin.

"Your brain must be like Mars," I said passionately. "There must be barren, dry canals."

"What caused your brain to dry up?" asked Tinkle, who of course had the opposite problem of overliquefaction.

"A young girl," said Mangrove. "A student at Columbia. She was in my writing class. I fell in love with her. She fell in love with me. For a semester. I've never recovered."

"When did this happen?" asked Tinkle.

"Ten years ago."

"You've been depressed for ten years over this girl?" I asked.

"Yes."

"Are you in touch with her at all?" Tinkle inquired.

"Haven't seen or talked to her in about nine years. But I've been stalking her."

"What do you mean?" asked Tinkle. "How can you stalk her if you haven't seen her?"

"I've been stalking her in my mind. Wherever I go, I look for her. I think she's in California, but even when I ride my bicycle here in Saratoga, I'm looking for her. If someone knocked at your door right now, I would hope for a moment that it was her. It's what has caused the ruts in my brain."

"More whiskey," I said to Tinkle. Pathos-wise this was almost as bad as Tinkle's confession of the night before, and it was eerily similar in theme to Kenneth's search for the man who had raped him. I thought of mentioning that Kenneth was in a similar boat, but it was too complicated to go into, and furthermore I didn't know if Mangrove would appreciate my drawing a parallel between Kenneth's rapist and his, Mangrove's, young coed.

"Yes, more whiskey," said Mangrove. "Though I probably shouldn't drink too much more. As it is, probably only two percent of my brain is functioning and I don't want to undo what the eye patch might be achieving."

"Maybe if you only swallow on the left side of your mouth," I offered. "That's what I do when I get mouth ulcers."

Tinkle generously poured out more medicine in all our glasses.

"I need to drink for my condition," said Tinkle to Mangrove. "So don't feel pressure to keep up with me."

"My condition *is* drinking," I said, not wanting to be left out of this discussion of maladies, though neither fellow seemed to take notice of my admission.

Mangrove said to Tinkle, "What's *your* condition?"

"Sexual problems," said Tinkle, and I thought to myself, Oh no, here we go again, and I girded myself, but before Tinkle could give me a second helping of penis cancer woes, there was a frantic knock at the door. It startled all of us, coming so soon after Mangrove had spoken of his long-lost coed knocking at the door. We froze. Could it be? Had she somehow tracked him down to the Rose Colony after all these years?

We were drunk enough to consider it a possibility, and we all *wanted* it to be her, because our hearts, united by the Rose Colony's strange hothouse forces, were momentarily beating and dreaming as one. What one friend wanted, we all wanted. Tinkle put his cigar in the windowsill and slowly walked to his door to answer the persistent knocking. Mangrove followed him with one depressed, expectant eye.

Tinkle opened the door and standing before us was not Mangrove's Columbia love. Rather, it was her spiritual opposite—Beaubien! The light of the hallway was behind her and her dark hair glowed like a solar eruption. It was not the first time a person seemed to be bursting into flames in front of me. A memory of Uncle Irwin superimposed itself over Beaubien, and this doubling of two nemeses added to my considerable discomfiture.

But it wasn't me she was after.

"Reginald!" she cried. "There's a bat in my room!"

For a man with a dried-out brain, who had just been hoping that the love of his life might at long last have come to him, he moved with incredible agility. Drink down, cigar in windowsill, he dashed out of the room. We all followed him, though I held back some, not wanting to be too close to Beaubien.

Mangrove, taking two stairs at a time, and holding on to the banisters like a gymnast, flew down to the second floor, went into his room, and came out wearing thick canvas gloves and carrying an enormous bat-catching net. The net was preposterously large, the kind of thing you'd see in the Three Stooges movies when a white-coated worker would be trying to catch people for a loony bin. Tinkle, Beaubien, and I then followed Mangrove down a carpeted, wood-paneled hall, until we were at Beaubien's room. For the moment at least, her hostilities toward me were dropped, as we now faced a common enemy.

The four of us went into her room, and I wondered if it was all right that no one took their shoes off, but maybe Beaubien didn't have a shoe policy, and only left slippers outside her door, which wasn't quite rational. Then I reasoned that whatever shoe policy she employed would most likely be dropped in an emergency situation, such as the one we were confronting.

Her boudoir was large and dominated by a four-poster antique bed, with a faded pink bedspread. Antique lamps and bureaus completed the picture of a very charming, turn-of-the-century bedroom.

"Where is it?" asked Mangrove with urgency.

We scanned the room, and then Tinkle spotted it: "In the corner, against the wall."

Sure enough, fixed to the wall, like a raised lump of light brown mud, was a bat with folded wings. Mangrove approached with great stealth, but the bat sensed something and suddenly was in flight, swooping right at us. I don't know if the others screamed, as all sound was drowned out by my own piercing yell. For once I had responded immediately to danger. It's clear that being at the Rose Colony was giving me greater access to all my emotions, including terror.

Luckily, Mangrove, with the concentration of a samurai, was not thrown off by my cry. He swung the net with a beautiful, harmonious motion and plucked the bat right out of the air. Then with an efficient twirl of the net handle, he made it so that the net closed upon itself, creating a pouch from which the bat could not escape.

"You did it!" exclaimed Beaubien.

"Try not to hurt it," said Tinkle, displaying his sympathies for bats.

"You're incredible," I said to Mangrove.

Mangrove smiled humbly, and then with humanitarian intent, he ran from Beaubien's room, with the three of us following at a safe distance, to free the creature outside.

We went through the mudroom, where a number of colonists were reading newspapers before going to Hibben's for drinks. They all exclaimed with great excitement at the sight of the bat. Then once outside, Mangrove heroically opened the net with another dexterous twirl, then laid it on the ground, leaving a slight opening. The bat, stunned, didn't move, then, sensing liberation, it scampered a few inches and took flight into the quickly darkening night sky to rejoin its brother and sister bats.

Beaubien approached Mangrove, who now held his net alongside him like Neptune's trident, and she put her pretty hand on his arm. Their former alliance could be seen in this touch.

"Thank you, Reginald," she said. She looked quite beautiful in that moment. Then she went back into the Mansion, without looking at me or Tinkle.

We three men stayed outside for a few moments, relishing the night air and Mangrove's triumph, and then went back in ourselves for one more counseling session with Tinkle's whiskey.

Back in our earlier positions, drinking glasses in hand, I said to Mangrove, "For someone who only has about two percent of his brain working, you're remarkable. Think what you can do when the serotonin is running freely."

"Thank you," he said.

"I think we only use about ten percent of our brains as it is," said Tinkle. "So all you need to do is get back that dried-out eight percent."

"That's the hope," said Mangrove.

"I wonder what Darwin would say about this ninety percent of unused brain?" I asked. "Did we ever use it? Or are we gearing up to use it? Maybe we use it and we're not aware of it. Maybe we're teleporting everywhere and leading multiple lives. Maybe the world population is quite small—just a handful of brains transubstantiating all around the globe. I wonder, though, if people collide in the ether if they're teleporting about like that. What do you guys think? Lately, I've been really hankering for an out-of-body experience."

Well, you have to be careful what you ask for—which our spiritual leaders are always reminding us—and in this case it held up. Right after delivering my speech on transubstantiation, I blacked out.

Luckily, I wasn't gone very long this time, roughly thirty minutes or so, and I came to at Dr. Hibben's drinks party. In my own special, alcoholic way, I had teleported across the colony grounds.

And when consciousness was restored to me at the party, I was alone, though in a large, hot group of people. I was standing in front of a mantel that was above a dormant fireplace, and I was looking right into Ava's dead eyes. I reached up and felt the contours of her dead nose and my soul shivered. You see, on the mantel was a life-size bronze bust of the woman I had fallen in love with.

CHAPTER 29

I encounter a fish, then a mythological creature ★ I try to survive a heated conversation with Dr. Hibben ★ The idea of using snorkeling equipment as a means of coping with cocktail parties is something to consider ★ Charles Murrin makes a brief appearance and I meet Mrs. Hibben and she makes quite an impact ★ Kenneth expresses his sympathies ★ Mangrove proposes something, which, to be honest, frightens me

As I touched my loved one's bronze features, a gigantic dead fish was slapped on my shoulder, probably a good-size Alaskan halibut. Someone must be playing a practical joke on me, I thought, and I was about to turn and tell Mangrove or Tinkle or whoever it was to cut it out, that they were going to destroy my seersucker jacket with a dead fish, but then the fish turned out to be alive and it bit my right shoulder in half.

Unable to scream—the pain was too great—I turned to face this halibut and I looked into two faraway little holes, gills of some sort, and then another, somewhat larger hole opened and I saw yellow, crushed-together dog fangs and was hit with a vicious breeze that carried the smells of garlic and decomposed animals. I closed my eyes and waited to die, to join Ava in some kind of bronzed heaven. I was obviously being attacked by a fish-dog that wanted to drag me to the underworld. It must be that dog from Hades, I thought. Cerberus. But no one knows he's part fish.

"You like Ava's sculpture?" asked a voice, and since I was sightless, eyes shut, I sensed that the voice was coming from the vicinity of the dog-fish and I couldn't recall Cerberus having the powers of speech, and adding to my confusion, I was sure it was a voice I had heard once before.

I didn't say anything and then the halidog let go of my shoulder and said, "I think it's a wonderful piece. I'm so pleased to have it."

As these words were spoken, I was smitten by a furnace blast of more garlic and dead animals, which caused me to open my eyes, and at that precise moment a few brain cells must have just been born to compensate for the ones I had been killing all night, and with this slight upgrade of brainpower and sobriety, I realized I was being addressed by Dr. Hibben and not some creature from Hades. He must have slapped his gigantic hand on my right shoulder in friend-liness and then given me a playful, affectionate squeeze, but not knowing his own prodigious strength had crushed my shoulder joint like it was a marshmallow. I don't know what he was doing running an artist colony. He should have been working in a gravel pit as some kind of human marvel.

Loosened from his grip, though it was now certain I would never pitch in the major leagues or even brush my hair again, I was able to say, "Yes, it's a wonderful sculpture." Then several thousand more brain cells were born, very good of them to multiply like that, and I continued, "I love it. I've never seen anything more beautiful."

"She gave it to me a few weeks ago. I saw it in her studio and I praised it, you know, and then she gave it to me. I tried to say no, but she absolutely insisted. Very generous of her."

Without being rude, I was trying to retract my neck so as not to inhale Dr. Hibben's fiery breath, which he was shooting down at me from his considerable altitude. I imagine that my posture must have been rather odd—my right arm was dead, and my neck prob-ably looked like something that could hang in the window of a Chinese restaurant.

Cocktail parties, I find, are always minefields of bad breath. If I ever get popular on some sort of social circuit and have to go to a lot of cocktail parties, I might use snorkeling equipment. This way people won't have to smell my breath, which I worry can be quite punishing, and I won't have to smell theirs.

But not having a snorkel or some other filtering device to contend with Dr. Hibben's breath, I looked to Ava's head for courage. "I really do love this sculpture," I said, which was a more than honest sentiment.

"So do I," said Dr. Hibben, who had exchanged his seersucker jacket for a harmless, ill-fitting green blazer, which could have upholstered a good-size couch, with enough left over for a nice set of drapes. "And this bust is one-of-a-kind; she literally broke the plaster mold after making only one copy. Dropped it, she said."

"You're very lucky to have it." I pushed my neck back another notch, which would have alarmed a chiropractor but might have impressed a yoga teacher.

"Yes, I think so, too," said Dr. Hibben, smiling.

"Can I buy it from you?" I asked with a sudden inspiration.

"No, no," he said, and laughed good-naturedly. "I couldn't sell a gift. Also, I adore it and so does my wife, though I'm sure Ava will be flattered to hear that you like her work so much. Maybe there's another piece you can buy. I think it's wonderful, you know, if you can all support each other."

"I hope to visit her studio and see her work," I said, and then I thought that better than buying that bust of her head, I would hold her real head in my hands and kiss it. Kiss all of it. Kiss her nose. Kiss her nose a thousand times! I tried to look past Dr. Hibben's considerable frame to see if Ava was at the party, but she didn't seem to be there. If she were, I would have spotted her immediately. Just about everyone else was present, though. We were in what must have been Dr. Hibben's living room. There was a couch and some chairs, and two walls were impressively adorned with loaded bookshelves.

But mostly there were people. All my mad fellow colonists. The place was a riot of conversation, and jazz breathed out of unseen speakers. Tinkle and Mangrove were in a corner, drinking. I longed to join them, both for the company and a fresh drink, but there was no easy way to leave Dr. Hibben, though the forces of the party were bound to separate us; the laws of cocktail parties dictated as much. How long this would take, though, was the unknown, disturbing factor. So in the meantime, I had to be brave and keep going. To distract myself, I threw a question at him, referring to Ava's head: "Is a sculpture of yourself a self-sculpture?"

243

"I don't know," he said, and for some reason he closed in on me. I had no more room to back up, neck-wise or body-wise. I was up against the fireplace, trapped. He continued, "No one has asked me that before. Self-sculpture. You're very good with these kinds of questions."

As he finished his speech, a fresh blast of hot garlic burnt my eyelashes down to their tiny follicle roots. I tried to console myself with the thought that garlic is very good for the immune system, perhaps even when inhaled as secondhand smoke.

The tide of the cocktail party then washed up tiny Charles Murrin onto our little blistered island of two. I blinked at him with unprotected eyes.

"We're talking about Ava's bust," said Dr. Hibben, addressing Murrin.

"I hope she doesn't mind," said Murrin mischievously, though none too brilliantly.

Dr. Hibben laughed and I looked from one man to the next, giving myself quite the workout—Murrin just about surpassed Dr. Hibben's belt. Looking at the two of them was like traveling from Miami Beach to the Bay of Fundy and then back again. That is, there was a lot of north-south head-wagging going on.

The party then had another tidal spasm and Dr. Hibben's wife was presented to me. She was a suitable mate. Tall enough to play Olympic volleyball—for the men—and shoulders broad enough upon which to hang several suits at Barneys. If you want numbers, she was about eight feet in men's height, six-four in women's, and she was wearing some kind of coarse brown dress, which in a previous life might have been a tent in the Spanish-American War. It nicely matched her brown eyes, brown hair, brown skin, and brown tongue, which I saw when she said very sweetly, "So nice to meet you, Alan."

She then offered me her right hand and I offered my right hand, which she proceeded to crush, though not as violently as Dr. Hibben had crushed it earlier that day or as violently as he had crushed my shoulder, but, regardless, it was a good crushing. She could have ripped off the back leg of an elephant with her grip. She and Dr. Hibben must have practiced on each other.

Then she politely gave my hand back to me, and I looked forward to its career as a jelly product.

The gods of cocktail parties, sensing that I couldn't take much more, released me from my torture, as I was somehow shifted away from Dr. and Mrs. Hibben and Murrin and was now facing the corner where Mangrove and Tinkle were sucking on wineglasses. I willed myself in their direction. Conveniently, they were located right next to one of those rolling bars. For some reason in my blackout, I had not acquired a drink. I must have seen Ava's head and gone right toward it—her appeal stronger than liquor, which was a good sign.

Halfway to Mangrove and Tinkle, through the thick crowd, I was stopped by Kenneth. "I saw you cornered by Hibben," he said. "My heart went out to you, but there was nothing I could do."

"I think I'm still alive," I said. "But I'm not sure."

"You appear to be breathing."

"Not happily. I'm sorry if this sounds rude, but I think Dr. Hibben ate a clove of garlic before the party. I think my nose may have had a setback in its healing process."

"I'm sorry to hear that. You did well in the pool today, icing it."

"I'll try to hold on to that memory; maybe that will remind my body of its earlier gains."

"Good thinking." Kenneth smiled handsomely at me, his nose straight and regal. Then he said, "I enjoyed our talk today."

"Me, too," I said, which was the truth, and then, lying, I said, "I have to get a drink; I'll be right back." It was the second part that was a lie. But it's the kind of lie that is spoken so often at cocktail parties that Kenneth simply nodded his head with approval and moved on to someone else, not at all expecting me to return.

I made it to Tinkle and Mangrove, poured myself a glass of wine, ate it, looked at the two of them, and Mangrove said, "Let's get out of here and smoke some pot."

"You have pot?" asked Tinkle.

"Medical marijuana for my depression," said Mangrove. "Do you guys want to?"

"Isn't it dangerous to smoke pot here?" I said in a whisper, like a real milquetoast. For some reason smoking marijuana at the Rose

245

Colony seemed terribly illicit. Also, I hadn't smoked pot since college, and back then it never worked well with a bellyful of booze.

"We're not supposed to, of course," said Mangrove. "But we weren't supposed to smoke those cigars either. At least not in the Mansion."

"I'd like some pot," said Tinkle, and I didn't appreciate him acting so bravely. In our little family of three, Mangrove was our leader, an older-brother figure, and I didn't want him approving of Tinkle more than me; I was an only child without brothers, but this was my natural, fraternally competitive response. I felt the need to vie against Tinkle for Mangrove's affection.

"I'd like some, too," I then said, with false bravery, and so we quit the party to go smoke pot, which was sure to mingle quite disastrously, I thought, with all the wine and whiskey I had consumed. But if it was truly medical marijuana, I reasoned, then there could also be benefits for my numerous and growing list of wounded organs—liver, brain, nose, bruised torso, and the most recent members of the infirmary, my right shoulder and hand.

CHAPTER 30

Serotonin Springs ★ **Paradise Lost in Space** ★ *We all join the navy* ★ *The escape pod is activated* ★ *We take the waters*

"I'm so glad I came to Serotonin Springs," I said, "and met you fellows."

"What did you say?" asked Tinkle. He looked at me as if he were peering up from the bottom of a deep well. The marijuana had sent him very far inside himself. He was lying on his bed; I was at the desk chair again; and Mangrove was in the easy chair, hunched over, preparing another bowl of his medical marijuana in his small ceramic pipe. We had smoked several already. I was planning on attending Woodstock and had made a mental note to finally read the poetry of Allen Ginsberg.

"I'm so glad I came to Serotonin Springs," I repeated.

"Saratoga Springs!" said Tinkle.

"That's what I said."

"No, you said Serotonin Springs."

"You did say Serotonin Springs," said Mangrove sagely.

I traveled back in time, replayed my speech, and realized that they were correct. I had said Serotonin Springs! How curious!

"You're right," I said to my two friends. In that moment, I loved them both very much. The marijuana had me feeling as benefi-cent as the Dalai Lama. "I guess it was all that talk earlier of sero-tonin. . . . But what if this place *is* loaded with serotonin? That would be incredible. Then people could really come here and get cured and not just pretend to be cured."

I was referring to Saratoga's history as a spa, which it was as well known for as its racetrack. In fact, it occurred to me in a stoned instant of great vision, as I sat there in Tinkle's room, that the wealthy people, the ones who had abandoned Sharon Springs for Saratoga Springs at the end of the nineteenth century, probably needed diversion while soaking in the baths and taking the waters and so had built themselves a racetrack. The two had gone hand in hand, I realized. Water and then horses. You can lead a horse to water, I said to myself, and maybe you can't make it drink, but you *can* make it run! The history of Saratoga was summed up in the phrase *you can lead a horse to water*! The town tourist bureau could use it as its slogan! It combined the track and the spa! Maybe the town would pay me for this sentence! I wanted to share my marijuana-induced bit of marketing genius and insight into the history of Saratoga with my friends, but before I could do so, Mangrove said:

"You know, they'd make millions if those fountains in town were coughing up liquid antidepressants."

"If you drank it," said Tinkle, "you could take off that patch and use both your eyes again."

Suddenly a new fantastic idea replaced my thoughts about a good touristic slogan for Saratoga. I could hardly keep up with myself. It was like the northern lights were going off in my head.

I said, with great cannabis-sparked enthusiasm, "Yes, Reginald, you could heal yourself. You see, we three are like space travelers searching for serotonin. We're searching because we're so depressed and crazed, each in our own way, sort of like superheroes, but instead of superpowers we have superafflictions. And because we're so depressed and screwed up, we landed in the wrong spot. We thought Saratoga Springs was Serotonin Springs. We read it wrong on our galactic map, and now we're stuck here. Our ship broke. . . . I don't know if this really happened, but it could be a science fiction movie. A science fiction movie that's also a comedy, since it's about reading a map wrong and being depressed. . . . I was going to write this screenplay about homosexuals taking over Nantucket after I finish my novel, but this serotonin movie could be the next thing I write. You guys could help me if you like. Screenplays often have numerous writers."

"What are you talking about?" asked Tinkle.

"I'm talking about a screenplay about the three of us as space travelers searching for serotonin."

"That's not a bad idea," said Tinkle, sitting up. "In *Dune* they're searching for spice. What would you call the movie?"

"I think just *Serotonin Springs.*"

"No, that's no good," said Mangrove.

"Lost in Space," offered Tinkle.

"That fits, but it's been used," said Mangrove.

"You're right," said Tinkle. "I can't believe I forgot. . . . But I never realized what a great title that is until just now."

"Lost in Space is very beautiful as a title," I said. "I guess anything with the word *lost* is always pretty good. . . . We could call it *Paradise Lost in Space,* which would be a funny mixture of two mediums, or just *Lost.*"

"The word *space* is also beautiful," said Tinkle. "Space. Space. Space. Hear how beautiful it is? I can hear Kirk's voice saying, 'Space, the final frontier,' at the beginning of *Star Trek,* and that sounds really beautiful to me right now. . . . But I wish I could watch an episode of *Lost in Space.* I haven't seen it in years. It's weird. I have mental munchies for a TV show."

"I think you should call the movie *The Lost Depressives,*" said Mangrove.

"I like that, too," said Tinkle.

"It's very strong," I said. "But what about *The Three Lost Depressives?*"

"No," said Mangrove. "Just *The Lost Depressives.*"

"You're right," I said. "It's unusual for a science fiction movie, but I think it's okay."

Pleased with our work on the title, Mangrove lit a match and took a luxurious hit from his pipe and passed it around. We then washed down our lungfuls of smoke with some more of Tinkle's whiskey. I was quite pleased that I seemed to be maintaining consciousness. I also wasn't vomiting, which had happened to me a few times in college when I mixed booze and marijuana, once notably destroying a white dinner jacket I had worn to parties all junior year as a fetishistic nod to my hero and fellow Princetonian Fitzgerald.

Mangrove excused himself and went to the bathroom. He

returned almost immediately. I said to them both, "Have you guys ever noticed that when someone else goes to the bathroom, it seems to take no time at all?"

"I've noticed that," said Tinkle.

"Me, too," said Mangrove. "Though I'm surprised you experienced that just now. Time is usually different on marijuana. It elongates. One minute would normally feel like ten minutes."

"Maybe the bathroom thing trumps the effects of marijuana," I said.

"Possibly," said Mangrove. "Anyway, I was thinking we should go to a spring in town and see if it has serotonin. It might actually have lithium. That would be good."

"I have a car," I said. "I can drive us in. I saw a mineral fountain near the library today."

"Let's go," said Tinkle. He was in a good mood now. Full of life.

"My car will be like an escape pod, since our main spaceship broke down," I said.

"Yes, let's get in the escape pod," said Mangrove.

"Reginald, you should be our commander, since you're like our leader," I said.

"I'm your leader?"

"I think so. There's something tragic and heroic about you, which is good for leading."

"Yes, you're our leader," said Tinkle.

"We're kind of like a space navy," I said. "And you, Alan, can be our science officer. You're Science Officer Alan Tinkle, played by Alan Tinkle."

"All right," said Tinkle.

"I'll be the sergeant, since I fly the escape pod. I don't know if they have sergeants in the navy, but maybe they have them in space navies."

"I think that sounds correct," said Mangrove.

So with that, we three intrepid spacemen issued out of the Mansion—we didn't see anyone, they were all still at Hibben's—and got into our escape pod, previously known as a Chevrolet Caprice Classic. As I revved the engine, preparing for takeoff, I said, "I think the future of space travel lies in the spiral. Previously rocket ships and space shuttles have traveled in straight lines. But if they really want to voyage great distances, they need to spin or corkscrew, mimicking the movement of the earth and the sun. The spiral is in, the straight line is out. I read in *The New York Times* Science section about the power of the spiral."

"Well, later dash off a note to NASA, Sergeant," said Mangrove. "In the meantime, warp drive, please."

Following the commander's order, we then careened, without getting arrested by any space constabulary, into town, and I am very fortunate that as a drunk and stoned driver—the roads were quite dark—I did not hit any innocent citizens of Saratoga, and in retrospect I condemn my selfish, impaired driving! But at that time, it was rather fun, especially since we all had taken to this notion of being spacemen searching for serotonin, and that my Caprice had transformed itself into a highly advanced escape pod.

"Commander," I said as we neared the library, "we're approaching the town vector and my instruments indicate the presence of serotonin."

"Very good, Sergeant," said Mangrove. "Decrease speed of main thruster engines." Under the influence of Mangrove's fine medical marijuana, we had fallen naturally and capably into the argot of space travel.

The library was just off Broadway, Saratoga's old-fashioned main street, the kind of main street America specialized in before the advent of the shopping mall and the great obesity plague at the end of the twentieth century. Visible to my scanners were restaurants, bars, clothing stores, coffee shops, newspaper stands, and drugstores. Most things were closed because it was evening, but the bars and restaurants—it was racing season—appeared to be doing a robust and healthy business. It was a Friday night and nearly 11 P.M., but things were lively.

I turned down the library's street, and behind the library was a grassy, elegant park where several sulfur-water fountains had been built.

"There is adequate docking space two hundred meters from the serotonin source," said Tinkle from the backseat, as the fountain closest to the library was now visible.

"Thank you, Science Officer Alan Tinkle," I said.

"By the way, I think we should be in the Federation, like the *Enterprise*," said Tinkle, who was turning out to be something of a master of contemporary culture, having referenced *Star Trek, Dune,* and inadvertently, *Lost in Space.*

"I have no problems with us being in the Federation," I said. "Do you, Commander?"

"I'm pleased to be a Federation officer," said Mangrove.

I then parked the escape pod. "Shields up, Commander?" I asked.

"Yes, shields up," said Mangrove.

"They should be photon shields," said Tinkle.

Using the master electronic window device, I put all our photon shields up.

"Commander," I said as a brilliant notion came to me, "after we drink from the spring, I suggest that we go to one of the alien bedding stations and locate their alcohol service area. I had discussed earlier with Science Officer Alan Tinkle the possibility of securing information regarding the whereabouts of a female alien comfort hospital."

"You're too stoned," said Tinkle.

"I am," I said. "But let's try to stay in our rôles."

"All right," said Tinkle. "But I told you I can't do that."

"What are you talking about, Sergeant?" asked Mangrove.

"In non-Federation speak, I was referring to the possibility of going to one of the hotels on Broadway, sitting at the bar, and finding out if there are any brothels in town."

"You're referring to docking procedures with female aliens?" asked Mangrove.

"Possibly, Commander. I know it's outlandish, but it's something I had thought of earlier in the day, and now that we're on leave, like sailors, the idea came back to me."

"You're against this plan of attack, Science Officer?" asked Mangrove, not indicating his own position on the matter.

"I am against it, Commander," said Tinkle. "I prefer to just drink from the serotonin fountain."

"I think then we should only drink from the fountain," said Mangrove, "but we might consider it as a future mission. Important things could be learned from the local female alien population. All agreed?"

"Yes," said both Tinkle and I.

"Let's have a moment of silence and then proceed to the serotonin fountain," said Mangrove, taking quite nicely to his appointed rôle as our commander, giving orders both practical and spiritual. He wanted us to gather our mental forces before venturing forth into the alien village.

But thinking I had better keep watch during our moment of silence, while Mangrove closed his one eye, and Tinkle closed both his eyes (as I observed in the rearview mirror), I noted that a lot of people were on the streets, either strolling off their dinners or barhopping. When Mangrove opened his eye after about a minute, an indication that our moment of s. had passed, I said, "There seems to be a good deal of alien-humanoid activity."

"Is it alien or humanoid?" asked Tinkle, a little fraternally competitive with me, possibly because I had put him on the spot yet again about this business of going to a brothel, which I probably shouldn't have done, though my intentions were good.

"I'm not sure," I said. "They look like humans but they must be aliens. Correct of you to point this out, Science Officer." I was trying to be conciliatory, to win him back over.

"They are aliens, but they have a very human appearance," said Mangrove. "So be careful."

"There appears to be a dairy-and-sugar station to the right of the serotonin fountain," said Tinkle, getting back into the swing of things. "Most of the aliens are drawn to that."

An ice cream shop was directly across the street from the bubbling mineral fountain. In fact, no one was at the fountain, but they were all on line at the ice cream place.

"Those aliens are ignoring the serotonin fountain," I said. "Must not be an advanced civilization."

We then got out of the escape pod and made our way to the spring. It was underneath a wooden pagoda and there were several benches surrounding it, where you could rest between sips. The spring was essentially a large water fountain that was perpetually gurgling. It had a three-foot-high ceramic base, topped by a round metal bowl, for collecting the overflow, and out of this bowl rose two upside-down, L-shaped pipes, or spigots, if you like, from which the sulfur-smelling water splashed.

We circled the bowl and studied the liquid. The bowl was stained orange from the water's rich mineral content.

"We have found the serotonin, Commander!" I said.

"Wait a second," said Tinkle. "Remember, it's not supposed to be serotonin; we made a mistake when we came to this planet."

"You're right," I said. "I'd like maybe to change the script. Could be interesting if it really was serotonin."

"No, we always have to be searching for it. We can't ever find it, if we want this to be a television series. . . . If it's a movie, we can find it," said Tinkle.

"I was thinking in terms of a movie, at first," I said. "But a TV series would be fun."

"Whether it's a movie or a TV series, I think we should think that it's serotonin," said Mangrove. "Then we drink it, and it works on us, but only because we're deluded. The placebo effect. And it's only later that we discover we're in Saratoga Springs and not Serotonin Springs, and we're so devastated by this that the placebo effect goes away. Don't forget we're at the start of our mission; we don't know yet that we've landed on the wrong planet. Then later, as ourselves, we can figure out whether it's for TV or a movie or both."

Mangrove then dipped his head and drank a snortful of the water. His eye patch got a little wet, but he didn't seem to mind.

"Delicious," he said. "And I feel happy." He smiled. I had never seen him smile so broadly before. Minuscule grins had been all he had previously dispensed. He sat on one of the benches and stretched out his long commander legs.

Then Tinkle went. He dipped his powerful jaw beneath the flowing water. "I like it," he said, and sat down, joining the commander.

I drank some, and to my stoned palate the water was fantastically charged, better and richer than the water I had drunk from that stream in Sharon Springs. I then sat on the bench next to the one inhabited by the commander and the science officer.

We three were happy and stoned on our warm summer night adventure. Every few minutes or so, we stood up to drink another mouthful of water. Then I had the brilliant idea that one of us should procure plastic cups from the dairy and sugar dispensary, a mission which Tinkle bravely undertook.

When he returned alive, the commander and I complimented him on his courageous action, venturing into an establishment overrun with aliens. Then we three space travelers sipped the waters like gentlemen, refilling our cups when we needed to. Occasionally, an alien or two would join us at the fountain and then move on, and we would keep a wary silence; Tinkle informed us that his "phaser is on stun."

It was all quite amusing and exciting.

Then I seemed to be sobering up; the passage of time and the drinking of the water was undoing the blissful effects of the marijuana and the booze, and right when I was about to propose that we head back to the main space station and absorb more alcohol and marijuana, a large, shapely female alien approached the fountain from behind us, walking between our two benches. She then bent over the fountain, showed us a rather lovely backside in a short blue skirt, dipped her head, took a healthy dose of the serotonin water, and then turned to us with a wet and smiling and beautiful face.

The female alien was Ava.

CHAPTER 31

*A delight ★ A fantasy ★ A bitter look ★ A talk in front of a door ★
A discussion of positions with Jeeves ★ A trap is laid ★ A slammed
door*

We all went back to the Mansion. Ava, in her blue skirt, was in the front seat next to me. She felt bad that she had displaced Mangrove from his earlier position of honor and insisted that he also sit up front. He tried to politely decline, but she persevered and he gave in to her wishes. So it was the three of us up front, and that put her right against me. Her bare thigh against my khaki pants. I tried to delight in this bit of incidental contact, putting my whole spirit into my leg, in case that was all I would ever know of her.

I pretended that it was the 1950s. Saratoga could pass for the 1950s, especially in the dark—the movie-set main street, the old houses, the tree-lined roads, the racetrack. I was the husband, Ava was my wife, Mangrove was our eccentric friend, and Tinkle, in the back, was our strange, gifted child.

"We're approaching the compound, Commander," said Tinkle.

He and Mangrove were still playing Federation, but I had moved on to this more adult fantasy of 1950s married life.

"Starboard thrust warp hyperspeed vector, Sergeant," said Mangrove, searching for the right nautical galactic terms.

"I can't believe how stoned you guys are," said Ava.

At the fountain, we had tried to explain to her the search for serotonin, and she had seemed amused but also bored by the whole thing and asked us for a ride back. She had walked into town and eaten dinner by herself.

"Yes, Commander," I said in a rather low voice, embarrassed to be playing space traveler in front of Ava, but I couldn't be completely disloyal to my two friends and abandon ship, so to speak.

I turned right and we drove down and through the narrow tunnel of dark trees, my headlamps illuminating the winding ribbon of driveway that led to the Mansion. After I parked the escape pod/Caprice, we all entered the mudroom together, and a few people were in there now, reading papers, playing cards, though it was nearly midnight. Hibben's party had obviously broken up.

We three space travelers felt sheepish, worried that the remnants of our stoned state might be visible. Beaubien was there reading *Artforum*. She gave me a bitter look. Whatever hostilities had been displaced during the capture of the bat seemed to have resurfaced. Seeing her, I remembered that I had to set up my slipper snare if I was going to clear up that trouble.

We passed through the mudroom, not really lingering. We simply mumbled hellos to our fellow colonists and advanced to the main hall. At the foot of the grand staircase, Mangrove declared that we should all convene in Tinkle's room. He invited Ava, but she begged off, said she was tired. I said I had to run to my room but would join them shortly.

As we climbed the red-carpeted stairs together, I tried to position myself to be alongside Ava, and while Mangrove and Tinkle continued on to the third floor, Ava and I proceeded down the wood-paneled hallway of the *deuixième étage*. We passed the rather lovely antique-filled library—velvet couches, a gold-leaf-trimmed desk, voluptuous chairs—and then walked past numerous closed doors which led to bedrooms.

I was starting to learn my way around the maze of the Mansion. If I continued down this hall, I would eventually descend a half-flight of stairs that led to the former servants' hallway and to my rooms.

I was pleased to have a few moments alone with Ava, though I also felt quite shy. We came to her door, which was just two doors down from Beaubien's chambers.

"Thanks for the ride back," Ava said. We stood at her threshold.

"You're welcome," I said, and then added, "I saw your sculpture at Dr. Hibben's tonight. It was really something. So beautiful."

She smiled. Her full mouth was even more lovely when cast this way. And her nose was fantastic. It looked different from one moment to the next, the light doing all sorts of things, casting shadows, revealing contours.

"I'm glad you liked it," she said. "I should read something you've written. You have anything here?"

"I've only written one book. . . . It's out of print . . . but I do have a few copies in the trunk of my car. I could get one for you. . . ."

"Give it to me tomorrow. What's it called?"

"It's sort of an immature title . . . *I Pity I.*"

"I like that title."

"I'll get it for you tomorrow then . . . first thing. . . . My new book has a better title, *The Walker.* . . . And I'd love to see more of your work. Maybe I could visit your studio?"

"Sure," she said, and then she looked a little uncomfortable. Her eyes darted away from my face. I'm boring her, I thought. Inwardly I panicked. How not to bore someone? But before I could solve this dilemma, she said, "I'm going to go to bed now."

"Okay."

"Good night." She gave me one more smile, then went into her room and closed the door.

There's nothing worse than boring someone. I limped off to my rooms and felt impotent and ashamed of myself, which was an overreaction. We'd had a nice enough talk, but it seemed to me that I had blown everything with Ava. It must have been the alcohol and the pot. I was speaking clearly and was able to walk a straight line, so I had the outer manifestations of sobriety, but my emotions were all distended and strange. It was that time of the night, bender-wise, when self-pity and melancholy come out and flex their muscles.

I went into my writing room, and Jeeves was there, sitting on his cot and reading Powell. He was dutifully keeping up with our club. He was on the first novel of the final movement, beautifully titled *Books Do Furnish a Room.*

"Hello, Jeeves," I said, and sat at my desk. It was good to see him, but I still felt rather inconsolable. I had a taste of what Tinkle was going through all the time—I didn't think I would ever be loved. Like I said, the pot and the alcohol were doing things to me. Not positive things now, as they had earlier, when they had freed me up to be a little boy again and play at space travel.

"Good evening, sir," said Jeeves.

"I'll be direct, Jeeves," I said, and loosened my tie. "No use trying to hide it. I got drunk again and I'm still drunk. I also blacked out again. Came to at Dr. Hibben's drinks party and was nearly killed by Dr. Hibben and his wife. Then smoked marijuana. Then drove drunk. If you want to call the FBI, I won't stop you, Jeeves."

I had told him everything, except for being a dull fool at Ava's door. That, I couldn't admit. I wanted to pretend it hadn't happened.

"You've done quite a lot, sir. It's not yet midnight."

"I try to be efficient, Jeeves. . . . And I'm going to do more. I'm hopeless. So I might as well enjoy myself, right, Jeeves?"

"That is a position one could take, sir."

"But it's not a position you would take, Jeeves?"

"I don't think I would be in a position to take that position, sir."

"That's a lot of positions, Jeeves."

"Yes, sir."

"Let me put it this way. Do you think it's a position that I should take? I want to go rejoin my two friends, Mangrove and Tinkle, and drink more booze and smoke more marijuana."

"I do not have an opinion, sir, on the position you should take in your position."

I squinted an oysterish glance at Jeeves, but it didn't have much effect. I wasn't very good at oyster looks. A snail was more my range.

"All right, Jeeves. I know that it's not very pleasant to talk to someone in their cups. If it's any consolation to you, the marijuana I smoked was medically approved."

"Very good, sir."

"I'm not sure who approved it or what organ of the state was involved, but nonetheless it was certified marijuana. So that eases my conscience. I still think it was illegal for me to smoke it, but maybe not *as* illegal."

"Yes, sir."

"All right, Jeeves, I can see you're not feeling very approving of me. I wish you wouldn't be so judgmental. I can't help it. There's something wrong with me. I'm mentally weak!"

"I'm not judgmental, sir."

"What are you then?"

"If there were a word, sir, to characterize me or my emotional state, though I'm not sure I need to be characterized, I would say that I am detached, as I explained earlier today, in response to your alcoholism and now your drug addiction."

"I'm not addicted to drugs! I smoked a little marijuana. Medical marijuana!"

"Very good, sir."

"All right, Jeeves. Be detached. Detach yourself until you don't know where you are anymore!"

I stood up in a huff. I didn't know what I was doing. I was behaving irrationally. In retrospect, I realize that I was taking out my frustration about Ava on Jeeves. I went into the bedroom and got my slippers and slammed them down in the hallway. I reentered the writing room. I shouted:

"I'm off to go drink and smoke more pot! And if you feel like detaching yourself from that bed if you hear someone removing my slippers, I would be very pleased. And if you don't want to catch the slipper nut, then that's all right, too!"

Before Jeeves could answer, I slammed the door.

I was aware that I was acting atrociously but I couldn't stop myself. Rarely had I behaved in such a manner. But I guess when we're feeling lonely in life, we attack those who actually do love us. It's one of the things that characterizes human nature and can be summed up in one word: FLAWED.

CHAPTER 32

An encounter in the hall ★ There's something wrong with the world ★ Stallions and babies are having a good time ★ X. is paid homage to ★ There's talk of phalluses of various nationalities ★ A minstrel stops playing and a flower dies ★ Somebody gets rough and somebody else likes it ★ The 1973 Mets are brought to life and Ed Kranepool plays a significant rôle ★ There's no need for dreams

Poor Jeeves. Nobody likes to be yelled at. But if anybody could take it, it was Jeeves. He knew that I was a complete idiot and not to be taken seriously. If anything, he was probably glad that I had left him in peace to continue his reading.

Nevertheless, I was pretty ashamed of myself, and so I walked rapidly down the hallway, and up the small half-flight of stairs, running away, as it were, from what I had just done. I was going to go to Tinkle's room, be with my fellow Federation members, and recapture my earlier, happier mood.

What I should have done, though, was to have gone back and apologized to Jeeves.

But if I had done that, I wouldn't have run into Ava. She was in a white robe, held tight to her beautiful frame. She had just come from the bathroom on her hallway and was returning to her room.

"Want to come in a second?" she asked.

She was inviting me into her room. I was a bad person. I had just yelled at Jeeves. The universe was showing its design: good things happen to bad people.

"All right," I said, and the words came out like cement. An incredible pounding was in my temples. There was so much fresh blood in me that I sobered up completely. I realized that I must have misread her earlier mood. Perhaps she had wanted to invite me in then.

She went first. I followed. She closed the door. She walked toward her bed—an antique four-poster, like Beaubien's. A small lamp was lit on an old, large wooden bureau. There wasn't much light. But Ava looked good in the shadows. I didn't move. Then she turned. She walked back toward me. She was barefoot. Shorter than me. Normal male-female measuring systems were in effect. Her arms reached out to me. I lifted my arms to take hold of her, but I was weak and frightened, each wrist had a small boulder fastened to it, but I managed to get my arms up and around her. She was a big girl, but even a big girl feels small in one's arms.

Her mouth pressed against mine. Then her lips opened and her teeth opened and her tongue was in my mouth. I didn't feel weak anymore, but I was self-conscious. I started worrying about my breath, all that wine and whiskey and pot and sulfur water. But she kept on kissing me, and I dismissed my neurosis. Her breath was warm and tasted good, like she had just been eating an apple. Maybe she had been. I kissed her and put my hand into her thick, dark brown hair.

I had the girl I wanted. But no one ever gets the girl they want. There was something very wrong with the world.

Her nose was against my cheek. My nose was against her cheek. We danced like that, backward toward the bed. She sat on the bed. I stood.

The robe opened up. She was naked.

I put my hand on her full, fat breast. Then I put my hand under her breast. Nobody had enjoyed weighing something as much since Archimedes. Her nipples were brown and large.

I bent down and kissed a nipple, and then I sat down on the bed and took the same nipple in my mouth, like a hungry baby. It must have felt good thirty years ago when I was an infant, and the charm hadn't worn off.

I put my face between her breasts and inhaled. All wars had come to an end. I loved the smell of her. I pushed both breasts together and was able to get two nipples at once into my mouth.

We did some more kissing. Then my clothes starting coming off.

My boxer shorts stayed on. We lay side by side, kissing. My broken nose was doing okay. Didn't hurt. Then again, I could have had an ax stuck in my back and I wouldn't have felt it.

I had her pulled tight against me. Her rear in my hand made me as hot as a stallion. Actually, I was already as hot as a stallion. The rear in my hand made me a stallion with a fever.

She said, "Your mustache is rough, but I like it."

I said, "I want to kiss your nose."

She smiled. She let me kiss her nose. I ran my lips up and down the bone of it. Then I kissed it lightly, delicately. I followed this up with an experimental suck, but I couldn't fit the whole thing in my mouth. But I liked sucking on it. It was different from sucking on her breast. It was like getting to the essence of her. I took my mouth off her nose. I felt sated.

"You're perverted," she said, and laughed. She didn't know the half of it—that there was only one other nose fetishist in the history of human sexuality. Well, recorded history of human sexuality, that is. Certainly there must have been a few unreported cases, though it definitely wasn't common.

I didn't want her to think I was too crazy, though, so I went back to work on her mouth. Sucked her lips. She rolled on top of me. I had one hand on her rear and one hand on her breast.

She put her hand down my boxers. I followed her lead and put my hand between her legs. The hair there was soft.

My shorts came off. She kept me in her hand. I took a breast in my mouth again and nursed. She moaned. She liked my nursing style. She squeezed me in her fist. I was a man. I was a baby. I was a man. I was a baby.

I couldn't get enough of her breast. I felt like an agitated tapeworm. Too hungry. Too excited. I slid back up and kissed her. Kept a hand down below, but didn't do much else, just warmed my hand there, like over a stove. Wanted to be a gentleman. Sucked on her nose some more and I was in nineteenth-century Germany, living out a dream. I was doing it for X, poor fellow. Hoped he was in heaven watching.

"What's with all this nose kissing?" she asked.

"You have a beautiful nose," I said.

"Thank you," she said softly. What I found beautiful, I was aware, may have been a source of ridicule in her life.

She encouraged, so I put a finger inside her, slow and respectful, like a Jew stepping inside a church. And her hand went up and down on me. We were enjoying each other. I took my slick finger out and rubbed it gently at the top of her sex. She liked that. Little cries escaped from her.

Then we took a break. The initial fury was over. We had to look at each other; get to know each other. So we just lay there. Side by side. She opened her fist and looked down. There was just enough light to see by. She said, "You're the first white guy I've been with in years."

This was unexpected. What does one say to that? I went the simple route. "How many years?"

"At least five . . . I've only been seeing Africans since I was thirty. But I haven't been with anyone for six months. I needed to stop for a little while."

"You're thirty-five?"

"Did you think I was older?"

"No, of course not. You look like you're twenty-five."

She did. She smiled. "How old are you?" she asked.

"Thirty . . . I don't mean to be rude, but how is it that you were only seeing Africans? Were you living in Africa?"

"No," she said, and laughed. "I live in Brooklyn. But I've been to Africa three times, mostly Nigeria. . . . I take African dance classes in New York. My whole life is dance classes. I don't really do anything else. Make art. Teach. But mostly I dance. That's my social life. Keeps me sane."

"Where do you teach?"

"Pratt."

"I've heard of Pratt. . . . You teach art?"

"Yes, sculpture."

I had been going easy on her, but now I threw her a fastball: "Why haven't you seen anyone for six months?"

She was Mickey Mantle. She ate my fastball. She didn't blink an eye. She said:

"It was getting to be too much. Everybody knows everybody in

266

that world. The African community. But I like being with them. You don't date. They come up to you and you know what's what. No hemming and hawing. I like it that way. But I fell in love with this one guy, Cholee. . . . But he had a wife back in Nigeria. They're Yoruba. They don't divorce in their culture. So after him, I had a whole herd of them. Was seeing every African in town. But that wasn't healthy. And I was still in love with Cholee. . . . So I trimmed down the herd until there was nothing. It's been good. . . . I was talking to this therapist on the phone. He encouraged me to take a break. It's crazy, but I got his number out of the back of the *Utne* reader. He said that because my self-esteem was so low, I thought only a poor African would be with me. He said that subconsciously I was a racist."

"I don't know if it's helpful for a therapist to call you a racist."

"His point was that I didn't think I deserved a white guy, or I thought that a white guy wouldn't love me, so I went to a lower class and this to him is racism. . . . I don't know, maybe he's right . . . I'm not calling him anymore. I didn't consciously think of them as a lower class. . . . The whole thing is complicated. . . . Sex is a big part of it. I do love their dicks. I don't know if that's racist. But a big dick does feel better. And black men do have bigger dicks. They just do. But I also love their bodies, their skin. They smell so good. They oil themselves up like seals. The men and the women. I don't know why white people don't do that. We should rub that stuff into our skin, they have a million products. . . . Their skin is like food." She grew thoughtful. "Sometimes there's a black guy who doesn't have a big one. But it's rare. There was one guy who was small and he was a mess because of it. When you're black and have a small dick, it's really devastating."

In light of the circumstances, this wasn't the most encouraging conversation to be having. In fact, I rather wilted in her hand, a cross between a dying flower and an accordion being shut down for the night by a beggar minstrel. And I felt insane and confused. I had been so happy just a few moments earlier. Also, I had heard of the *Utne* reader magazine, but I had never actually seen one, and who knew that you could get a therapist from its back pages. It was all rather baffling.

"But I don't always need a big dick," she continued. Was she talking about me? "Before this African phase, I was in love with a Mexican boy. He was only nineteen. I was twenty-nine. He was beautiful. Had long black hair to his ass. Everyone stared at him. Made me jealous. But he had a small dick. But I still loved him. And before that I was with this Japanese guy, and he had the smallest one ever, but I was crazy for him."

I was thinking that maybe I should kill myself. Usually, I have suicidal thoughts when I'm alone. So it was rare to have one in the company of another person. But after this conversation about other men's penises, and the possible inference that I could keep company with her underendowed Mexican and Japanese lovers, there wasn't much left to me, mentally *and* physically. The flower-accordion, which was still in her hand, was practically inverting. My belly button had greater length.

"Where do I fit into all this?" I whispered. My shattered ego was gasping for air.

"I like you. You're weird; I like weird guys."

"Weird?"

"Weird in a good way . . . And I needed to be touched. I've been lonely at this stupid colony. I had a terrible day today. I went to the track and lost a lot of money."

"How much?"

"A lot."

"I'm sorry."

"It doesn't matter. But listen, I'm attracted to you. I like your beat-up face."

Then she kissed me passionately. I didn't say no.

She drew me on top of her. Her eyelids closed halfway over her green eyes. I could see the pulse beating in her neck. Her breasts, like giant eggs-over-easy, lay on her chest. That might not sound appealing, but I happen to love eggs.

I had to ask: "Am I as small as the Mexican and the Japanese guys?"

"No," she said huskily. "You have a nice fat one. I just hadn't seen a pink one in a while. I'm not used to the color, but you're nice and hefty."

That did it. Praise a man's penis and there's not much he can't do.

So the beggar minstrel decided to unpack his accordion and wait for a few more tourists. He unfurled a long, happy song!

I was also a little upset. She shouldn't have made that speech about other men. But these things happen. People always say the wrong things. I've done it. And Ava was probably unbalanced. But what did I expect at the Rose Colony? And who was I to judge? I wasn't exactly a Libra myself, if you know what I mean.

Well, I was on top of her. Straddling her hips. Her legs were closed. My sex was just above her pubis. She looked up at me. I kissed her some more.

Her right arm was to the side of the pillow, inching up. I could see that she wanted to adopt the position of a woman being taken, and so I raised both her arms over her head and pushed the wrists down with my left hand.

She had shaved her armpits. They were bare and sexy and hollow. I have always been drawn to women's armpits. Don't know why.

She arched her back. Her breasts rose into the air. Her lids closed completely over her green eyes. I took the pillow out from beneath her head and threw it to the floor. Her dark brown hair splayed out on the white sheet. She fought against my hand on her wrists, but I was strong. And she wouldn't have wanted me to let go anyway. She wanted the rough stuff.

I wasn't really myself. But few people are when they make love. It's a lesser self. Or at least, a less thinking self. So I kissed her hard. I took a breast in my right hand and squeezed it. I gave her nose a suck, like taking a hit of adrenaline, and then I sucked her neck.

I rose up and drew the back of my right hand across her cheek, like a caress, but I was testing something. I did it again. This time she swung her face against the back of my hand. I knew it. So I backhanded her lightly across her cheek. She moaned. She kept her eyes closed. I did it again. She squirmed beneath me, excited. I still had her wrists pinned with my left hand. Then I slapped the other side of her face with my open palm. Not too hard, but enough to thrill her. Delight her. I slapped her some more. She was breathing heavily.

I let go of her wrists, lay flat on top of her, and kissed her cheeks

269

where I had slapped them. Then I slapped her again. Good to keep her guessing. Then I gave her more sweet kisses, almost like apologies. She opened her eyes and looked at me and gave me little kisses.

"Please go in me," she whispered.

I roughly pried her legs apart with my knee. Rubbed myself against her wetness, her hair. It felt beautiful. I threw her legs on my shoulders and rubbed against her that way. I liked tossing her around like that. "Do you have a condom?" I asked.

"No. Just don't come. Pull out."

We all weaken in these situations. I was no exception. But there was something I had to do first. I was acting tough, but if I went in her, I probably wouldn't last very long, and the whole thing would be a sham.

So I kissed her face, her nose, her neck, her breasts. "Go in me, please, I don't care about the condom," she said.

"Not yet," I said.

I worked my way down her body. When I was in front of her sex, I lifted up her thighs. Then holding on to the thighs, I rolled her onto the small of her back, lifting her sex off the bed. Her legs were up and open. I held the thighs to keep her legs in place. To the right and left of her mound, I kissed the insides of her legs. Left leg. Right leg. I inched closer to where she wanted me to kiss her. But didn't.

Then I did give a little lick there, got a taste of her salt, then back to kissing the right leg, left leg, with a stop in the middle. Right leg, left leg, a stop in the middle. She caught on to the pattern and pushed up to meet that stop, wanted more, but I was like the hummingbirds on my tie. Too fast. Right leg, left leg, a stop in the middle. She was crying. Good crying.

I was teasing her. But I couldn't take it anymore myself. So I put my whole face in there. A baptism. I let go of her thighs and put them on my shoulders, pinning my head in place. She then fastened her legs, imprisoning me completely. She had strong legs. My eyes were closed. I sucked on her. I licked her. The lower half of my body made love to the bed. I took as much of her sex in my mouth as I could, and when it was in there, I licked it with my tongue.

Her legs squeezed my head tight. I could hear the ocean. I stayed in there a long time drinking from her. I loved it in there, and I knew I was making her happy, which was my insurance if I failed at making love, if I came right away.

For quite a while, I did only one thing: I licked very fast on the right spot—that little swelling that feels like your own fat lip after you get hit in the mouth. Then finally she cried out, her body spasming. When she was still, I pried open her legs, freed myself, and went and rested my wet face on her chest. I could hear her heart pounding.

Then she hugged me and kissed me. We were tender with each other.

"Go in me now," she said. "Please."

I got between her legs.

"I'm going to have to go slow. I might have to pull out right away."

"I don't care. Just put it in."

I went in. Slow. Cautious. Being in her was a revelation. I had nearly forgotten what it felt like to be in a woman. When it comes to sex, I think we all suffer from a kind of amnesia. We can never fully recollect what it's like. Our memory doesn't allow it. So we're compelled to do it over and over, again and again. I think this memory loss must be a function of the brain. Good old Darwin! He knew what he was up to.

"Please don't move," I said.

I tried to remember to breathe, to stay calm. I was my own minefield. I had to not set myself off. I made it through the first minute. Maybe I can do this, I thought. I began to apply some strokes. She was sensitive, knew I was struggling, and so she didn't do anything too dramatic. She just made small movements, lifting her hips just the slightest.

Then I got the hang of it. Wasn't in immediate danger. We began to move together more rapidly. I kissed her. I grabbed her breasts. We kept moving. I got her arms above her and pinned her wrists again. She liked that. Her legs were wrapped around me. I was fucking her. It kills me to use that word, but that's what I was doing. She was moaning and crying out quite a lot now. I pinched her nipples. Kept the wrists pinned. I gave her some slaps with the back of my hand and the palm of my hand. Never too hard, but enough to make a sound like a clap.

Then we found our spot together. I was kissing her and my pubic bone was rubbing against her pubic bone. That was the spot.

Then I had to stop kissing her. It was too exciting. Too intimate. I had to be alone. So I nursed on her neck and kept rubbing that bone. I didn't think I was going to make it.

"Keep doing that," she said.

The more she got excited, the more I thought I couldn't hang on. But I had to last. I had to make her come. I had to be good. I had to be better than all those Africans and Mexicans and Japanese. I hid in her neck and rubbed. I fell back on that old male trick of thinking about sports. In my mind, I began to recite the Mets lineup from 1973, which was the year I became truly conscious of sports and the Mets went to the World Series but lost.

I started with the catcher and then went around the infield and then started over.

Jerry Grote. Ed Kranepool. Felix Millan. Bud Harrelson. Wayne Garrett. Cleon Jones. Don Hahn. Rusty Staub. Jerry Grote. Ed Kranepool. Felix Millan. Bud Harrelson. Wayne Garrett. Cleon Jones. Don Hahn. Rusty Staub.

I did a few of the pitchers.

Tom Seaver. Jerry Koosman. Jon Matlack. Tug McGraw.

Then she really started to moan. Come, goddammit, I shouted in my mind. I visualized each player. Felix Millan's batting stance. Wayne Garrett's red hair. Cleon Jones's Afro. Rusty Staub's belly. I tried to think of the ugliest Met: Ed Kranepool. I remembered his swing. A lefty. He had dark stubble. Thinking about him was very good. He was completely unfeminine. I couldn't think of anything feminine. So I kept thinking about Ed Kranepool, and all the while I was thrusting and rubbing.

I was able to be detached from my body as long as he was in my mind. I said his name backward in my head.

Loopenark. Loopenark. Loopenark. Loopenark. Loopenark. Loopenark.

Then I did the whole team. I've always been good at speaking people's names backward.

Etorg. Loopenark. Nallim. Noslerrah. Tterrag. Senoj. Nhah. Buats. Revaes. Namsook.

Then there was a cry like no other cry. Just had to give her a few more thrusts to finish it off. Loopenark. Loopenark. Loopenark. Another cry.

She had to be done. I gave one deep final thrust, like Brutus. Something inside me screamed; I was ready, beyond ready, but I had the presence of mind to yank the knife out, rub it wet and alive against her belly and spill all over her.

I rolled to her side. We were silent. Then I asked, "Do you want me to get a towel, clean you up?" I was embarrassed that I had made a mess; suddenly, I felt like I hardly knew her.

"No, it's okay," she said.

We lay there quietly. I kissed her shoulder, but it was a phony move, just something a man does to keep the peace with a woman. You see, I was starting to commit what a friend of mine once called *mentacide*. This is when your brain tries to kill you. My thoughts went like this: What if I dripped a little? She could be pregnant. She seems very fertile. If she's pregnant, I'm doomed.

Then I thought: She's been with Africans. Almost all Africans have AIDS according to *The New York Times*. But she's been celibate six months, she would know if anything is going on. And I'm sure she's safe with those Africans. But she wasn't safe with me. Why should I think she's safe with them? But how does a man get AIDS from a woman? They never explain this. They're very prudish when it comes to this. I have to have a cut? There's a cut on my nose. When I went down on her, I could have gotten AIDS in the cut on my nose.

So I wasn't exactly plotting our honeymoon. I was depressed and fearful and committing mentacide, but there's a scientific explanation for this. It's my understanding that one's testosterone level dips dramatically after orgasm, and this loss of testosterone deprives a male of his unconscious sense of purpose, which is to impregnate women, despite whatever conscious fears one might have about that.

And without purpose we get despondent. We don't know why we're alive. We don't know why we just made love. Our testosterone does all our thinking for us, and in those few minutes without it, having just spilled it, we're lost.

Well, a few minutes later, my body had begun to regenerate and I was feeling much better. My fears and paranoid worries disappeared. New testosterone had been manufactured. I had purpose again. I was happy now to be lying next to this beautiful woman. Happy to have just made love to her, with very good prospects of making love to her again. I didn't want to impregnate her, but my testosterone did, my body did, and it was looking forward to the chance to manipulate me into taking another shot at it.

She was very quiet. Just lying there, staring at the ceiling. What was she thinking?

"Are you all right?" I whispered, a little worried about how rough I had been.

"Yes, I'm all right," she said. "I feel really good."

"Did you come?" I then asked selfishly, needing confirmation that I had indeed proved myself a capable lover. Every now and then, one does encounter women who scream quite magnificently and you think you've done it, only to find out you haven't, and this can be terribly disappointing.

"What do you think?" she said sweetly, teasingly.

"I hope so. I mean it sounded like you did."

"I did. Twice. When you were licking me, and then now, and it was a long one. I think I'm still coming."

I hugged her. I was myself. How could I ever have slapped her? Who was that fellow? I knew he would come back; that she would want him back; but for now he was gone. She demurely turned away from me, proffering her rear for me to snuggle against, and so I held her that way. I felt her stomach. It was still slick.

"Are you sure you don't want me to clean you up?" I asked.

"I'll do it," she said.

She got up, took a towel from the closet. She looked beautiful, standing at the end of the bed, naked.

"I'm going to go to the bathroom," she said. "I'll be right back." She put on her robe and went out.

I lay there. It was all so improbable, but it had happened. I had just made love to a sexy, gorgeous woman. I was quite pleased with myself. And exhausted, too. I assumed she wanted me to spend the night. But I had to be discreet. Couldn't let anyone see me leaving her room. I'd leave early before people were awake.

She came back, turned off the little lamp on the bureau, and got into bed. She offered me her rear again, for me to slide into place against it. We fit nicely. I kissed the back of her neck.

"Thank you for making love with me," I said.

"Thank *you,*" she said.

We were silent. Ready to sleep. Then I felt a terrible gastric pressure. There was a rumbling noise, like thunder. This didn't bode well. Where there's thunder, there's lightning. You see—and to further borrow from the world of meteorology, to be even more explicit—one of the earth's elements was trapped inside me. Wind. Oh no, I thought. No. No. No!

I shifted it around inside me. I could go to the bathroom, but that would mean getting dressed, possibly being seen coming from her room if someone was up late. Therefore, I tried to redirect the pressure as best I could, finding emergency valves, but I felt like I was doing structural damage. I'd buy myself a few seconds reprieve with these maneuvers, but then the wind would start to howl again. For several minutes, I was in one of the circles of hell. Experiencing gas while in the presence of a new lover is one of the worst tortures known to man.

Then the wind absolutely insisted on being released or something very bad internally would occur. With my last bit of strength, I tried rationing its dispersement, like slowly opening a bottle of seltzer and releasing the gas in small measures so that the seltzer doesn't come bursting out.

Well, this seltzer method seemed to work. No sound effects, anyway. If there were other effects, which for the moment were being held up by the sheets, I figured that Ava had been with many men, that she knew I was human and would accept me, not judge me. So I opened the seltzer bottle a little more. I sniffed the air, pretending to take a deep breath. No odor, thank God. She seemed to be drifting off. I held her close to me. I emptied out the rest of the bottle. The crisis had pased. The gods had been kind to me: odorless wind!

She wasn't asleep; she said, "I have to go to New York tomorrow. I have to go to my gallery. Can you take me to the train? There's an early one at six-thirty. I was going to call a cab."

"Yes, I can take you, of course. . . . How long will you be in New York?"

"I'll be back Sunday."

Then there was talk of how we would wake up; she had already set her alarm before having run into me in the hallway. So then we tried to sleep, but she kept pushing her rear against me, seeking me out, and I responded. She reached around and put me in her. Then she was on her knees and I was in her and staring at her beautiful back, this heavenly letter *V,* leading to the globes of her bottom, where I was hidden. As we made love this way, I was struck anew by the utter vulnerability and submissiveness of women. How do they do it? I kissed her neck and reached under her and took hold of her breasts. Everything about her was so sumptuous.

"Come," she whispered.

"Are you going to?"

"I want you to."

Then she violently pushed back for more and cried out, and this was terribly exciting, so I pulled out and spilled on her back. This time I got the towel.

We lay there silently. I was holding her from behind again. There was no despondency this time, no mentacide. I felt myself slipping into that thick black sleep that comes after pleasing sex, but I asked, "What are you thinking?"

"How I lose control of myself," she said.

Then we slept, just a few hours, and in the morning, she packed a small bag and went and performed her toilet. I dressed and put my tie in my jacket pocket, which made me feel like a rogue. We left her room together and no one saw us. It was too early.

I stopped in the bathroom, and then we went out to the parking lot. Everything was very still and quiet and so we dared to hold hands. It was unspoken between us, but at a place like the Rose Colony, the need for secrecy and discretion and privacy, at least at the start of an affair, seemed very important.

"You like these hummingbirds, right?" I pulled my tie out of my pocket with a flourish like a magician as I opened the car door for her. She sat down in the car and looked at me: the tie was this beautiful blue ribbon of birds.

"I like them," she said. "They're pretty. But your black eyes are even prettier."

When I got in the car and looked in the rearview mirror to back up, I saw that the colors beneath my eyes were changing, there was some yellow and green and purple.

I drove her to the train, we got there just in time, and I kissed her good-bye on the concrete platform, and for good measure I kissed her playfully on the tip of her gigantic sexy nose. She smiled. The train was a big silver Amtrak. I almost said *I love you,* but I knew better than that. So I said, "Thank you for last night."

She smiled, then she said, "I'll see you tomorrow. I'll take a taxi back. I'm not sure what time I'll get in."

She got on the train. I took my tie out again and waved it like a handkerchief, being silly. I don't know if she saw me. The windows were impossible to look into.

Then the train left. I stood on the platform, waved my tie a few times, then shoved it in my pocket and watched the train until it had completely disappeared and the long, rusted track was empty.

It was an overcast day, gray and cool, especially for summer. I didn't know if the weather would change. I liked being up while the world was so quiet, and I felt a little relieved to be alone. I drove back to the Rose Colony and went to my room. There was still the hush of sleep to the Mansion. I wondered for a moment why my slippers were outside my door and then I remembered and collected them. The trap had failed. I thought of Jeeves: I owed him an apology. Then I crawled into bed and slept for hours. There were no dreams. I didn't need any.

CHAPTER 33

An apology ★ I'm jaundiced but not jaded ★ Jeeves explains to me the nature of time and memory and nearly gives me a seizure ★ The utter meaninglessness of life tries to bite me in the neck ★ I crave some Raymond Chandler ★ Is it Great Britain, England, or the UK? ★ The parable of a young girl on a toilet ★ A walk in the woods with Jeeves, not Robert Frost ★ I don't fly with the Federation ★ One of those glorious mornings ★ A chant and a spell

I was sick the whole day. There was something wrong with me. I was nauseous, fitful, itchy. The booze, the marijuana, the vigorous lovemaking—it all had done a number on me. I was a wreck. Also, there was the collective trauma and strain of everything I had been through since New Jersey, and I finally just collapsed. You would think it would be a day of celebration after my conquest of Ava, but it was the opposite. I was utterly dissipated and tormented. For hours and hours, I stayed in bed, reading, twisting about, sometimes sleeping, and sometimes talking to Jeeves.

When Jeeves first attended to me around 1 P.M., bringing me a glass of water, I said from my sickbed, "I'm so sorry about last night, Jeeves. I feel terrible about it."

"There's no need to apologize, sir."

"But I was rude and histrionic. . . . Even if you say there's no need, I'd like it known for the record that I'm apologizing and that I hate myself for talking to you like an idiot."

"Try not to hate yourself, sir. I wasn't offended by your remarks."

Jeeves was a statue of forgiveness. I perceived no rancor in the man.

"You're kind and generous to me, Jeeves."

"Very good, sir."

"I see we didn't catch the slipper thief," I said, shifting the conversation from the emotional realm to the practical.

"No, sir."

"Well, we can try again tonight."

"Very good, sir."

"I don't feel much like working on the novel today, Jeeves."

"You do seem a bit jaundiced, sir."

"My eyes are yellow, Jeeves?"

"Yes, sir."

"That medical marijuana didn't live up to its reputation. . . . Oh, well, live and *don't* learn, that's my motto. . . . Jeeves, how long has it been since we left New Jersey? Three, four weeks? This trip has taken a good deal out of me."

"We left New Jersey four days ago, sir."

"Don't be insane, Jeeves!"

"I'm not being insane, sir."

"Today is Saturday, Jeeves."

"Yes, sir."

"We left New Jersey . . ."

"This past Tuesday, sir."

"Oh, God, Jeeves, you're right. That's only four days. Or is it five? Do we at least count today?"

"I believe, sir, that most people would say that we had left New Jersey four days ago."

"Oh, Jeeves, I think I'm losing my mind . . . I can never tell if life is long or if life is short. . . . Do you have an opinion?"

"I have noticed, sir, that small increments of time can feel quite long: an hour, ten minutes, a day. But that over the course of one's life, longer stretches—ten years, fifty years—feel quite short."

"Do you know why this is, Jeeves?"

"It may have something to do with memory, sir. We do not have the capacity to recall each instant of our lives, so experience becomes compacted, summed up, dismissed. An affair is reduced to a sentence: 'We were together three years.' This makes the life lived seem rather short. . . . The whole thing is a conundrum, sir. It takes us sixty, seventy, eighty years to live a life, and it appears to go by so quickly, and yet we also know how long it took to get where we are. . . . I think of the world of cinema. A two-hour film is the result of hundreds of hours of shot footage. The same thing with a life. It can all be remembered and reviewed quite quickly, but it took millions of moments to create it."

"Don't torture me, Jeeves. My brain just jumped up and banged its head on the inside of my skull. Go easy with me intellectually. I can hardly spell my name today."

"I apologize, sir."

"It's my fault, Jeeves, I asked the question."

"Very good, sir."

I was somewhat eager to tell Jeeves that my romance with Ava had escalated considerably—my impulse to confide in him was a mixture of vanity, confession, and a desire for counsel—but I didn't want him to think poorly of me, to think that I was the type of man who spoke of his lady friends in a less-than-discreet manner. So I remained silent on the issue. He, of course, was aware that I had been out all night, but he probably thought I'd been toping with Tinkle and Mangrove until dawn and so didn't suspect that I had been with Ava.

"Jeeves, I think I'll go back to sleep."

"Very good, sir."

About an hour later, I woke up, threw on some clothes, and retrieved my lunch pail and thermos from the mudroom. Then I sat at my letter-writing desk. I sipped coffee and stared out the window. The day had continued to be gray and overcast. More of a cool spring day than a summer day. One of the male poets, a middle-aged Jew with a classically round bald spot, went jogging by. Why do we Jews bother? I thought. We're doomed.

The man's little ego, his desire to be fit and maybe to be attractive to the females at the colony, his ruminating on his poems as he jogged, his vulnerable bald head, his bad posture, his poor running style, his mirroring of my own hopelessness—well, the whole thing came roaring at me like a comet. So I moved my head to the right and it scorched past me and shot out the other side of the room. I wondered if it would make it to the third floor and strike poor Tinkle.

Jeeves entered a moment later. I didn't want to go into the whole thing, but I said, "Every now and then, Jeeves, I almost grasp the utter meaninglessness of life, but then it eludes me."

"I understand, sir."

I tried to rally. I ate my lunch and then took a bath. When I shaved, I leaned against the sink and felt a pain above my groin. I had bruised myself with Ava. I smiled for a moment. But then the sourness in my whole body took over and I went and lay back down.

Jeeves brought me a glass of water. Stood over me.

"Jeeves, can you go into the writing room and get me my Raymond Chandler novel. It's on the desk, under the Hammett collection. Chandler writes beautifully about hangovers. I think I need to be in the presence of a fellow sufferer."

"Yes, sir."

Jeeves came back with *The Long Goodbye*.

"You know, Jeeves, all I really need in life, reading-wise, is Raymond Chandler and Dashiell Hammett. I wish they had written more. I do love Anthony Powell, but I think it might be a temporary infatuation."

"I certainly am enjoying Powell, sir."

"Well, your forebears are from England, so he speaks to you."

"Yes, sir."

"England is completely nuts, so he doesn't speak as coherently to me. I mean, what the hell is going on over there? I don't get it, really. It has too many names. Great Britain. Britain. The UK. England. Sometimes people are British or English or Britons. There's also the Irish and the Scottish, both of whom drink heavily to deal with the complexity of it all. And some people say they're from Wales. I think that might be an island, like Martha's Vineyard. They must be Welsh. So we have to add that to the mix. And let's not forget that their public schools are actually private. So what the hell do they call their public schools?"

"I can try to explain everything, sir."

"No, I'm still reeling from your dissertation on time and the cinema, Jeeves. You nearly gave me a brain aneurysm with that one. But I'd be happy to hear your British lecture another time, though I'm not a very good Anglophile, I'm afraid. I just dress like one, which is doubly pathetic since an Anglophile is ostensibly dressing like someone English or British or whatever the hell they are, so I'm mimicking something once removed from the authentic as it is. I'm an Anglo-Anglophile. I hadn't considered this before. . . . So I don't know what I am anymore. I think I'm a Wandering Jew. . . . That would be a good name for a musical group, The Wandering Jews. Of course, they could only play at bar mitzvahs, but there certainly would be an income."

"Yes, sir."

"You know, Jeeves, if I wasn't Jewish, I would find the attention paid to Jews very annoying. In fact, I do find it annoying. There are definitely more articles and TV shows and movies and world crises about Jews than any other people, and when you consider our percentage relative to the human population, it's completely out of control. As far as news coverage goes, you'd think there were more Jews than Chinese. . . . I do wish, though, we Jews were more like the Chinese—have great frightening numbers but keep a low profile. I mean, I've seen more articles in *The New York Times* on klezmer music alone in the last five years than anything having to do with the Chinese. . . . I find it all very nerve-racking. The more attention the more hatred. And everything with time gets bigger, so can you imagine if the Holocaust is trumped?"

"Try not to think of such things, sir."

"You're right, Jeeves . . . I'm awfully splenetic today. . . . I'm suffering from humors, but it's not very funny."

"Yes, sir."

"Jeeves, could you write down that last line? I may have to use it, but I'm too weak to hold a pen."

"Yes, sir." Jeeves sat at the letter-writing desk and I repeated the line: "I'm suffering from humors, but it's not very funny."

Jeeves printed out the line on some scratch paper.

"Thank you, Jeeves."

"You're welcome, sir."

"At least I got *some* writing done today. One good line isn't bad, especially for someone as sick as I am."

"I'm sorry that you are feeling ill, sir."

"No need to feel sorry, Jeeves. You and I both know I brought it on myself and that I'm utterly hopeless, so I won't bore us by claiming to get on the wagon. . . . I really did it last night, though. All my organs must be in a state of shock. My spleen has got its head in the toilet and is vomiting. My liver is passed out in front of a Bowery mission, and my kidneys are in the fifteenth round of a brutal fight and my opponent has illegally removed the stuffing from his gloves."

"Apt metaphors, sir."

"Thank you, Jeeves. But no need to jot those down. Not that good. I do like the idea of you taking dictation. I could be like Milton or Henry James."

I don't think this notion appealed to Jeeves, because he didn't say anything. So I read a little Chandler, and Jeeves effervesced over to my writing room. A few pages into *The Long Goodbye,* I fell asleep. When I woke up, Jeeves was standing over me again. It was around 4 P.M.

"Would you like to go for a walk, sir? It might be good for you."

"I don't think so. . . . A glass of water, please."

Some H$_2$O in the system, I squinted a yellow eye at Jeeves. He stood by the letter-writing desk, waiting for my next solicitation. But I had nothing to ask of him. I felt intolerably sad and pathetic. How dare I want anything for myself? I thought. How dare I even dream for a moment that I could have something with Ava beyond last night?

It was probably the dreadful hangover, but I sensed a shadow over everything. Before it had even begun with Ava, I felt like it was over. There was no way I could be loved.

"Jeeves, bear with me a moment. Please sit down." He sat down. "I'd like to try to get to the root of today's melancholy, the psychological root, not the physical root due to last night's pollution. . . . I can almost put my finger on it."

"I am more than happy to listen, sir."

"Well . . . you see . . ." How could I convey what I was thinking and feeling? Then a parable of sorts came to me. "I think, Jeeves, this might explain it: One time I was baby-sitting—this was when I was living in Princeton—and I was looking after twins, a young girl and boy, about five years old. I was playing with them and then the young girl went into the bathroom. A few minutes later, she sang out, 'I'm done.' I had to go in there and help her off the toilet, which was perfectly fine. But what I've never forgotten is her saying, 'I'm done.' . . . It was her supposition that someone cared, that someone would come to her. She was still, of course, very much in the bubble of her parents' love, that when she went to the bathroom and called out, 'I'm done,' they'd come running and they'd praise her, make her feel important, make her feel like her little life was important. . . . So maybe it was seeing the birth of an ego . . . her use of the word *I* and how under the sway she was of the illusion of her own significance. And so I felt terribly sad thinking how life was going to crush her in the years to come."

"Maybe life won't crush her, sir," said Jeeves.

"I think life crushes everyone."

"I'm not sure I agree with you, sir. . . . Are you sure you don't want to go for a walk?"

"You said you'd listen! . . . I'm almost done, Jeeves. . . . I know I'm a bore. . . . I just want to say that I think the word *I* is the saddest word in the English language. To me it means failure, disappointment, heartbreak, and death. Nothing good comes of being an 'I.' Know what the saddest word in French is? *Je* . . . I don't know any other words for *I*. . . . Wait, *yo* is *I* in Spanish. But *yo* doesn't sound sad. Maybe that's why Latins are in a good mood most of the time. *Ich* is the German one. My grasp of foreign tongues is better than I thought. *Ich* sounds like they're disgusted with themselves. Maybe that's why Germans are so insane. They do seem to be better lately, though. I don't think they'll give the world trouble again, but you never know. . . . Almost all peoples have a dark period, though theirs was very dark. America is in a dark period right now, since we're leading the way in boiling the oceans and killing everything. . . . Even the Scandinavians, who are sort of perfect—clean streets, good health care, active sex lives—had a dark period, a brief Viking phase, but since then they've been very well behaved."

"A walk, sir?"

"All right already, let's walk."

I hadn't quite expressed what I wanted to, but some bilious crap had managed to get out, which was helpful, I guess. It was just this overall feeling of despair, futility, and hopelessness, both universal and personal. It had started with the jogging Jew and culminated with my memory of the young girl on the toilet. Oh, well, I really am an idiot.

We went for a stroll. We crossed paths with no one. I will say this for my fellow colonists: they may have been absolutely crazy but they were also quite serious about their work—hiding out all day in their studios and their writing rooms.

As we made our way through the green woods, I felt a sugar attack coming on—the booze had my blood all messed up—so we sat on a fallen tree to give me a few moments to gather myself. Despite the sugar attack, the trees and the fresh air had me feeling a little better mentally, so I said, "The thing is this, Jeeves. The key to life is to *not to want*. If you want, you have pain. I picked that up off a tea bag. . . . So whenever you want something, you have to think of giving something instead. That's the way to have a good life."

"That sounds like a wise approach, sir."

"So I want Ava's love, but what I have to do is think about giving Ava love. That's something I can count on. The reverse I can't."

"Very good, sir."

"I haven't said anything to you, Jeeves, but last night Ava and I . . . well, something was consummated."

"I am pleased for you, sir."

"You don't think it's bad form for me to have said something?"

"No, sir."

"Well, since I've alluded to this consummation, can I ask you something as a younger man to an older man?"

"Yes, sir."

"Have you noticed that women like you to be rough with them in the boudoir?"

"Very good, sir."

"'Very good, sir' is not an answer to a question, Jeeves!"

"Yes, sir."

"All right, stonewall me. Sorry to put you on the spot, Jeeves. I'm just full of nerves today, and I'm feeling concerned about the way I make love. I'm not always very tender. In fact, I'm a little violent. But I attack the woman to make her happy. . . . I guess what it comes down to is that they want to be defiled, like everyone else, which I can understand. They also like to be kissed and licked, but that's usually a buildup to defiling. Sylvia Plath said something about every woman loving a fascist who puts his boot on her throat. It's just that it's hard to feel good about yourself when you're the one playing the fascist, if you know what I mean."

"Yes, sir."

"Also, I explored things in the nose area. I kissed it several times. They say, 'Once a philosopher, twice a pervert.' But what if you do something three times or a thousand times? Are you a philosopher-pervert, like a philosopher-king?"

"I don't know, sir."

"I wouldn't mind that title—philosopher-pervert, though philosopher-king is better, of course."

"I agree, sir. Philosopher-king would be the preferred title."

"Well, my sugar seems to have stabilized, Jeeves. Let's head back to the Mansion."

"Yes, sir."

It was nearly time for the predinner drinks, but I was hit by a fresh wave of nausea, lay down, and skipped dinner. It really was an all-day hangover. Jeeves took off to fend for himself and around eight o'clock there was a knock at my door. I wondered for a gleeful, happy moment if Ava had returned early, and I said, propping myself up on my elbow, "Come in, come in."

It was Tinkle. He issued into the room and, upon seeing me lying in bed, said, "Are you all right?"

"I'm still sick from last night, if you can believe it."

"It hits you hard," he said. "Can I do anything?"

"No, I'm fine. . . . Thanks for asking. How are *you*?"

"I'm fine. Had a good day of writing and now the commander is coming up to my room for some whiskey, but I guess you're not up for it."

"It's tempting . . . I'd like to fly another mission with the Federation. . . . But maybe tomorrow?"

"Sure."

"Any news or gossip? Anything on the slipper scandal?"

"Nothing," he said. "Everything is quiet. No fires or thefts."

"Well, have a good time with the commander. Tell him the sergeant is in sick bay, but will be ready for duty tomorrow."

"Okay," said Tinkle. "Feel better."

He left the room. I missed being with him and the commander,

287

and despite my feelings of foreboding, I missed Ava terribly. It was odd to miss someone I hardly knew, but I did miss her.

I didn't eat anything, just drank water, which was probably healthy for my system, and I curled up in bed with Hammett, Chandler, and Powell. They were a wonderful substitute for living people, and for most of my life such fellows have been a substitute.

It was quite rare—I usually only read one book at a time—but I read bits and pieces from all three authors, like sampling different wines.

Jeeves came back around ten. He had probably been down to the fountain of nymphs with one of the cooks. I made a mental note to take Ava down there when she returned.

"How are you, sir?" he asked.

"To be honest, Jeeves, I'm still nauseous, and I'm also anxious, fearful, nervous, and ill at ease."

"I'm sorry, sir."

"Along with being physically unwell, I feel like I have homework that I'm avoiding and it weighs on me. But I always feel this way at my core. I think my nervous system still hasn't recovered from high school."

"Try your yoga breaths, sir."

"Good idea, Jeeves. I think I'll also pray. For an agnostic, I take a lot of comfort in prayer."

"Very good, sir."

"Well, good night, Jeeves."

"Good night, sir."

"You know, Jeeves, before I met you, I used to say, each night, before going to sleep, 'Good night, cruel world.' So it's much nicer to say good night to you."

"I'm pleased, sir."

Then Jeeves dutifully set out the slippers and closed my door. I read a little more, then went to sleep.

When I woke up, rather early, there were lovely shafts of light filtering into the room. It was one of those summer mornings where you forget that the world is on the verge of environmental collapse. Outside my window, the green leaves were turning to face the sun, and I put my face out the window to get some sun, too. All dreary and gloomy thoughts from the day before had vanished, and my body felt splendid. I was so eager now for Ava's return that it was almost unbearable.

I got dressed and headed out and the slippers were still there, unwanted, unstolen, which was a good thing—I had slept so heavily I wouldn't have heard anything anyway.

I went down to the dining room and it was practically empty, it being Sunday morning and most people were sleeping in. Charles Murrin and I sat alone at one of the small tables and I ate a full and delicious breakfast, drank many cups of coffee, and he and I talked about the writing process. His advice to writers if they were stuck was to "Torture the heroine, torture the heroine. When in doubt, just give your heroine a hard time. It always jump-starts the plot."

"What if you don't have a heroine?" I asked, thinking of *The Walker.* "Can you torture the hero?"

"Yes, that would work," said Murrin.

I thought this was very good advice, and I thanked him for his wise words. Then I finished my breakfast and was at my writing desk by 9 A.M. I tried to work on the novel, but couldn't. I was too nervous, thinking of Ava's return. I couldn't wait to kiss her. To squeeze her to me. So I wrote over and over again, like a lunatic, on my yellow pad, "I can't wait to see Ava. I can't wait to see Ava."

I did this almost like a chant or a spell to bring her back from New York as soon as possible.

CHAPTER 34

Foot-dangling ★ A blow ★ A startling discovery ★ The Spa City Motel! ★ Forgiveness? ★ Tears

Around 1 P.M., there was a knock on my door. I had long ago stopped my mad repetitive scribbling and had taken to just staring out the window or reading some Chandler. At the moment, I was practicing dangling my foot off the edge of the desk.

"Come in," I said.

She walked in, more beautiful than ever, which was becoming a habit of hers—looking more beautiful each time I saw her. She was wearing a white skirt and a tight blue T-shirt. There was the expected radiant skin, love-object nose, green eyes, and lustrous dark brown hair. I stood up, smiling and excited.

"Ava—"

She stepped toward me and punched me with all her might in my stomach. My hands, reflexively, went to my abdomen. I was hurt, but not terribly. She hadn't knocked the wind out of me. She was no Hill.

There was a real look of anger on her face, but I wanted to pretend that this blow to the stomach was her silly, affectionate way of greeting me, so I said with a smile, "Why'd you punch me?"

"You know why, asshole."

Being called asshole was more painful than the shot to my stomach. Something had gone dreadfully wrong. So the part of me that always expects disaster came to the fore, like a ghost stepping out of a body it has inhabited.

I said in a very quiet voice, "I really don't know why you punched me."

291

"You have to," she said, and she went to punch me again, but this time I blocked her fist with my hands, and I stepped back to put myself out of her range.

"Please don't hit me," I said. "I don't know why you're upset. . . . Are you pregnant?"

It seemed inconceivable that this would be the case, that she would already know, but what else could it be?

"I hope not," she said in such a way that it was evident that carrying my child might make a good sequel to *Rosemary's Baby*.

"So what's going on then?" I asked, desperate to understand.

"You really don't know?"

"I don't know. I swear."

"I don't believe you; you have to know. . . . You gave me crabs."

Crabs? For a very long moment, I didn't know what she was talking about. Then I had a very good idea what she was talking about.

"You mean pubic lice? I gave you pubic lice? That's not possible."

"Well, I have crabs . . . and I haven't slept with anyone for six months. So there's only one person who could have given them to me and that's you."

"But I don't have crabs," I said, pleading with her. "Maybe you're just itchy."

"I know what crabs look like. I had them in college. And when I woke up this morning, there was a nice little crab in there and a lot of eggs."

"Maybe you got them from a toilet seat."

"You're an idiot." She looked at me. She could see that I was both sincere and frightened. "You really don't think you have them?"

"I don't think so; I haven't noticed anything—"

"Go to the bathroom and check." Her voice was cold.

I left her in my writing room and went to the bathroom. I recalled observing what looked like a bug bite or a pimple on my thigh two days ago, but I hadn't thought anything more of it. And then I did think that I had been rather itchy yesterday, but I assumed it was just my skin acting funny during a hangover.

In the bathroom, I slowly lowered my pants and underwear.

With dread, I examined myself.

I had crabs.

I felt the beginning of a mad panic coming over me.

Tiny, crumblike sacs were at the base of my pubic hairs, and in the top left corner of my pubis, a miniature brown spider appeared to be embedded. Suddenly I felt very itchy. An itchiness I had mentally been dismissing as having no relevance or importance, such that it had barely registered. But it was there.

I couldn't believe I had crabs. I had never had them before. I picked at the spider-thing with my nail; I couldn't get it out. Then I managed to get my nail under it and the thing lifted up and walked off, very easygoing and nonchalant, oblivious to the fact that it was destroying my life. It had several little legs and moved like . . . a crab! I had a sand crab in my crotch! It disappeared into the dense forest—relative to its size—of my pubis. Come back, you bastard! It left behind a red sore spot, like the sore spot on my thigh. This was all too disgusting.

I pulled up my shorts and pants. My mind sought an explanation. I hadn't slept with anyone for months and months. Where had I been? What toilets had I sat on? Then the solution came to me: the Spa City Motel. The blankets had smelled of cigarettes. The place was a dive. They changed the sheets but not the blankets and not the coverlet. I had gotten crabs from a damn motel! And I had given them to Ava, to the girl I loved, and now she clearly hated me.

I went back to the writing room.

"I didn't know I had them," I said weakly. "But you're right, I have them."

"How could you not know?"

"I did feel a little itchy, now that I think of it . . . but it wasn't overwhelming. . . . I must have gotten them from the Spa City Motel. I stayed there the night before coming here. I had gotten my nose broken in Sharon Springs and then came here—"

"I know about your stupid nose. . . . I don't care how you got them, but you gave them to me. I never should have slept with you. I wanted to be celibate for a year. This is really gross. You don't have any other diseases, do you? Any other surprises?"

"No, I don't . . . I swear. I'm so sorry."

"I can't believe you didn't notice."

"I know . . . I'm an idiot. . . . What should we do?"

"I don't know what you should do, but I've already shaved myself. I didn't want to bother with those shampoos. So I shaved my whole thing. And now I'm going to wash all my clothes and all my sheets and blankets; anything you might have touched. . . . If we're lucky, we'll give the whole colony crabs."

"I feel like a leper," I said, and I actually started crying. I turned away from her, mortified with shame.

She put her hand on my shoulder. I was too embarrassed to face her.

"It's just crabs," she said.

"But I really like you. . . . I forgot to give you my book. . . . I've wrecked everything." I couldn't stop crying.

She was quiet. She took her hand off my shoulder.

"You sort of did wreck everything. . . . But don't worry about it; it's not that big of a deal, if you really think about it. Just get some of that shampoo and wash everything you have in really hot water. I'm going to go do my laundry now. There's only one machine, so if you want to do a wash, you can probably find a place in town."

"I'm really sorry." I still couldn't turn and face her. I tried to stop my tears with my hands.

"Okay, okay. I accept your apology," she said. "I was pissed. I thought you knew you had them and didn't care, that you just wanted to get laid. But I believe you didn't mean it. . . . I'm just really annoyed by the whole thing. I have a lot of problems at the moment and I didn't need this at all . . . but I can handle it. So let's just forget about Friday night." Then she said with a greater urgency, "Please, please, don't tell anybody anything."

"Of course not," I said. She was ashamed on many levels to have slept with me. I felt so bad that a numbing shock had set in and my tears stopped.

I was able to turn now, but I looked down at her feet, couldn't meet her eyes. How embarrassing, on top of everything else, to have cried. I said, "I hope you can forgive me. I'm really sorry—"

"I believe you."

She moved to the doorway to leave, then turned and faced me, though our eyes didn't meet. I was still looking down. She said, "So let's just act like we hardly know each other and get through the rest of our time here. I think that's the easiest way to go."

"All right," I said with a quiet voice. I was heartbroken and wanted to ask for a second chance, but more than that I wanted to do whatever she asked of me, and she was asking me to become a stranger, and so that's what I would do.

CHAPTER 35

Jeeves is spared ★ A murder cover-up and a military occupation ★ Hello, Dorian Gray ★ Good-bye, Douglas Fairbanks Jr. and Errol Flynn

"Jeeves," I whimpered. "Jeeves."

Ava had left. I was sitting at my desk with my head in my hands.

Jeeves melted over from the bedroom to the writing room.

"Yes, sir."

"Oh, Jeeves."

"I know, sir."

"You know, Jeeves?"

"Yes, sir. Your door was open and the relevant aspects of your conversation with the young woman were conveyed to me."

"Oh, Jeeves . . . what are we going to do?"

"There are a number of necessary steps to take, sir."

"Fleeing and then suicide?"

"No, sir."

"Don't you think we should just leave? We should go back to the Spa City Motel. That's the one place on earth where we'd fit in . . . well, where I'd fit in. . . . Oh, my God, Jeeves. What about you? Do you have the scourge?"

"I don't believe so, sir."

"I didn't think I had it either, but I do. . . . Jeeves, you have to go inspect yourself."

"I am sure that is not necessary, sir."

"Jeeves!"

"Very good, sir."

Poor Jeeves. Working for me had to be the worst assignment in the history of valetdom. First my alcoholism and now crabs.

He retreated to the bathroom. I did some more temple squeezing. Then I looked out the window. A two-story jump probably wouldn't kill me, I thought. I'd most likely only break a leg, and when the paramedics came, I'd have to tell them I had crabs. So I can't jump, I mused, but I can break a windowpane and take the edge to my neck. That might work. And this would also be an effective way to kill the crabs, I reasoned; I didn't think they could exist on a corpse for very long, and if I was cremated, that would really show them.

Jeeves came back.

"I do not appear to be afflicted, sir."

"Your bed at the motel must have been all right. . . . Well, better me than you, Jeeves. Everything about me is a disaster, so one more thing doesn't really matter, whereas you're more or less perfect so you'd feel the effects of a disaster more dramatically. . . . So let's get the hell out of here. I say we go to the Spa City Motel and I rub myself all over the place. I'd like to give my crabs to the crabs. Can I recrab a crab? What can you give a crab as revenge? Fleas? I could pet a lot of dogs and rent a room at the motel and let the fleas and crabs go at it."

"What I suggest, sir, is that we take all your bedding and the clothing you've worn the last few days and do a wash in Saratoga. We can also go to a pharmacy and purchase the proper ointments and medications."

"Do they sell loaded guns at pharmacies? That's the only kind of medication I need. A forty-five in my mouth, ready to dispense a lead pill."

"Try to be reasonable, sir."

"But shouldn't we just leave this place?"

"It's an honor, sir, that you were accepted here to pursue your writing. I think it would be a terrible waste to run away, to allow the current distressing circumstances to deprive you of an excellent opportunity. We can clear up this situation rather easily, and then you will have a few weeks to concentrate on and finish your novel. You're nearly done, aren't you, sir?"

"Well, nearly . . . A few months of hard work and I'd be done."

"So it is my feeling, sir, that we should not flee, as you put it, but stay here, face things, and do the best we can. If you left prematurely, sir, I think you'd later feel that you had squandered something quite precious."

"I've already lost something quite precious. . . . I feel like I love Ava, even if it's too soon to feel that, and now she wants nothing to do with me."

"Her attitude toward you might soften, sir. She strikes me as a reasonable person, and once a little time passes, she may yet come around."

"You think so, Jeeves?"

"It is certainly a possibility, sir. It is only a case of lice, which is exceedingly common throughout the world. There are far worse things that could happen to two people who feel affection for each other."

"I know, Jeeves, but it *is* pretty bad . . . but I'll do whatever you say. I can't really think straight. Maybe a crab crawled in my ear and is eating its way through my brain. Just tell me what to do."

"Very good, sir."

Jeeves outlined a basic plan of action, and so the next several hours were like a combination of a military assault and a murder cover-up.

First we had to get my clothes and bedding out of the Mansion without arousing suspicion. Jeeves directed us to a service exit, which I hadn't noticed, at the foot of my staircase. This saved us from having to traverse the mudroom, where we might be spotted. Using my two enormous suitcases and garment bag, like taking out parts of a dead body, we loaded the trunk of the Caprice with the incriminating evidence. While packing, I had forbidden Jeeves from handling any of my clothing.

"A crab could alight on your wrist hair and find its way to where it wants to go," I had explained to him.

"If that were the case, sir, I would already be suffering from an infestation."

"But now that I know what's going on, Jeeves, I can't put you any more in harm's way."

After much back-and-forth, he acceded to my wishes, though I did allow him to help with carrying the bags, thinking that the crabs couldn't chew through canvas and plastic.

I did suggest that we simply burn all my clothing, but Jeeves counseled against this.

We found a Laundromat open near the library, and the place was empty—only one or two machines were making noise. Whoever was doing a wash was off somewhere else.

My sport coats and ties couldn't be washed since it was a Sunday and all the dry cleaners were closed. So we left those in the garment bag, under quarantine. I would have to go a few days without wearing a jacket and tie, but I was prepared to make this sacrifice. I was even going to clean my spring, fall, and winter jackets; Jeeves felt, and I concurred, that it was best to conduct a Stalinesque purge of all my garments. And my blue linen jacket still needed to have the blood washed out from my beating in Sharon Springs.

I loaded four machines with my clothing and the Rose Colony bedding and towels. I set the temperatures to boil. I still wouldn't allow Jeeves to touch anything, and this frustrated him, but he continued to comply with my wishes.

While Jeeves watched and stood guard over the hypnotic machines, making sure no crabs crawled out and attacked any innocent Saratogans, I got in the Caprice and made my way to an enormous Rite Aid emporium. The place was indecent. Everything that is wrong with American culture can find its expression in the modern pharmacy.

I wandered hopeless and lost through the aisles of shampoos, chocolate bars, power tools, crayon boxes, and hemorrhoid creams, but, naturally, I couldn't find the pubic-lice medicaments, which necessitated an unpleasant conversation with a terrifying pharmacist. He was in his forties and his eyes were unusually close together. His dead, lifeless hair was patchy; you might have called it brown in a black-and-white movie. His nose was wide at the bottom, and his nostrils were upturned, so regarding him was like looking into the barrel of a shotgun. He was probably taking one pill from every prescription he filled, like a chef sampling his own dishes, which may have explained his frightening appearance.

"Excuse me, sir," I said.

"Do you need something for your nose?" he asked, curt and to the point, like most pharmacists I have encountered.

"No, thank you, my nose is under control . . . healing and all that. . . . I know it's bruised, still, but it's getting better. I'm here because my nephew picked up lice at a summer camp, and we need to treat him. Where might I find the lice products?"

"Head lice?"

"Yes, the young boy has head lice."

"You know you have to wash everything in very hot water. All clothing, bedding. And spray the house, too."

"We were thinking of burning the house, killing the lice, and collecting the insurance."

"Are you being obnoxious?" The barrels of his nose dilated.

"No, I'm sorry . . . a bad joke. . . . It's just that this poor boy is really suffering and it has me upset and not thinking correctly."

"Aisle five. There's nontoxic stuff, too. If you want. Works pretty well."

"Thank you."

I reasoned quite intelligently—I did go to Princeton, after all—that pubic-lice products would be next to their cousins the head-lice products, and I was correct. There were several brands to choose from and I was tempted to buy them all, fill the bathtub with the stuff, and bathe myself, or I could just find a nuclear reactor and jump into its waste pool. I settled on one product called RidX, which was a whole kit—shampoos, house spray, special comb, blowtorch, and a free piece of chewing gum. It was toxic as opposed to nontoxic. This was not the time to join the Green Party.

I purchased this humiliating RidX product from a young, overweight teenage girl, who seemed to be taking no visible notice of what I was buying. I figured that high school illiteracy rates were as bad as the newspapers said. She lasered the thing with her fazer, I thought momentarily of Science Officer Tinkle, and a report was sent through the scanner to the FBI that Alan Blair had crabs.

She gave me an enormous plastic bag for the lice kit, and my mind drifted back to good old Jerzy Kosinski with a bag over his head, but I decided to be mentally strong and just fight these crabs, not have them take my whole life, though having plastic bags around is like having a piece of rope with that elaborate noose knot all set to go.

I returned to the Laundromat, and when everything was ready, I allowed Jeeves to make the transfer to the dryers, which we set to incinerate.

We both reasoned that the hot water in the washing machines had probably made the clothes and bedding and towels safe for Jeeves to touch, and I didn't want to touch them and possibly recontaminate everything.

I went out and got a newspaper and we passed the time reading, and I felt terribly itchy, physically and mentally. It was quite upsetting to think that my pubis was a nursery for dozens and dozens of crab eggs. During my inspection, I had only spotted that one crab, which must have been the mother, and when all her children were born, I would be vastly outnumbered. I wondered if they were hatching as we sat there in the Laundromat.

Finally, the clothes were dry, and I didn't want to put them in the suitcases, which quite possibly were infected. We would have to spray them later. One has to think of everything when battling crabs. So I ran out and bought a bunch of black suicidal plastic garbage bags at a supermarket, and Jeeves loaded those up.

We snuck back into the Mansion with just a few garbage bags, containing enough clothing and bedding to get by. As soon I was in my room, I stripped down and we put the clothes I was wearing in yet another plastic bag and sealed that, with the idea that later we'd put it in the trunk of the car with the other quarantined clothing.

Crab kit in hand, I sprinted naked to the bathroom—didn't want to recorrupt any towels—and locked myself in there and went to work. I was lucky that almost no one else used my hallway and that I had the bathroom all to myself. First thing I did was read the voluminous instructions, which were terribly depressing—it was like a correspondence course on pubic lice; I learned about their nasty little life cycle, from nit to nymph to full-blown adult menace.

After receiving my diploma in the mail, I coated myself with the stinging cream, which upon contact with water would turn to shampoo, but I had to leave it on my person for fifteen minutes before rinsing myself. Then after rinsing I was to comb the hairs in question over the toilet bowl, removing nits and nymphs and trolls and spotted owls, and then rinse again.

So it was a very long fifteen minutes waiting for that RidX cream to do its job. They were fifteen of the longest minutes of my life. I thought of Jeeves's lecture on time. At the end of those fifteen minutes, I was going to be eligible for Social Security.

As I stood about, I examined my armpits in the mirror. The educational materials had made mention that once in a while pubic lice enjoy taking vacations in the armpit. I didn't see anything up there, but then I looked again, and I saw one of those embedded brown creatures! This was too sickening. I realized that the little bastard had followed the tributary of hair that ran up my belly to my chest, and from there it had swung on a few chest hairs, like Tarzan, until it had made it to my pit, where it had taken sanctuary.

So now I soaked my pits with the cream, but this was a few minutes after I had started the cream in my groin, and I worried about the timing being off, but said to hell with it, figuring it wasn't an exact science.

After twenty minutes I showered off the cream and then did the work with the comb. I regarded myself in the long mirror that was on the back of the door. I got the bright idea of shaving the tributary that ran up the middle of my torso. This way if any crab lived, it wouldn't have transit. So I shaved that off, and then a kind of mania took over, and the next thing I knew, I was hacking away at every hair on my body, except for the hair on my head, which the materials had said was not appealing to pubic lice, having something to do with air temperature.

I slathered shaving cream all over myself; no area felt safe from crabs, and in part I was driven to this shaving frenzy because I didn't fully trust the medication; the directions said that the whole process might need to be repeated several times, which didn't exactly fill one with confidence.

Thus, if I removed every hair—as Ava had done—the little buggers would have nowhere to hide! I went through five disposable razors.

I even bent over and shaved where I had never considered putting a sharp object. But I did it and was more ready than ever for my prison fantasy to come true. I was as hairless as young Kenneth must have been when he was first happily defiled.

I looked in the mirror at my bare legs, groin, belly, chest, and armpits. Except for the bruises the Hill had given me, I was confronted with a body I hadn't seen in many years. It was like a reunion with the past, with my younger self. I felt a sad affection for the young boy I was who didn't know yet how much trouble there was going to be, how much he would lose. It was different from nostalgia: by shaving my body, it seemed as if I had physically gone back in time, not just mentally.

Then I regarded my mustache. That would complete this strange Dorian Gray shaving trance, and also I couldn't risk keeping it. Maybe a crab, as a last resort, would hide in there. Off the mustache came. After the scarring of my legs, the removal of my thin lip hair was just a moment's handiwork.

"Good-bye, Douglas Fairbanks Jr.," I said in a maudlin voice. "It's been nice knowing you. And good-bye to you, too, Mr. Errol Flynn." I sounded like an Oscar telecast, during that moment when they worship dead stars.

Then I took a long hot shower and it soothed my raw body. Dripping wet, I dashed to my room. I dried myself with a crab-free towel and got dressed in crab-free clothing—khaki pants and a dark blue shirt from Brooks Brothers. I told Jeeves that I had shaved off every hair on my body.

"I had grown fond of your mustache, sir, but you look more youthful without it. I do hope you won't be too uncomfortable elsewhere."

"I already am, I can tell. But I deserve it. It's my penance. Kind of the opposite of a hair shirt, but with the same effect."

Our next task was to spray my mattress and pillows and the whole room, and then the writing room. We held handkerchiefs over our mouths, and I had some sense of the sadistic power that exterminators must enjoy. We opened the windows, though I hoped that wouldn't nullify the effects of the Agent Orange. Then we sprayed and cleaned the bathroom. Finally, our labors were over.

I felt violated underneath my clothes, but I was also quite relieved. No crab could possibly have survived. They had taken my girl from me; they had taken my mustache; but their attack on me had come to an end, I felt. We put all the elements of the crab kit in a plastic bag and planned to dispose of it off-campus. If the kit was discovered in the colony garbage, a witch hunt could ensue. What kind of note would Hibben leave on the mail table then?

"Well, thank you, Jeeves, for all your help." We were back in the writing room. "I couldn't have killed these crabs without you."

"Very good, sir."

It was a few minutes past six. Out the window, I could see that people were gathering on the back terrace.

"I'm going to go get drunk, Jeeves."

"I understand, sir."

CHAPTER 36

A possible explanation as to why dogs are so beloved ★ A recap of dinner ★ Mangrove's coed is at the door? ★ I'm going to play both rôles in a Cole Porter song—the top and the bottom ★ I'm no Philip Marlowe

"I think dogs must have a lot of free-flowing serotonin," I said. "More than humans, anyways. I wonder if scientists should be studying their brains for depression cures. I think their high serotonin levels might be why we like to have them around. When I pet a dog, I get some kind of contact euphoria. I may be getting extra serotonin subcutaneously or however things are transferred through the skin."

Mangrove didn't respond to my comment; he said, just noticing, "Hey! Why'd you shave your mustache?"

"Yeah, I thought you looked different," said Tinkle.

"It was getting too itchy," I said.

We were in Tinkle's room having another skull session with a freshly opened bottle of whiskey and a new packet of medicinal cannabis. It was around 10 P.M. I was drugged and intoxicated, but I hadn't yet blacked out, though I wish I had earlier in the evening.

Dinner, you see, had been a total nightmare. The gods had really laid it on thick, even for them.

We had been served, of all things, crab cakes. It was too macabre. We were also served corn. Corn on the macabre.

Naturally, I thought some kind of conspiracy was at play. That the staff knew someone had crabs, but didn't know who, and they were trying to push the guilty party over the edge and force out a confession.

But I didn't crack. I ate the things, though it was like being the royal taster for Hitler or Caesar, except I *was* Hitler and Caesar. So it was like being my own royal taster.

All the colonists were thrilled with the entrée and there was a happy buzz of talk and laughter. A grayish light came through the windows; the day, after its promising start, had been steadfastly overcast. The large chandelier was lit.

I was at a satellite table with just Mangrove and Tinkle and was doing my best, while gumming the crab cakes, to bludgeon all available nerve endings with a lot of white wine, taking more than my usual dosage.

I was halfway through my third bottle when Ava arrived late, just as she had my first night at the Rose six months ago, though according to Jeeves's bookkeeping that was probably three nights ago.

I saw her blanch when she approached the buffet line. Then she made eye contact with me as she went to find a seat at the big table. I saw that her plate only had salad and a piece of corn. No crab cakes. She smiled just a little at me, enough to make my heart pause, and then she sat down.

I drank two more glasses of wine and then Beaubien came to our table and addressed me: "When are you going to return my slippers?"

I had spent the day battling crabs and had now gone through three bottles of the thin white wine, and the combined effect of the trauma and the booze was a sort of plastic surgery on my personality. I didn't cower. I had guts. If I could face crabs, I could face anything. I was sitting down, but I stood up, so to speak, to Beaubien. I said, "Just be patient. I'll have them for you in the middle of the week. They're at Tiffany's getting bronzed."

Her eyes widened and she walked away, and Mangrove and Tinkle laughed. She turned back and said, "I expect better of you, Reginald," and then she left the dining room.

Reginald was a little wounded by this, but not terribly. After dinner we three then went up to Tinkle's room to see how his whiskey was doing. It was doing fine, and after two hours of reacquainting ourselves with it, Mangrove brought out the marijuana. Under the influence of the cannabis, conversation had worked its way back to the failed mission to find a serotonin spring, and that's when I brought up the possibility of dogs being serotonin carriers, which for some reason had triggered Mangrove to perceive with his one eye that I had removed my lip hair, as recorded above.

"And you're not in jacket and tie," said Mangrove. "What's gotten into you?"

"You're only just now noticing this radical transformation of my person?"

"Well, this side of my brain isn't that fast yet."

"I understand," I said. "But what's your excuse, Tinkle?"

"I don't know," he said. "I don't really look at anybody too closely."

"That's honest," I said. "But a science officer should be a master of close observation."

Just then there was a knock at the door. We were all startled. Yet again, we three shared the same telepathic thought: Mangrove's coed?

Tinkle went to the door.

It was Ava. She asked to speak with me. I got up from my chair and was a little wobbly. I was rather drunk and stoned but was thinking and speaking clearly.

"Let's go to my room," she said, seemingly not caring that Mangrove and Tinkle would infer some intimacy between us.

"See you later," said Tinkle.

"Okay," I said.

I submissively followed Ava to her room. Maybe Jeeves was right. She was already softening. She shut the door and sat on her bed. I sat at her desk chair, thinking that was my proper place.

"Are you doing okay?" I asked.

"Yeah, I washed everything. I think it's going to be all right. . . . You didn't tell Reginald and the other Alan, did you?"

"Of course not," I said.

This seemed to please her. Then she said, "Can you believe they had crab cakes?"

"Do you think they were trying to force our hand?"

"What do you mean?"

"I thought maybe they somehow knew that someone had crabs and were letting us know they know."

"Don't be nuts. . . . But you could be right in some crazy way;

those cleaning ladies see everything. . . . Did you wash all your clothes?"

"Yes, I boiled all my clothing, and I bought a kit with the shampoo and stuff, but then I went a little berserk and shaved my whole body."

"Oh, God," she said and laughed.

I smiled at her. This was going very well. She was being very nice to me! I said, "My kit came with a spray; you might want to spray your room."

"All right," she said.

"You want me to get the spray right now?"

"No . . . there's a favor I want to ask you."

"Anything. I'll do anything for you. I feel so bad about this crab craziness."

"I'm going through a really bad time financially," she said, suddenly very serious. "Friday, when I went to the track, I lost almost fifteen hundred dollars. . . . I had never really gambled before and I lost control; it was a real rush. I got lucky and won the first two races, and then I lost eight straight times and went to a cash machine . . . and the rent is due on my studio in Brooklyn and I don't have any money—" She stopped a moment. She must want a loan. This I could do! "And I went to my gallery yesterday. There's a buyer who likes my stuff. But there's only one piece he wants. He saw a photo of the bust I gave to Dr. Hibben. He wants that. The price is two thousand dollars. Selling that would solve everything. But I need the bust."

"Just ask Hibben for it back," I said. "He'll understand."

"No, I can't do that," she said. "It would look really bad. He's on the board of a lot of things, like the Pollock-Krasner, which gives a ton of money to sculptors. He really likes the piece, and if I ask for it back, I'll look like a flaky artist. . . . I want you to steal it."

This was like her punch in the stomach and her discussion of African lovers. She was volatile and unpredictable. I didn't know what to say. She wanted me to commit a crime.

By giving her crabs, had I put myself that much in her debt? I couldn't think straight. The booze, the pot. I can't think straight when I'm not on booze and pot.

"I don't know. . . . I'll be caught. . . . Can I give you two thousand dollars? I'll be happy to. You don't have to pay me back . . . it's a gift."

"I don't want your money," she said. "And I've thought this out . . . I want this collector to have my piece. It will look good for me. He'll buy others if he gets this one."

"But Hibben will report it stolen. This collector will think it's stolen."

"No, it will come from me. I can always tell Hibben there was one more copy I made from the original, if he somehow heard this collector had it. . . . And the piece will have greater mystique if a copy of it is reported stolen; even though there is no copy."

Ava was nuts. I had suspected as much when she'd unfurled that story about the therapist from the *Utne* reader, though her personality *was* deceptive. She was capable of appearing sane, but I could now see that she was mentally ill. But this was par for the course. Everyone at the Rose was mentally ill. In fact, most everyone I meet is mentally ill. It's just all too hard. We can't handle being alive.

"I'm sorry . . . I don't think I can do it," I said. "Why don't you do it? I'll stand lookout, if you like." I wanted to help her; I hated letting her down, but I was too much of a coward.

"I want you to do it. If I got caught stealing my own piece, it would just look absurd. You have to do it. You gave me crabs! You know how disgusting that is?"

"But what if I'm caught? I could go to jail. . . ." Then I thought maybe that wasn't such a bad idea. What the hell, this was my chance. Either way I came out on top or on bottom, and both were appealing. If I was successful, I'd have my fantasy girl back, and if I failed, then I'd have my defiling fantasy come true, and then afterward I could hang myself in my cell. Hanging one's self in one's cell is perfectly reasonable. For once my suicidal tendencies could be justified.

"It'll be easy," she said, "the Hibbens don't lock their door." She came over and kissed me hard on the lips. She put my hand on her full breast. She knelt in front of me. "Please," she said.

I weakened and strengthened at the same time. Morally, I was collapsing, but my capacity for stupidity and bravery was increasing. I squeezed her breast, and then I said boldly, with masculine intensity, "I'll do it."

Why not? For Ava! Don Quixote would do it for La Dulcinea!

"Get it tonight," she said, smiling. "Then I'll take the head to New York tomorrow; the collector will have it before Hibben even notices that it's gone. . . . I know it's crazy, but I think it will work."

"I'll do it around two A.M. The Hibbens should be asleep by then," I said, signing my own death warrant or suicide note, or whatever you call it when you know that you are being willfully irrational.

She gave me another delicious kiss, then led me to her bed. I lay on top of her. "Is there anything else you want me to steal, while I'm there?" I asked.

She responded by putting her tongue in my mouth. I was a novice, but a life of crime was showing that it had its attractions.

We quickly stripped down to see each other's naked, hairless bodies.

"I guess there's no chance that we could recrab each other?" I asked.

"I don't think so."

Below the waist, she looked perversely like a prepubescent young girl, and I looked like a boiled chicken with an erection.

I got to suck her nose again a little, but she said she didn't want us to make love, that she was worried that Alan and Reginald would guess at the truth if I was gone too long. But she promised me that if I came back with the head, we could again lie down together. I got dressed, kissed her good-bye, and said, "I'll be back with the head in a few hours." I went up to the third floor and rejoined Tinkle and Mangrove. They were eager to know what Ava had wanted, and I said, "She wants me to sit for a sculpture. She's intrigued by my broken nose."

Along with several other less than admirable traits, I was becoming a very good liar.

CHAPTER 37

A code word ★ We almost have enough for a minyan, but not quite ★ I said, she said ★ A walk in the dark ★ Navy scores a touchdown ★ A social gathering of sorts ★ A transposed head ★ What happens if there is a gun in the last act, but not the first act— does it still go off?

Mangrove left Tinkle's room around midnight.

"Good night, Commander," I said.

"Good night, Commander," said Tinkle.

"Carry on!" said Mangrove, and made his exit.

I wanted to keep fueling myself with Tinkle's whiskey to help me commit my felony appointment at 2 A.M.

I had bravely not said a word to either Federation member; I was, of course, going to have to do this alone. Also, I had to protect Ava, and furthermore, I didn't want to implicate Mangrove and Tinkle in any way—knowledge could make them accomplices.

I was worried, though, that I might black out and not go through with the thing. I said to Tinkle, "Please check every now and then to see if I'm blacked out."

"How do I do that?"

"Ask me if I'm blacked out."

"But even if you're blacked out, you might tell me that you're not blacked out."

"That's true. I'm probably not very trustworthy in that condition. We have to come up with a password. Something only my current consciousness would know."

"How do we know you're not in a blackout right now?"

"I don't think someone in a blackout would worry about being in a blackout," I said, getting exasperated. "That just doesn't happen."

"Maybe . . . but sometimes when I'm dreaming, I know that I'm dreaming."

"Well, even if I am in a blackout or I'm dreaming, let's just come up with a password. What's your middle name?"

"Spencer."

"Alan Spencer Tinkle?"

"Yes."

"I like it. That'll be our password: Spencer."

"My mother thought I might be the first Jewish president with a middle name like Spencer. That was her hope."

"I should have known you were Jewish," I said. "I can't believe we haven't established our fellow Yiddishness before. There are a lot of Jews here. This place should be called the Rosenberg Colony."

Tinkle chose this moment to get a cassette-player/radio out of his closet, and he produced from his desk drawer several tape recordings of Jewish comedy albums. He had Sid Caesar, Mel Brooks, Woody Allen, Carl Reiner, and Lenny Bruce.

"You're halfway to a minyan!" I said.

We started listening to a Mel Brooks album, and half an hour into it, Tinkle said, "What's my middle name?"

"Spencer!"

"I guess you're here."

"I think so. . . . If I am in a blackout, then I'm in a blackout within a blackout and so I know what's going on. That's what's key."

"That's what I was trying to say before."

"Then we're in agreement."

"Okay," said Tinkle.

At one-thirty, I took my leave.

"Thank you as always, Alan, for your whiskey," I said. "I now must go kill myself."

"You're joking, right? I'm the one with cancer of the penis."

"Yes, I'm joking. And you don't have cancer of the penis. I told you before that all men see things on their penis. I can't begin to tell you the things I've seen. Just lately even . . . I wonder if anyone has seen the Virgin Mary on their penis. You know how there's always these sightings. This would be a very vulgar sighting, of course, and I'm sure the Church wouldn't recognize it, but anything is possible."

"What's my middle name?" asked Tinkle.

"Spencer. Alan Spencer Tinkle, the forty-eighth president of the United States of America, land that we love to destroy."

"You're definitely drunk," said Tinkle, "but I don't think you're blacked out."

"I'll take that as a compliment. . . . Well, so long. I'll see you in the next life, or tomorrow, whichever comes first."

We parted without shaking hands because of Tinkle's hyperhidrosis.

I went down the stairs to the second floor and I was feeling, despite what I'd said to Tinkle, rather maudlin and suicidal. I had done a lot of things in my life, but I had never broken into someone's home to steal a sculpture of a human head.

I didn't stop by my rooms. If Jeeves was awake, I wouldn't be able to keep a secret of this magnitude from him, and I'd hate to see the look of disappointment on his face when I confessed that I was about to go commit a crime.

Thus, from Tinkle's room, I went to Ava's. No one was on the hallway. I knocked lightly at her door. She let me in.

"I'm off to go murder them in their sleep," I said.

"You're totally drunk," she said.

"I was totally drunk a few hours ago, too," I said.

"You didn't show it then," she said.

"I'm sorry, I forgot to," I said.

"You better not do it tonight," she said.

"If I don't do it tonight, I'll lose my nerve," I said.

"You'll fuck it up," she said.

"The whole thing is fucked up," I said.

"Fuck you," she said.

"This isn't the send-off I was hoping for. I can do this better drunk than sober. Sober, I'd chicken out. I know it," I said.

"All right, just bring me back the sculpture," she said.

"Can I have a good-luck kiss?" I said.

Her face seemed to soften. That was the end of our "I said, she said." We both shut up and she gave me a nice kiss. I held her to me. She felt good in my arms.

I left the Mansion and went down to the Caprice. I removed a flashlight from the glove compartment, thinking that's what a good burglar would use.

I walked across the silent, black grounds. Nice starlight and moonlight were coming through the roof of the colonnaded trees; the sky had cleared. Crossing the large colony was like moving through a manicured forest, and there was just enough light to walk by. I didn't want to use the flashlight until I was in Dr. Hibben's. I was afraid the beam might catch someone's eye should they glance out a window from one of the outlying buildings where some colonists were housed.

My heart was pounding, but I stealthily made my way. I stopped by the pool and sat Indian-style next to its shimmering, black surface. I dipped my hand in and put the cool water to my brow. I felt resigned to my fate, but I decided to pray. I said in my mind, "God, please help me. Please help me to not get into trouble."

Then I just sat there for a little while. From watching movies, I had the idea that professional criminals were very disciplined and operated on a tight schedule, so I was trying to be obsessively punctual; and according to my watch, which I shined the flashlight on for a split second, it wasn't yet 2 A.M. Of course, being scheduled is more important when breaking into museums or banks, and not so important for going into a house with an unlocked door, but romanticizing my activity was helping me to go through with it. I regretted now shaving off my mustache. It would have given me courage, made me feel dashing. But I could always grow it back, if I wanted to continue this new career of thievery. That's the good thing about mustaches. If you rashly shave one off, you can always get another just like it.

Well, at 1:57 A.M., I made my intrepid way over to Dr. Hibben's house. There was a short path through the trees from the pool. In front of the house there was a wide stretch of lawn; behind the house were thick woods.

A light was over the front door. I hadn't really observed the Hibben structure too closely on Friday night, owing to having

316

arrived in a blackout, but I now saw that it was an attractive, boxy, two-story, modernish affair.

Not from booze, but from nerves, I nearly vomited as I quietly approached the front door. Just keep going, I urged myself. There was a screen door and then the main door. With a squeak that could wake the dead and the living, I opened the first door. I waited. No response to the squeak. I turned the handle on the front door. Locked! Ava was wrong. The damn Hibbens had locked themselves in. I slowly closed the screen door and stepped back from the house and returned to the shadows.

Should I quit? Return to Ava, having failed?

I put my massive intellect to work on the situation. I came up with nothing.

Then I noticed that there was an open window right where the living room should be, according to my hazy memory of Friday night. The window was large enough for a person to get through. I went and stood in some shrubbery beneath it. A screen was in place, but it was loose. I put my flashlight in my pocket. I was able to get my fingers under the screen and push it up its little runners, and then it clicked in place. I stuck my head in and right below the window was a little table that held a vase of flowers, a lamp, and an ashtray. It was a narrow table, and I would be able to swing my leg over it, once I swung my leg through the window, which was about four and a half feet off the ground.

I moved the vase to one edge of the table and the lamp to the other edge. The room was dark and I took out the flashlight and gave the room a quick sweep. Directly across was the mantel that held Ava's bronze bust, which glinted gold when the light hit it. I then turned off the flashlight and put it on the table. I swung my leg through, cleared the table, but the force of such an action was a bit much, some kind of kinesis was at play, I wasn't fully in control of my body, and so I spastically tried to follow my leg with my head and torso and smashed my broken nose into the window frame, not lowering my head quite enough. I involuntarily let out a loud gasp of pain, slung my other leg through, but it bounced on the table. The lamp was knocked over and made a hell of a racket falling to its death, and the flashlight fell to the ground, lost to me, but the vase held steady.

The room was pitch-black and I was temporarily insane. Some bone chip in my nose, dislodged by the windowsill, may have shot into my frontal lobe. I ran for the mantel in the darkness, blasting my shin into a coffee table, which I don't think had attended the drinks party. That made some kind of noise, but at this point the West Point marching band was playing in my head and so it didn't register too much. Then Navy scored a touchdown and the Annapolis crowd screamed.

I made it to the mantel, grabbed the head, which weighed a ton, at least twenty-five pounds, and limbs flailing, got back to the window, tried to kick my leg through, and shattered the vase. Got a leg through after that, and then the whole room was lit up and Dr. Hibben was in the room, wearing a gigantic pair of white boxer shorts but no shirt. His torso looked like something out of a medical text for venereal diseases, and he shouted, "What the hell are you doing, Alan?"

When he said my name, the gravity of the situation struck me full on. I had been recognized. My nervous-system response was to suddenly cry out. It was a cross between a wolf howl and the sort of shrieking that has been bouncing off the walls of Bellevue for some time.

Dr. Hibben took a step back, a scared look on his face. He was about ten feet from me. Then my cry stopped. I was still straddling the table and the windowsill. My shin was gashed, my nose was rebroken and starting to bleed, I was having an insane fit, and I held the sculpture of Ava's head under my right arm.

Mrs. Hibben came into the room wearing a diaphanous gown and holding a shotgun, pointed in my direction. Beneath her gown, I could see swinging breasts that would have made nice medieval wine jugs. Maybe I was in one of Tinkle's wet nightmares. I did note— despite the trying circumstances—that they were fairly sexy medieval wine jugs; the dark nipples looked rather fecund and erotic.

Dr. Hibben addressed his wife sternly, "Put the gun down. We don't want that thing going off. It's Alan Blair." Then to me he commanded, "Get in here."

I had some muscle function left, which was a small miracle, and I was able to climb back in and put Ava's weighty bronze head on the table, as if I had just happened to be holding it. Mrs. Hibben put the shotgun on the couch. I stood in front of the window, frozen as a chess piece. At least my parents are dead, I thought. Can't shame them.

"I'm going to call the police," said Mrs. Hibben.

"Don't," said Dr. Hibben. "We can handle this. He reeks of whiskey. I can smell it from here. He wanted Ava's sculpture." He looked at me with a disturbing intensity. "What are we going to do with you? You're worse than Goldberg."

I wondered for a moment if he was making some kind of general anti-Semitic remark, as if *Goldberg* was a code word for hebe or kike, and then I remembered that Goldberg was the Brit who had peed in teacups. I felt ashamed that I had momentarily accused Dr. Hibben, in my mind, of anti-Semitism.

"Do you have anything to say?" he asked me.

I was mute with shame and terror.

He walked over to me, all seven long feet of freckles, and his enormous boxer shorts were billowing like a parachute, in fact there was enough material there for a parachute, so if he was ever ejected from a plane unexpectedly, he would probably survive.

He took me by the back of the neck, the way you would handle a schoolboy, and he paralyzed several nerves, including my spinal column. He pushed me along to the couch and threw me down onto it, and my rear landed on the end of the shotgun. He didn't say anything about that, and I thought I should just continue sitting on it. I was afraid to move.

"You're a sick person, aren't you?" asked Mrs. Hibben.

"I think I am," I said.

"Your nose is bleeding," said Hibben. I wiped my wrist across the base of my nostrils. I wasn't bleeding heavily.

Just then there was a knock at the door. Dr. and Mrs. Hibben gave each other a look as if nothing could surprise them at this point.

Dr. Hibben went to the door.

I heard a familiar voice say, "We heard a scream." It was the commander. Had he come to save me?

"Might as well come in," said Dr. Hibben. "We've got quite a situation going on here."

In came Mangrove and Beaubien. Looking Neptunish, Mangrove had his bat-catching net with him. He and Beaubien perceived the wreckage on the floor of the lamp and the vase. Then they took in the fact that I was sitting, like a prisoner, on the couch, a shotgun barrel pressed right against my rectum, though this latter detail they might not have exactly registered; they probably only saw that I was sitting on a shotgun poised in the general area of my buttocks.

"What are you two doing up?" asked Dr. Hibben.

Beaubien stared at me with incredulous eyes.

Mangrove said, "Sigrid had a bat in her room, and I caught it and brought it outside and the two of us decided to go for a walk. . . . We heard this terrible scream. Is everyone all right?"

"Alan, here," said Dr. Hibben, "came through the window and tried to make off with the bust of Ava's head."

"I want to call the police," said Mrs. Hibben.

"I don't want that kind of publicity," said Dr. Hibben.

"What did you do, Alan?" asked Mangrove with concern.

"I'm not really sure," I said. "But the police should be called, I deserve to be arrested and shot."

"He's very sick," said Mrs. Hibben.

"I knew there was something wrong with him," said Beaubien.

Just then, out of the corner of my eye, I saw Ava's head lift up, as if on its own; then I saw that two inky hands appeared to be grasping it by the ears, and then the head was gone and materializing in its place were a pair of slippers.

Mrs. Hibben caught the tail end of this supernatural transaction and screamed. This set off a chain reaction of screams. First me, then Beaubien. Mangrove and Dr. Hibben held strong and only grunted in fear. Mrs. Hibben, while screaming, had the presence of mind to grab the shotgun, but I was still sitting on it. So the shotgun lifted up at a strange angle, and as is often the case with firearms, it went off accidentally with a violent explosion, proving that guns are dangerous, though Uncle Irwin would be the first to argue that it's people who are dangerous and not guns.

CHAPTER 38

Navy is really putting it to Army ★ A bullet wound ★ I'm called a maniac, not for the first time, and I deserve it ★ Mangrove and Beaubien ★ Ava in my bed ★ If they hang you ★ I always liked Batman ★ Loose ends

The force of the shotgun blast had a catapulting effect on me. I was sent over the arm of the sofa, bounced off a little side table, cracked it in half, and took down with me to the floor a nice antique lamp. The lamp and I snuggled together and dreamed of getting married. The side table tried to intrude, but we told it that three's a crowd.

While the lamp and I tried to go to sleep on the floor, there was also a lot of noise. Apparently, Navy had scored another touchdown.

Then Beaubien, single-minded to the end, could be heard definitively shouting through the cheers of the Annapolis crowd, "Those are my slippers!"

That woke me from my shotgun-blast reverie, and I looked about me. Dr. Hibben, seemingly oblivious to my having been shot, which is perfectly understandable since I had broken into and entered his home, raced to the front door, flipped a switch, and went outside. From my vantage point on the floor, I could see out the window a massive illumination. He had turned on a floodlight for the front of the house, though I could have pretended it was that white light we've heard so much about.

The commander dropped his bat net and knelt at my side. He seemed rather emotional, and so he shifted his eye patch onto his forehead, the better to inspect me, his fallen sergeant.

"Where did she shoot you?" he asked, nearly crying.

It was strange to see two eyes beaming out of his severe, melancholic face. The eye patch, in the middle of his forehead, looked like one of the components of Jewish phylactery—the ceremonial prayer box that Uncle Irwin donned each morning.

"I'm not sure," I said.

Mrs. Hibben was standing erect, in shock, never having shot someone before, or so I presumed. She still held the murder weapon, but, mercifully, it was pointed at the floor.

Beaubien stood behind Mangrove, peering down at me, holding her slippers to her chest.

I reached under myself and felt my buttocks through my pants. Then I rolled to my side and put my hand in the seat of my pants— there was no bullet hole or bleeding. If any crabs were left, I hoped they had been permanently deafened.

"I don't think I've been shot," I said.

Mangrove helped me up. My right buttock felt numb as if I had been kicked by a horse, but that was the extent of the damage; well, there was some blackening of my pants in the rear area, but this could be cleaned.

Hearing that I hadn't been shot seemed to bring Mrs. Hibben to life. "You're all right?" she asked.

"Yes, I wasn't shot."

"Thank God," she said, which was very kind of her.

"You could have been killed," said Beaubien sweetly and sympathetically. This shooting was bringing out the best in everyone.

We all looked at the sofa. When Mrs. Hibben had lifted the gun, changing the angle of the weapon, my buttocks had been spared, but the sofa had been critically wounded. There was an enormous charred hole in the cushion, revealing stuffing, and down through the stuffing we could see the springs of the sofa-bed mattress.

Dr. Hibben then came back inside. His face was flushed in between the freckles. He looked as if he might combust from the stress of it all.

"Is he shot?" he asked, looking at me standing there in full health, relatively speaking, but he had to be sure.

"No," said Mrs. Hibben. "It went through the couch. . . . Let's call the police."

"Shut up with the damn police. . . . There's no one outside. I should have seen someone. They couldn't run across the lawn that fast. . . . Who's your accomplice, Alan? Tell me!"

"Let's call the police," said Mrs. Hibben.

"You shut up," Dr. Hibben roared at Mrs. Hibben. "We don't have a permit for that fucking gun of your brother's! And put the fucking thing away before you shoot somebody else!"

Beaubien, Mangrove, and I all lowered our heads. It was unseemly, even in this florid moment, to witness a quarrel between the director of the Rose Colony and his wife.

Mrs. Hibben sat down on the good end of the couch, gingerly lowered the shotgun to the floor, put her head in her hands, and started weeping.

This created a sympathetic stress response in Beaubien and myself, and so there was a chorus of crying. Mangrove put his arm around Beaubien. My nose, which had stopped bleeding, began to trickle once more.

"Who took the head and returned the slippers?" Dr. Hibben demanded of me.

"I don't know," I said, still crying, and holding my hand to my nose so that I didn't bleed all over everything.

"It was the ghost of the Rose Colony," said Beaubien with a hysterical note to her voice.

"Who took the damn head?" shouted Dr. Hibben.

"I don't know," I moaned, though in my heart I knew. Only one man could have moved that efficiently and eerily; only one man would have come to my aid:

Jeeves!

"It was a ghost," repeated Beaubien, weeping.

Mangrove held her tight under his arm and said, "It's all right, Sigrid. It's all right."

Then Dr. Hibben said, "Everybody out of here. This is the worst night ever in the history of the colony. I'd wake everyone up right now, but I don't want there to be any more pandemonium. . . . In the morning, I'm going to have an assembly and find out who took that head. And after that, Alan, you are to leave immediately, and I might yet call the police!" I could see that he had made this last statement to threaten me, but also to make some amends to his wife.

"I'm so sorry for all this, Dr. Hibben," said Mangrove, acting as a general representative of the colonists, and I was grateful to him, because I was unable to summon up the will to apologize, knowing that anything I said would sound so paltry and unequal to the damage I had caused.

"You have nothing to apologize for, Reginald," said Dr. Hibben, then he went to his wife and put his hand on her shoulder, but she was still crying.

Mangrove picked up his bat net and said to Beaubien and me, "Let's go." But as we stepped toward the door, Dr. Hibben started breathing rapidly and his naked torso began to quiver and heave. He was having a delayed reaction, and simultaneously Mrs. Hibben stopped crying. Her hysteria had transferred to him, which is often the case with hysteria; very rarely are two people hysterical at the same time; they tend to bandy it back and forth.

Mangrove passed me the bat net and alertly went to the mobile bar and produced from behind it a bottle of scotch and a glass. He poured Dr. Hibben a shot and brought it to the man. Hibben swallowed some of it and spilled the rest. It seemed to have a calming effect.

He sat down next to his wife. He was above the hole in the cushion, but his bottom was large enough that he didn't sink in. Mrs. Hibben reached her arms around Dr. Hibben and kissed him on the cheek. Then they sat there side by side, slumping, and looked very tiny for half-naked human giants.

"You're both all right?" Mangrove asked.

"We're fine," said Dr. Hibben, some of his normal composure returning. "Thank you for the drink."

"Is there anything else I can do?" Mangrove asked.

"Just make sure this Blair maniac doesn't burn down the Mansion. Keep an eye on him. We just have to get through to the morning."

Dr. Hibben's words pained me, but I deserved it, and it wasn't the first time I'd been called a maniac by a doctor.

The three of us then left. Nobody said good-bye. It wasn't the kind of gathering that called for any sort of farewell. I gave Mangrove his bat net and he used it as a walking stick and put his free arm around Beaubien. My severely bruised buttock was causing me to limp, but it was amazing that I could even continue on at all.

We walked in silence. Amid the horror of everything, I was glad to see that a rekindling of affection was occurring between Mangrove and Beaubien. When all was said and done, Beaubien wasn't so bad.

"Alan," Mangrove said, breaking the quiet, "tell me what's going on. Who took that head and put back the slippers?"

"I really don't know." I wasn't going to incriminate Jeeves, not even to the commander.

"So you didn't take my slippers?" asked Beaubien.

"I know I'm not the most credible person, but I really didn't take your slippers."

We resumed our silent march. When we got to the Mansion, Mangrove asked Beaubien to step inside the mudroom, said that he needed to speak with me privately. She didn't protest. It was clear that she would do anything he asked. She was radiant. Their affection was reignited and she had her slippers. She was at peace. She went inside.

Mangrove looked at me. His eye patch was still in the middle of his forehead, blocking his third eye, if he had one. If anyone has one.

"We've only just gotten to know each other," he said, "but I like you. . . . So why did you sneak into Hibben's? Did you do it because you're drunk? I shouldn't have let you smoke that pot. . . . Did Ava put you up to it?"

"Of coure not."

Mangrove was silent. Then: "You really don't know who took the head and returned the slippers?"

I lied with all my might, "I don't know."

"Okay," said Mangrove, resigned. He lowered his head, exhausted, then looked at me. "You're not going to get into any more trouble, are you?"

"No," I said.

"Are you all right?"

"My buttock is sore, but not bad."

"There's dried blood under your nose."

"I know,"

"I guess you'll be leaving in the morning."

"As soon as Dr. Hibben tells me to go, unless he does call the police."

"I don't think he will; he has to answer to the board, and I'm sure he'd like to avoid a scandal . . . but who knows."

We went into the Mansion then. Beaubien was waiting. We all said good night, and he and Beaubien held hands. Off they went to the main hall, and I went up the back staircase.

Jeeves wasn't in my room and I had a fright—Ava's head was on my pillow, which was a rather dramatic gesture for Jeeves to have made, I thought. I then took the pillow out of the white pillowcase and put the head in it, using the pillowcase like a sack at the base of a guillotine.

I went over to the writing room. "Jeeves," I whispered, outside the door.

"Come in, sir," he said.

I went in, closed the door. He stood up from his cot and put down his volume of Powell.

"How can you be reading?"

"I couldn't sleep, sir."

The man had polar ice for blood. He was completely unflappable.

"Well, I thank you, Jeeves. I owe you everything."

"You're welcome, sir."

"So how'd you do it, Jeeves? I didn't hear you following me. . . . And how'd Hibben not see you? You ran behind the house, into the woods?"

"I did not run behind Dr. Hibben's house, sir."

"You heard the gun go off? I was nearly shot, you know."

"I was unaware of this, sir."

"You ran that quickly?"

"Your questions mystify me, sir."

"I just want to know how you eluded Dr. Hibben after you took the head." I swung the heavy pillowcase, to indicate the skull inside. "And where'd you get Beaubien's slippers?"

"I did not find Miss Beaubien's slippers and I didn't take the head, sir. If the head belonged to Dr. Hibben, then it was Mr. Tinkle who took the head from Dr. Hibben. He came by your room several minutes ago and put it on your bed. I observed him through the crack in the door, and when he left, I went to your room and saw the head on your pillow. I imagined that he was playing a prank on you, so I didn't think it was my place to remove it. . . . But how is it, sir, that you were nearly shot? Also, you have dried blood on your lip. I would like to get a washcloth for you."

I sat at my desk and tried to absorb what Jeeves had just told me, but there wasn't much room in my brain after all I had done and witnessed, so it took a few moments. Then all at once a course of action presented itself to me.

"Jeeves, I'll be right back and explain all." I stood up.

"Do you want to wash your lip first, sir?"

"No."

"There's a blackened area on the seat of your trousers, sir."

"I know, Jeeves. That's where I was nearly shot. . . . I'll be right back and tell you everything."

Hidden in my desk drawer was the plastic bag that contained the crab kit. From it, I grabbed the crab spray and put that in with the head. Then I ran-limped to Ava's room. No one saw me. I went in. She was sitting in bed. Wearing a sleeveless T-shirt.

I stormed across the room and put the pillowcased head in her lap.

"It's a long story, which I don't have time to tell," I said. "But here's the head and the spray. I'm fleeing. I adore you, but . . . well, maybe I'll see you in Brooklyn someday. I'll come find you at Pratt. . . . So, listen, the police might be here tomorrow, but I doubt it. Hibben is afraid of publicity. Regardless, I'm going to disappear, that will put all suspicion on me and leave you in the clear."

She was speechless. I leaned forward and kissed her. "You're beautiful," I said.

"There's blood on your face."

I started for the door.

"Alan, tell me what happened!"

"I got the head for you. That's all you need to know. If you knew more, you'd have to lie. This way you can play dumb and it will be believable. . . . But if they hang you, I'll always remember you."

327

"What are you talking about?"

"Just joking." I had always wanted to say that to somebody. "So just hide the head. It won't occur to them, anyway, that you'd have it, but let things cool down. Don't go to New York right away. Let the gallery know you'll be bringing it in a few days. Have them advance you some money if you need it."

I opened the door.

"Alan!"

"I have to go. Please let me go!"

She just looked at me. I closed the door. I didn't want her to know about Tinkle. Had to keep him out of the loop if she was grilled.

I limp-bolted up to Tinkle's room. Without knocking, I penetrated his chambers and shut the door behind me. Tinkle spun around and faced me. With a damp towel, he was cleaning his blackened face. There were several charred wine corks on his desk—his blackening agent.

"You followed me to Hibben's," I said.

He nodded mutely. His face was half-black, and he had on dark jeans and a black turtleneck. He had cleaned his hands, but there were still smudges on his knuckles from the cork.

"You saved me," I said.

"The Bat saved you," he said, and he bent down and picked up, like a swordsman, a large, black, rolled-up umbrella. He pushed a button and the umbrella fanned out, and then he crouched down and hid his small frame behind the black shield. The effect was as if he had disappeared. He stood up and closed the umbrella. "It's my cloaking device. It works well in shadows."

"You're brilliant. That's how you eluded Hibben."

"That's how the Bat eluded Hibben."

"Listen, there's going to be a search tomorrow, but I'm going to take off now with the head, and that will shut the whole thing down. But if they talk to you, play dumb. And get rid of those corks."

"Are you sure you have to take off?"

"I'm being kicked out anyway, and if I stay here another minute . . . well, I don't think I can take it."

"I understand. But all for that head. Well, enjoy it."

He had followed me to Hibben's, but he hadn't known about Ava sending me there. I was counting on that. He believed I still had the head, which was perfect.

"By the way," I said, "I should have realized you were behind the slipper thing from the start."

"I was planning on putting them back tonight, to get her off your back, but then when I saw her at Hibben's, it was the perfect opportunity."

"Well, it worked beautifully. A good, weird diversion . . . So thanks for everything." I went to shake his hand. He hesitated. "Come on," I said.

We shook. It was nice and wet. Good old Tinkle.

"How'd you keep the black stuff on?"

"Two coatings of it."

We shook hands again.

"I hope to see you on the mainland someday," I said.

"Me, too," he said.

I dashed out of there. Tinkle was protected from Ava, and Ava was protected from Tinkle. There were loose ends, but there always are; that's why you have the phrase *loose ends*.

CHAPTER 39

Let's flee! ★ A busman's holiday ★ International laundry and massage techniques ★ Note to self with a dash ★ My mother's song

I went to the writing room and told Jeeves, with a certain manic intensity, everything that had transpired, and at the end of my police report I said, "So I think you'll agree with me this time that fleeing immediately is the best course of action."

"Yes, sir, I do think fleeing is the appropriate response."

Since most of my clothing was already in the car, it didn't take us long at all to pack up. By three-thirty, the Caprice was loaded and we were on our way.

We traversed the winding driveway for the last time. The trees of the long colonnade, like dark mourners, reached across the way to one another, holding hands above us as we escaped.

At the main road I said, "Oh, God, where should we go?"

I had been so intent on leaving that an actual destination hadn't occurred to me.

"I was thinking, sir," said Jeeves, "that to properly flee we should leave the country. Montreal is just a few hours' drive from here on Route Eighty-seven."

"That's absolutely a magnificent idea. One usually associates fleeing the country with getting on a plane with a false passport and going to Venezuela, but escaping to Canada is a perfectly reasonable alternative. It's kind of like a busman's holiday for fugitives such as ourselves."

"Very good, sir. I am glad you are in agreement."

Route 87 was less than a mile from the colony. I piloted the

331

Caprice in the necessary direction, and in less than a minute we were on the highway, moving along at an excellent fleeing speed of 70 mph.

As we rocketed northward, I saw a sign that said MONTREAL 183 MILES. I said to Jeeves, "This is one of your best ideas of all time. All my sport coats need cleaning and decrabbing, and they probably have a lot of French laundries up there. . . . It's interesting that only the French and the Chinese have distinguished themselves when it comes to dry cleaning. You don't hear anything about Portuguese laundry. I wonder what the difference between French and Chinese laundry is? It's sort of like shiatsu and Swedish massage. The Swedes, of course, have made a name for themselves in the massage arena, but not laundry."

"Yes, sir," said Jeeves.

"You know, Jeeves, it might have been nice to return to Montclair and try to reform and go to AA and be a good nephew, but if I'm not over these crabs, I'd hate to pollute Aunt Florence's sheets and possibly expose her to my condition. I wouldn't mind, though, in a weak moment, giving Uncle Irwin crabs, but that's only in a weak moment, Jeeves. . . . Anyway, Hibben could find me in Montclair. . . . So Montreal really is our best choice. . . . You know, the Frenchness of the word *Montclair* never struck me before. I guess the French were in New Jersey for a little while. Not much trace, though."

"Many towns have French-sounding names, sir. Bel-Air and Belmar, for example."

"That's true, Jeeves. . . . Was it only a week ago that I spilled that coffee on Uncle Irwin in Nouvelle Montclair?"

"Yes, sir. Today is Monday."

"See, I'm getting better with this time business. Still, it's rather uncanny."

"I would agree, sir."

Then we lapsed into silence and got down to the business of taking flight. For about half an hour, we purposefully cruised along on the nearly empty highway, and then my adrenaline, which had made me decisive and fearless and capable, as well as immune to physical and mental pain, was completely gone. A more normal, fear-based consciousness began to assert itself. I had been so pragmatic and charged up that I had been nearly oblivious to what I had wreaked, to the utter mess I had left behind at the Rose Colony. Now this grace period of numbness was over. My whole body ached—shaved skin, broken nose, gashed shin, fired-upon buttock—and my mind was tormented with shame.

"Oh, God, Jeeves," I whimpered, letting the horror of my actions nip at me. "I don't think I could have behaved worse. What a humiliating disaster."

"It was not one of your triumphs, sir."

"The poor Hibbens. They may never be the same."

"They are probably stronger than you realize, sir."

"I hope so. . . . They certainly have great physical strength. . . . But, God, what a mess. I failed in every way possible. I upset people and destroyed my name. . . . And I didn't achieve any of my goals. I didn't fall in love. Not really, if I'm to be honest. I didn't finish my novel; in fact, I hardly worked on it. And I didn't stay sober."

"You tried, sir."

"Not very hard."

"An argument with that as its central thesis could be made, sir."

"My problem is that I'm too self-destructive, self-absorbed, self-obsessed, self-centered. . . . Anything with *self* and a dash, that's me."

"Try not to be self-critical, sir."

"Are you teasing me, Jeeves?"

"Yes and no, sir."

I laughed. Jeeves was a wonder.

"You're too good to be true, Jeeves," I said.

"Thank you, sir."

"Not too many people are too good to be true, Jeeves, but you definitely fall into that category."

"Very good, sir."

We drove on. After a while, the road grew smoky and then completely black. My headlights failed. I acquiesced. I let myself drive without light. It was like falling in a dream. When I was a child, my mother would tuck me in and sing to me every night the same song:

333

Little boy, you're tired,
little boy, you're blue,
you've had a busy day today,
so go to sleep, my sweetheart,
and dream all your cares
away.

I'd try to stay up so that she'd have to keep singing it, but then the darkness would come, and she'd be gone. And so I drove without light. The road was black and the drop was sheer and frightening. Then from far away, I heard a voice calling out. There was no more darkness. A concrete embankment replaced it. The voice called to me again, just in time.

"Wake up, sir! Wake up."